The TEMPTATION *of* GRACIE

Also by Santa Montefiore

The Affair
The Italian Matchmaker
The French Gardener
Sea of Lost Love
The Gypsy Madonna
Last Voyage of the Valentina
The Swallow and the Hummingbird
The Forget-Me-Not Sonata
The Butterfly Box
Meet Me Under the Ombu Tree
The House by the Sea
The Summer House
Secrets of the Lighthouse
The Beekeeper's Daughter

The Deverill Chronicles

Songs of Love and War
Daughters of Castle Deverill
The Last Secret of the Deverills

Santa
Montefiore

The TEMPTATION *of* GRACIE

SIMON &
SCHUSTER

London · New York · Sydney · Toronto · New Delhi

A CBS COMPANY

First published in Great Britain by Simon & Schuster UK Ltd, 2018
A CBS COMPANY

1 3 5 7 9 10 8 6 4 2

Simon & Schuster UK Ltd
1st Floor
222 Gray's Inn Road
London WC1X 8HB

Simon & Schuster Australia, Sydney
Simon & Schuster India, New Delhi

www.simonandschuster.co.uk
www.simonandschuster.com.au
www.simonandschuster.co.in

A CIP catalogue record for this book
is available from the British Library

Hardback ISBN: 978-1-4711-6958-8
Trade Paperback ISBN: 978-1-4711-6959-5
eBook ISBN: 978-1-4711-6960-1

Typeset in Bembo by M Rules
Printed and bound by CPI Group (UK) Ltd, Croydon, CR0 4YY

In memory of my beloved sister, Tara

I am sending a dove to heaven
With a parcel on its wings.
Be careful when you open it,
It's full of beautiful things.
Inside are a million kisses,
Wrapped up in a million hugs
To say how much I miss you,
And to send you all my love.
I hold you close within my heart
And there you will remain
To walk with me throughout my life,
Until we meet again.

ANON

Chapter 1

England, March 2010

The muffle of cloud that had settled over Badley Compton Harbour was so dense that the little fishing boats tethered to buoys in the middle of the bay had completely vanished. So too had the pretty white cottages which were stacked in rows up the hillside and the crown of green at the top where Ruby Red cows grazed on sweet grass and clover, and small birds played about the hedgerows. It was all gone now, as if it had never been.

Gracie Burton sat at the mirror of the salon, her short hair wrapped in tin foil, her diminutive body draped in a black gown, and gazed at the fog through the big glass window. She swept her eyes over the shimmering pavements and glistening stone wall to where one would normally see the sea, then turned back to the photograph in the magazine on her lap where a Tuscan castle glowed like amber beneath a bright Italian sun. She was seized by a deep and urgent craving. She had read the article several times already, but she read it again now, and it was as if she were growing a small sun inside her that was all her own.

❧

Set high on top of the undulating Tuscan hills, with an uninterrupted view of the breathtaking Italian countryside all the way to the sea, Castello Montefosco is a rare jewel. Built by the Montefosco family in the twelfth century it can boast a long list of prestigious guests including Leonardo da Vinci and various popes. The widowed Count Tancredi Bassanelli, whose mother was a Montefosco, has now opened the doors of his beautiful home to paying guests, who will have the privilege of learning how to cook authentic Italian food under the expert eye of his octogenarian cook, Mamma Bernadetta. Don't expect to see much of the count, he is a private man, but you will enjoy the outrageous beauty of the gardens and terraces, the magnificence of his ancestral home full of treasures and the cookery lessons with the eccentric and talented Mamma Bernadetta.

Gracie let her eyes linger on the photograph. The castle was everything an Italian *castello* should be: harmoniously proportioned with a crenulated roof, tall shuttered windows set beneath half-moon pediments, sandstone faded to a pale grey-yellow by centuries of burning summer sun and bitter winter winds. It dominated the crest of the hill like a grand old king, rising majestically out of the cluster of medieval houses that had grown up around it in a forest of stone. Gracie closed her eyes and inhaled. She could already smell the wild thyme and rosemary, the honeysuckle and jasmine, the luxurious gardenia, dewy grass and aromatic pine. She could hear the gentle chirruping of crickets and see the velvet sky twinkling with a thousand stars like a vast canopy of diamonds spread out over the Tuscan hills. Her chest flooded with longing, a longing that she hadn't felt in years, deep in her heart. It frightened her, this feeling, because she had forgotten what to do with it. She had forgotten what it felt like to be young, to be in love, to be reckless, adventurous and brave. She had forgotten how to live. She had stuffed herself into a shell and remained there, hidden and safe, for decades. Now this photograph had forced her out like a cork from a bottle and all the fizz was coming with it and she didn't know what to do, except to go to Tuscany, as soon as possible.

She looked at her reflection and the fizz died away a little. She was sixty-eight and although relatively well-preserved, she was still old. Where had the years gone? she asked herself. Not that she had ever been beautiful, so mourning the loss of her looks was never going to be her misfortune. However, there is a loveliness about a young woman simply because she is young, and that quality in Gracie had withered a long time ago.

She ran a rough hand down her cheek. Time had sucked the juice out of her skin but the elements had also played a part during her daily dog walks up and down the beach in all weathers. Her nose, she noticed, hadn't changed. It still dominated her face with its aquiline curve, giving her the look of a bird, an old bird now, a strange bird then, never a beautiful bird. Her eyes had always been special, though. Everyone used to say so and she had clung to that compliment when as a girl she had yearned to be pretty. They were large and grey-green, the irises encircled by a darker shade of grey, which had given her a feral look that people had once found compelling. *Her eyes were less noticeable now,* she thought, *on account of her wrinkled face.* Time had stolen the one thing that had set her apart. She hadn't cared how she looked since she was a young woman, but she cared now, suddenly, very much.

'You all right, dear?' said Judy, who cut her hair and gave it a colour rinse every now and then. Young and fashionable, Judy had a pierced nose, a tattoo and a ring on every vividly manicured finger. 'Won't be long,' she added. 'Would you like another cup of tea?'

'Thank you,' Gracie replied, still gazing at her reflection. She feared she'd look a hundred if she didn't tint her hair brown. She glanced down at her hands, the rough hands of a potter and gardener; the coarse hands of a woman who had never bothered with creams or manicures. The article drew her gaze again and she stared at it and allowed it to swallow her whole.

'Oh, that looks lovely,' said Judy, returning a few moments later and putting the mug of tea on the little shelf in front of the mirror. 'Where is it? Spain?'

'Italy,' said Gracie.

'Lovely,' the girl repeated.

Gracie sighed with longing. 'Yes, it is. Would you mind if I borrowed the magazine?' she asked.

'You can take it. It's out of date now anyway. I think it's the February issue.' Judy knew that Mrs Burton never went anywhere and she gave her a sympathetic smile. 'Doesn't cost anything to dream, does it, dear?' she said.

Gracie returned home to her small whitewashed cottage that looked out over the harbour. The two rescue mongrels she had bought after her husband died eight years before greeted her enthusiastically. 'You'll be wanting a walk, I suspect,' she said, putting the magazine on the hall table and bending down to give them a pat. She changed into boots and squashed her freshly coiffed hair beneath a woolly hat. A moment later she was making her way down the foggy road in the direction of the beach, the two dogs trotting excitedly beside her.

Gracie Burton had lived in Badley Compton for just over forty years. Ted, her late husband, had taken her to the Lake District for the occasional holiday, but like her he had preferred to remain at home. They hadn't had much money, but even if they had, they wouldn't have indulged in extravagant cruises or expensive trips abroad. Ted, who had been twenty years older than Gracie and a freelance journalist by trade, had liked his golf, his evenings in the pub and his books. Gracie liked books too. She travelled the world vicariously through the pages of the stories she read, but until now she hadn't been inspired to go anywhere. As she strode down the pavement she smiled, a nervous and excited smile, for she had decided, quite spontaneously and extremely uncharacteristically, that she was going to go to Italy. For a woman as cautious and unadventurous as Gracie Burton, this decision was extraordinary.

Gracie was by nature a solitary woman. She didn't crave company but she knew that if she allowed herself to withdraw completely from the community she might disappear altogether, and Ted had made her promise, on his deathbed, that she would make an effort to reach out to people. Consequently, she had allowed herself to be drawn into the Badley Compton Ladies' Book Club rather like a small stone that gets carried downriver by much bigger ones. It had started as a book club, but evolved into an anything-we-can-do-to-be-busy club, and was organised by the self-proclaimed queen of Badley Compton, Flappy Scott-Booth, whose husband was very rich, and attended by a flurry of four eager women, who, like attentive ladies-in-waiting, agreed with everything their queen said. Gracie, the fifth and lowest in the pecking order, found herself doing all the menial tasks in the arrangement of charity events, bridge nights, coffee mornings, the annual town fête as well as book club lunches and other small get-togethers. She wondered, while her mind drifted, how on earth she had allowed herself to be so zealously gathered up and taken for granted. But she didn't complain. She was patient and accepting, working quietly and diligently while the limelight shone on the other more enthusiastic ladies. Gracie relished her dog walking, because, for those precious hours alone on the beach, she was entirely in her own company.

This sudden notion of going to Italy had only just seeded itself in Gracie's mind when she casually mentioned it to Harry Pratt, who liked to sit on the bench near the bus stop and watch the coming and going of boats in the harbour. She came across him on her way back from her walk and asked if he was all right. After all, there was nothing to see but cloud. He enjoyed the tranquillity of it, he replied, for he was reminded of his flying days when he had been in the RAF during the war. He'd often flown into thick fog over Dover, he explained. Gracie was so excited at the thought of the adventure ahead that she told him. Harry Pratt stared at her in astonishment, for not only did Gracie rarely talk about herself, but she barely ever left Badley Compton. She was as much a feature of the town as the bench he was sitting on. 'Good Lord,' Harry exclaimed, bright blue eyes gleaming. 'What the devil do you want to go to Italy for?'

'I'm going to learn to cook Italian food.' Gracie beamed such a wide smile that Harry wondered whether she was on something. It made her look like a young girl and Harry blinked in wonder at the sudden transformation.

'And you have to go all the way to Italy for that, do you?' he asked.

'That's the fun of it,' she replied, before walking off with an unusual bounce in her step.

Harry Pratt had to share the news and share it at once. No sooner had Gracie disappeared down the road than the old man hurried into Café Délice opposite the bus stop, which was always full of people he knew. He pushed open the door and was greeted by a noseful of warm, sugar-scented air and a number of expectant faces looking up from their coffee and croissants. Big Mary Timpson was behind the counter hovering over the feast of sticky buns, pastries and gateaux displayed enticingly behind glass. 'Good afternoon, Harry,' she said, and her Devon drawl curled softly around her words like icing around a cake. Fat and cheerful with plump, rosy cheeks, a ponytail of platinum-blonde hair and a perky candy-cane-striped apron stretching over her voluminous bosom, Big Mary Timpson had time to talk to everyone, and time to listen too. Since she had opened fifteen years before, Café Délice had been the hub of town gossip.

Harry Pratt took off his cap and ran a rough hand through thinning grey hair. He swept his twinkling eyes over the faces and was spoilt for choice. He knew every single one. 'Double espresso with whipped cream for you, Harry?' Big Mary asked, taking down a pink cup and saucer from the shelf behind her.

'And a slice of apple tart,' he added and pulled out a stool. He sat between two small tables, not wanting to commit to either one, and decided to share his news with the entire café. 'Did you know that Gracie is going to Italy?' he said. He directed his question at Big Mary, but his gaze darted from face to face, delighting in their surprise.

'Gracie? Gracie Burton? *Our* Gracie? What do you mean, going to Italy?' Big Mary gasped, forgetting about the coffee and putting her hands on her wide hips. '*Really* going to Italy?'

'She's going to learn to cook Italian food,' Harry announced gleefully.

'Why?' Big Mary asked after a long pause.

Harry grinned raffishly. 'For fun,' he said and he didn't elaborate, not only because he didn't have many more details to share, but because the idea of Gracie Burton going to Italy for fun was so completely extraordinary, unbelievable even, that Harry wanted to savour it – as well as the effect it was having on everyone in the café.

It was exactly five minutes before the news leaked further. John Hitchens, who had been in the café having tea with his son and granddaughter, told his friend Pete Murray, who was on his way to the newsagent's, who in turn shared the gossip with Jagadeesh behind the counter as he paid for cigarettes and a National Lottery ticket. When John arrived home he informed his wife, Mabel, who hurried to the telephone to tell Flappy, hoping that no one had got to her first. Flappy liked to be in the know about everything and Mabel liked to be in Flappy's good books. *It would be a mutually beneficial telephone call*, she thought excitedly. 'Please, please, please . . .' she mumbled to herself as she clamped the telephone to her ear and waited for Flappy to pick up. A good seven rings later – Flappy always answered *after* seven to give the impression that she was busy – the queen of Badley Compton's pompous voice resonated down the line.

'Darnley Manor, Mrs Scott-Booth speaking.'

'Flappy, it's me, Mabel. I have news,' Mabel hissed urgently.

'Do tell,' said Flappy in a tone that suggested she was interested but not too eager.

'Gracie's going to Italy,' Mabel blurted breathlessly. Then she waited for the shriek of delight, followed by, 'Goodness, Mabel, who told you?' or, 'How good of you, Mabel, to let me know.'

Instead there was a long pause. Flappy inhaled through her nostrils to control her surprise. How could Gracie be going to Italy and she not know about it? Gracie was the only 'doer' in the group, if *she* went away there'd be no one to do all the tedious organising of Flappy's many events. Flappy was so affronted she could barely speak, but speak she did because she was a master at keeping up appearances. 'Yes, I know, isn't it extraordinary!' she said at last in a tight voice.

Mabel was deflated. 'You know already?' she asked, put out.

'But of course I know, my dear. I'm always the first to know everything in this town.'

Mabel rallied a little at the prospect of further details. 'Then you'll know more than me,' she said. 'When is she going?'

There was another pause, then Flappy said, 'How about *you* tell me what *you've* heard and I'll fill in any gaps.' Mabel was too admiring of Flappy to notice the flaw in that suggestion and hastened to tell her what John had heard in the café. She waited keenly for something more from Flappy, but Flappy was not forthcoming.

'We must hear it from the horse's mouth,' Flappy declared, her mind whirring with ideas. Gracie was notoriously secretive, but if she had told Harry Pratt of her plan then she wasn't intending to keep it secret. Harry was famously loose-tongued. 'I will give an impromptu soirée tonight,' she announced impulsively. 'Kenneth is away and I have the house to myself. Yes, I'll summon the ladies and cook a splendid dinner.'

'What will the soirée be for?' Mabel asked eagerly, because she loved an occasion and Flappy's soirées were *always* an occasion. The last one had been in celebration of the money they had managed to raise to repair the church roof and Flappy had hired a string quartet from Exeter to play especially for them. But there wasn't enough time to put on that level of entertainment tonight. Flappy went silent for a moment as her busy mind made space for a new idea.

'But for Gracie, of course. If she's told Harry Pratt, she'll know the whole town will have heard by now. We'll have pasta and Prosecco and *parlare Italiano* . . .' Flappy sighed contentedly. 'Yes, it will be fun to *parlare* the *bella lingua*. After all, I've spent so many holidays in *Firenze, Roma* and *La Costa Amalfitana, Italiano* is second nature to me.'

Mabel wasn't in the least surprised that Flappy was fluent in Italian. She always said a very hearty '*bonjour*' to the French teacher who taught at the primary school and liked Big Mary's cakes, and just from the way Flappy said '*bonjour*' Mabel could tell that she was fluent in French too. *There is no end to Flappy's talents*, Mabel thought admiringly.

'Be a dear and summon the ladies, Mabel,' Flappy commanded. 'I will call Gracie myself.' She hung up and hastened across the hall to the library to find the Italian dictionary so that she could flash a few well-chosen phrases at the dinner table.

Gracie was sitting in an armchair beside the fire, drinking a cup of tea and gazing longingly at the photograph of the castle, when the telephone rang. She wrenched her thoughts away from the Tuscan countryside and lifted the receiver. 'Hello?' she said.

'Good, you're home,' said Flappy officiously.

'Flappy!' Gracie exclaimed and put down her mug.

'Now, I know it's short notice, but your presence is required at Darnley this evening.'

'This evening?' Gracie repeated. She'd rather been hoping to stay in and warm herself with the thought of that hot Italian sun in the blissful silence of her pottery room.

'This evening, at seven-thirty to be precise. I'm having a small, informal get-together and it's imperative that you're here.' There was a determined tone to Flappy's voice which Gracie immediately recognised. A tone that suggested she would not accept any excuse Gracie might give in order to avoid going out on this damp and foggy evening. Besides, Flappy knew very well that Gracie had no reason to decline; it wasn't as if she had anything else to do.

'How lovely,' Gracie replied weakly, feeling decidedly *un*lovely about it. Italy beckoned. She was already there. But tonight she would be firmly embedded in Devon – her pottery and her planning would have to wait until the morrow.

'Good,' said Flappy, then she added cheerfully, '*Ciao*.'

Gracie frowned. She had never heard Flappy say '*Ciao*' before.

❧

Flappy's husband Kenneth had made his money in a chain of fast food restaurants that became popular in the 1970s. He sold it for millions in 1983 and promptly retired, buying the big house in Badley Compton and building a golf course for which the people of Badley Compton were enormously grateful. It had been Flappy's idea to join their names together when they married, but no one in Badley Compton knew that. For all they were aware the Scott-Booths were an old English family with a house in the Algarve and plenty of money to spend on holidays in the Caribbean where they invited their four children and ten grandchildren for Christmas every year.

Darnley was a pretty white house with a grey slate roof that boasted fourteen bedrooms, an indoor swimming pool and an outdoor tennis court. The gardens were open to the public for three weeks in June (when Flappy could be spotted floating around the borders in a big straw hat and summer dress wielding a pair of secateurs with which she lopped off the occasional dead rose). Tonight Karen, the girl who came to cook, managed to disappear in time for Flappy to put on an apron and start stirring the Napoli sauce before any of her guests arrived for dinner. The first to appear was Mabel Hitchens, who made it her business to arrive before anyone else. She had brought Sally Hancock with her in her small green Golf and the two of them were more excited than ever, ringing the doorbell three times with impatience.

Flappy let them in, wooden spoon in one hand, glass of prosecco in the other, looking elegant and serene in an ivory silk blouse, floaty black trousers and pearls, her shoulder-length blonde hair immaculately coloured and blow-dried. At sixty-six she was still strikingly beautiful and aware of it. '*Buona sera*,' she said, closing the door behind them. 'What a *bella* evening this is going to be. Come, you must have some prosecco. I've been slaving in the kitchen all afternoon so I took the liberty of helping myself to a teeny tiny glass before you arrived.'

The two women followed Flappy's willowy figure across the black-and-white chequerboard floor to the spacious kitchen, which was warmed by a large Aga and scented with the savoury smells of fried onions and garlic. Both Mabel and Sally had dressed up for the occasion because Flappy's interpretation of the word 'informal' was notoriously understated. Always chic with a Continental air and a permanent suntan, Flappy wore silk and cashmere and lots of gold jewellery even when she had no plans to see anyone. She detested denim and never wore boots. She abhorred trainers even on the young, and her shoes were dainty with a low, discreet heel. She professed that it was vulgar to show off one's wealth (and came down very heavily on the modern celebrity who flaunted theirs) but managed to let the other women know by allowing the odd detail to slip out in conversation that her clothes were expensive designer items bought on Net-a-Porter and delivered to her door, then waving her manicured fingers in the air and adding breezily, 'I don't care for that sort of thing but Kenneth expects it, you know.'

As the two women stepped into the kitchen Flappy caught sight of Sally's sparkly gold stilettos and gave a little sniff. Anything sparkly besides diamonds was enormously vulgar to Flappy. But this small act of rebellion was as far as Sally would dare go. Being on the wrong side of Flappy Scott-Booth was an experience none of the women wanted to risk. Eileen Bagshott had been foolish enough to call a meeting at *her* house and worse, to *chair* it, an act of outright rebellion which had resulted in the end of her membership of the Badley Compton Ladies' Book Club as well as invitations to Darnley. Eileen was now a sorry figure sitting in the shadows in the back row at church on Sundays, and had to practically beg for tickets to concerts in the town hall. So, besides her stilettos, Sally, who had written unashamedly trashy romantic novels for thirty years under the pseudonym Charity Chance, wore burgundy trousers (a touch on the tight side), a pink blouse and her red hair swept into what she believed to be a modern take on the 1960s beehive. Her leather trousers and glittery tops were reserved for dinners at home with her family.

Unlike Sally, Mabel would have rather died than induce Flappy to think ill of her. She was a nervous, conventional creature and eager to please. Mabel wore a busy floral blouse fixed at the throat with a pastiche diamond brooch, navy-blue slacks and gold buckled pumps on her small feet – a high street version of Flappy, worn with less flair. Her hair was shoulder-length, grey-brown and too thin to copy Flappy's billowing bob. If it hadn't been for the glasses that exaggerated the size of Mabel's watery grey eyes, which had an unsettling habit of staring, she would have looked decidedly unremarkable. Now they stared at Flappy who had gone to such trouble to lay the table beautifully. Really, Mabel thought it remarkable how Flappy had thrown together a soirée at the very last minute, and for a moment she forgot about Gracie going to Italy and gazed in wonder at the clusters of candles, flower displays and starched blue-and-white Provençal tablecloth with matching napkins. 'I don't know how you do it,' she murmured, propelling Flappy, already on a pedestal, to even greater heights.

'*Fa niente,*' said Flappy, taking credit for Karen's good taste and hard work and feeling very pleased with her Italian, which sounded flawless to her ignorant ear. She handed them crystal flutes of prosecco and then swept into the hall to answer the door. A few moments later Esther Hancock and Madge Armitage, who had spent the previous couple of hours reading the book club choice in case Flappy asked them about it, hurried into the kitchen, bursting in their enthusiasm to talk about Gracie.

Flappy had taken care to invite Gracie half an hour later than the other women so that they'd have time to discuss her decision to go to Italy before she arrived. Once Flappy was satisfied that the women had witnessed her cooking apron and the few professional-looking sweeps of the wooden spoon around the tomato sauce, she hung the apron on the back of the door and led her guests into the drawing room where Karen had lit the fire and scented candles. The four women had spent many evenings in Flappy's cream-and-taupe-coloured drawing room and yet they hovered about the chairs until she invited them to sit down.

'We need to talk about Gracie,' said Flappy in her slow, well-articulated voice, and the other women listened respectfully. 'I've been thinking about her ever since I heard the news. I believe *I* was the first. I've decided that the worry is *not* about Gracie going to a foreign country on her own, even though she hasn't gone anywhere on her own for as long as I've known her, and really, as her friends, we must discourage her, it's about her running away. What is she running from? What has happened to induce her to take such drastic measures?' Flappy looked at each lady individually, fixing them with her topaz-blue eyes and silently asking them to think carefully and not all reply at once.

'How clever you are, Flappy. Running away had never crossed my mind,' gushed Mabel, enjoying the taste of prosecco but trying not to gulp it. 'I just assumed she wanted a holiday.'

'No, she's never wanted a holiday. She's running from *something*,' Flappy persisted. 'And we must find out what it is.'

'She must want to run away very much to venture so far from home,' said Esther, who had the deep, gravelly voice of a man and the ruddy, weathered skin of someone who has spent most of her life on horseback. 'She could run to Land's End, but to run to Italy . . . That's very far.'

'Boredom?' Sally suggested with a grin that might have won support had the others not been so nervous of Flappy.

Flappy put her head on one side and gave Sally a look as if she were a teacher ticking off a student who had said something unkind. 'Just because *you* might think her routine a little dull does not mean to say that it *is* dull, Sally,' she said. 'Gracie is comfortable in that routine and she's very happy to be given things to do for the book club. There's nothing boring about being busy, *I* know *that* better than anyone! Gracie is not a woman who wants to be adventurous and social like us.' Sally took a swig of prosecco and noticed that none of the others were willing to catch her eye.

'I wonder what her daughter thinks,' said Mabel, knowing

that the mention of Gracie's daughter would please Flappy, who enjoyed criticising the girl for not taking trouble with her mother when Flappy's four children and ten grandchildren made such a fuss of *her*.

True to form Flappy inhaled through dilated nostrils and shook her head gravely. 'That girl should be ashamed of herself. She hasn't been down to see her mother for over six months. If my memory serves me right, which it usually does, I believe her last visit was in August. However busy her life is in London, she should spare a thought for her poor mama who is alone in that house with only her dogs for company. I know what comfort children can be. I can't imagine being ignored like poor Gracie is ignored. Without us she'd have no one.'

'Perhaps she just wants to see Italy,' said Madge with a shrug. 'After all, there's nothing wrong with wanting to go to Italy, is there?'

Once again Flappy put her head on one side and smiled patiently at Madge, whose bohemian clothes and unkempt grey hair more typically drew her sympathy. 'My dear, if it were anyone else we wouldn't be having this conversation, now would we? Of course, there's nothing wrong with wanting to go to Italy, or with simply *going* to Italy, I've been many times and it's a *paese incantevole*, but this is Gracie we're talking about. Gracie can't possibly go on her own. She can't possibly go. She's not up to it. It'll be a disaster. Gracie—' And at that point the doorbell went.

'Gracie!' Madge gasped, and as Flappy got up to open the front door four pairs of eyes followed her eagerly.

Chapter 2

Gracie was stunned and a little embarrassed to find herself the centre of attention. She usually arrived at these get-togethers unnoticed, but now every eye in the room was upon her and every ear cocked to hear what she had to say. 'My dear Gracie,' said Flappy, towering over her (for Flappy was very tall and Gracie quite small) as she thrust a glass of prosecco into her hand. 'We're having an Italian evening in your *onore*.' Gracie frowned. 'Don't look so *sorpresa*. You're the talk of the town. Do tell us all about it. We're longing to hear. When are you going? Where are you staying? Is it true you're going alone? Who will look after the dogs? Is your daughter stepping in at last?' Flappy ushered Gracie into a chair and no one said anything. They all waited.

Gracie would normally have shrunk beneath the weight of such scrutiny. But she didn't. Not this time. Italy was already coursing through her veins like sun-warmed olive oil, giving her a heady sense of escape and adventure and courage. Yes, courage. She lifted her chin and replied, 'I'm going to Tuscany, in April, for seven days. I'm going to learn how to cook Italian food.'

The four pairs of eyes which had been fixed upon Gracie now fixed themselves upon Flappy. What would Flappy say to that? Flappy was almost too aghast to say anything, for April was one of the busiest months in Badley Compton and she needed all five women to be on hand, but she knew the ladies would depend on her to get to the bottom of it and she wasn't going to let them down. 'To cook?' she exclaimed with a chuckle that implied she thought the idea preposterous and a little quaint. 'Do you really have to go all the way to Tuscany to learn how to cook? I have some very good cookery books on Tuscan food I can lend you, I'm sure.'

'Thank you, Flappy,' said Gracie, knitting her fingers on her lap. 'But I'm going.' The determined way she said 'I'm going' was surprising in itself. Gracie had never sounded so determined in all the years they had known her. This determination further aroused their curiosity, and a touch of resentment, for no one likes it when people are not themselves.

'But surely, you're not going alone?' Flappy continued.

'I am,' Gracie replied.

'What would Ted say?'

'I think he'd be very happy.'

'And surprised,' Flappy added wryly. 'Where are you going to stay?'

'In a lovely old castle on a hill.'

'Is it an hotel?'

'Sort of . . .' Gracie didn't seem very certain about this.

'But you're paying, obviously?'

'Yes, it's quite dear.'

Flappy looked at each of the four other women and took a sharp breath. Then she looked back at Gracie. 'I don't want to sound vulgar, as you know I *never* discuss money, but I find myself having to bring up the dreaded subject, just this once. Where is the money coming from, Gracie?'

'My savings,' said Gracie.

'What, *all* of them?' Flappy gasped.

'Much of them,' Gracie corrected. Flappy was now more than astonished, she was irritated. There was an air of recklessness about Gracie that she had never seen in her before. It was as if someone else had taken over her body and was being very unlike Gracie in it. Flappy took this as a personal affront and felt compelled to get the old Gracie back, the one they knew and could depend upon.

'Well, I think that's very rash. I'm sure we all agree.' Flappy looked at the other women again, this time quite sternly. They all nodded, except Madge, who was staring at Gracie with admiration.

'Oh, yes, we do,' said Mabel, who was always quick to agree with Flappy.

'Quite rash,' Sally agreed.

'I don't think Ted would be very happy about *that*,' added Esther in her gravelly man's voice.

Then Madge surprised them. 'You only live once,' she said, and Flappy resolved not to refill her wine glass.

Gracie smiled at Madge who was looking a little cross-eyed. 'I read about the place in a magazine while Judy was colouring my hair and I thought just that. Just what Madge said: that you only live once.'

Madge chuckled and drained her glass. 'I would say you haven't even lived once, Gracie. Now is the time. Seize the day. Before that daughter of yours stuffs you in an old people's home and you can't ever go anywhere again.' That was a rather depressing thought, but it made space in Flappy's mind for an idea to present itself. It was high time that daughter of Gracie's stepped up to the mark. *She'd* dissuade her mother if Flappy presented a persuasive argument.

After the women had left and Flappy had stood on the doorstep and shouted '*Ciao*' into the wind in her most authentic Italian accent, she hurried back into the house to make a telephone call. It wasn't yet ten – she thought it incredibly rude to telephone *after* ten – and she had Carina's number from the time she had thrown Ted a surprise birthday party (he and Kenneth had played golf together, Kenneth rather better than Ted). She hoped the girl hadn't moved or changed her telephone number. To her immense relief, she hadn't.

'Hello?' said Carina in the refined voice she had cultivated since leaving Devon and settling in London twenty years before.

'Darling Carina, it's Flappy Scott-Booth.'

There was a moment's hesitation before the name registered. 'Ah, hello, Flappy.' Carina glanced at her watch, it was a quarter to ten, very late to be telephoning. It must be important. 'Is Mum all right?'

'That's why I'm calling. She's decided to go to Italy.'

'Italy?'

'Yes, Tuscany. In April, for seven days.' Flappy liked to be in possession of the facts.

'She's said nothing to me,' said Carina.

'When was the last time you spoke to her?' There was a disapproving tone in Flappy's voice.

'About a month ago, I think.' Flappy tutted but it wasn't her place to berate Carina for neglecting her mother. 'I've been so busy, you know, at work. I'll call her tomorrow. Thank you for letting me know, Flappy.' Carina hoped that her decisive manner would end the conversation, but Flappy was used to calling the shots and continued stridently.

'Well, she came up with the idea only recently, but I thought I should tell you so you can talk some sense into her. Your father would be very unhappy to think of her going all the way to Tuscany unaccompanied, and using all her savings.'

'She said that?' Carina asked. '*All* her savings?' *That has done it,* Flappy thought triumphantly. If Gracie were to return to an empty pot, Carina would have to support her.

'I'm afraid she did. Now you see why we're so worried about her.'

'I'll call her tomorrow and see what's going on.'

'I don't like to get involved in other people's business, but we're very fond of Gracie down here. My daughters would never allow *me* to spend seven days in a foreign country on my own even though I've travelled the world extensively and speak four languages with the fluency of a native. If she does go to Italy, and she's most determined to go, I would hate anything to happen to her. I'm sure you agree.'

'Absolutely,' Carina replied, somewhat tensely. 'As I said, I'll call her tomorrow.'

'Do. That would put my mind at rest. Really, when something dramatic happens the family must rally round, and you, Carina, are the only family she's got. I'm sure your father, wherever he is, would be very pleased you're taking control. And you know, April in Badley Compton is a very busy month. We have the Easter fête for a start and I really can't do without your mother. She's wonderfully competent at doing the behind-the-scenes administration I don't have the patience for. I really don't know what's got into her. It's so unlike her, which is why we're all terribly worried. I'm sure you will change her mind. You're our only hope.'

When Flappy put the telephone down she gave a contented sigh. Carina would no doubt put a stop to her mother's ludicrous plan and talk some sense into her. With any luck, the old Gracie, the Gracie they knew and loved, would return – and be around in April to help with the many events Flappy was planning for Badley Compton.

Happily, Flappy settled into bed and reached beneath the pile of glossy historical biographies and literary fiction there for show to find the one she really wanted to read, in private, without anyone knowing: *The Heat of Passion* by Charity Chance.

❧

Carina hung up and gave a sigh of irritation. She did not need this right now.

'Who was that, darling?' her husband called from the dressing room next door.

'Flappy Scott-Booth, aka pain in the neck,' she replied, marching in to share her annoyance. 'She's one of my mother's ghastly friends and a meddler. She called to tell me that Mum has decided to go to Italy.' Carina laughed joylessly and rolled her eyes. 'Mum must be mad! Perhaps she's lost her mind. God! Now is *not* a good time. I'm frantically busy at work. I don't have time to deal with her losing her marbles.'

Rufus, who was undressing, stood in his stripy boxer shorts and shirt and stared at his wife. 'Did you just say that Gracie is going to Italy?'

'Yes, but she's *not* going,' Carina replied firmly. 'Not if *I* have anything to do with it. One, she doesn't have the money to go hopping all over the world, and two, she's totally incapable of going anywhere on her own. She never went anywhere when Dad was alive, why she has to go now is beyond me. It's just silly. I'll call her tomorrow and talk her out of it. But that Flappy woman is a right pain. I thought she'd called me to tell me something terrible had happened!'

Rufus ran a hand through rust-coloured hair and grinned. 'It does sound very out of character. Do you think she's joined a cult?' His grey eyes twinkled, but Carina did not find him funny. It was late and she was tired and her guilt at not having spoken to her mother in so long made her tetchy.

'Not in Italy,' she retorted. 'God! As if I haven't got enough on my plate at the moment.' She lifted her long brown hair off her neck and turned round so that Rufus could unzip her black dress which had received many admiring comments at the cocktail party that evening.

'Before you go in there like a bulldozer, you might want to find out why she's going away. There's probably a perfectly logical explanation.'

'No, there isn't. You know Mother. She's shy and timid and likes her routine.'

'A late-life crisis?' said Rufus, then he added mischievously, 'Perhaps she's got a lover!'

Carina was unamused. 'That's not funny.'

'Just a joke,' he chuckled.

'Still not funny.' The truth was that while Gracie was tucked away quietly in Badley Compton, going about her usual routine and not causing Carina any worry, Carina could focus on the really important things, like increasing the success of her business and expanding her net of contacts and suitable friends.

She stepped out of her dress and wandered back into the bedroom in her underwear. As she put her jewellery away in the chest of drawers, she caught sight of herself in the long mirror that was leaning up against the wall. She knew she shouldn't have eaten the canapés. It was rare that a carbo-hydrate passed her lips, but she had weakened at the tray of duck pancakes. She stood straight and pulled in her stomach, regretting the pancake (only one) very much. At forty-one she was in pretty good shape. Who would know just by looking at her body that she was a mother? She worked out with a personal trainer three times a week and avoided a long list of unhealthy foods most of the time. Wine was a nightly necessity in order to unwind from a stressful day at the office. If dieting didn't keep her thin, being frantically busy did. Running her own public relations company was enormously demanding, especially as she found it very hard to delegate. She hadn't worked like a dog for the last fifteen years to loosen the reins now. Each of her clients had to believe they were the only ones who mattered. That kind of attentiveness required her to be in a dozen different places all at the same time – looking sharp, glamorous and in control. She turned away from her reflection, slipped out of her underwear and into silk pyjamas.

The en suite bathroom was designed especially so that she and Rufus had their own space. They each had a sink and capacious cupboards. Carina filled hers with beauty products from the companies she represented, but she didn't have much time to enjoy them. If she wasn't racing to a drinks party she was hurrying to a dinner party, and the odd night they stayed in she was so tired she lay in bed watching television like a zombie. Once, before they had made money, she and Rufus had shared the tiniest bathroom in a flat in Wandsworth – that was when their daughter Anastasia was a baby. Carina couldn't imagine living like that now. She'd got used to finer things. She certainly couldn't imagine living in her parents' cottage in Badley Compton where she'd grown up. She'd left that dull and uneventful life long ago and closed the door resolutely behind her.

As she removed her make-up and washed her face she didn't

dwell on her childhood by the sea or the early days of her marriage, she was busy thinking about the breakfast meeting she was due to have at eight-thirty the following morning with a prospective client, a cosmetics company, which was going to have to be persuaded to change not only its packaging but its advertising as well if it wanted to compete with the bigger and more successful brands. However, her mother kept drifting into her mind like an annoying grey cloud.

When she climbed into bed Rufus was reading *The Economist* with his glasses on. He looked old slumped against the pillows with his chin on his chest. Rufus didn't work out very often. He had a slight paunch which irritated Carina because, unlike her, he had the time to look after himself. He was a successful property developer, although the market was pretty slow at the moment, but even when business wasn't thin on the ground he seemed to have all the time in the world to do exactly as he pleased. He knew how to delegate and did, very efficiently. Like many public-school boys Rufus was laid-back and optimistic, the sort of man who made time to have a drink with a friend and didn't complain if he was having a bad week. He saw the funny side of every drama, mostly hers, and tried to encourage her to be as philosophical as he was, but Carina was much too busy being busy to have time to let her guard down. She wasn't from his world and had to work hard to convince everyone that she was. Having left Devon and married well, she had taken great trouble to reinvent herself. The thought of her mother pulled her straight back to a place she didn't want to be.

Carina would have liked to read in bed but her eyes were stinging. Her bedside table was piled high with award-winning books, which she intended to read just so that she could keep up with her erudite friends, but she hadn't read a single page of any of them. Her head sank into the pillow. She'd start on one tomorrow.

'Night, darling,' she said, pulling a silk mask over her eyes.

'Night,' said Rufus, without looking up from his magazine. They both knew the routine. It hadn't changed in years.

Carina dreamed that her mother was lost in Florence; a lonely, bewildered figure, shuffling down shady alleyways.

The following morning, after the breakfast meeting, during which the client had agreed to all her suggestions, Carina telephoned Gracie. She had closed her office door so that no one could listen in, having asked her assistant to go out and get her an almond milk decaffeinated latte from the coffee shop around the corner. She felt a moment's guilt when she heard her mother's voice, because it had been a long while since she'd heard it, but that was swiftly gone, along with the pleasantries, as she went straight to the point.

'Your friend Flappy called me last night, very late, I might add, to tell me that you've decided to go to Italy.' Carina was sitting perched on the end of her desk, throwing her gaze over the framed photographs on the wall of herself with a glittering array of celebrities. 'Is this true?'

'Yes,' Gracie replied. Her daughter's educated vowels still sounded strange to Gracie. She hadn't been brought up that way. 'I've only just decided, but it seems the whole of Badley Compton is talking about it.'

'Why do you need to go?' Carina asked, trying to mask her irritation with curiosity.

'I'm going to learn to cook Italian food.' There was a brightness in her voice that Carina didn't recognise. Wasn't she a bit old for a mid-life crisis?

'But, Mum, isn't this a bit rash? I mean, how are you going to afford it?'

'I have some savings.'

'But they're for your old age.'

Gracie chuckled. 'I'm already in my old age, dear.'

'Only just. You may have another thirty years ahead of you.'

'I'm not the Queen Mother.'

'And you're planning on going alone?'

'Yes,' said Gracie. 'But you mustn't worry about me. I'm very capable of—'

Carina cut her off briskly. 'Mum, you can't go alone. What are you thinking?'

'Of going alone,' Gracie replied simply and firmly.

It was clear to Carina that she wasn't going to talk her mother out of it, at least not today, not on the telephone. She sighed heavily. She didn't have time for this nonsense and yet she couldn't allow her mother to travel abroad on her own. It didn't feel right. She knew her father wouldn't have allowed it. He'd expect her to step into his shoes and go with her.

There came a knock on the door. 'Hold on, Mum,' she said. 'Come in, Jenny.' Her assistant put the coffee carton on the desk, beside a photograph of Carina shaking hands with the Countess of Wessex. Carina put her hand over the receiver. 'Jenny, call Theo Fennell and book in a lunch at the earliest. I have an idea that might interest him. And tell Jonathan I need that report on my desk before I lunch with Bruce.' She glanced at her watch. 'Which means *now*,' she added. Then, speaking back into the telephone, she continued. 'Look, Mum, what's the rush? Why don't you wait a year?'

'A year? Who knows where I'll be in a year?' It was clear from Gracie's tone that she really didn't care one way or the other, what mattered was *now*. 'You really don't need to concern yourself over this, Carina. It's my decision and my treat.

I'm very excited about it.' There was that buoyant, cheerful voice again that Carina didn't recognise.

'If I hadn't so much on I'd come with you,' Carina said weakly, but she knew that was a lie. She bit her lip and dropped her gaze to her feet. If she hardly ever visited her mother in Badley Compton, she was hardly going to go all the way to Italy.

'You're busy with your life, dear. But thank you for the kind thought.'

'Why don't you go with a friend?'

'Because I don't want to,' said Gracie. 'I'm going alone and my friend Esther has offered to look after the dogs.'

'I thought I'd talk you out of it, Mum, but it seems you have everything worked out.'

'Oh, I do.'

'So, you're going in April?'

'For seven days.'

'Can I get Jenny to book your flights, at least . . .?'

'I can manage myself, thank you.'

'Well, if you're sure you're okay, I'd better run. Full-on day. You know.'

'Oh, yes. Off you go. You're such a busy girl.'

Gracie listened to her daughter hang up and then, regretfully, did the same. She remained in the kitchen, looking out over the harbour, and the sense of loss which ran like a hidden stream beneath the veneer of contentment rose suddenly to flood her heart. She put a hand on the side of the sink and took a deep breath. Carina was a successful businesswoman, she told herself. Of course, it was hard for her to come all the way down to Devon to visit. The last thing Gracie wanted was to be a burden. And yet, in spite of the well-worn arguments, she felt an emptiness inside where Carina had once been.

All around the cottage were photographs of Carina, as a little girl in school uniform, grinning at the camera, as a rebellious teenager with spiky hair and black eyeliner, as a young woman already morphing into the sophisticated woman she would later become. Her wedding day, she and Rufus one Christmas, with Anastasia as a small baby, and then the gaps grew wider. Those windows into her daughter's life became less frequent until there were no more windows. Carina had made it clear by her absence that she didn't want her mother to be a part of her life. Gracie had lost her daughter and she had never really got to know her granddaughter. The truth was too painful to acknowledge, that for some reason she was unwanted, so she put Carina's distance down to a very hectic and successful life and told herself to be proud of her daughter's achievements, to be unselfish and undemanding; to let her go.

Gracie returned to her chair by the fire and to the magazine which lay open on the table beside it. Her battered heart recovered a little at the sight of that magnificent castle as if the amber glow surrounding it were honey being poured straight into her chest. What did it matter to anyone if she went to Italy? Who would miss her? Why should anyone care? She felt a surge of defiance, a stirring of an old and forgotten courage, an almost imperceptible reawakening of a part of her that had been in deep hibernation for many, many years. She smiled then as she remembered the girl she had once been and, in that moment, she felt young again.

❧

Carina hurried off to her lunch meeting and then on to the various evening events that her position as a top London PR director required her to attend. Yet, as the week advanced, the irritating grey cloud that was her mother refused to drift away.

In fact, it only grew heavier. It brought guilt and annoyance. By Thursday night she was in an extremely bad mood. What made matters worse was the text she received from Anastasia. Her seventeen-year-old daughter was in the school sanatorium, with the flu, demanding to be taken home.

Carina gave a loud sigh. 'Why does she always get sick at the worst possible time?' she asked Rufus, who was in his usual place on the bed, reading the *Spectator.* 'I mean, I haven't got time to drive all the way to her boarding school to pick her up. She'll just have to sweat it out in the san. Isn't that what we pay the school for anyway?'

Rufus smiled in that lackadaisical manner of his which Carina now found exasperating, because everything always seemed so *easy* for him. '*I'll* bring her home,' he volunteered.

'But I don't *want* her at home. We've got people for Sunday lunch and I don't want her moaning and groaning around the house, giving everyone the flu.'

'Darling, she'll stay in bed watching TV. She won't be a problem.'

'Then I'll have to drive her back—'

'*I'll* drive her back,' Rufus interjected, taking off his glasses and looking at his wife in bewilderment. 'What kind of mother refuses to have her daughter home when she's sick?'

Carina sat up. 'Are you accusing me of being a bad mother?'

'Since you ask, right now that's what you look like.'

'How dare you, Rufus!'

'Look, Carina, I'm accepting of you not making time for *me*, I'm used to that and I'm fine with it, but I won't allow your job to monopolise you to the extent that you find no time for your own child.'

Carina folded her arms defensively. 'So, you're now saying I'm a bad wife *and* mother? That's just great.'

'I'm saying that you're married to your job, which is fine, but *Anastasia* is your child, not your business.'

'That's just perfect! I'm a success and you chastise me for it. If I was a lowly secretary I'd have all the time in the world to bring your slippers and cook your dinners and pick up Anastasia from school when she's sick, but this isn't the 1950s! I have a career, like you, and yet, as a woman, I'm expected to do all the domestic stuff as well. Those feminists have a lot to answer for as there's a fault in their argument. I'm a bad wife because I go out and earn a living. Perhaps you should have married one of your Sloaney friends whose only goal is to raise kids and spend their husband's money. I'm not going to let you make me feel bad about my career. I'm a success, a *huge* success, and I've done it all on my own. I've come from nowhere. I didn't have the contacts and privileges that you had. My parents were provincial, unambitious people and if I hadn't left Badley Compton I'd still be there working in the gift shop!'

Rufus frowned. It was the amusement in it that infuriated Carina. He never took anything she said seriously. 'How did we get from Anastasia's flu to the Badley Compton gift shop?'

She glowered at him. 'You're the most annoying man!' she snapped.

'But *you* married me.' He grinned, but Carina looked away. 'I'll fetch Anastasia tomorrow. You don't have to cancel any of your meetings. God forbid your daughter infringes upon your business life.'

'That's unfair. It's a rat race out there.'

'And you're queen rat, I know.'

She sighed dramatically, turned her back on him and pulled her mask over her eyes. 'I've had enough of this. I'm going to sleep. Some of us have to get up at dawn to go to work.'

'While you're lying there lamenting your lot, chew on this: I think you should accompany your mother to Italy.'

'You're so predictable, Rufus. I knew you were going to say this. It was only a matter of time . . .'

'You need a break. It will do you good to go away for a week. Gracie won't be around for ever and she's your mother. She's a widow. She lives on her own and you barely see her.'

'Devon is a five-hour drive from London,' Carina mumbled.

'The telephone is in your hand, all the time.' Carina had nothing to say to that. 'One could even go as far as saying you've disowned her in favour of *my* mother,' Rufus continued.

'Diana lives around the corner,' she retorted wearily.

'But you still feel the need to telephone her most days.'

'You don't understand,' she said.

Rufus picked up his magazine and began to read again. 'The trouble is,' he said. 'I understand too well.' Glamorous society queen Diana Cavendish was just the sort of mother Carina wished hers could be. 'By the way, did you really work in the gift shop?'

Chapter 3

Anastasia lay in bed, shivering, and waited for the school nurse to inform her that her father had arrived to take her home. The rain was tapping cheerlessly on the window pane and it was already getting dark, even though it wasn't yet four. The room in the health centre was just as desolate: thin, nondescript curtains which served no purpose, stark white walls, practical linoleum floor and iron beds with lumpy mattresses. Suffering from a temperature and a sore throat Anastasia was feeling sufficiently sorry for herself to have persuaded the school nurse that she was sick enough to be sent home. In any case, they needed the beds as there was a bug going round and the ill overseas girls had no option but to remain at school. The nurse was really quite pleased to be getting rid of Anastasia.

In the next-door bed was a girl in the year below Anastasia whose mother was on her way from Suffolk to pick her up. Anastasia had listened to their telephone conversation with mounting irritation. The mother was obviously a neurotic fusspot, she decided, asking ridiculous questions: Was she drinking enough liquids? Was she warm enough? Was she comfortable and had she been able to sleep? Then she had asked to speak to the nurse and had gone over every detail again. By the end of the call Anastasia knew the minutiae of the girl's condition and longed for the silly woman to arrive and take her daughter away.

Anastasia hadn't even spoken to *her* mother. She had texted but it had been her father who had telephoned the school and arranged to fetch her, but only after the doctor had come to see her at 2 p.m. and signed her out. *Her* mother clearly wasn't worrying about *her* warmth and comfort. She'd texted this morning to tell her that Daddy was coming and that there was an M&S cottage pie in the fridge in case she wasn't back in time to cook supper. Anastasia knew she wouldn't be back in time. She never was. She picked up her smartphone and began to play a mindless game to pass the time.

'I'm so excited I'm going home,' said the girl in the next-door bed. Anastasia didn't respond. It was an unwritten school rule that younger girls did not speak to older girls and Anastasia was not only in the year above, but considered by most to be quite intimidating. But the girl went on regardless. *Perhaps she believed sick bay to be a kind of neutral territory*, Anastasia thought grudgingly. 'Once when I was sick Mummy came to get me and I lay on the sofa with the dogs for a week watching telly while she brought me hot chocolate and biscuits. It was heaven!'

Anastasia didn't look up from her phone. 'Well, when I was suspended for smoking, my mother was on a business trip abroad so I didn't even see her.'

'Who looked after you?' the girl asked, and Anastasia was cheered a little by the amazement in the girl's voice.

'No one. I looked after myself.' Which wasn't entirely true because her father had stayed home, but if she revealed *that* detail the story would lose its clout. 'I'm an only child of working parents. I've had to learn to be independent.'

'I suppose you were lucky not to have been expelled.'

'I don't know,' Anastasia said with a shrug. 'Wouldn't have been too bad. I'd rather fancy going to a sixth form college in London, but Mum doesn't want me at home.'

Anastasia grinned into her smartphone as the girl seemed to dry up and the conversation came to an abrupt end. They spent the following hour in silence, Anastasia on social media, the girl reading a book, which annoyed Anastasia too because not only did she have a mother who made her hot chocolate, but she was reading a highbrow novel, and seemingly engrossed in it. She was much too wholesome for Anastasia's comfort. Then the girl's mother appeared and swept into the room like a tornado of goose down. 'Darling, are you all right? I've been so worried about you.' She embraced her child, holding her close and stroking her hair. Anastasia glanced up from her phone to see the girl's arms around her mother's big coat. She swallowed the rising jealousy and went back to her phone, telling herself that she'd hate it if her mother smothered *her* like that. 'Come on, let's get you home where I can look after you and make you well again,' the mother said in the same voice she had probably used when her daughter was little. Then, as the girl was dressing, the woman turned to Anastasia. 'You're not going to languish here, are you?'

'Nope, my dad's coming to pick me up,' Anastasia replied politely. She hadn't expected to be spoken to.

'That's good. Not very nice being sick at school. Home is the best place for a speedy recovery.' She turned back to her daughter. 'Well done, darling. Now, got everything?'

'Yes,' the girl replied, picking up a floral overnight bag. She smiled at Anastasia. 'I hope you get better soon.'

'Thanks,' Anastasia replied. She couldn't very well be mean-spirited in front of the mother. 'You too.'

For a while the room was empty and quiet. The rain had

stopped but the wind continued to moan through the bare branches of the plane trees that shivered in the cold. Anastasia felt empty too, and forlorn. That mother had brought something warm and tender into the room, but now it had gone. She imagined the girl lying on the sofa with her dogs, watching television in front of a boisterous fire, eating biscuits and drinking hot chocolate. She imagined the mother would sit with her and check her forehead every now and then with the back of her hand. Every time *she* was ill, which wasn't often, Carina made her feel like an inconvenience. She'd once heard her parents arguing in their bedroom on the floor below hers. Carina had been complaining that this was the worst time for Anastasia to be sick, as if Anastasia had chosen it on purpose, because she had important meetings she couldn't miss. Her voice had risen with anxiety as she went through all the things she had to do and the people she had to see. Rufus had offered to remain at home and look after the patient, as he had affectionately called her, and her mother had ended the conversation by grumbling that once again she was cast as a bad mother because *she* had a job that demanded one hundred per cent of her time, whereas *he* could pick his up and put it down as he wanted. Anastasia imagined that argument had been replayed last night when they'd received her text. *Well,* she thought defiantly, *I might be an inconvenience, but I'm a* sick *inconvenience so I'm not going to waste away at school just to make Mum's life easier.*

A beam of bright light shone through the curtains as a car turned into the forecourt. She sensed that was her father and her annoyance dissolved at the thought of going home. When the nurse came in to tell her that it was indeed her father who had come to collect her, she had already dressed and was sitting on her bed with her overnight bag packed.

Rufus gave Anastasia a big hug before throwing the bag over his shoulder and setting off down the corridor. Once in the car he patted her knee with his big hand. 'Poor old you,' he said in his usual jovial voice. Rufus was positive about everything, always. 'We'll get you well again.'

'I feel rotten,' Anastasia complained.

'Of course you do. That sanatorium is enough to make a healthy person sick. You'll feel better at home.'

'Don't suppose Mum's there,' she said, hating herself for caring.

'I'm afraid she's—'

'Got a meeting,' Anastasia interrupted. 'What's new?'

'Well, *I'm* home and we're going to have cottage pie together.'

'Good. My throat feels like it's made of sandpaper.'

'Do you want me to stop at a garage and get you a hot drink?'

Anastasia looked at her father steadily. She felt a wave of gratitude and relief. 'Yes please,' she replied. 'And a biscuit?'

❧

It was late when Carina put her key in the lock. She'd been to two parties and a charity dinner all the way out in the East End of London, and was now not only a little tipsy but exhausted. She stood at the door of her house but didn't open it. She knew Rufus was inside with Anastasia. The lights were on in the upstairs bedrooms. They would have had supper together and both would have silently cursed her for being absent.

Since Carina had learned that her mother was taking herself off to Italy she had felt a growing sense of disquiet. An uncomfortable weight, like a stone in her conscience, reminded her of her refusal to do what was right. And it seemed she couldn't do right by anyone at the moment. Her mother made her feel like a bad daughter, her daughter made her feel like a bad mother and Rufus made her feel like a bad wife, all because she had a very demanding career. How did other women manage it? How did they succeed in making the people around them feel valued? How did they find time to share? *She* didn't have time even for herself.

Carina reflected that it wasn't so long ago that Anastasia had been caught smoking and suspended. The girl didn't do a scrap of work at the massively expensive school they sent her to, and was going through that grunting, negative stage that so many of her friends with teenage daughters complained of. Was it so very surprising that she didn't jump into the car the minute Anastasia got flu and demanded to be taken home? As for Gracie, she was a grown-up. If she wanted company in Italy she could invite Flappy to go with her, or one of her other friends. She did *have* friends, Carina reflected, or Flappy would not have telephoned in a panic. Carina wouldn't allow herself to feel guilty about her mother. And Rufus? He claimed to understand her, so understand her he would just have to do, and be a little more tolerant while he was at it!

Yet, as she pushed open the front door and walked into the hall, she still felt that uncomfortable feeling in her conscience, despite the arguments in her favour.

The mirrors on the walls and the polished oak floor gleamed in the golden light of the chandeliers, which raised her spirits a little. She cast her mind back to the cottage where she had grown up and considered how far she had come. She was proud of her ascent from small-town girl to big-city success, although it hadn't come without a great deal of effort. She had worked hard to build her business and transform herself into a better version of the person she had been. Not a day went by when she didn't appreciate her beautiful home and the glamorous social life she had acquired. The trouble was, having spoken to her mother, she was reminded of her humble roots and that made her uncomfortable. She felt guilty for having turned her back on them and resentful for feeling guilty. She did *not* want to remember that she had humble roots. She wanted to be who she was *now*.

She hung up her coat and tossed her handbag onto the marble-topped island in the kitchen. She paused at the bottom of the stairs, almost afraid to go up and face her husband and daughter. What was she afraid of? she asked herself. Two cross people or discovering that they were doing very well without her. She began to climb briskly.

She found them lying on the bed in the master bedroom, watching a movie – or rather, Rufus was watching the movie while their daughter seemed to be more interested in her smartphone. Anastasia didn't look anything like as sick as Carina expected. Her face looked a little flushed, to be sure, and her eyes were perhaps a touch on the glassy side, but had she been *very* ill she would have taken to her bed. Carina deduced that she had a heavy cold rather than the flu, and was slightly irritated that she had managed to manipulate them into bringing her home.

'Hello, darling,' she said and gave a small wave from the doorway. She didn't want to catch her cold by kissing her. She certainly couldn't spare the time to be sick.

Anastasia didn't lift her eyes from the phone. 'Hi,' she mumbled.

'Come and join us,' said Rufus, patting the bedspread. 'We're watching *The Princess Bride*.'

'Well, *you're* watching *The Princess Bride*. Anastasia is on social media,' retorted Carina.

'I'm not on social media,' Anastasia corrected her grumpily.

'I think you should go to bed, Anastasia,' said her mother. 'If you're sick you shouldn't be up and about.'

'I'm not up and about. I'm lying on your bed.'

'I think you should be lying in *your* bed.'

Rufus looked at his watch. 'Your mother's right. It's nearly midnight. Off to bed, darling.' He leaned over and kissed her cheek. *He's clearly not worried about catching her cold,* Carina thought resentfully. Rufus switched off the movie with the remote.

'Night, Dad,' Anastasia replied, getting up. 'Night, Mum,' she added as she passed her and shuffled through the door.

'What a day I've had,' said Carina, stepping out of her shoes.

'Anastasia seems all right. She's got a temperature, but I've given her Nurofen and it's gone down. She'll feel better tomorrow, after a good night.'

'Great,' Carina replied, absent-mindedly. 'She doesn't look too bad,' she added, to show that she too was concerned. 'Thank you for picking her up.'

'You don't need to thank me. That's what fathers do.'

'Most fathers are too busy,' she said, sitting on the edge of the bed.

'No one is too busy for the important things.'

Carina was too tired to take offence. She turned to him suddenly. 'Why do you love me?' she asked.

Rufus frowned. 'What do you mean?'

'I'm a horrible person. I'm a bad mother, a bad daughter and a bad wife. What's there to love?'

Rufus smiled indulgently. He seemed to have endless patience and energy to be positive. 'You don't stop loving someone because they're too busy to make time for you. I love you because you're *you*,' he said simply.

Carina was not satisfied. She wanted something more concrete to hold on to. 'But what *is* that? What *is* me?'

'I know what you are, but perhaps you need to make time to find out for yourself. You've spent twenty years on the run. Why don't you just stop running for a moment and look about you.'

'I don't know what you're talking about.'

'That's because you've drunk too much.'

'It's made me sad.'

'No, the wine hasn't made you sad. You were sad already, the wine has just let it out.'

Carina nodded. 'I'd better go and say goodnight to Anastasia.'

'She'd like that,' he said.

'I don't think so, but I'll go anyway.'

When she opened her daughter's bedroom door, the lights were off. Anastasia was a mound beneath the duvet. Carina walked over and bent down to pat her. 'Night night, darling.'

'Night,' came the muffled response.

'I hope you feel better in the morning.'

'So do I.'

Carina made to leave the room when the mound moved. 'I hear Granny is going to Italy on her own.' She poked her head out of the duvet.

'Yes, she is.'

'Daddy told me.'

'Well, we've been worrying about her.'

'Then I think you should go with her,' Anastasia urged and Carina heard herself reply, 'If I do, then *you're* coming with me.'

There was a long silence as each was as surprised as the other by Carina's response. Then Anastasia finally spoke in the dead tone of a person accustomed to being disappointed. 'Pigs might fly,' she said and pulled the duvet over her head.

There was something terribly shocking to Carina in the way her daughter had so readily and automatically written her off that she was left reeling in the doorway. Her response suggested, in its pessimistic tone, that she had *never* given her daughter time or attention. As she closed the door, Carina wondered whether the girl was, in fact, right.

If there was one thing Carina relished, it was a challenge. Provoked by her daughter's lack of faith in her, she was now determined to prove that she was a mother who could be counted on.

The following morning, being a Saturday, Carina went for a run around the park before Rufus woke up. The rain had passed in the night and now the sky was a freshly washed duck-egg blue. The tarmac path glistened beneath her running shoes and the weak winter sun rose slowly in the eastern sky, causing the raindrops to sparkle prettily on the bare trees like little Christmas lights. Carina was feeling positive. She had made her decision and the uncomfortable feeling in her conscience was now replaced by a buoyant sense of doing the right thing. She'd go to Italy with her mother and Anastasia. She could work from there. After all, with internet and her computer her absence would hardly be noticed by clients or employees. She'd delegate what she could and take care of the rest from Tuscany. Rufus would be happy she was doing as he suggested, Anastasia would get a week's holiday in the sun and her mother would not have to go on her own, which would have made her father happy too. It was a win-win for everybody concerned. She could do seven days, she reasoned. Seven days; and then things would return to the way they were.

As she was running back up the street towards her house, who should be walking towards her with her overweight basset hound waddling at her booted feet but Diana Cavendish, her mother-in-law. Carina removed her earphones and waved. Diana smiled. Even in a headscarf and coat she looked glamorous. 'Look at you!' Diana exclaimed. 'You never stop!'

'It's a beautiful day,' Carina replied. 'And I can never lie in anyway. There's always too much to do.'

At seven-thirty in the morning Diana was wearing a full face of make-up. She was a handsome woman with eyes the colour of gunmetal, high, pronounced cheekbones and a long, straight nose. Her pedigree was unmistakable even before she opened her mouth and released the clipped consonants and lazy vowels of the upper class. 'Quite right. If you lie in, you miss the whole morning,' she said.

'Anastasia's home. She's got the flu,' Carina told her.

'Gracious, poor girl. I hope you don't catch it.'

Carina laughed. 'I don't have time to catch the flu.'

'Well, I don't want it either, so don't bring her over until she's better. Just give her my love.'

'I'm taking her to Italy in April, with my mother. I thought it would be nice for the three of us to spend some time together.'

Diana's reaction was gratifying. 'Aren't you a good girl!' she exclaimed, sending Carina's spirits soaring. 'What a lovely thought.'

'I don't get to see my mother very often.'

'Well, she does live awfully far away,' said Diana sympathetically.

'Rufus has told me I need to take a break.'

'You do work terribly hard. Really, modern girls like you put an awful lot onto their plates. I think we had it much easier in our day.' The overweight basset hound spotted another dog across the street and pulled on its lead.

'I won't keep you. Bernard wants to get on,' said Carina.

'Pop over later for a cup of tea. I want to hear all about Italy. What a good daughter you are, and Anastasia is a lucky girl. Show her some culture. It'll be good for her. Young people these days watch much too much television.'

When Carina arrived at her front door she was feeling very pleased with herself. Diana's praise had soothed her bruised morale and given her a welcome boost. She found Rufus in the kitchen in his dressing gown, reading the papers and drinking a cup of coffee on a stool at the island. He looked up when she entered. 'Morning,' he said.

'I've decided to go with Mum to Italy and to take Anastasia with us,' she said breezily.

Rufus frowned and took off his reading glasses. 'Good Lord, what's come over you?'

'I've had time to think about it—'

'I didn't think you had time for anything!' he interrupted with a grin.

Carina ignored him. 'I've had time to think about it and have realised that you're right. Mum can't go on her own. It's not fair to let her. Anastasia can come if she wants to. She might prefer to go somewhere with her friends, but I'll ask her. Of course, you're very welcome too.'

Rufus put his glasses back on. 'I think it's a girls' trip and when it comes to cooking, I'm unteachable.'

'Okay, as you wish.'

'You can come back and bring me my slippers and cook me pasta for dinner.'

'As Anastasia would say, pigs might fly.'

Rufus laughed. 'You'd better call your mother before you tell Anastasia. Gracie might not want you to go with her.'

That possibility had not occurred to Carina.

Gracie had just returned from walking the dogs when the telephone rang. She sensed it might be Flappy and had a good mind not to answer. For some reason she had become Flappy's latest cause. Having practically been ignored, or at least taken for granted, by Flappy for years, her sudden elevation in status was making Gracie uneasy. Was it really such an extraordinary thing to decide to go to Italy? Didn't *everyone* choose to go somewhere at some point? Was she so very different? Before she announced her intention no one ever took any notice of her; now she couldn't walk down the street without people smiling and saying hello and detaining her for a chat. It was as if she had become a celebrity overnight, and why? Because she had simply decided to take a trip. She wandered over to the telephone and reluctantly picked it up.

'Mum, it's me,' said Carina. *Her voice didn't sound nearly as brisk as it had the other day*, Gracie thought with relief.

'Hello, dear,' said Gracie.

'I've been thinking, about you going to Italy.'

'You're not going to try and stop me, are you?'

'Of course not. You must go. I think it'll be good for you to get away. You haven't been anywhere since Dad died and even then he only took you to the Lake District.'

'I only ever wanted to go to the Lake District,' said Gracie.

'Would you mind terribly if Anastasia and I came with you?'

Gracie didn't know what to say. Having dreaded the caller being Flappy, she was now surprised that not only was it Carina, but her daughter and granddaughter wanted to accompany her to Italy. She sank into the armchair. 'Of course I wouldn't mind. But you're not coming because you feel sorry for me, are you? I'd hate to be a burden.'

'Mum, you're not a burden. It'll be fun. We could all do with a break in the sunshine and Tuscany is lovely in April.'

'Yes, it is,' said Gracie wistfully and the longing that had gripped her heart since reading that article in the hairdresser's tightened its hold.

'Then that's settled,' said Carina decisively, defaulting to the officious tone she used in the office. 'Send me the details and I'll get Karen to book us all in.'

'I've already booked and paid,' said Gracie. 'But I'll give you the details so you and Anastasia can book as well.' The magazine was on the table beside her. She glanced at it. 'You won't be disappointed, Carina. It's a very beautiful place.' She lifted it onto her knee and watched it fall open on the right page. '*Truly* beautiful,' she emphasised with a sigh. She couldn't believe that she was going to share Castello Montefosco with her daughter and granddaughter. She felt the sudden urge to tell Flappy, but then overcame it. She'd keep that information to herself. She was used to keeping secrets, after all, and habits are hard to change. It was deeply gratifying that Flappy, who thought she knew everything, knew absolutely nothing about *this*.

And no one knew, not even Carina, that Gracie had been to Italy before. That Italy was embedded deep in her heart, like a pearl in an oyster. Only *she* knew that.

Chapter 4

London, 1955

As a little girl, Gracie Robinson knew how to count to ten in Italian. She had been taught by her uncle Hans, who was Dutch but lived in Italy and came to visit his sister, Gracie's mother, whenever he travelled to London on business. As a reward for her quick learning he had given her a box of paints, brushes and paper. Uncle Hans was a gifted painter and there was every chance that *she* would be too, for Gracie had shown a keen interest in drawing ever since she had first held a pencil. 'It's in your blood,' her mother would tell her, 'from Oma's side.' *Oma* meaning grandmother in Dutch. 'The Dutch are the best painters in the world, along with the Italians,' her mother added proudly, for although she had committed to a life in England, her blood would always be orange. Gracie dipped her brush into the paint and dabbed it gingerly on the paper. She wanted very much to be a gifted painter like Uncle Hans.

Gracie wanted to be rich too, like Uncle Hans. He'd arrive in front of their modest house in Camden in a big shiny car, dressed in an expensive suit and tie, a thick coat draped over his wide shoulders, a hat set at a raffish angle on his head. He smelt of lemons and spice and sported a dashing moustache. He smoked Cuban cigars, drank Irish whiskey and wore a large gold signet ring on the little finger of his left hand. Like Gracie's mother he spoke English with an accent and often slipped into Dutch when he was in the house, especially in the evenings when he was tired. He never arrived empty-handed. He brought presents for his sister, his elderly mother who lived with them, Gracie, and for Gracie's older brother, Joseph. The children, who had lost their father in the war, loved Uncle Hans and looked forward to his visits in the same way that children look forward to Santa Claus at Christmas. In their eyes he was magical, larger-than-life and omnipotent.

Greet, Gracie's mother, was not rich like her brother so she depended on him for money to subsidise the small amount she earned from dressmaking. Hans and Greet's father, who was English, had left their mother and run off with his secretary – the cliché would have been laughable had he not broken his wife's heart and left her destitute – so Hans had to support *her* as well Greet and her children. But Oma Hollingsworth was no trouble. She helped Greet in her workroom in spite of being unable to thread a needle even with the help of spectacles, and was a splendid cook. Whenever Uncle Hans visited there was meat on the table and Oma's famous *stamppot*, for which she claimed to add secret ingredients to the mashed potatoes and other vegetables, which set it apart from the traditional Dutch recipe and gave it a uniquely delicious flavour. She told them that even though people begged her for it, she would take the recipe to her grave, but Uncle Hans confided in the children, with a lopsided grin and a wink, that her *stamppot* was just the same as everybody else's.

Gracie knew more about Uncle Hans than she did about her own father, whose photograph was exhibited in a frame on the dresser in the parlour. A black-and-white photograph of a formal-looking young man in uniform who was a stranger to her, for Gracie had been born the year before he died. The little she knew about him was this: He had been called Frank Robinson and had met Greet, Gracie's mother, when he was working in Amsterdam for her father, who ran an art gallery. They had married in 1938 in Holland, but when war was declared he had insisted they return to England so that he could enlist. Greet had dutifully gone with him and set up home in the small house in Camden, north London, which he'd just been able to afford. Joseph had been born in 1940 and Gracie two years later. Frank had been killed in France in 1943. Greet kept his letters in a shoebox, but Gracie had never had the courage to ask if she could read them. Uncle Hans, albeit living far away in Italy, soon filled the void and became the father figure she could look up to. Her mother would read her brother's letters aloud at the dinner table and then she and Oma would discuss him in excited tones for the rest of the meal. Gracie and her brother would devour every word, adding more glitter to the already dazzling image of Uncle Hans Hollingsworth.

Uncle Hans took trouble with the children, encouraging them to paint and learn about art by gifting them big picture books of the world's most famous painters, but it wasn't until one visit in 1955, when Gracie was thirteen, that he saw something in her that he hadn't noticed before. It all started with a discussion around the kitchen table when Oma commented on Gracie's gift. 'She's a natural artist, just like you were at her age, Hans,' she said in her slow Dutch drawl.

A shadow of alarm swept across Greet's face. 'It is an entertaining hobby, nothing more,' she cut in.

Hans turned his sharp blue eyes onto Gracie and raised a

bushy eyebrow. 'Are you a natural artist, Gracie?' he asked and Gracie nodded shyly.

'Ever since you gave me paint I have practised,' she replied, eager to please her uncle.

Joseph, jealous of Uncle Hans's attention being so intensely focused on his sister, interjected. 'But copying doesn't count,' he scoffed. This seemed to darken the shadow of alarm on Greet's face.

Now Hans raised *two* bushy eyebrows. He looked at Greet. 'You didn't tell me that Gracie can paint.'

'She wasn't really any good until recently,' Greet explained, flustered. 'And Joseph is right, copying isn't the same as painting with one's own expression.'

'There is a place for everything,' Hans said, almost to himself. He turned back to Gracie, who was itching to be invited to show him. 'May I see what you have painted?' he asked, and Gracie was already off her chair and hurrying to her bedroom before he had finished the sentence. She was too eager to flaunt what she knew was a talent to notice the rising tension in the kitchen.

Gracie had painted many pictures, all copied from the books her uncle had given her. She had a wide range of good examples, from Raphael, to Johannes Vermeer and Van Gogh. She knelt on the floor and went through them, anxious to choose the best examples to show her uncle. *Sure, they were copies,* she thought to herself, *but they were* excellent *copies.* As she bent over her work she suddenly sensed someone standing behind her and spun round. She expected Joseph and was ready to respond firmly to his derision, but to her surprise it was her uncle and the look on his face was one she had never seen before. She thought, at first, that he was angry, for his cheeks had gone the colour of red wine and his mouth had twisted into an unattractive grimace, quite unlike the humorous smile which usually hovered about his lips. But then he shook his head and muttered something inaudible under his breath. A second later he was kneeling beside her, carefully studying each painting. Gracie said nothing as he scrutinised her work, lifting the paper into the dim light coming through the window, moving it slightly this way and that to fully appraise the brushstrokes.

At last he turned his incisive gaze on *her.* 'You are a fine painter, Gracie,' he said in a voice that was quiet and steady and full of intention, though Gracie didn't know what that intention was. 'These are very good. I am impressed.'

'They are only copies,' Gracie mumbled humbly, but her pale face flushed with pride.

'They are exceptional copies.'

At that, Gracie's heart flooded with happiness. For her beloved Uncle Hans to praise her in this way was more wonderful than any other praise she had received. It lifted her as if she were a balloon filled with hot air. Inspired by his interest she pulled out her sketchbook from under the bed and showed him that too. They sat, the two of them, on the rug, going through every drawing Gracie had ever done, and Gracie wanted the moment to last for ever. She felt special, singled out in this way, and her love and respect for her uncle swelled.

At length he stood up and smoothed the creases in his trousers and jacket. 'Come downstairs. I want to talk to your mother.'

Gracie followed him, excited that he was going to share his admiration with everyone, triumphant that Joseph would be proved wrong. Her mother, grandmother and brother were still in the kitchen. Her mother was washing up while Joseph dried with a tea towel. Oma had nodded off in her chair and was quietly snoring.

'Greet, I am disappointed that you never told me what an accomplished artist my niece is.' Greet glanced at her daughter warily. Joseph stopped what he was doing. Gracie now sensed the strain in the air and bit her lip anxiously. She didn't understand the silent communication passing between her mother and her uncle. 'She has a promising future as a restorer,' he went on. 'With training and experience she could be very good.'

'She is only thirteen,' said Greet and her voice trembled in spite of the effort she was making to keep it steady.

'The perfect age to learn.'

Greet's throat grew tight and Gracie felt a chill ripple over her skin. She stared at her mother, trying to read her thoughts. Uncle Hans turned to Gracie and engaged her with his sharp blue eyes. His smile, now broad, held within it the promise of glamour and sunshine. 'My dear child, how would you like to come and live in Italy? How would you like to learn to paint as well as the great masters?' Gracie now realised why her mother was so upset. Greet knew what her brother was going to ask, and as he was supporting her financially she wasn't in a position to refuse. Only Gracie could do that, but Gracie wasn't sure she wanted to. She'd grown up on Uncle Hans's stories and often imagined what his life must be like in Italy. She'd studied the paintings in the books he brought and longed to see pomegranates and lemons growing on trees and those comical umbrella pines that grew so tall. Everything about Uncle Hans was exotic. Everything about him was *superior.*

'I would like to learn to be as accomplished as you, Uncle Hans,' she said. 'But perhaps Mother is right and I am too young.' She hoped he would disagree.

'You are nearly fourteen, are you not?' he countered. She nodded. 'It would be a terrible waste to remain here when you could be apprenticing the greatest picture restorer in Europe.'

At this Gracie was unable to hide her enthusiasm. 'Please, Mother,' she begged. 'Perhaps I could go for a short time, to see if I like it. You wouldn't mind that, would you?'

Joseph, who had said nothing and now didn't need to dry the plate he was holding because it had dried all on its own, spoke up. 'Can't she learn to restore in London?'

'Yes,' Greet rejoined swiftly. 'London has the best art galleries in the world.'

'But I don't live in London,' said Uncle Hans and the undertone of impatience in his voice silenced both sister and nephew. 'I live in Italy and it is there that I have my studio, my restorer and my materials. If Gracie is going to learn she has to do it under my supervision.' He smiled then at Greet as if he understood a mother's anguish. 'I will take care of her, don't you worry,' he said gently. 'She is a daughter to me. A precious daughter. No harm will come to her. But I will give her a trade, Greet. A means to earn a decent living. Do you want her to follow you into the business of making dresses which barely pays enough to put food on the table? Is that the future you want for your girl?'

'No, I don't want that for Gracie,' she answered quietly.

'Then give her this opportunity,' he urged. 'I'll arrange her passport. Leave everything to me.'

A long silence followed. Gracie gazed at her mother, watching her mind whirring as she weighed up the advantages for her daughter against the disadvantages for her. At last she dropped her shoulders and Gracie knew that her uncle had won. That *they* had won, for she wanted to go to Italy with all her heart.

'Very well, Hans. You have your way,' Greet said softly. 'I just hope I don't live to regret it.'

❦

And so it was, on a drizzly day in May, that Gracie set off to start a new life in Italy. Dressed in her best Sunday frock and hat usually reserved for church, she said goodbye to her family, embracing her mother tightly and feeling only a momentary pinch of sorrow. Oma dabbed her eyes with a handkerchief and even though Joseph's eyes shone, he didn't cry. 'It's not for ever,' Uncle Hans laughed as he put her small suitcase into the cab which would take them to London Airport. 'I'll bring her back soon enough, I promise, and you'll see for yourselves that I have treated her like a princess.'

Gracie had never been further than London. She had never travelled in a cab and she had never been anywhere near an aeroplane. Now she was heading out of the city into a new world, and everything she saw through the windows of the cab enthralled her. She didn't feel nervous because she was with Uncle Hans. He, however, wasn't in the least interested in the passing fields and hamlets and sat with his ankle on his knee, reading the newspaper.

Gracie tried not to gawp as she followed her uncle through the airport to the check-in desk. Everything sparkled, from the shiny floor to the glass windows, even the lady in the blue suit and hat, who took their passports and tickets, glowed with an otherworldly glamour. Gracie watched her small suitcase disappear on a trolley loaded with luggage and wondered with a sudden lurch of panic whether she'd ever see it again. But she knew she'd sound gauche voicing her fears so she put her trust in her uncle and followed him through the terminal. It was very busy and everyone looked as if they had chosen their very best clothes for the occasion. She wondered, as she sat in front of a cup of tea and a slice of cake, whether the other travellers noticed that this was her first time or whether she looked just like them, sophisticated and insouciant. Uncle Hans sipped a large gin and tonic and opened his newspaper again. He had travelled so much as to be bored by all the things that excited Gracie. She watched him light a cigarette and then she noticed the waitresses giggling and whispering in the corner, and glancing in their direction. This was the first time she had ever appreciated her uncle's good looks. He had always been dashing, of course, but now she knew he was handsome too. How proud she was to be with him.

Nothing could have prepared her for the flight. Nothing she had been told about flying compared to the reality. She sat in the squashy leather seat and gazed out of the round window as the aeroplane raced down the runway and then took off. The ground fell away beneath her and the countryside grew smaller, and for a moment she felt as if she had left her stomach on the tarmac. Uncle Hans chuckled, amused. 'Not regretting you came?' he asked.

'Not at all,' Gracie replied and the thought of home and the family she had left behind caused her not the slightest twinge of homesickness.

Gracie lost her heart to Italy the moment she set eyes on it. It was as if she had always been incomplete, as if she had been missing some vital part of her essence and had only now, at this extraordinary moment of recognition, realised it. She breathed in the warm, aromatic smell of foreign plants and flowers and felt her spirits come alive, like buds opening in sunshine. Uncle Hans's driver was standing to attention in a navy suit and cap beside a gleaming white Lancia, the kind of car Gracie had only seen in magazines; the kind of car that belonged to film stars. The light bounced off the bonnet and it was dazzling, brighter than the brightest summer's day in London.

They motored into the countryside. Gracie sat on the back seat and looked out at umbrella pines and undulating green and yellow hills, soft as velvet, aglow beneath an azure sky, and the Italian her uncle was speaking to the chauffeur grew distant until it was a drone, like the distant buzzing of a bee. Wild poppies grew among emerging crops, pretty farmhouses with terracotta roofs nestled among plumes of cypress trees and Gracie had never seen anything more beautiful. While she had gone about her daily life in grey, smoggy London, this paradise had existed here and she had never known it. It seemed impossible somehow that this great wealth of splendour had been hidden from her, that had it not been for Uncle Hans, she might never have seen it. Her gratitude for him swelled; this magician who had spirited her away to heaven, and she wished her mother, Oma and Joseph could see it too.

Uncle Hans lived at the end of a long farm track, in a big, square-shaped villa built in the same sandy-coloured stone as the farmhouses Gracie had seen en route, with a tiled roof and large windows with green shutters. It enjoyed a wide view of uninterrupted hills and forests, and was just the sort of place she expected her wealthy uncle to live in. Three men in uniform appeared to take their luggage (to Gracie's relief her suitcase *had* miraculously appeared in Pisa Airport) and a young woman with olive skin and shiny brown hair hurried out to welcome her master home. Gracie returned their smiles and said a shy hello, which they understood perfectly. Her uncle put his hand in the small of her back and showed her around the manicured gardens where topiary had been clipped into perfect spheres and borders of lavender saturated the air with their sweet perfume, and everything was set against a chorus of chirruping crickets and twittering birds. There were fig and lemon trees which Uncle Hans told her would bear fruit in September, and olive groves from which he made his own oil. The gardens seemed to swell with fecundity, as if they could barely contain their enthusiasm to grow and propagate. Gracie could feel the energy rising up from the soil like heat on her skin. It made her feel alive, and she was seized by a childish desire to roll about on the grass and laugh out loud.

Her bedroom was simple but comfortable, with windows giving out onto two sides of the garden. On one side lay a terrace, where there was a table and six chairs, partially shaded by a fig tree, and on the other side a lawn, with a stony path lined with topiary, leading towards a pagoda and an arrangement of garden chairs. Gracie could imagine her uncle sitting there, smoking and reading the newspapers away from the sun.

It didn't take her long to unpack, she didn't own much. When she went downstairs she searched among the rooms for her uncle, airy, comfortable rooms, lavishly but tastefully decorated with tapestries and shelves weighed down with books and objects. The girl who had greeted them on arrival appeared and directed her to a converted barn at the back of the house. When Gracie pushed open the big door it was clear at once that this was the hub of Uncle Hans's business, the workshop he had told her about. It smelt not as she imagined an artist's studio should smell, of oils and turpentine, of dusty wooden frames and canvases, but of something else she didn't recognise. It was immaculately clean and tidy, more reminiscent of the chemistry laboratory at school than the art room. Paintings were displayed on and stacked up against whitewashed walls, easels carried old and damaged pictures waiting for attention, shelves were crammed with bottles of coloured liquids and tubes of paint, shiny jars with brushes and instruments she'd never seen before. There were cupboards and drawers and everything seemed to be clearly labelled. The large windows were blocked with shutters to cut out all natural light and the overhead electric lights and lamps secured onto the easels gave the room a scientific feeling. Gracie noticed a large fan extractor with a long tube which hovered over a small trolley on wheels on which were a tray of paints and small jars of chemicals. The place reeked of toil and industry.

A man looked round from behind one of the easels. The top of his head was bald and so shiny that the light attached to his easel seemed to bounce off it. The little hair he had was the colour of straw and curled around ears as large as the *stroopwafels* Oma made for breakfast. His face was kind with an aquiline nose and small eyes twinkling through a pair of round spectacles. 'You must be Gracie,' he said in a slow, deliberate voice, lifting his brush off his work. She nodded. 'Then you are to be my apprentice,' he added and Gracie noticed that he spoke English with a strong Dutch accent like her grandmother.

'Yes, I am,' she replied, looking round for her uncle.

'My name is Rutger. I have known your uncle for nearly fifteen years. How old are you, Gracie?'

'Nearly fourteen,' she replied.

The man nodded gravely. 'Your uncle tells me you have a fine talent.'

'Where is my uncle?' she asked.

Rutger nodded towards a door at the back. 'He is in his studio.' Gracie began to make her way towards it, but Rutger stopped her. 'No, you are not allowed in there. That is Hans's place of work and he does not like to be disturbed. Why don't you help yourself to an apron and bring that stool over here so you can see what I'm doing.'

Gracie did as she was told and sat down. 'I am restoring part of a Renaissance altar piece,' he told her. 'It is my job to restore it to as close to its original state as possible. One can only do one's best to reach an *interpretation* of the original work, you understand. To do that, patience and understanding are required, of course, but above everything, the ability to interpret. *That* is the prime job of a conservator. That is what I am going to teach you to do.' Rutger began to carefully dab the surface with his brush. 'When you look at a painting you have to first look *beyond* the image. You have to appreciate all sorts of things, like when it was painted, what it was painted for, what it is painted on, what is the material of the frame, and you have to have sufficient knowledge of the history of materials and the ageing process to have a good idea of the artist's intent. To be a skilful painter is only the first step and it is a very small step. You have to be a detective.' He looked at her steadily and Gracie saw that his eyes were amber brown. 'And I am going to teach you everything you need to know.'

'Uncle says that you are the greatest restorer in Europe,' said Gracie.

'He flatters me,' Rutger replied. 'But I am not too modest to admit that I am, indeed, very good.'

At that moment the door at the back of the room opened and Uncle Hans stepped out. 'Ah, I see you two have met,' he said, noticing them at once.

'The first lesson has begun,' said Rutger.

'Good,' said Uncle Hans. Gracie's eyes strayed into the room behind him but her uncle closed the door and locked it with a key. There is nothing more alluring than a locked door and Gracie's curiosity was at once aroused. But she wouldn't be invited into that room for many years, and when she was, at last, permitted to enter, there would be no going back from what she would see within it.

Chapter 5

Italy, 2010

Heathrow had changed since Gracie had last seen it, but Italy hadn't. Not really, not in its soul. The beauty was still as arresting as it had been the first time she had experienced it. When she was young it had filled her with excitement and joy, now it was charged with melancholy.

The journey out had been tense. Carina had spent most of the time at the airport on her mobile phone either talking to her assistant, or reading and replying to texts. Anastasia had barely looked up from her phone either. She had said a vague hello to her grandmother on meeting, but avoided Gracie's questions by looking busy and complaining of being tired. Gracie was patient. Her thoughts were far away anyhow, returning cautiously to another time, before either Carina or Anastasia were born.

Gracie had noticed that her daughter had been getting increasingly pale and thin over the years. She was far from the plump girl she had been when she had left Devon and gone to London in search of her dream. The intervening decades had not been kind. She looked harassed and responded to Anastasia's demands for food and drink with exasperation, as if her daughter was a nuisance. Gracie had managed to make her granddaughter smile by buying her a croissant and a juice while Carina had crouched beneath the escalator taking an important call. But the smile had soon vanished as Anastasia returned to the game she was playing or the friends she was communicating with on social media. Gracie didn't understand these modern telephones. In her day people had talked to each other.

In spite of her sulkiness, Anastasia was a very pretty girl. Gracie recognised Rufus's features, which translated particularly well onto a feminine face. But more than anything Gracie recognised her own eyes, grey-green encircled by a darker shade of grey, and she smiled proudly because it was the eyes that gave her granddaughter's beauty its uniqueness. She didn't think the girl was even aware of how lovely they were. Gracie considered Carina, who had her father's brown eyes, and wondered whether it was through dieting or stress that she had lost her bloom. Anastasia was fortunate, for at her age bloom was something that was given freely, and entirely taken for granted. Then Gracie considered herself and the loss of bloom, and she remembered the saying, 'Youth is wasted on the young,' and thought how very true that was. A woman only really appreciates beauty when she is beginning to lose it. But Gracie had never been beautiful like Anastasia. In her little floral dress and pink pumps Anastasia didn't realise the effect she had on the men around her. Gracie didn't imagine she'd be able to ignore their attention once she got to Italy.

Gracie's prediction was spot on. The moment the three women arrived in Pisa Anastasia was drawn away from her phone by the ill-disguised interest on the faces of the Italian men. 'Don't look them in the eye,' Carina told her as they marched through the airport towards the taxi rank outside. 'Just keep your head down and don't give them any encouragement.'

'It's a compliment,' said Gracie, trying to keep up.

'No, it isn't,' Carina retorted. 'They'll look at anything in a skirt.' *Well, considering they weren't looking at Carina, that was clearly not true*, Gracie thought. As for *herself*, no one had really noticed her even when she'd been young.

Castello Montefosco was in a town called Colladoro, an hour's drive away. Carina and Anastasia sat in the back, giving Gracie the front and allowing her to be alone with her thoughts, for the driver did not expect her to speak Italian, or did not care to find out. Carina had told him where to go in pidgin Italian, but he seemed to know it, nodding enthusiastically. There was a crucifix hanging from the rear-view mirror and a photograph of his wife and children clipped to the dashboard. The sight of the happy family brought a lump to Gracie's throat. She put her fingers to her lips and turned her head to look out of the window. If she was emotional now, how was she going to feel when she got there?

The countryside swept her back into the past, to the place where the other life she had lived remained abandoned and ignored. The sight of the acutely familiar veil of dusk that was now settling over the hills, turning them pink, revived her memories, and it could have been yesterday that she was walking across the fields, soaking up the majesty of sunset. It could have been yesterday, and yet it wasn't. She felt tears stinging the backs of her eyes and opened them wide to keep them at bay. How could something so old feel so alive? It had been over forty years, and yet, her heart was beginning to beat faster and the palms of her hands were beginning to sweat, and she felt the nerves churning her stomach to liquid. Was it rash of her to come? What did she expect? How great would be the disappointment if . . . She reined in her thoughts as they suddenly ran ahead of themselves. No, she wasn't rash to come, she told herself. She was old. Time was running out; she didn't want to die without knowing.

Carina and Anastasia sat on the back seat, busy on their phones, unaware of Gracie's growing apprehension and the magnificence of the world outside their windows. Occasionally the landscape caught their attention and they turned their eyes to the glass and looked out. But their attention was soon caught again by the buzz of the phone and they pulled their eyes away, unmoved by the splendour of the Italian twilight.

It was dark when they saw the lights on top of a distant hill. The sky was a deep indigo blue, the first stars twinkling brightly like moonlight catching the waves on a dark sea. Gracie caught her breath and realised that up until that moment her whole body had been rigid with anticipation. She ached all over. 'There it is,' she said, and Carina and Anastasia looked up from their screens.

The town that clustered round the hillside beneath the castle glittered like fairy lights and Gracie thought how little it had changed. It could have been 1955; as if the years that had opened up like a great canyon between then and now had suddenly closed. The silhouette of the hills set against that royal-blue, eternal sky was as it had always been, even before Gracie's heart had claimed it. '*Eccoci qua*,' said the taxi driver and Gracie nodded, relieved that it was now dark so he couldn't see her stricken face. The car motored slowly along the narrow road and then began the climb that meandered gently up the hill. Gracie rolled down the window and inhaled the scent of pine, wild rosemary and thyme, and let the rhythmic sound of crickets soothe her, like a melody, drawing her out of her thoughts and into the still, balmy night. She gazed at the familiar buildings as the road swept round a corner and entered the town. At once the place came alive. Locals sat at small tables outside the trattoria drinking wine and eating pasta, women walked with their arms linked on their way to dinner, children played freely and scrawny mongrels trotted along the pavement in search of supper. The town was busy with activity, the air thick with the smell of cooking onions and grilled meat, and Anastasia switched off her phone and began to look around with interest.

At last they reached a pair of iron gates held up by ancient-looking stone pillars. The driveway was lined on either side with cypress trees, which stood to attention like shadowy sentinels, and there, at the top, was the castle. Gracie caught her breath. She could see it glowing through the trees. It hadn't been lit up like that in her day. 'I'm hungry,' said Anastasia.

'I'm sure they'll have a big plate of spaghetti waiting for you,' said Carina. 'Personally, I could do with a large glass of wine,' she added, cheering up at the thought. Gracie was too emotional to speak. She was too stiff to move. She didn't know how she was going to get out of the car. Suddenly she was paralysed with fear.

The taxi reached the top and swung round to the right to draw up in front of the big *portone*. Carina and Anastasia climbed out, happy to stretch their legs, eager to get inside. Gracie waited, gripping the handbag on her lap with pale hands. She turned her eyes to the young man walking towards them from the castle entrance, presumably to fetch their bags, then peered behind him, half expecting to see someone else. Her door opened unexpectedly and she nearly jumped out of her skin.

'*Ci siamo arrivati, signora.*' It was the taxi driver, smiling at her kindly.

Gracie composed herself. '*Grazie*,' she murmured, taking his hand and letting him help her out of the car. '*Finalmente. Sono stanca morta*.'

'*Lei parla italiano*!' he said, surprised.

'*Si, un po*,' she replied.

Then her daughter was beside her, looking concerned. 'Are you all right, Mum?' she asked, feeling guilty for not having been more attentive. 'You must be tired. Let's go inside. Shall we eat first or go to our rooms and then eat?'

'Our rooms,' said Gracie, yearning for solitude.

'I'm starving,' moaned Anastasia.

'Granny wants to go to her room first, so you'll just have to wait.'

Gracie was too distracted to notice her granddaughter roll her eyes impatiently.

Gracie let her daughter help her up the steps and through the big door. She felt ancient, as if she'd aged a decade in the short time they had been in the taxi. Her heart was beating very fast. She didn't think it was healthy to be in such a fluster. She gripped Carina's arm and staggered inside.

It was apparent the moment they entered the castle that this was not a hotel but a private home, and a rather threadbare home at that. There was no reception desk, no lobby, no formality at all. Dusty old paintings hung around the hall in gilt frames, the red walls looked as if they could have done with a fresh coat of paint and the antique furniture with a good polish, and yet the place vibrated with warmth and hospitality. An enormous shaggy brown dog lay sleeping on the tiled floor and the woman who came forward to greet them had to step over it to reach them.

'You must be Mrs Burton,' she said in a thick Italian accent, taking Gracie's trembling hand in her big, squidgy one and squeezing it gently. 'I am Ilaria, Mamma Bernadetta's daughter, and I am here to welcome you to Castello Montefosco. You must be Mrs Cavendish and you,' she said, smiling broadly at Anastasia, '*Miss* Cavendish.' Her energy was so effervescent that Carina and Anastasia felt immediately restored.

'Do call us by our first names,' said Carina graciously. 'Gracie, Carina and Anastasia.'

'What beautiful names. Now, you must be hungry.' Ilaria laughed. 'We are always hungry in the Castello. But there is food and plenty of it.' She gesticulated to her fulsome body restrained behind the fabric of her black dress. 'Do I look like a woman who holds back at the dinner table? Now, come, I have cooked a delicious pasta for you. It is Mamma Bernadetta's own recipe and you will learn how to cook it yourselves tomorrow. Let me give you a feast now so that you sleep well, no?'

Gracie would have preferred to hide in her room, but she followed Ilaria through the castle to the dining room, propelled by a growing sense of curiosity and wonder. It was just as it used to be. It even smelt the same, of ancient walls and lavender. There was even lavender beneath her feet and every step she took released another whiff of perfume.

They were shown into a big room with a high, vaulted ceiling, two sets of large double doors and a vast tapestry that took up the entire opposite wall. At the far end was a fireplace obscured by a vast round pot of red geraniums, for it was April and there was no need to light a fire. In the middle of the room was a long table and sitting around the table was a group of people drinking wine and eating Mamma Bernadetta's pasta. The pasta must have been good because no one was talking.

'Don't get up or move from your delicious pasta,' Ilaria exclaimed, patting down the air with her hands to make sure they all remained in their seats. 'May I introduce Gracie, Carina and Anastasia. They have just arrived from London and are very hungry.' She pulled out a chair and helped Gracie sit down. Carina's spirits were much restored by the sight of the wine bottles and Anastasia by the handsome young man at the other side of the table who was looking at her with interest. Ilaria proceeded to walk around the table introducing everyone. She clearly had an astonishing memory and loved to flaunt it. 'This charming man is called Rex Bryce,' she said, putting her hands on the shoulders of a man who looked about the same age as Gracie. 'Rex is from California where he owns a beautiful ranch and produces wine. I think he has very good taste in wine because he has given our wine ten out of ten for excellence. Now this trio of lovely ladies are from Manchester,' she said, moving on to the young woman with dyed blonde hair, long purple nail extensions and a deep tan, who was sitting on Rex's left. 'This is Wendy Knowles,' she announced. 'And this is Tiff Beale,' she added, touching the shoulder of the girl beside Wendy who had very short auburn hair and was wearing a grey V-neck T-shirt with the word 'Whatever' emblazoned across the front in silver glitter. 'And the third of the trio is this lovely creature with angel hair. She is called Brigitte Dunne and don't call her Bridget unless you want a black eye. We do not like black eyes at Castello Montefosco!' Brigitte's ash-blonde locks almost reached down to her small waist. She wore a crop top with a big picture of a bee appliquéd above her breasts, exposing a tanned stomach and the occasional glimpse of a pierced tummy button. 'They have left their husbands behind to starve while they eat like queens. But fear not, their husbands will grow fat when they return home and cook them the delicious recipes they have learned from Mamma Bernadetta.' The three young women glanced at each other and laughed with the readiness of people who laughed often and mostly at themselves. Then Ilaria put her hands on the shoulders of the young man who had been looking at Anastasia. 'And this handsome and charming boy is called Alex Strauss-Jones and he has come with his mother, a little reluctantly he has admitted, because his mother Lauren, who is over there' – she pointed at Lauren who winced and gave an embarrassed smile – 'was meant to come with a friend but the naughty friend let her down at the last minute, so Alex has come in her place, rescuing his mother like a knight in shining armour. They are American but they live in London. And lastly, but not least, is beautiful Madeleine who is from Belgium. Her husband, the poor man, is very hungry because Madeleine does not feed him at all. So, she has come to learn how to cook so she can make her husband happy. I can promise you, my dear, that your husband will be very happy when you return home and cook him all of Mamma Bernadetta's recipes. I make a deal with you. If, after a week, he is still thin and hungry, I will give you your money back.' Everyone laughed. 'You have all arrived today, very punctually I might add, and I welcome you on behalf of Count Tancredi Bassanelli. We hope you will enjoy his home and treat it like your home for the duration of your stay. Nothing is out of bounds except the top floor, which is the private apartment of the count. Now eat! And enjoy! Eating and enjoying are the two most important ingredients for your stay at the castle.'

Carina had already helped herself to wine, because it didn't seem to be the sort of place where waiters hovered to serve the guests, and she was now feeling quite sociable. She resolved not to touch the pasta or the bread, but she would eat the salad which looked as appetising as a salad *could* look. Anastasia tucked into her pasta and revived instantly like a wilted flower that is given water. Gracie, who never drew attention to herself and certainly didn't expect anyone to give her any, sat quietly, sipping her wine and eating the pasta, which was a classic tomato and basil recipe, but far tastier than anything one would find at home, and listened to the conversations around the table.

The three girlfriends, Wendy, Tiff and Brigitte, were very excitable. They appeared to be in their early thirties and were clearly thrilled to be there. They chatted away without inhibition, fuelled by large glasses of wine, cigarettes (which they left the table to smoke on the terrace), and a general exuberance, telling the guests all about themselves and infecting them with their irrepressible *joie de vivre.* The old man, Rex, was quiet like Gracie, and listened to the girls' chatter with an amused look. *He had a wise face*, Gracie thought, *the kind that reflected a patient and philosophical nature.* He wore a khaki safari jacket with lots of pockets, an open-neck blue shirt, which emphasised his bright, china-blue eyes, and suggested, from the deep crow's feet at his temples, many a hot day squinting into the sun.

Madeleine, it transpired, was from the Flemish side of Belgium. Indisputably beautiful with lustrous sugar-brown hair to her shoulders, radiant, suntanned skin and a friendly, open face, she looked like she was in her early fifties but Gracie deduced from her hands that she was probably ten years older. She sensed, too, a strong character in the determined line of her jaw and in the strength of her features, but she was gracious enough to hold back and allow the younger women to take centre stage, watching them with her green cat's eyes and clearly enjoying their banter. Lauren had begun to talk to Carina. They looked about the same age and the same sort.

Gracie predicted they'd make good friends and was relieved that Carina might find a kindred spirit and consider the effort of coming to Italy worthwhile. Lauren's son Alex kept looking at Anastasia, which didn't surprise Gracie in the least. He had scruffy brown hair, striking grey eyes and an intelligent, alert expression. She wondered whether Anastasia would find him attractive. Anastasia seemed too engrossed in her food right now to notice, or perhaps she was just playing it cool.

Dinner was soon over. No one had spoken to Gracie, other than to welcome her, which was a relief because she wanted to be left alone to tackle her memories, which were stirring from their long sleep and coming at her out of the shadows. Ilaria and the young man who had carried their bags into the hall showed the guests to their rooms. Carina and Anastasia were together in a spacious bedroom with twin beds, brightly coloured quilts and shuttered windows.

Once in the privacy of her bedroom Carina called Rufus. 'We've arrived,' she announced, sinking onto the bed. 'And the Wi-Fi works beautifully so I don't have to be out of touch. Such a relief!' Anastasia took a selfie, making sure Carina was in the picture, and posted it on her Facebook site above the caption: *Sharing a room with Mother! LOL.*

Gracie was next door, in a similar room. As soon as she was alone she threw open the shutters. The walls were thick and she leaned on the sill, closed her eyes and breathed in the scents of the garden. She could smell the grass, the pine and the lavender. The night was dark but the creatures were busy for there were rustlings in the undergrowth and the chirruping of crickets was loud and constant. She longed to lie on the lawn and look up at the stars.

As she inhaled the night air Gracie began to feel a tingling inside her body, down every limb, right to her fingertips and toes, as if she was becoming aware of the inner self that remained always the same, untouched by time. It was only the outside that had changed, she realised; her skin that had aged, her bones that had grown brittle, her hair that had lost its lustre. Inside she hadn't changed at all. She was still Gracie.

The following morning Carina opened her eyes to small beams of light leaking through the gaps in the wooden shutters. She watched them a moment as they caught little specks of dust and made them glitter. The sight was mesmerising and it was a long moment before she remembered where she was.

Her first thought was of the office and she panicked that she might have overslept and missed something important, but then she remembered that Italy was an hour ahead, which gave her some breathing space. She turned over and reached for her phone. It was only eight-thirty. She gave a sigh of relief and turned her attention back to the specks of dust and was lost once more in their hypnotic dancing.

Anastasia stirred in the next-door bed. Like all teenagers, if Carina left her to sleep she would not emerge until lunchtime. Aware that they had a cookery lesson to attend, which wasn't Carina's idea of holiday fun – she'd rather have lain by a pool in her bikini – she climbed out of bed and went to open the shutters. It was then that she heard the chorus of tweeting. *It was loud and vibrant and didn't sound real,* Carina thought. It sounded like those meditation tracks therapists put on during massage treatments in spas. She pushed open the shutters. The light was so bright she had to shield her eyes.

'Mum!' came a cry from the bed behind her. 'I'm sleeping!'

Carina didn't respond. She was staring at the most beautiful sight she thought she had ever seen. Everywhere she looked there were flowers. Heaps of purple bougainvillea, cascades of white and pink roses, indecently large gardenia bushes, and the smell, oh the smell, it was heavenly. Beyond the cypress trees and umbrella pines were hills, roly-poly velour hills and lush valleys, disappearing into the mist as far as the eye could see. The sight of such splendour caused something to snag inside Carina's chest. She put her hand there and sighed. A long, drawn-out sigh. The sort of sigh she never had time for in London. But now she inhaled deeply and let out a groan, which disturbed the sleeping Anastasia and induced her to demand again that her mother close the shutters.

Carina ignored her. She stood at the window and savoured the view and the bouquet of smells rising to her window from the garden below. The sun was warm on her skin, penetrating her chest and filling the place where the snag had now become a gentle tug. Oh, she had missed this, she thought to herself. Living in a damp, grey city, she had missed colour and sunshine and beauty; yes, she had missed *beauty*. For the while that she stood there she did not think about the office, or her clients, or anything else. She relished the glory in front of her which had hijacked her senses and caused tears to sting her eyes. And she did not want it to stop.

Carina had been standing there quietly for some time when Anastasia joined her sleepily. 'I'm hungry,' she complained and then she looked out of the window. 'Wow, this place is awesome!' she said, waking up with a jolt. 'Clever Granny to have found it.'

'Isn't it wonderful?' said Carina.

'Let's go to breakfast,' Anastasia urged. 'Do you think they'll have pancakes?'

Chapter 6

When Gracie came to their room, Carina and Anastasia were ready. Carina noticed at once that her mother's cheeks were pink and her eyes were bright. *In fact, her eyes were strikingly pretty,* Carina thought. A good night's sleep had clearly done her the world of good. She looked very different from the pale and fragile woman she had been the day before. 'Have you seen the view?' Gracie asked.

Carina smiled in rapture. 'It's paradise,' she replied.

Anastasia nudged her mother. 'Come on, Mum. I'm starving.'

'Me too,' said Gracie and she followed her daughter and granddaughter down the corridor towards the smell of freshly baked pastries wafting up from the dining room downstairs.

A buffet was set up on the table where they had eaten dinner the night before, but the pair of double doors were now wide open, leading out onto a wide terrace where some of the guests were already enjoying breakfast. Terracotta pots of red geraniums were placed at intervals along the top of the balustrade, and jasmine and rose entwined playfully as they climbed the castle wall. The three women walked out to find a table and discovered that it was not only they who had been affected by the beauty of Castello Montefosco. Madeleine, the Belgian, looked up from her coffee cup and smiled cheerfully, showing off a set of dazzling white teeth. 'Isn't it a stunning morning,' she said in a thick Flemish accent, which reminded Gracie of her mother. 'I feel like a new person today.' At another table Alex, the handsome young man who had come with his mother, was spreading jam onto a croissant.

'I can highly recommend the buffet,' he said. 'It's hard to restrain oneself!' He smiled at Anastasia and she smiled back shyly, but said nothing. He looked older than the boys she was used to.

'Why don't you go and take a look,' Carina suggested to Anastasia. Gracie noticed the young man's indecision while his knife hovered over his croissant. He looked as if he was about to accompany her but then thought better of it.

As Lauren appeared with a bowl of fruit Gracie slipped away to find a table. Like everyone else, Lauren had been touched by the magic. Her eyes gleamed and her smile was that of someone who has slept deeply and woken to find that her cares amount to nothing. 'How did you sleep?' she asked Carina. 'I haven't slept so well in years!'

'Wonderfully well,' Carina replied. 'That looks good,' she added, glancing at Lauren's breakfast.

'Ilaria has just been telling me that they grow all their own fruit and vegetables here at the Castello, and raise their own poultry and pigs. She says we can wander around the herb garden later and pet the animals. Isn't it glorious!'

'I don't know how I'm going to resist the carbs,' said Carina, pulling a face.

'Me neither,' Lauren agreed and it was apparent to both women that they had found a kindred spirit in their fight against carbohydrates.

'But we will,' Carina said firmly. 'We can give each other

strength.' The two women laughed and Carina was thrilled to have found a soulmate. She hadn't expected that. She had expected to be bored by a lot of elderly people.

Carina stopped to talk to Rex, who was at a table on his own, drinking coffee and reading the news on his iPad. 'I feel like I've woken up in heaven,' he said.

'But then you read the news!' Carina replied with a grin.

Rex frowned and put his iPad down. 'You're right. I'm not going to switch it on again.' He turned his eyes to the hills and sighed, as if expelling the negativity he'd just absorbed. 'I'm going to tune out and enjoy the view. And what a spectacular view it is too.' Carina had barely noticed him the evening before, but with thick silver hair and a wide face he was undoubtedly handsome. The deep lines that fanned into his temples were attractive and his eyes were startlingly blue, like Spode china. She imagined him galloping across the plains on his ranch in America, which gave him a Paul Newman kind of glamour. *He must have been a real ladies' man when he was young*, she thought.

She joined her mother, who had already chosen a table and was sitting gazing at the view with a beatific smile on her face. A moment later the young man who had taken their luggage and showed them to their room the evening before appeared to ask if they would like tea or coffee. Carina asked for a double espresso and Gracie a cup of tea with milk. When Anastasia returned with a plate full of pastries, she informed them that the young man was Carlo. 'It's a family business,' she said, sitting down and placing her phone on the table in front of her.

'But where is the count?' Carina asked. She made it her business in London to meet the important people, she might as well do the same here. Gracie dropped her gaze. 'I'll ask

Ilaria when we're going to meet him,' Carina continued. 'He must greet his guests, surely?'

At that moment the three Manchester ladies spilled onto the terrace in a flurry of squeals and laughter. 'They're drunk on beauty,' said Gracie and Carina laughed. Anastasia grinned, unused to this new, lighter version of her mother.

'I think we all are,' Carina agreed.

While they enjoyed breakfast, Anastasia took photographs and posted them on her Facebook site. Carina sent off some emails. Gracie just enjoyed the panorama. She didn't want to be anywhere else in the world but *here*.

❦

After breakfast they were shown to the kitchen where Mamma Bernadetta awaited them. The room itself was as old as the castle, but it had evidently been modernised for the business of the cookery school. In the middle was a large island with a white marble surface. On the marble were ten clipboards with paper, ten pencils and ten white aprons embroidered in red with the words *Mamma Bernadetta's Cookery School* and ten white stools placed around it.

Anastasia put on her apron at once. She tied her hair into a ponytail and sat down, toying with her phone. Carina lingered outside with hers, speaking to her assistant, while Gracie took the stool beside her granddaughter. Everyone slowly took their places and Gracie saw that Rex chose the stool beside her. She gave him a small smile. 'Well, isn't this fun?' he said. 'I mean, these women are a pair of characters, don't you think?'

Gracie looked at Ilaria who was talking to a short, rotund old lady in a black dress who was undoubtedly her mother, Mamma Bernadetta. Her black stockings had gathered in rings at her thick ankles and she was wearing a pair of old leather lace-up shoes. With her grey hair pulled back into a bun she might have looked severe had it not been for her eyes, which were small, chestnut brown and twinkling with humour. 'They're the best examples of Italian women,' Gracie answered. 'They're as warm as sun-ripened olives.'

Rex laughed and looked at her curiously, as if he had only just noticed her. 'You're right,' he said, nodding enthusiastically. 'They really *are* as warm as sun-ripened olives.'

'Good morning, class,' said Ilaria, silencing the conversations in the room. As she began to speak Carina crept in and took the free stool at the end of the row, beside Lauren. 'I would like to introduce you to my mother, Mamma Bernadetta.' The old lady nodded but she didn't smile. Gracie sensed her shyness at once. Mamma Bernadetta turned to her daughter and her face softened. Ilaria continued. 'My mother claims not to speak English,' she informed them. 'But it is amazing how she understands when I say something that she does not like. For example, mic-rowave . . .' At that moment Mamma Bernadetta's face came alive and she slapped her right hand on her forearm and raised her left in a gesture of fury. She muttered something in Italian that no one understood except Gracie, who began to laugh. Mamma Bernadetta caught her eye and the tiniest, almost imperceptible smile twitched at the corners of her mouth. 'So, Mamma cooks while I tell you what she is doing and you write down everything you want to remember. These are her recipes. You will not find them in cookery books. They are full of her little secrets because she has been cooking since she was a small girl. She has never measured any of the ingredients, so we have had to work out the amounts for your notes by looking at her hands. Mamma Bernadetta measures everything by feel, but you cannot take her hands home with you.' Everyone laughed. Ilaria's humour and ebullience were infectious. 'We are going to cook lunch every day. A starter, a main course and a dessert and then *you* are going to enjoy the feast. We do not restrain ourselves when it comes to food or wine. Life must be enjoyed. People who do not enjoy food do not enjoy life.' Carina did not agree with that last statement and resolved to pick at her food and push it around her plate. She did not want to return to London as round as Mamma Bernadetta and Ilaria.

And so the lesson began. As Mamma Bernadetta made the tomato and basil sauce, Ilaria entertained them with a running commentary. 'Tomato in oil sounds like a wedding, a happy sound,' she said exuberantly. 'Put ripe cherry tomatoes in to sweeten, but don't bother them by stirring. Leave them to get to know each other. They are honeymooning.' She grinned broadly as her guests laughed at her jokes. Gracie wrote notes. Carina listened and Anastasia doodled. Ilaria reminded them that everything they would eat here at the Castello came from the gardens. 'Even the wine,' she said with a grin, winking at Rex. 'We make our own wine and it is delicious. During the break take a good look around the gardens and enjoy yourselves. This is more than a cookery school. This is a school of the soul. The beauty here will enrich it, if you let it.' Anastasia lifted her eyes off her doodles and saw that Ilaria was staring directly at *her*.

In the half-hour break Carina took the opportunity to sit in the shade with a cup of coffee and make some calls. Anastasia found herself exploring the castle grounds with her grandmother. She didn't really know her grandmother but the fact that Gracie had chosen to come to this magnificent place raised her in Anastasia's estimation. The castle was romantic, the weather glorious and Alex provided entertainment and the possibility of a flirtation. What was there not to like? 'Let's go and find the animals,' Gracie suggested and Anastasia agreed with enthusiasm.

'I'd like to see the pigs,' she said. 'I can post some photos on Facebook.' Gracie didn't know what that meant so she made no comment. They walked down a narrow path that meandered through the wild grasses until they reached the vegetable garden. Olive trees shimmered in the breeze, their grey leaves rustling gently. Rosemary, thyme and sage gave off a splendid aroma as they grew warm in the sun and neat rows of lettuces, radishes and other vegetables were planted in tidy plots. Butterflies fluttered about the lavender and fat bees bumbled from flower to flower, *drunk on beauty too*, Gracie thought happily. At last they came upon the animals. There were chickens, geese and an enormous turkey. When Anastasia saw the pigs she clapped her hands with excitement. 'Look, Granny. Aren't they cool!' Without a care, she climbed into the pen and began stroking them. They were very friendly pigs, Gracie mused, considering they would eventually land on a plate. Gracie rested her arms on the fence and watched her granddaughter who had suddenly transformed from a sulky teenager into a joyful young woman. 'I'm going to call this one Gus,' Anastasia announced, as Gus grunted in agreement. 'And this little piglet is Snorter. This one will be Captain Pugsy, because he's very big and important-looking. Now, now, Snorter, my flip-flops are not for lunch!' She was playing so contentedly she didn't notice the young man, *perhaps a brother of Carlo*, Gracie thought, who was clearing out the rabbit hutches a little way off and watching her furtively. Gracie noticed him. He was as handsome as a movie star.

'Your granddaughter has beaten me to the pigs,' said a voice beside Gracie. She turned to see Alex standing next to her, dwarfing her with his lofty height. Anastasia looked up from the pigs and grinned. 'I'm glad they're not eating *you*,' he said.

'They're adorable! Come and stroke them. They're so friendly.' Alex did not wait for further encouragement. He jumped over the gate with the ease of a natural athlete and Anastasia began to introduce him to the pigs, which were now *her* pigs. Gracie wondered whether she should leave the young people to their fun. They wouldn't want her watching them, she knew. She made to walk away but Anastasia started talking to her.

'Granny, what do you think Mum would say if I decided to buy a piglet?' she asked.

'I don't think she'd object to the piglet, but when it grew into a pig it might be less welcome,' said Gracie, edging away.

'I wish I lived in the countryside, then I could have one.'

'How about a rabbit?' Alex suggested, wandering towards the hutches.

'Come on, Granny. Come and see the rabbits.' Gracie was flattered that Anastasia should want her company and walked round the pig pen to where the Italian was working among the hutches. The rabbits were free to hop about an enclosure and it was into this patch of grass that Alex and Anastasia now entered. They crouched down and began to play with them. The surly Italian watched from a distance, but Anastasia didn't notice him.

Anastasia warmed to Alex. She found that, with the animals to give her something to talk about, her shyness evaporated. She was keen for her grandmother to remain so that she wasn't left alone with him, however. *That* would have been awkward. But with Gracie there she felt confident.

'I must say, I didn't expect to find someone my age here. I thought they'd all be old, like Mom,' said Alex with a grin.

'Or like Granny,' Anastasia replied, lowering her voice.

'*I* filled in for Mom's friend. How did *you* get here?'

'Because Mum didn't want to let Granny come on her own. Mum couldn't very well ditch me. Though, if she'd had the chance she would have. She's a workaholic. I'm an only child – and an inconvenience,' she added, enjoying the sympathetic look that he offered readily. 'I'm usually ditched in the holidays because Mum can't get away from the office. Or Dad steps in. I'm not an inconvenience to him.'

'Then it's good that you're spending some time here with your Mom,' said Alex.

Anastasia looked horrified. 'If you think we're going to bond over cookery lessons, think again.'

'You may be pleasantly surprised. Places like this, I mean, magical places, have a funny way of directing your focus onto the things that are really important.'

'Like what?'

'Friends, family . . .' He smiled playfully. 'Food!'

'My mother doesn't like food.'

'Then she's missing one of life's greatest pleasures!'

'I'm not,' Anastasia replied with a grin.

'Me neither,' he agreed.

❧

Gracie was surprised when Rex began conversing with her again. He had discovered a medieval round tower at the back of the castle, and was very excited about it. It stood within the castle walls, on a small hill. Had it not been for the giant cedar tree behind it, it would have had the most spectacular views of the valley. 'I took the liberty of going inside,' he told her, lowering his voice. 'I wasn't sure I was allowed in, but as there was no one around to stop me, I snuck inside like a thief. It's an artist's studio. I didn't know the count was a painter, and quite a good one too.'

Gracie couldn't tell him how she knew the tower. How she knew every inch of it. She couldn't tell him how fast her heart was racing now at the very mention of it. So, she just smiled enigmatically which encouraged him to continue. 'I'm going to explore the place after lunch,' he told her, giving her a wink, drawing her into his confidence. 'After all, we've been encouraged to treat the place like home, right?'

'Good idea,' said Gracie. She longed to wander round too, but she wasn't sure she wanted company when she summoned the courage to do it. Italy was having a strange effect on her, in spite of her years she didn't feel old at all. Regardless of how she looked on the outside, inside, the girl she had once been was beginning to awaken.

At last it was lunchtime. Anastasia was so hungry she was feeling a little faint. She sat next to Alex with Gracie on her other side. Her mother sat opposite, next to Lauren. *The two had clearly bonded over their eating habits*, Anastasia thought. Why they avoided the most delicious foods, she couldn't imagine, especially as Wendy, Tiff, Brigitte and Madeleine were all eating bread with olive oil and lots of it. But then something miraculous happened. Ilaria noticed that Carina had not put any pasta onto her plate. 'At the Castello we always start with pasta,' she had told them and she clearly wasn't going to stand for anyone not eating it. She stood behind Carina and leaned over her shoulder. 'Why you don't eat the spaghetti?' she asked quietly, but the whole table heard and the conversations stopped.

'I'm not good with carbs,' Carina replied with a blush.

'Nonsense. Everyone is good with carbs. Avoiding a whole food group is like living half a life. Living half a life is like being half a person. And being half a person means that I could eat you and no one would notice.' Laugher filled the awkward silence and Carina felt a little foolish. 'We are in Italy. The land of plenty. Don't hold back. Let yourself go. Savour the flavours. Let them transform you. Let them take you to paradise. Try a little, at least, for Mamma Bernadetta.'

With every eye upon her Carina was in no position to refuse. Besides, Ilaria had made a pretty persuasive argument. It did seem trivial to be in this magnificent place, learning how to cook the most delicious food, yet not eating it. Gingerly, Carina wound a little onto her fork. The smell of garlic reached her nose and made her mouth water even before the sauce passed her lips. Then, when it did, an explosion of flavour burst onto her tongue, flooding her senses with an almost indecent feeling of bliss. She let the flood of pleasure wash over her. It careered through her body, awaking senses dulled by monotonous, tasteless food and years of denial, and the strangest thing of all was that it made her want to laugh.

'Delicious, no?' said Ilaria, watching Carina's cheeks flush now with delight. 'There is nothing bad about pasta. You see, your body is coming alive with the glorious taste. God gave Italy the most beautiful climate, the most succulent food, the world's best art and architecture and a people who are warm and generous like the sun. So, enjoy His bounty, Carina.' She swept her twinkling eyes over the amused faces of the other guests. 'We won't talk about the dishonest politicians. God did not give Italy those. *We* gave *them* to Italy and what a mess we made. But eat, enjoy, and taste a little wine. You can then sleep in the sun afterwards. That is good for your body too.'

'Oh, Lauren, you have to try this!' Carina whispered as Lauren reluctantly dipped her fork into the spaghetti. 'I'm going to grow fat out here, I can see it,' she added. Then she laughed – a laugh that spouted from somewhere deep inside her and took her as much by surprise as it did Gracie and Anastasia, who looked at each other in bewilderment. 'But I don't think I'm going to care!'

Lauren put her fork into her mouth and experienced the same explosion of pleasure that Carina had. She closed her eyes and moaned, as if she, too, had been secretly longing for someone to bully her into ending the years of self-denial.

Ilaria smiled with satisfaction. It was always a joy to see the first falling away of old skin as her pupils began their gradual and unavoidable metamorphosis, which was Castello Montefosco's most precious gift.

❧

After lunch Wendy, Tiff and Brigitte decided to lie in the sun on the top terrace. They changed into the tiniest bikinis, smothered their bodies in suntan oil and gossiped and smoked until their eyes grew heavy and the alcohol lured them into a pleasant doze. Rex invited Gracie to join him for a wander around the castle grounds, which she felt unable to refuse. Lauren and Madeleine chose a couple of chairs on one of the lower terraces and chatted over cups of coffee, while Alex and Anastasia went in search of the swimming pool.

Carina switched off her telephone. Eating a whole plate of pasta had resulted in a strange kind of domino effect which now extended to her telephone. She didn't just switch it off, she left it in her bedroom. Never had she been without it by choice. The few times it had been mislaid or broken had caused her the most monumental panic, but now, albeit still a challenge, it did not affect her in the way she had expected. It gave her a pleasing sense of freedom. A mischievous kind of satisfaction. She hurried out of her room as quickly as she could before she changed her mind.

Down the path she went, but not towards the vegetable garden. This particular path led in the direction of olive groves and vines, and she was all alone. Blissfully alone. Alone as she hadn't been in such a long time. Without her telephone to hijack her attention she was able to appreciate her surroundings. It was as if she was seeing the splendour of the countryside for the very first time. She breathed in the sugar-scented air, listened to the chirping of crickets and the twittering of birds, and felt the warm sunshine on her face. Her spirits soared and her heart melted like ice cream in the heat and spread into every corner of her chest. She felt happy. So happy that she had to sit on the grassy slope and savour it so that this wonderful feeling might last a little longer. In that moment of ecstasy her mind wandered into fantasy. She imagined she had left her frenetic London life behind and lived here among umbrella pines and olive groves. She imagined a simple life where the days were long and time was only evident in the slow movement of the sun as it made its way nonchalantly across the sky. Her happiness gave her a sudden sense of perspective, like cloud that opens briefly to give a glimpse of blue sky, and she wondered why she had spent so many years rushing around, ignoring the important things. She'd become so focused on her work, her clients, her strategies and her networking that she'd lost sight of Rufus and Anastasia who were far more important. She had lost sight of her mother too. She wasn't sure how it had happened, but it had and she felt ashamed. Gazing out over the soft Tuscan countryside she was made aware of a hardness inside *her.* She didn't want to be like this. She didn't want to be a hard person who was always running around being busy and missing the simple pleasures of life like spaghetti bolognese.

Sitting there on the hillside Carina made a pact with herself.

It would start right here, right now. She would email the office and inform them that she wasn't to be disturbed until she returned. She would switch off her phone. Right off. The idea gave her a shiver of wicked excitement, as if she were a schoolgirl again, flouting the rules. But she was the boss and the rules had been created by her. She could do whatever she wanted. She inhaled deeply and felt the tightness in her shoulders begin to relax. She noticed a couple of old men on horseback plodding slowly along a distant track and their unhurried pace made her sigh with longing. London seemed very far away.

❧

Rex had invited Gracie to join him in such a polite and gallant way that she felt it would be rude to refuse. Besides, she was flattered. She wasn't used to strangers noticing her, least of all taking trouble with her. So she set off with him to explore the castle grounds, drawn by the irresistible pull of nostalgia.

On the western side a wide stretch of terracing ran the entire length of the castle. On the first terrace a long table was placed beneath a canopy of trellising woven with vines where baby grapes were beginning to bud. Gracie remembered that table crowded with people. She remembered the spread of prosciutto and pecorino cheese. She remembered the wine, the laughter and how she tried to follow the conversations in Italian. She shook her head to dispel the memories and followed Rex to the second terrace which faced a low, crenellated wall in a semicircular shape. Here the trio of Manchester ladies were now quietly enjoying a siesta on sun loungers. Gracie put her hand on her chest and continued up the wide steps which ascended behind the dozing women. To the right was a chapel, to the left a side door into the castle. Gracie knew that this led into a library. She could feel the cool darkness of that room as if she were standing in it. But Rex was not so interested in the inside of the castle. He climbed the steps and followed the terracing round to the back. There, positioned on the rise of ground, was the medieval tower.

Gracie caught her breath. The tower seemed to loom out of the past like a relic. It stole her breath. She felt a lump lodge itself in her throat. 'I'm feeling a little tired, suddenly. I think I'll go and lie down,' she said to Rex as he began to walk towards it.

He looked disappointed. 'Are you sure? You really should take a look. It's a jewel,' he said, trying to convince her to stay.

'I'm sorry. I hope you don't mind.'

'Of course not, Gracie. You go and put your feet up. There is always tomorrow.' He raised his hat. 'The food has made me sleepy too, but I'm old. I don't want to waste a moment.' He chuckled, gave an apologetic smile, and replaced his hat. 'One only realises how precious every moment is in the autumn of one's life.' Gracie wanted to agree with him, but she could no longer speak.

Just then Rex raised his eyes and looked beyond her and he shouted, 'Well, good afternoon!' Gracie turned round to see who he was talking to. But the sudden cramp in her stomach told her it was him, their host, Count Tancredi Bassanelli. She stared at him up there on the balcony and he looked down at them and raised his hand in greeting.

As Rex took off his hat again, Gracie froze. She couldn't move. She couldn't speak. She was paralysed with anxiety and longing. Tancredi was an old man now and yet, to her, he was still the same Tancredi. His hair was no longer dark brown but peppered with grey, and wavy, swept off his wide forehead and curling behind his ears and at his neck like it always had. He wore an open-neck blue shirt with a matching scarf tied loosely at his throat, and Gracie remembered how stylish he had always been. Yes, she remembered in a deluge of memory the smell of him, the feel of him, the sound of him, but *he* seemed not to know *her* at all. He gazed down, his smile polite but impersonal, and there was not even a flicker of recognition. She was not too far for him to see her and yet she felt invisible.

The moment felt as if it lasted minutes and his failure to recognise her cut her deeply. At length, Tancredi withdrew inside and Rex said something about how charming he was to wave, but Gracie didn't hear. The blood throbbed in her temples, drowning out everything but her sorrow. She knew she had to hide, like a dog seeking a bush beneath which to lick its wounds; she needed to be alone.

She knew her way round the castle already. She entered through the back door and climbed the stairs to her floor with legs that felt like lead. She staggered along the dark corridors to her room, suppressing the sobs that were rapidly building in her chest, and closed the door behind her. Then she lay on the bed, shut her eyes and allowed her grief to pass through her like a tornado. How could a man who had loved her so deeply not know her? She now asked herself whether he had really loved her at all. Perhaps what had been the most significant love of her life had been only one of many to him. She looked back now, searching the past for evidence to prove that she hadn't been wrong in believing.

He had loved her, surely he had loved her. If not, she had spent the last forty-odd years hankering after a dream.

Chapter 7

Italy, 1955

If Gracie had thought she would be living a glamorous life in Italy she was proved wrong. There was nothing glamorous about studying with Rutger, and he worked her very hard. She had much to learn and in the beginning most of it was studying the history of art, all the way back to the Greeks. Rutger gave her books and she sat at a desk in the corner of the studio and read, after which he would test her. He was a hard task master. Gracie realised very quickly that the man with the kind and twinkly eyes was in fact a man of high standards and expectations, a man who did not tolerate anything short of excellence.

In London Gracie had found school uninspiring and she hadn't felt particularly clever. Here, however, she realised she was much cleverer than she realised. She absorbed the art history with surprising ease and with her gradual learning grew her curiosity and interest. She had always enjoyed painting but the tools she had had at home were far inferior to the ones at her disposal in Uncle Hans's studios. In the warm room with its bright electric lights and the sound of doves cooing on the roof, she would copy paintings while Rutger restored his. She enjoyed the sense of industry, the peace and quiet, and the satisfaction of pleasing her tutor.

Uncle Hans kept a sharp eye on her progress. When he spoke to Rutger he often spoke in Dutch, but even if Gracie hadn't been able to understand she could tell by the look on his face when he was pleased. He would smile a very special kind of smile which lifted her heart as nothing else could. He studied her work closely, holding her paintings to the light, scrutinising her brushstrokes through his magnifying lenses, and she sensed there was something else propelling his interest, as if he saw some sort of potential beyond her imaginings and was keen to realise it for his own ends. Gracie strived hard for his approval. She wanted to be as good a restorer as Rutger. She didn't want her uncle to regret having brought her to Italy. So, she worked conscientiously and her reward was his praise.

When Uncle Hans wasn't in his studio – and he could be there for weeks on end, emerging only to eat and sleep – he was away travelling. When he returned he brought new paintings to be restored, or to be sold. Gracie loved looking at the works of art he had found and they always came with an interesting story. An elderly widow here who didn't realise she had been sitting on a masterpiece; a young man there who had hit hard times and had to sell a family heirloom to keep the wolf from the door; a painting of little value found in a small country sale that Rutger restored to reveal the work of a great master. Uncle Hans always told wonderfully elaborate stories and Gracie loved listening to them. Rutger would shake his head and declare Hans Hollingsworth a man with the Midas touch.

When Gracie had first arrived at La Colomba, for that was the name of the house, she had enjoyed exploring the gardens and surrounding countryside. She learned that Rutger lived in a picturesque cottage just outside the walls of Uncle Hans's property, nestled among bushes of pink oleander. There were undulating fields of farmland, crops that would turn to gold in August, vines that would produce grapes in September, olive groves that gave up their fruit in November. For Gracie, who had never been to the countryside, Tuscany was like heaven. The freedom she experienced was intoxicating, the beauty mesmerising. She missed her mother and grandmother and was surprised that she occasionally missed Joseph too, but she knew she was fortunate and believed that giving in to homesickness was insulting to Uncle Hans, who had given her such an exotic and privileged life.

She wrote to her family every week, describing her life in minute detail, knowing that her mother would read her letters out loud at the dinner table just like she read Uncle Hans's. Gracie knew the pleasure those letters would give her mother and grandmother, and how envious Joseph would be, which gave her a wicked thrill. Uncle Hans bought her pretty dresses from Rome and Paris and spoiled her like the daughter he'd never had. She wondered why he hadn't ever married, for she was sure he would make a loving husband and father, but that wasn't a subject she could raise with him. She respected him too much to ask such personal questions.

As the months went by Gracie grew more confident. She walked the mile and a half to the town, which was a cluster of Tuscan stone houses built on a hillside beneath a magnificent castle. The streets were paved, the ancient houses shuttered and adorned with pots of red geraniums, the occasional wall embellished with extravagant bushes of bougainvillea and oleander. There were a few shops where one could buy the essentials, a butcher's, a bakery, a fruit and vegetable shop where they also sold pasta and biscuits, a few cafés and the church of Maria Maddalena where the entire population would congregate regularly for mass. There were also a couple of simple restaurants and an inn. The first time Gracie had visited, the locals had stared at her as if she were some strange creature from outer space. She had felt so self-conscious that it had been a few weeks before she had dared go again, and this time with Rutger for company. The Dutchman had explained that their community was a small one and that any new face aroused curiosity. Especially a child on her own, dropped into their midst as if by magic. But soon she was able to go without fear and, as the summer days shortened and autumn ripened the grapes on the vines, her Italian improved and she began to talk to people. It wasn't long before they knew her by name and considered her much like the stray dogs and cats that wandered the streets, only not as thin and uncared for.

Uncle Hans and Rutger were both fluent in Italian but neither bothered to teach her. It was Gaia who taught her, the sultry-eyed young woman with shiny brown hair which reached her waist in a thick plait, who worked around the house and cooked. Gracie enjoyed the long evenings when Uncle Hans was away, when the two of them sat outside beneath the pagoda, in the balmy, fragrant air, chatting about their lives, Gracie faltering in Italian, Gaia gently correcting her, a woman and a child forging an unlikely friendship. Had it not been for Gaia Gracie might have been lonely.

Gaia's family lived a mile down a track. Her father was a farmer and her mother raised their other six children, but Gaia lived in a small bedroom at the top of the villa and had done so for five years. Gracie was surprised to discover that she had started working for Uncle Hans when she was the same age as her.

When Gracie turned sixteen she began to go to town in

the evenings with Gaia. They cycled along the track that wound its way up the hillside and Gaia introduced her to her friends. Gradually Gracie became part of a large and boisterous group of young people who spent their evenings in the piazza, flirting and sharing gossip. It was there that she first heard of Count Tancredi Bassanelli.

Castello Montefosco dominated the town not only because it was positioned on top of the hill, but because many of the locals worked there. Gracie learned that the countess, who was a widow, was a flamboyant, creative woman who lived in Rome during the winter months and spent the summers at the castle, which had been a wedding present from her wealthy father, Count Gaetano Montefosco. She loved to entertain lavishly and, according to Donato Fabbri who worked in the gardens with his father, she took lovers without so much as a blush. Every year there was a different man but they were all very much of a type. They were rich, arriving in shiny motor cars and swaggering about the terraces in expensive clothes with gold watches glinting on their wrists. Donato told Gracie that the countess thought nothing of kissing these men in front of her employees and that he had seen her, on various occasions, in a passionate embrace in the pavilion next to the tennis court.

The more Gracie heard about the headstrong countess, the more her curiosity grew. The woman sounded so glamorous and carefree and Gracie admired the independent way she lived her life. In Gracie's experience a woman was nothing without a husband, her mother was an example of that, but the countess was a sovereign power who seemed to please no one but herself and, according to gossip, had no intention of marrying again. Damiana Conti, who was a maid in the castle and a close friend of Gaia's, told Gracie that the countess's father was an avid art collector and was so rich he bled gold. The countess's son, Tancredi, was fast going through his inheritance, however. Damiana's face lit up when she talked about *him*. Dashing and handsome, he had a bad reputation for womanising and partying. He roared up the street in his sports car and turned every head in town. According to Damiana, girls wanted to bed him, men wanted to *be* him. Gracie longed to see this swashbuckling count for herself.

Gracie was aware that she wasn't a beauty like Gaia and Damiana. She did not assume that men would be interested in her, even Italian men who loved to flirt. At sixteen she was now a woman, but she did not exude sex appeal like Italian women did. She did not walk with a swinging gait, nor smile with promise. She did not believe she was attractive so she did not draw attention to herself. She was shy, self-contained and watchful. She applied to life the same attention to detail that she applied to her work, and this made her acutely perceptive. She noticed everything going on around her, from Donato's foot toying with Gaia's beneath the table, to the teasing glances he was simultaneously throwing at Damiana. She sensed romance before it blossomed and she intuited the bitter end as it withered. She knew that the young men who flirted with her were not in love, but full of lust, and she was not going to be fooled by them. She did not know how she knew this. She was young and inexperienced, but somehow she saw through them. Perhaps they were clumsy. Perhaps their intention was poorly concealed in their lascivious eyes, perhaps she just knew that, when they told her she was beautiful, they were lying because she knew she wasn't. She longed to be, but nature had not blessed her with beauty. Nature had, however, endowed her with a beguiling mystery, but Gracie did not know that. Uncle Hans did. He had recognised that quality in her when she was a small child, for she'd inherited it from him. Mystery was one of the key ingredients required for the very specialised job he had in mind for her.

Three years passed before Rutger allowed her to start restoring paintings herself. She had learned how to study the work, to ascertain the date and place of conception, to read what should be there but was lost due to damage, age or intervention. She was accomplished now at removing the discoloured varnish, repairing tears, restoring a painting to an interpretation of its original state using the specific materials and techniques available to the artist at the time. She had learned to be a detective as Rutger had said she would, although she had nothing like the knowledge the Dutchman had – only experience could give her that. So when the bookshelves were deficient in the information she needed to correctly analyse a painting she had to rely on Rutger to advise her. But generally he allowed her freedom to work independently. 'It is only with freedom that you will grow,' he told her and left her to work it out for herself.

After five years Uncle Hans was pleased with her progress and her genuine interest in the skill of restoration. 'You have shown patience, intelligence and skill,' he said one afternoon after he had just returned from Paris with a crateload of paintings, old frames and canvases. He was standing behind her as she toiled at her easel, watching her intently. 'I think it is time,' he said.

Rutger tossed another cotton swab into the bin and stood up. 'I have been waiting for you to say that, Hans. I believe she is ready too.'

Gracie took off her magnifying lenses and looked at the two men with curiosity. 'Ready for what, Uncle Hans?' she asked.

'Follow me,' he said. He put his hand in his pocket and took out the key to his studio. Gracie's heart began to race. She had longed to know what was behind the door ever since Rutger had told her she was not allowed inside.

Uncle Hans put the key in the lock and turned it to the right. He opened the door and stepped into the room. 'Come,' he said to Gracie, who hovered nervously on the threshold. 'I am now going to bring you into a secret.'

Gracie looked around expecting to see something special. What she saw was a typical artist's studio. However, that in itself was a surprise because she had learned how different a restorer's studio was to an artist's, and this was definitely an artist's place of work. There were paintings stacked against the walls, canvases rolled up and placed on specially designed shelving, bookcases full of books and ledges lined with pigments in small glass jars, brushes and paints. Easels stood ready to be of use and everywhere was evidence of Hans's toil. Paint splattered the wooden floorboards and furniture. The air smelt of oil paint, linseed, turpentine and wood – all the things a studio would normally smell of. Uncle Hans was not restoring works of art in here; he was painting them.

Uncle Hans closed the door behind Rutger and locked it. For the first time in her life Gracie felt fear. What was so secret that it required the door to be locked when all three of them were in the room? She looked at her uncle and he must have noticed her panic, because he was swift to reassure her. 'Do not be afraid, my dear,' he said. 'You are about to join a very exclusive club. I know I can trust you. You are like a daughter to me. My own flesh and blood. So, you must never speak of what you are going to do to anyone. Do you understand?' Gracie nodded, wondering frantically what it was that she was going to do.

'Come,' he said. He directed her to a large canvas leaning

against the wall in an old gilt frame. 'What do you make of this?' he asked. Gracie studied the painting. It was quite obviously a Matisse. She was excited to see such a famous painting up close. 'Well? If you know your art you should know this,' said Uncle Hans.

'It is a Matisse,' Gracie replied with a shrug. *Even a child would know that*, she thought. 'However, I cannot pretend that I have seen this particular work before.'

Her uncle laughed, delighted with her reply. 'It is not by Matisse,' he said and there was a triumphant inflection in the way he said the artist's name. 'It is by Hans Hollingsworth.'

'You are a genius, Hans,' said Rutger, who had evidently never seen the work either.

'It is a brilliant copy,' said Gracie, impressed and much relieved. If her uncle wanted her to copy paintings there was nothing to worry about. She was very good at copying. She always had been.

'Yes, my dear,' said Uncle Hans. 'It is indeed a brilliant copy. But it is more than that, Gracie. It is a brilliant *forgery*.'

Gracie felt the air still around her. Her stomach clenched again with panic. Now she knew why he had locked the door, why he didn't want anyone to come in, why this room was out of bounds for everybody. Uncle Hans was painting forgeries and selling them. And this is what he now wanted Gracie to do. She stared at him in horror. 'But you could go to prison for this, Uncle,' she said, aghast.

'I could, but I won't. I have got away with it for twenty years. There is no reason why anyone is going to catch me now.'

'And you want me to . . .' Gracie could barely say the word.

'Yes, you are going to forge paintings and I am going to teach you how to do it. Rutger has prepared you but now I will take you to the next step.' He registered his niece's anxiety and changed his tone, as he had done that day in the kitchen when his sister Greet had tried to dissuade him from taking her daughter away. 'You have the potential to be brilliant, Gracie. I recognised that quality in you, which is why I brought you here. I knew you had the skill and the temperament to be a master forger. Who knows, you may one day make more money than I do.'

'But I can't,' she said in a small voice. 'I mean, it's breaking the law.'

Uncle Hans smiled in the calm, deliberate way he did when he wanted to manipulate someone into doing his bidding. 'Do you want to travel the world, Gracie? Do you want to meet the most creative and dazzling minds? Do you want to live in a world that is exciting and opulent? Of course you do, because you are like me, Gracie. We are the same. I was once a child from a home like yours, with little money and no prospects, but I could paint. I could paint well and I had ambition. I rescued myself and made my fortune. Now I have rescued *you* from a life of toil and struggle, from the life you would have had had I not brought you here and given you the finest education that money *cannot* buy. No, money *cannot* buy you the knowledge that Rutger has given you, because Rutger is priceless. Do you see? I have given you something *beyond* value, as I promised your mother I would. We will work together, you and I, and you will help build my empire.'

'But I could go to prison if I'm caught?'

He shrugged and chuckled as if the idea of being caught was ridiculous. 'But you won't.'

'Can't I just continue to restore and work with Rutger?' She looked to Rutger for support, but Rutger shook his head solemnly. He had known all along what Hans's intentions were. Indeed, he had been key in their conception.

'There is so much more you can do,' he said.

'I'm afraid.'

Uncle Hans put a firm hand on her shoulder and she felt the weight of it even in the pit of her belly. 'I have given you a roof over your head, an education beyond the wildest dreams of even the most talented artists, clothed you, fed you and looked after your every need. Have I not done enough?' Gracie stared at him in bewilderment. Uncle Hans lowered his gaze, downcast. He shrugged in defeat and removed his hand. 'Perhaps I have fooled myself into believing I have managed to fill your father's footsteps. Or perhaps you know only of taking and nothing of gratitude—'

'No, you've given me so much,' Gracie cut in, desperate to show her appreciation. 'This is more than a girl like me could ever have wished for.'

'Good, so we understand each other,' said Hans. Gracie nodded. She realised now that she could not deny Uncle Hans anything. Had he asked for her right arm, she knew, as she stood before him like a mouse before a snake, that she would have given it without hesitation, and offered him her left. How could she refuse after everything he had done for her? He was more than an uncle, he was the father she had never had, and she loved him. In any case, what was the alternative? She didn't want to return to Camden, to a life of drudgery and poverty. She had flown beyond that now and seen new horizons. She did not want to look back.

'If you really believe you can teach me how to paint a forgery that will dupe the art world, I am your willing student,' she said and the smile that transformed her uncle's face melted her fears and the horrifying prospect of committing a crime.

'Then we have work to do,' he said and Rutger nodded in agreement.

'You have graduated from the School of Rutger,' said Rutger with a wry smile. 'Now you are to commence at the higher School of Hollingsworth. My job is done.'

'I shall miss your lessons,' she said and the old man patted her arm.

'My final piece of advice,' he said. 'There is always more to learn. Just when you think you know it all you find there is another horizon. Don't ever forget that.'

And so, under the guidance of a cunning and skilled forger, Gracie learned to paint with the intention of deceiving. She didn't consider the consequences of being found out. She was young, she was reckless and she was trusting of her uncle. The most thrilling part was in discovering how very good she was at her new craft.

Art forgery was not the only secret Uncle Hans Hollingsworth asked Gracie to keep. The other was not one he would have asked her to keep by choice and it was certainly not one he would have ever talked about. But a few nights after he had told Gracie about his true occupation, she had been gripped by a terrible hunger in the middle of the night and decided to sneak down to the kitchen for something to eat. She didn't want to wait until morning and besides, excitement had made her restless. The world was now opening up to her and filling with endless possibility. She tiptoed down the wooden staircase and across the flagstone floor. The old grandfather clock ticked loudly in the hall. As she approached the kitchen she sensed someone there. It wasn't the usual patter of mice, but a breathing sound, staggered and sharp. The lights weren't on, but moonlight shone through the window, flooding the villa with an eerie silver radiance. She wondered what on earth it could be making this panting noise.

She padded in on her bare feet. There, in his dressing gown, with his back to the wall, was Uncle Hans. On his knees in front of him was Guido Vanni, one of the servants. Gracie stared at Uncle Hans. His eyes were closed and his mouth was agape and he was panting like a dog. Sweat glistened on his forehead and nose and the veins stood out on his neck. Guido Vanni's head was moving but Gracie wasn't quite sure what he was doing. She knew, however, that it was something she shouldn't be witnessing. Just as she realised she had caught her uncle doing something unsavoury, he opened his eyes. He stared at her and for the first time she saw horror in his bulging, glistening eyes. Gracie was frozen with panic. They seemed to stare at each other for an agonisingly long moment. Guido Vanni continued oblivious. Then Gracie managed to move her feet and hurry away.

How she wished she hadn't seen him. How she longed to turn back the clock. How she hated the sight of it re-enacted every time she closed her eyes. And yet, the following morning, when Uncle Hans appeared beneath the fig tree for breakfast, it was as if nothing had happened. He knew, as she did, that his secret was safe with her.

Chapter 8

The first time Gracie set eyes on Count Tancredi Bassanelli was in the summer of 1961. The whole town had gathered in the streets to witness the wedding of Tancredi's sister, Costanza, who was marrying a wealthy Austrian in the local church of Maria Maddalena, which dominated the Piazza della Chiesa with its tall bell tower and grand *portone* as it had done for hundreds of years.

The day could not have been more splendid. The bright green fields of spring had mellowed to softer hues of gold and the air was saturated with the floral scents of jasmine and rose. Sunshine blazed in a bright blue sky and birds soared overhead on a gentle breeze. Red geraniums shimmered on windowsills and purple bougainvillea fluttered on the ancient stone walls like clusters of exotic butterflies. Gracie had been in Tuscany now for six years. She had only been home to see her family once, and had felt so out of sorts there, among the childish things she had since outgrown, that she had been only too ready to return to Italy. Now she stood beside Gaia and Damiana in a pretty white dress Uncle Hans had bought her from Venice to watch the guests arriving in their finery, and she felt as much part of the place as they did.

Damiana, who was notoriously catty, enjoyed criticising

the ladies' clothes as they walked across the cobbled piazza to the church of Maria Maddalena. 'She should not have chosen that colour,' she said about a woman in an orange dress. 'It is very unforgiving and makes her look ill. And those shoes,' she sneered about another. 'Really, she is a young woman not a grandmother!' But Gaia and Gracie thought the orange dress extremely glamorous and the shoes very elegant and laughed at Damiana's observations, which they suspected were largely made for their amusement.

Gracie could barely stand still for the excitement. There were many festivals which punctuated the year with pageantry and partying, and local weddings, which were always entertaining to watch, but nothing had ever happened in Gracie's experience that was as thrilling as the Montefosco wedding. It was like a royal wedding and although Damiana was enjoying criticising it, Gracie knew she was as electrified as everybody else.

After the guests arrived the families of the bride and groom were driven right to the steps of the church in carriages drawn by white horses. The ancient carriages, which Damiana told Gracie had been in the family for hundreds of years, were adorned with so many flowers one could barely see the people inside them.

It was then that Gaia grabbed Gracie's arm. 'There he is!' she exclaimed as a clamour of clapping arose from the crowd. Gracie didn't need to ask which one he was. He stood out from the other members of his family on account of his dashing good looks. He was tall, broad-shouldered with dark, wavy hair that bounced a little as he moved. His face was wide, handsome and when he smiled at the crowd Gracie felt a sudden jolt as if she had been struck in the heart. 'Isn't he delicious!' Damiana groaned. 'How lucky is the girl who wins *him.*' Gracie said nothing. She just stared with her lips parted, not wanting to miss a moment.

Count Bassanelli turned and lifted down a young girl from the carriage. She must have only been about twelve, but Gracie wished that *she* were that child, in his arms, grinning at him and saying something to which he responded with an affectionate chuckle. He took her hand and they walked up the steps together towards the ushers who stood on either side of the big doors. Count Bassanelli wore the same pale grey suit as the other men and yet his jacket seemed to be more defined at the waist and sharper at the shoulders. Perhaps it was just the way he walked, but to Gracie he was like a superior species of man. She barely blinked until he had been swallowed into the dark gullet of the church. She couldn't wait for the ceremony to end and for him to walk out again so she could get another glimpse.

Ten minutes later the bride arrived with bridesmaids in white dresses, their long hair adorned with little white flowers and pearls. Gracie thought they looked like a herd of lovely swans as they fussed about their dresses and the bride's long train. Again the clapping rose into a crescendo and the bride smiled sweetly behind her veil and waved. 'What a beautiful family,' said Gracie.

'They are very blessed,' said Gaia.

'I think the bride's nose is a little on the pointy side,' Damiana added and Gracie smiled at her eagerness to see fault where there really was none.

'I think only beautiful women see fault in other beautiful women,' Gracie said.

'Are you saying that, because you're not beautiful, you don't?' Damiana retorted. Then, realising that she might have caused offence, she added quickly, 'You have a sweet face, Gracie, and beautiful eyes. There are many kinds of beauty.'

Gaia was mortified that Damiana might have hurt her friend's feelings. 'No, Gracie, *you* don't criticise other women because you're kind, that's why you have a nice face and Damiana has a mean face.' She put her arm around Gracie's shoulders. 'Damiana here is a witch. I dread to think what she says about us behind *our* backs!' They laughed together and Gracie was not in the least offended for Damiana had only stated the truth. They continued to chat until the church bells rang out and the big doors opened and the bride and groom stepped into the sunshine.

But Gracie's eyes were not on the bride and groom. She was anxiously standing on tiptoes and straining her neck to see the count. When he emerged at last it was as if the entire town stilled around her. Only *he* moved, elegantly, down the steps, smiling and clapping, white teeth bright against brown skin, and Gracie was sure she could hear him laugh.

Then the world moved again and the guests threw rose petals at the couple who posed for photographs before climbing into a carriage to be driven up to the castle. Gracie watched the count until he too disappeared up the street with the child by his side, his arm around her, his head inclined to hear what she had to say. Gracie put a hand on her heart and sighed. *How would it feel to be loved by him?* she mused. But then she laughed at the absurdity of such a thought. A man like him would never look twice at a girl like her. He wouldn't even notice she was on the planet.

There was a party that night in the Piazza della Chiesa, courtesy of the Castello Montefosco. The surrounding houses were lit with strings of fairy lights that twinkled in the dusk. Long tables were laid out with bottles of wine and a banquet of ham and meat, pasta and vegetables, and the smoke from the barbecues attracted stray dogs which trotted out of the shadows to join the feast. A band played heartily and there was dancing. Gracie loved to dance. She let go of her longing and allowed the wine and the music and the heat to take her over. She danced with anyone who invited her, both young men and old, and kicked off her shoes to skip more easily over the cobbles. She laughed with abandon, flirted in a way she had never previously flirted, for her heart had been touched and now it ached for love.

She wanted to be held, to be kissed, to be cherished and although she was realistic enough to know that a man like Count Bassanelli was beyond her reach, she did not believe it naive to hope that someone was out there somewhere for *her*. For the first time in her life she wanted to be desired. For the first time since arriving in Tuscany as a girl, she looked at the men with the eyes of a woman. The alcohol gave her a confidence she would never have otherwise had, her yearning for the count a recklessness which was out of character. She allowed Donato to hold her close, to press his cheek against hers and to brush his lips across her cheek. She didn't care that he flirted with all the pretty girls, in fact, she was flattered that he was now flirting with *her*.

When he took her hand and led her at a run down a dark alley, far from the music and the dancing, she didn't resist. She *wanted* him to want her. He pushed her against a wall and pressed his lips to hers and she closed her eyes and parted hers so that he could kiss her more fully. She hadn't the experience to judge whether it was a good or a bad kiss, but the tingling feeling of awakening that careered through her whole body was sublime. He wound his arms around her and she slipped her hands beneath his jacket to feel his back through his shirt, which was damp with sweat. He kissed her neck and the bristles against her skin caused her to laugh out loud with pleasure and nervousness, for the strange feelings now building in her belly were new and alarming. Donato cupped her breast and the sensation was exquisite. He traced his thumb over the thin fabric of her summer dress and fell on her mouth again, kissing her deeply. Her mind drifted to the count and suddenly it was *his* thumb on her nipple and *his* lips on hers and the sublime sensation turned into something far more intense. She heard herself moan, which woke her abruptly from her reverie. She gasped in horror and pushed Donato away. He looked at her with dark eyes, feverish with lust.

'You are driving me crazy, Gracie!' he said, putting his hands on her waist. 'Was that your first kiss?' She nodded and he grinned. 'How was it?' But he didn't wait for her reply. He kissed her again, more softly this time, and it didn't matter to Gracie that he didn't love her, that she didn't love him. She loved the way he kissed her and, right now, that was all that mattered.

Donato walked Gracie home as the pinky-orange light of dawn glowed in the eastern sky. He held her hand, pulling her close to kiss her every now and again, which made her laugh. 'You're a desirable woman, Gracie,' he said. 'I don't know what happened to you tonight, but you changed. You became a butterfly.'

'Or a swan,' she replied with a wry smile.

'Or a swan,' he agreed, failing to detect the cynical tone in her voice. 'I cannot stop kissing you.' He laughed, kissing her again.

'It was the wine, the music, the summer heat. The flowers, the beauty ...' She paused and savoured the tender play of light on the gently undulating hills and the wisps of mist that lingered in the valleys. 'It's just too beautiful,' she said with a sigh. 'Too beautiful sometimes to bear.' And she thought of the count and wished he were holding her hand and kissing her instead of Donato.

'Then you should drink more wine, dance to more music and enjoy the beauty more often.' He smiled at her and she saw a sweetness in it that she hadn't noticed before. 'And kiss me more often,' he added huskily.

Gracie laughed. 'It's nice, kissing.'

'Only with me,' he replied.

'Are there any girls here who you haven't kissed?' she asked.

He looked offended and put his hand on his chest. 'I only want to kiss *you*.'

'For now,' she added. 'And for now, *I* only want to kiss *you*.'

He frowned at her candour. 'You are a strange woman, Gracie. A mysterious woman. I like that.'

They reached La Colomba. The emerging light was turning the garden to gold and birds heralded the awakening day in the umbrella pines. Gracie thought of Gaia asleep in her bedroom on the top floor. She wondered whether she knew what Gracie had got up to with Donato. She wondered whether the whole town knew. 'Thank you for walking me home,' she said and kissed him.

'Is your uncle home?' he asked.

'He's away travelling.'

'Good.' Donato pulled her against him and pressed his lips to hers.

She gently pushed him away. 'I must go. I have to work tomorrow.'

'It's already tomorrow.'

'Then I need to get some sleep.'

'You even work on a weekend?' he asked, astonished.

'There are many paintings to be restored.'

'Then I will let you go, little butterfly.' And he reluctantly dropped her hand.

Gracie was too agitated to sleep. She waited for Donato to leave and then she stole down to the pagoda where she lay on one of the reclining chairs and watched the garden slowly awaken. She thought of the wedding party up at the castle. It was strange to think of Count Bassanelli there, breathing the same air as her, watching the same dawn. If he looked over the crenellated wall he'd see La Colomba. If he looked through binoculars, he'd see *her*. Yet, he didn't know she existed and probably never would. Maybe she'd end up marrying a man like Donato and be content with that. She'd always remember the first time she'd set eyes on Count Bassanelli and lost her heart. Perhaps she'd tell her daughters one day and they'd laugh at her romantic nature. But she would always count herself lucky that she could remember the very moment she had first learned about love.

❧

Gaia and Damiana were surprised to discover that Donato, the wild and flirtatious Lothario who had kissed all the girls in town, had not only kissed Gracie, but apparently fallen in love with her. He appeared at La Colomba with a large bouquet of flowers the day after the wedding only to be told by Gaia that Gracie was working and couldn't be disturbed. On the Sunday Uncle Hans arrived back having successfully sold a fake Renoir to an American collector. He was in high spirits. He had bought Gracie two new dresses from Paris and letters from her mother and Joseph, who he had seen in London. When Donato turned up at the house every evening the following week with more flowers, Gaia told him that

Signor Hollingsworth was now home and working Gracie to the bone. Donato would have to wait.

When Gaia asked Gracie about Donato, Gracie was frank. 'He's a good kisser,' she replied with a grin. 'But so he should be with all the experience he has gleaned over the years.'

'But do you love him?' Gaia asked.

'No,' Gracie replied.

'I think *he* loves *you*.'

'Perhaps he thinks he does, but he doesn't. I'm another conquest, that's all. If I chased him round the piazza he'd soon tire of me.'

'So wise for one so young,' said Gaia with a frown. 'But will you go out with him?'

'When I have a free evening, perhaps,' Gracie replied with a shrug. 'But while my uncle is home, I am very busy.'

It was a month before Uncle Hans went away again. Rutger continued to work in the studio while Gracie toiled in her uncle's, behind the door that always had to be locked. In the evenings she went to town with Gaia, who had begun a tentative romance with a young man called Filippo Pieri, and saw Donato. They held hands in the shadow of the castle, and Gracie gazed up at it and wondered whether she'd ever lay eyes on Count Bassanelli again. She pressed Donato for details about the Montefosco family and he was only too happy to indulge her curiosity with elaborate stories of their grand house parties. He promised to take her up to the castle in the autumn when the countess had returned to Rome. By the light in her eyes he could see that a private tour of the castle grounds interested her more than bunches of flowers ever could. However, in spite of the promise of wandering the gardens of Count Bassanelli's home, Gracie remained just out of reach to the man who was used to having any woman he wanted.

At the end of the summer Gracie's grandmother died. Uncle Hans informed her gravely and by the stricken look on his face, his mother's death had cut him deeply. They returned to London for the funeral, a sad, subdued pair. As the plane descended through thick cloud Gracie watched London come into view through the round window. In spite of the season, the city was damp and miserable in the rain, and looked even more so after the vibrant colours of Italy. For the first time in her life Gracie knew what it was to lose someone she loved. Her father didn't count, because she had never known him. But her grandmother had been a constant, reassuring presence throughout her childhood. With a dry sense of humour and an eagerness to avoid being a burden to her daughter, she had involved herself in the raising of her grandchildren and Gracie had never imagined she wouldn't be there, nodding off in her chair after tea. She realised now that by moving to Italy she had not only gained a new life but had lost her old life in the process. It would have been impossible not to – she couldn't have lived in both places simultaneously even if she had wanted to.

Italy had changed her and she no longer fitted the small terraced house where she had grown up. She no longer knew her brother Joseph and she understood now her mother's sacrifice. She didn't feel guilty for leaving them, for life is about change and nothing stays the same, but she felt sad that her grandmother had ceased to be a part of her life and now it was too late. That moment of awakening at the wedding had touched Gracie's heart and opened it to love, but with love always comes the pain of loss. As the plane descended into Heathrow Gracie experienced loss for the first time and sobbed quietly into her handkerchief.

After the funeral Gracie spent time with her mother and

Joseph while Uncle Hans met important people from the art world in London's West End. The house felt very different without Oma in it, but they put on brave faces and Gracie cheered them up with tales of Italy. Her mother loved listening to Gracie's stories and Gracie delighted in seeing the smile on her face as she told them. Joseph now worked in a hardware shop and received a small wage. He was dating a local girl and Greet told Gracie in confidence that he would probably marry her. Greet sewed and was grateful for the money her brother sent her every month. When Gracie thought of Uncle Hans's wealth she was surprised he didn't send them more. He could have bought his sister a palace with the money he earned from his forgeries. But Greet didn't complain. She wasn't used to luxuries, she said.

Gracie, on the other hand, was. She found her old home stifling and was uncomfortable wearing the fine clothes Uncle Hans had bought her in front of her mother, who never had time to make dresses for herself. She would have happily given her mother her dresses on leaving had Greet lived the sort of life that required stylish clothes. But she didn't and they would have languished in her cupboard being eaten by moths, so Gracie packed them for Italy and gave her a couple of cardigans instead.

'Why don't you and Joseph come and live with Uncle Hans now?' Gracie asked on the last evening as they were in the kitchen drying their soup bowls. She wondered why they hadn't all moved out there years ago. There was certainly room in La Colomba for the lot of them.

Her mother smiled at her sadly. 'I would love to, but my home is here,' she said quietly.

'But it rains all the time in London. Tuscany is like heaven.'

'This is the house your father bought for us,' she explained.

'It is the home he would have come back to at the end of the war had he lived. It is all I have left of him, Gracie.' She swept her weary eyes over the shabby walls and dingy furniture. 'And I like it,' she added firmly. 'I like it just the way it is.'

'I wish I had known him,' Gracie said suddenly.

Her mother's smile faltered. 'I wish you had too, Gracie. He would have been very proud of you. I think he would have wanted more for Joseph, but he is young. There is time for him to find a better job.'

'Are you going to be all right without Oma?' Gracie asked.

'I am stronger than I look. I will be fine. You mustn't worry about me. We survived the war, didn't we?'

At the mention of the war Gracie thought of Uncle Hans. He had never talked about those years when he had lived in Amsterdam. 'What did Uncle Hans do during the war?'

Greet's face seemed to snap shut and she began to wipe the sink and surrounding wood with vigour. 'Well, as you know Holland was occupied by the Germans in 1940. Hans did the best he could under the occupation. He did what he had to in order to survive. He restored and sold paintings, just like he had always done. As soon as the war was over he moved to Italy. He was accused of collaborating with the Germans, selling them works of art, and would have been in trouble had he not left. Of course he restored and sold paintings to the Germans. How could it be avoided?' Gracie wondered whether he had sold them fakes. She hoped he had.

❧

Gracie returned to Tuscany in the middle of September. The autumn sun was still hot, but it hung lower in the sky, turning the harvested fields a tender pinky-orange, making everything about the land look soft. Gracie's happiness at returning to the country that had claimed her heart was marred by the sorrow of having left her mother. She wished Uncle Hans had insisted she come and live with them at La Colomba. She didn't understand why he hadn't. Gracie hated thinking of her grieving for her mother with only Joseph to take care of her.

In Colladoro life continued from where it had left off, but something inside Gracie had shifted. Just knowing that Oma was no longer in the world filled her heart with a heavy sorrow. She regretted not visiting her more. She regretted not talking to her more. She regretted not telling her she loved her. It was too late now. All she could do was whisper her love into her pillow at night and hope that Oma heard her, wherever she was.

Gracie spent time with Donato. She managed to enjoy evenings with her friends in town and resumed her work. She forgot about Donato's offer of a private tour around the gardens of the castle, not because she was no longer curious, but because time had assuaged the urgency and reality had eclipsed the fantasy. She enjoyed being with Donato. She didn't love him but she was fond of him and that was ample for the girl who was neither rich nor beautiful nor, in her opinion, special. Damiana had married a farmer's son from across the valley and she now worked on the family farm instead of at the castle, which she much preferred because there was greater opportunity to slack off, her new husband being indulgent and enamoured. However, she no longer had tales to tell of the countess and her flamboyant son so the blood supply of information from the castle to Gracie's heart was duly cut off and, as a consequence, her ardour waned. Together with Gaia and Filippo the six of them were a tight group of closely bonded friends. Gracie rarely raised her eyes to the castle walls and dreamed and, if she caught herself doing so, she swiftly reined in her thoughts.

In the spring of the following year Rutger studied a Monet she had painted. It took him three days to test it for a forgery. When he had reached his conclusion, he discussed it with Uncle Hans, falling easily into Dutch. Gracie listened, half hoping that they would declare the painting not good enough so she would not have to become the criminal her uncle wanted her to become.

At last Hans turned to Gracie and nodded. 'You are ready,' he said. 'It is time to launch your work into the world.'

Chapter 9

Convincing a buyer that a painting is genuine is far more complicated than the actual painting of it. It is one thing to mimic the style of a painter long dead but quite another to convince the contemporary mind of its validity. This is where Hans Hollingsworth applied his genius. He worked alone, found his own middle men and stage-managed the swindles himself. He also pocketed all the money. A master storyteller, he invented credible stories to give his forgeries the solid provenance required to hoodwink the buyer. With the charm of a boulevardier and the steady gaze of an honest man he had earned the reputation of being both decent and trustworthy. His English surname and sheen of wealth gave him a certain respectability, not to mention the contacts high up in the art world which he had cultivated over the years. Hans Hollingsworth was the perfect front man for a very dubious business.

Gracie learned that Uncle Hans had an office in the centre of Paris where he would meet clients and representatives of clients. He never brought anyone to La Colomba. Now he went to Paris with Gracie's painting and began negotiations with a client in Texas who was an avid collector of French Impressionist painting. While her uncle was busy trying to sell her forgery, Gracie returned to Rutger's studio, helping him restore pictures.

Then one day in June Rutger invited Gracie to accompany him on a special assignment. Countess Bassanelli's father had died, leaving her half of his art collection. It had, up until now, been stored in Rome, gathering dust. The countess had decided to bring it to the castle to be catalogued and valued. The paintings in need of restoration would be sent to La Colomba for Rutger and Gracie to work on. The fantasies which Gracie had repressed now shifted sharply into focus.

Gracie sat in the passenger seat of Rutger's small car while Rutger drove up the track towards town. On either side fields of sunflowers turned their pretty faces to the sun and birds frolicked in the cypress trees. The sky was the brightest indigo blue and Gracie's heart grew buoyant at the thought of visiting the count's home. She didn't imagine he would be there; she didn't dare hope.

They drove through the town to the imposing iron gates at the top, gates that Gracie had so often dreamed of entering. The paradise she had imagined was only too real. Donato's father saw them from the lawn where he was mowing and hurried down to open the gates, his red face sweating beneath his cap. Somewhere among the gardenia and oleander was Donato, but Gracie was too busy gazing about her in wonder to think of him. This was the realm of fantasy where Donato had no place.

The car made its way slowly up the slope, over stripy shadows which the avenue of cypress trees threw across the drive, and on towards the castle that peeped enticingly out from between them. At last they reached the summit and all the images Gracie had conjured up in her mind paled in comparison to the real castle. Its magnificence took Gracie's breath away, not because it was big or grand, in fact, it was neither, but because of its age and quiet dignity, which reminded her of a cherished grandfather. There was something very wise about its expression, like an old farmer whose wrinkled, gentle face reveals a deep understanding of the magic that lies beneath the land. It was built in the Tuscan stone which is common throughout the land, but these walls had weathered over the centuries to the colour of milky tea and looked almost battle-weary, as if they had witnessed dramatic things before this tranquil retirement. The windows were framed by sage-green shutters and placed either side of the big door were enormous terracotta pots of purple bougainvillea, heaped high and cascading over the sides in an extravagant overflow. The beauty of the place delighted Gracie, whose English heart would never tire of such splendour.

A short, grey-haired man in a black Nehru jacket greeted them with a warm smile and showed them into the hall. It was cool, with high ceilings and putty-coloured walls, and Gracie immediately smelt lavender and looked around until she found the source, huge urns full of it, like purple grain, giving off an exquisite perfume. They followed the man through the castle and Gracie couldn't help but peep inquisitively through open doors which gave tempting glimpses into rooms steeped in history and heritage and comfort. They emerged into the light and were led across a lawn to a terrace where a woman rose from a big wicker sofa to greet them. Gracie knew instantly that she was the countess. In a wide-brimmed sunhat, floral blouse tucked into wide-legged trousers and white espadrilles on her feet, she was elegant and understated. Her dark hair was tied into a chignon at the back of her neck and, as Gracie approached, she saw that the countess was not beautiful in an obvious way, but handsome with an aquiline nose, a dark, penetrating gaze and a sensual mouth that smiled with the confidence of a woman sure of her appeal.

The countess put out her hand. 'Very nice to meet you, Signor Janssen,' she said, and the way she spoke Italian was soft and melodious, garnished with a timbre of laughter. 'My father spoke highly of you,' she said to Rutger and Gracie could tell that she was the sort of woman who couldn't help but flirt with everyone. 'And who is this?' she asked, putting out a graceful hand to shake Gracie's.

'May I present Hans Hollingsworth's niece, Gracie,' Rutger replied.

Those dark eyes scrutinised her and Gracie felt like a mouse before a bird of prey. 'And you work for your uncle?' the countess probed.

'Yes, I do,' Gracie replied.

'And you are not Italian?'

'English. I have been here seven years, Contessa,' she said.

'Congratulations. You speak Italian beautifully. I'm glad you brought an assistant, Signor Janssen,' said the countess to Rutger. 'My father left me a considerable number of paintings. Come, let me show you.'

Accompanied by the smiling retainer, they followed the countess, who seemed to float over the grass, to the other side of the lawn. They passed a medieval tower that looked like it had been built even earlier than the castle. It stood on the crest of the hill beside a giant cedar tree. 'That is where my son paints,' she told them and the mention of Tancredi gave Gracie a jolt. 'The tower was built in the thirteenth century,' she went on and Gracie longed for her to tell them less about the tower and more about her son. But as they walked down the grassy path towards an old chapel the countess was only too eager to show off her knowledge of history.

The retainer opened the heavy door with a rusty key. 'This used to be the family chapel,' the countess informed them, stepping inside. 'But it has not been used for a hundred years. It is a good place to store my father's paintings.' Indeed, it was. Stacked against every wall were frames hidden under white sheets. Gracie couldn't wait to see what treasures lay beneath.

'Bagwis will bring you water and lemonade. There is a lavatory through that door,' she said, pointing to a small wooden exit to the right of the nave. 'Is there anything else you need?'

'We shall start at once,' said Rutger, putting his bag on one of the chairs randomly placed around the chapel.

'Very good. If you need me, you only have to shout, or ask Bagwis, and when you feel like a break, please, enjoy the gardens. I imagine it will take you a few days to go through all the paintings.'

'At least,' said Rutger, running his eyes around the room.

The countess departed, leaving a lingering scent of tuberose, and Gracie and Rutger took the sheet off the first painting and turned it into the light. It was a portrait of a girl in a green dress by Johannes Cornelisz Verspronck, a seventeenth-century Dutch painter. Gracie gasped. 'This is stunning!' she exclaimed.

'As you know, Verspronck was a Golden Age Dutch portraitist, probably a pupil of Frans Hals,' Rutger said. 'He painted mostly Catholic sitters. You see how delicately he painted the lace on the dress. It is so fine, so intricate, you can almost touch it.'

Gracie was excited. If the first painting was a Johannes Cornelisz Verspronck, what were the other ones going to be? Rutger gave her his ledger and pencil and dictated notes, which Gracie dutifully took down in her neat hand. Bagwis entered with a tray of glasses and a jug of lemonade and placed it on the floor, away from the paintings, for there was no table available. But Gracie and Rutger were much too engrossed in their work to notice.

They had been toiling for a couple of hours when the door opened and a man stepped into the chapel. Gracie assumed it was Bagwis and didn't even look up from the ledger. Rutger glanced over the rim of his spectacles and stopped what he was doing.

'*Buon giorno, Signor Janssen*,' said the man and Gracie's pencil broke onto the paper. She looked up. Standing in the doorway was Count Bassanelli. 'I'm sorry to disturb you, but I wanted to say hello,' he said and strode across the chapel to introduce himself to Rutger. It was as if he hadn't seen Gracie, sitting on the chair with her face in her ledger. 'Quite a collection, eh?' he said after the pleasantries, and Rutger laughed and took off his glasses to wipe his eyes.

'A lot of work for a man who is no longer young,' he chuckled. 'But I like to be busy.'

'I suspect some of these will need restoring.'

'They will.'

'You may even find one or two old friends,' said the count. 'I gather Signor Hollingsworth sold my grandfather the odd painting.'

'I haven't come across them yet.'

'Perhaps they are in my uncle's collection. My grandfather left half to him and half to my mother.' Gracie noticed a bitter edge sharpen his tone as he mentioned his uncle. It was subtle, so subtle that the count would not have noticed it himself even if it had been pointed out to him, but Gracie heard it. She missed nothing as she sat there quietly observing the man she had loved from afar for so long.

'The countess tells me you paint,' Rutger continued, speaking with the assurance of a man who is unimpressed by titles and wealth.

'Very badly,' Tancredi replied.

'Beauty is in the eye of the beholder,' Rutger said wisely.

'It would take an exceptional beholder to see beauty in mine,' Tancredi replied.

As they talked Gracie watched the count from her chair. He was just as handsome up close, but he seemed diminished somehow, as if a little of his glitter had worn off. In spite of his graciousness he was subdued, unlike the man she had watched at the wedding whose smile had been broad and insouciant. He took an interest in the paintings they had already studied and when Rutger called Gracie over, to show him her ledger, he said a polite hello, but gave her no more attention than that. Gracie was relieved he didn't talk to her because she wasn't sure she'd be able to reply without saying something gauche, or without getting her tongue in a twist.

Tancredi looked at her ledger and discussed the paintings with Rutger. Gracie tried not to stare, but she noticed everything. The wavy hair that curled at his collar, the shadow of bristle on his chin and jaw, the long dark lashes that framed eyes so blue God must have used the same colour with which to paint the sky. He was much taller than her, but most men were, Gracie was only five feet six inches and he must have been well over six feet. His hands were clean, his nails trimmed short, but his cuticles were rough, especially on the thumbs, as if they had been relentlessly chewed. It was those ragged cuticles that made her realise, suddenly, that he wasn't a fantasy but a real person with fears and anxieties like everybody else, and her heart went out to him. As soon as she noticed one flaw, she began to see others: the lines on his brow; the downturn of his lips when he wasn't smiling; a heaviness behind the eyes that belied the humorous twinkle in them. *He must have loved his grandfather very much*, Gracie thought and she felt a gentle wrench on her heartstrings. She understood loss and how it leaves a hole in the soul that can never be filled.

After a long while he left them to their work. He handed Gracie the ledger, thanked her and left. Rutger made no comment on the man Gracie could have discussed until sunset. He returned to the painting he had been analysing when the count entered and Gracie sharpened her pencil and began to write again.

It wasn't until the following day that she saw him again. Rutger was sitting on a bench in the shade, eating his packed lunch, while she sat on the terrace in the sunshine, gazing out over the hills that quivered like mirages in the midday heat. She was thinking of Tancredi, imagining him in the tower, painting, when he marched onto the terrace. She was so surprised to see him that she leapt to her feet. She was about to tell him where to find Rutger, for she was certain it wasn't *her* he wished to speak to, when he shook his head apologetically and put his hands on his hips. 'I am a very rude man,' he said and his face creased into a bashful frown. 'I never introduced myself yesterday and my mother tells me you are Signor Hollingsworth's niece.'

'Gracie,' she said and smiled, because he looked so ashamed of himself she felt sorry for him.

'Tancredi. Please accept my apology.' He shook her hand and the touch of his skin was almost too intimate to be comfortable. 'I hope I'm not disturbing you. You deserve a break.'

'Not at all. I was admiring the view.'

'Isn't it magnificent? One never grows tired of it.' He stood beside her, tall and charismatic, and looked out. 'You know the colours change every day.' Then he chuckled. 'Of course you know, you've lived here for seven years. My mother told me that too. She makes it her business to know everything about everyone.'

'As an English girl I appreciate the changing colours every day. I don't think I'll ever tire of them either. I think I could travel the world and never find a place more beautiful.'

'I *have* travelled the world and I can tell you that you won't.' He laughed and seemed relieved to be doing so. Then he sighed, as if expelling something heavy. 'Would you like to look round the gardens?'

She hesitated a moment, fearing they'd bump into Donato. But then her longing got the better of her. She wanted more than anything to extend their meeting, even though he must have only wanted to be kind to make up for having ignored her. 'I would love to,' she said.

'My mother is very proud of the gardens,' he said as they set off. 'She has a team of gardeners who do all the work for her. She just gives orders and shows it off.' Gracie did not mention that one of those gardeners was her boyfriend.

They wandered slowly from terrace to terrace and Gracie admired the trimmed box hedges, the rows of lavender, climbing roses, jasmine, periwinkles and violets. The loveliness of the flowers and the abundance of them touched her heart and she heard herself say, 'I'm sorry your grandfather died.'

Tancredi looked surprised. The muscles in his face tightened and Gracie realised she had touched a nerve and wished she hadn't been so forward. 'Thank you,' he replied, putting his hands in his trouser pockets. 'He was a very special man and I miss him.'

'My grandmother died last year,' she said softly. 'She was special too.'

His expression softened when he realised that she, too, had suffered loss. 'Then we are both grieving,' he said.

'Yes,' she replied. 'I feel I have crossed a bridge and can never go back to where I was before.'

He looked at her with an intensity that told her he had crossed it as well. 'Did she live in Italy, your grandmother?'

'She was Dutch, but she lived in London with my mother. I left home when I was thirteen to come and apprentice Rutger. I regret that I spent so many years away from her, but if I went back in time I would make the same choice.' That sounded silly to Gracie, but Tancredi seemed to understand and not think her silly at all.

'You must not regret anything. I could regret many things if I allowed myself to, but one has to live in the moment and not lament the past. It is what it is. One has to accept it and look forward.'

'Very true,' she said.

'That's what my grandfather would say.'

'He sounds like he was a wise man.' Tancredi smiled and Gracie sensed the sadness in it and couldn't look at him. She fixed her eyes on the gardens and changed the subject. 'It must be lovely to live in such a beautiful place . . .' but Tancredi wanted to talk about his grandfather.

'There was a painting in my grandfather's house in Rome which I especially loved. It was by an artist called Piero Bartoloni. Have you heard of him?'

'Of course, I have. A Baroque painter,' Gracie replied and Tancredi was impressed.

'He is not very well known,' he said.

'Perhaps, but art is my business,' she replied with a shrug. 'What was the subject?'

'A voluptuous woman in a beautiful garden, faced with a snake in a tree, entitled *The Temptation of Eve*. As a child, I found it fascinating. For a start, Eve's body was so sensual and beautiful, I was spellbound, and then the snake was so menacing. It stirred in me a mixture of delight and fear. Light and dark. Sweet and sour. It also stirred something in me which was beyond the understanding of a child.'

'It sounds wonderful. I'd like to say I am familiar with it, but I'm not. Where is it now?'

'My grandfather promised me he would leave it to me when he died.'

'But he didn't,' said Gracie. She looked at him and saw the tension in his profile. 'He forgot.'

'How do you know that when I didn't tell you?' he asked, astonished.

'I don't know. A good guess? Intuition? If he had given it to you, you wouldn't look so sad.'

He sighed, venting frustration. 'He either forgot, or he didn't want me to have it. I suspect the former, but my uncle, who now owns it, suspects the latter, which is why he will not give it to me.' He chuckled bitterly. 'I'm sorry, I don't know why I'm telling you this. Perhaps because you are nothing to do with my family. It is easier to confide in a stranger than in someone you know well.'

'Is there no way your uncle will give it to you? A Bartoloni would not be very valuable right now, though, of course, that might change. The Baroque period goes in and out of fashion. Why don't you buy it off him?'

'He won't sell.'

Gracie grinned. 'Is he an unpleasant man?'

'Yes.' Tancredi laughed. 'To put it as bluntly as you, he is a *very* unpleasant man. He will hold on to it just to spite me.'

'I'm sorry you can't have the painting you want. But it is only a painting. That's what my grandmother would say.'

'And she's right, of course. But I hazard a guess that you don't believe that any more than I do. To me, it's more than a painting. It's part of my childhood. Part of a time when I was very happy. And my grandfather wanted me to have it.' He shook his head as if berating his own folly. 'I don't want to bore you with my woes.'

'You're not. And your guess is correct. If it has sentimental value, then it's priceless. Perhaps your uncle will change his mind one day.'

'Perhaps,' he replied, but Gracie could tell that he didn't believe it.

They returned to the chapel. 'I must not take up any more of your time,' he said, hovering at the door.

'Rutger will be wondering where I got to,' she said.

'You'd better go inside then and open that ledger of yours.'

'Thank you for showing me the gardens.'

'It was a pleasure.' He walked away and Gracie entered the chapel with a bounce in her step. Rutger looked up at her over the top of his spectacles. He didn't ask where she'd been. Perhaps he knew. He began to tell her about the Picasso he had just uncovered.

That evening Gracie told Gaia that she had met the handsome count. Gaia was fascinated and wanted all the details and Gracie told her. 'Lucky you to be given a private tour of the gardens by him. Do you think Donato saw you? He'll be very jealous.'

'I didn't see him, but he has no reason to be jealous. It was hardly a romantic walk. The count was just being gracious.'

'Of course, but Italian men are very possessive, Gracie, and Donato has a high opinion of himself. Probably the only man capable of making him jealous would be Tancredi Bassanelli.'

'Then I will use him if I need to.'

'You won't need to,' said Gaia. 'Donato is besotted with you.'

'I can't think why. If he could have anyone, why does he want me?'

'Because you are out of reach.'

'I'm his girlfriend,' Gracie protested.

'But you're still out of reach.'

'I have so much work to do.'

'I know, so I tell him. Perhaps that is what keeps him keen.' She grinned. 'If you want to marry him, keep working.'

Gracie felt uneasy. The idea of marriage hadn't occurred to her. 'I'm too young to marry,' she said.

'No, you're not. If Filippo doesn't ask me soon, I'll be too old.'

'He will ask you,' said Gracie, watching Gaia picking her nails anxiously.

'I hope so.'

'And you'll have a wedding like the Montefosco wedding and the whole town will come out to watch.'

Gaia laughed. 'I hope you're right. I love Filippo.' She narrowed her dark eyes at Gracie. 'Don't you love Donato?'

'I'm very fond of him,' Gracie replied carefully.

'That's not the same.'

'I know. But not everyone will find the kind of love you have for Filippo. For some people being fond is enough to make a life together.'

'I'm too romantic,' said Gaia. 'I would always hold out for love. Fond would never be enough for me.'

'But it's enough for *me*. I'm not saying I want to marry Donato, but I could be happy with a man like him. I don't expect the earth to move. I don't think it does for girls like me.'

Gaia looked appalled. 'What do you mean for girls like you?'

'For *ordinary* girls.'

'Why ever do you think you're ordinary? Why ever do you think you won't fall madly in love with someone?'

'Oh, I don't doubt that I will fall madly in love, I just doubt that the man I fall in love with will fall madly in love with *me*.' She couldn't confess that she was referring to Tancredi.

'Do you think men are so shallow that they only fall in love with great beauty? If you're beautiful on the inside it will shine on the outside, however plain or pretty the features. You doubt yourself too much, Gracie. Someone has told you that you are undeserving and they are wrong. If Donato is not the man for you, there is someone out there somewhere who is and he will find you.'

Gracie laughed cynically. 'You really are a romantic,' she said.

'But I believe it.'

'If we all believed it like you, most of the girls in the world would never marry. We'd all be holding out for Rhett Butler. But I'm not a beauty like Scarlett, Gaia. I will settle for less and I'll be content. One can't ask for more than that.' But she did, in the heart of her heart, ask for more than that.

Chapter 10

Over the next four days Tancredi visited the chapel often. He looked at the paintings he had known from childhood and discussed them with Rutger and Gracie. Rutger was able to expand on the knowledge Tancredi already had and Tancredi listened to the Dutchman with interest. Once he discovered that they brought their lunches to eat in the garden he asked them to join him and his mother and any guests she had invited for lunch on the terrace. The countess *always* had guests. At first Gracie was embarrassed. She felt awkward in the company of grand and important people, but Tancredi introduced Rutger as one of the finest art restorers in Europe and Gracie as the niece of the well-known art dealer Hans Hollingsworth, and Gracie discovered that the countess's friends were well-educated, cultured people who enjoyed talking about art. They discussed history and politics too, and gossiped, which thrilled the countess, and if ever Gracie felt shy Tancredi grinned at her across the table and made her smile.

As Gaia predicted Donato was jealous. Gracie reassured him that a man like Tancredi would never look at a girl like her, and even though Donato believed her, it didn't prevent him from spying on them from the garden where he worked with his father. He watched them having lunch and he made sure he was weeding and dead-heading around the chapel when Tancredi happened to be in there.

When, on the seventh day, they came to the final painting Gracie was sorry. It would mean they would no longer be coming up to the castle. She would no longer have the opportunity to see Tancredi. Rutger had chosen fifteen paintings to be cleaned and five to be restored. Bagwis agreed to have them crated up and driven round to La Colomba. The countess swept into the chapel in a cloud of linen and tuberose and shook their hands, thanking them for their trouble. Tancredi appeared just as they were climbing into the car. He bent down and peered in through Rutger's window to say goodbye. He didn't linger, but waved as Rutger started the engine, then walked back through the *portone* into the castle. Gracie felt wretched. She knew he would never love her like she loved him, but it didn't matter. If she could be near him, that would suffice. She wished she worked for the countess like Donato. If her job took her to the castle she would see Tancredi and that would be enough.

That evening Gracie stood in front of the mirror in the bathroom and studied her face. If she were beautiful like Damiana and Gaia he might be attracted to her. She unpinned her hair and let it fall about her shoulders. It was the colour of a mouse, bleached on the top by the intense Italian sun. Her skin was tanned, which accentuated the one asset she had, her eyes. They were large, almond-shaped and grey-green. She knew they were unusual, not just because she had been told so, but because she could see for herself. She wished her nose was smaller and prettier and that her mouth was more sensual, like the countess's.

The following morning Gracie started working on the

Baroque painting of the girl in the green dress. It was quiet in the studio and dim, for the shutters were drawn. Outside, birds could be heard cheeping in the umbrella pines. Rutger was busy looking through his magnifying lenses at a very valuable Renaissance painting. Neither talked as they worked. They both needed silence in order to concentrate. Gracie loved the peace. She enjoyed the challenge of her job and the excitement of seeing what lay beneath the yellowed varnish.

Engrossed in her toil, Gracie was released from her compulsive thinking about Tancredi. It was a relief to focus on something else. But, at the end of day when she packed up her tools, her mind was once more filled with him. It made her morose. She didn't want to go out, she didn't want to see Donato; she just wanted to lie beneath the stars and think of him.

A few weeks later Hans returned from Paris with good news. He had sold Gracie's forgery for a very large sum of money. Gracie, who received a small salary from her uncle, was now rewarded with a bonus. He didn't tell her how much the painting had gone for and she didn't ask. The bonus was more money than she had ever seen. She decided she would share it with her mother and Joseph. If her brother did indeed marry, it would pay for his wedding and give him a good start in his new life.

Uncle Hans was very interested in the countess's paintings. He looked through the five that Rutger and Gracie were restoring and had a long conversation with Rutger in Dutch. Gracie was used to them slipping into their mother tongue and thought nothing of it. They both decided that Gracie should finish work on the countess's paintings before starting another forgery. Uncle Hans disappeared into his studio again and locked the door behind him.

On the weekend Gracie bicycled into town to see Donato. She knew she had to accept what she had and not crave a man who was so totally out of her reach. Donato was happy to see her. He held her hand as they wandered up the cobbled streets, browsing in shop windows, and he swung her round to kiss her at every opportunity, *like a dog marking his territory,* she thought cynically. They passed the church of Maria Maddalena and Donato pulled her inside. She had never crossed the threshold before because she was not Catholic and Uncle Hans was not a religious man. The church was very old, with faded frescos painted onto the walls and a mosaic on the floor. Behind the altar was an enormous statue of Christ on the Cross, the crimson blood on his hands and torso painted brightly, which Gracie found alarming, and on the altar candles burned in silver candlesticks. Gracie let Donato take her round, wondering why he wanted to show her the church. She had an uneasy feeling in the pit of her stomach, which she tried to ignore. Well aware of what that feeling suggested, she talked incessantly out of nerves. They weren't alone, old ladies in black sat on chairs like crows, and a young couple were talking to the priest in low voices in a little chapel to the left of the altar.

Suddenly Donato dropped to one knee and Gracie's fear was confirmed. He was going to ask her to marry him. 'Gracie, I love you,' he said, taking her hand and gazing up at her with pleading eyes. 'You are the only woman for me. Will you do me the honour of being my wife?' Gracie blanched. She knew she should say yes. She knew she wouldn't do better. It was absurd to hold out for a man she couldn't have. Donato was kind. Perhaps he had a roving eye, but didn't all Italian men? He would make a good husband. Give her children. She knew she'd be content. She loved Italy, she loved Colladoro, did it really matter that she didn't love *him*? Wasn't being *fond* of him enough? She hesitated. 'Come on, Gracie,' he cajoled. 'Are you going to leave me waiting here on one knee? The floor is very hard.' He grinned raffishly and Gracie wanted her heart to leap. She wanted her stomach to lurch, she wanted to cry with emotion, but she couldn't. She felt nothing but awkwardness.

'Give me time to think about it,' she said, trying to let him down gently.

'That is as good as a no,' he replied sulkily. Then, swiftly changing tactic, he added in a wheedling tone, 'Gracie, we are good together. Come on, baby. You know we're good together.'

'We are,' she agreed. After all, it was true, they *were* good together. She knew it was foolish to refuse marriage on account of Tancredi – *that* was as good as holding out for a ghost. But what could she do?

'You like the way I kiss you.' He smiled and she couldn't help but give a little smile in return.

'I do,' she replied.

He stood up and whispered in her ear. 'You will like the way I make love to you, I promise.' Gracie didn't doubt that and yet, the idea of marrying Donato felt like a dead end.

'Give me time,' she asked, kissing him. But she felt him stiffen.

'All right. But not too long, eh?' Although he smiled his lips now curled with resentment rather than mirth. 'You don't want me to start looking somewhere else, do you?'

'No, I don't.'

'I didn't think so. I'm a patient man, Gracie, but I'm not an idiot.'

He took her hand a little roughly and walked towards the entrance of the church. Gracie's gaze was on the mosaic floor as her mind clamoured with questions she couldn't answer. She felt miserable. Miserable for disappointing Donato and miserable because the love she secretly harboured was an impossible one. Not looking where she was going she didn't see the tall man striding in the opposite direction and bumped straight into him. She drew back with a start. 'I'm so sorry . . .' she stammered and lifted her eyes to see that the man now regarding her with amusement was none other than Tancredi.

'Gracie,' he said and smiled.

'Tancredi, I'm sorry. I wasn't looking—'

'Please, don't worry.' He turned to Donato. 'Signor Fabbri.'

'*Buon giorno, Conte Bassanelli*,' Donato replied. 'I have just asked my girlfriend to marry me,' he blurted and Gracie knew why he had said it and wished he hadn't.

Tancredi's smile widened. 'Congratulations,' he said, patting Donato in the way that men do. 'This is a beautiful church to marry in,' he added.

'I know, I was just showing it to Gracie.'

The manner in which he said 'Gracie' was a way of marking his territory too, Gracie knew. She wanted to let go of his hand, to explain to Tancredi that she hadn't said yes and that she probably wouldn't. But she didn't. She just hid her misery behind her smile. After all, Tancredi looked delighted. If he had had any feelings for her at all he would have looked disappointed.

Tancredi didn't talk for long. He bade them a good day and walked on into the church. Gracie felt sick in the heart. Donato's grip tightened and he led her into the piazza. 'Let's have something to eat,' he suggested. Gracie tried to be cheerful, but it was a challenge. Donato was dispirited because she had in effect rebuffed his proposal of marriage and Gracie felt guilty. *I'm a fool in love*, she thought bleakly, *and yet I can't stop myself being a fool.* She wished she could talk to someone about it, but there was no one. Her mother was miles away and knew little of her life anyway and Uncle Hans had no experience of women.

It was only when she was in the studio the following week with Rutger that she found herself taking advice from *him*. 'You are not happy, Gracie,' he said, without pausing in his work. 'What is it?'

'Donato asked me to marry him,' she replied, pausing hers.

'And what did you say?'

'That I would think about it.'

'Ah, I see,' he grunted. 'If you have to think about it, it is not right.'

'I should have said yes,' she replied.

'But you have to think about it, so you didn't,' he said with a shrug.

Gracie sighed. 'I don't know why I have to think about it,' she said, annoyed with herself.

'Because it isn't right,' he said matter-of-factly.

'But why isn't it right?'

'Because your heart is elsewhere.'

This astonished Gracie. Was it so obvious? 'It is?'

He grinned and peered at her around his easel. 'I have watched you blossom before my eyes from a plain young woman into a beautiful one. A woman in love glows. She beams. She transforms. She is made lovely by love. How could I not see that?'

'What can I do?' Gracie asked.

'Because one loves you and the other doesn't?'

Gracie's chin trembled. It sounded harsh when said out loud. 'Yes.'

'Ah, that is the question. Are you a gambler or are you not?'

'I don't know.'

'A sensible person would tell you to marry the one who loves you and be grateful for that. A gambler would tell you to win the heart of the one who doesn't, but there is always a risk that you will not win it. Then you will be left with neither.'

'That's not very helpful, Rutger,' she said.

'Then you have to think about it.'

'Which is where we were at the beginning of this discussion.'

'I cannot think about it for you.'

'But if you could, what would you advise?'

He peered around his easel again. 'I am not a gambler, but I am a risk taker. I would sit on the fence and wait. If you marry Donato you close the door for ever on love, if you wait, you leave a gap and love might shine into it. If it doesn't, then you can close the door.'

'You're telling me to wait?'

'In a philosophical way, yes.' He smiled. 'Keep your options open. You are young. There is no need to rush into marriage and Donato will wait.'

'What if he doesn't?'

'He will, because he loves you. After all, isn't that why you are waiting for Tancredi?' Gracie took a sharp breath at the mention of his name. 'Some wait a whole lifetime,' he added. 'Some believe it is worth waiting for. I suspect *that* is the sort of woman *you* are.'

Gracie returned to her work. 'I didn't think I would be that sort of woman, Rutger.'

'Of course, you didn't. Nobody thinks they're going to waste their lives pining for someone they can't have, but love takes them over and they are incapable of doing otherwise.'

'What about you, Rutger? What sort of man are you?'

'If I was young I would be the sort of man who waits,

but' – he brushed aside the idea with a click of his tongue – 'I am old and tired of waiting, so I have given up. I work, I eat, I sleep and I dream. I am happy this way. Acceptance, that is the key. When you are old you will understand.' Gracie wanted to press him further, but somehow she knew she would get no more out of him.

She would wait. She would think and she would sit on the fence and hope, although it clearly hadn't worked for Rutger.

❧

Gracie and Rutger finished cleaning four of the paintings at the beginning of September. Bagwis sent a van to pick them up. Gracie wished she could accompany them up to the Castello, just to see Tancredi, on the off-chance that he was there, but no invitation was forthcoming.

Gaia married Filippo in the church of Maria Maddalena in the golden light of an early autumn evening. Gracie and Damiana were bridesmaids. Donato looked handsome in his suit and Gracie thought she was an idiot for not wanting to marry him. Damiana had told her as much and everyone in town knew and disapproved of her hesitation. No one could understand why she refused the best-looking man in Colladoro.

A few weeks later Rutger came across an exciting discovery. He had had a hunch that one of the countess's portraits was in fact a Gainsborough, not, as catalogued, a portrait by an inferior artist. The head was painted with the hand of a master but the body was ungainly. It was as if it belonged to an entirely different picture. Rutger hadn't said anything to Gracie, because he hadn't been entirely sure, but now, having found that the body of the gentleman had been overpainted to hide damage and discolouration, he was certain. He showed

Gracie. 'When one comes across a discovery like this, it is thrilling. It makes my job worthwhile.' He wiped his hands on a cloth. 'All the hours labouring in this studio reach a beautiful climax. You must inform the countess at once.'

'You should telephone her.'

'I spoke to Bagwis and as luck would have it she is there. I have told her that *you* will go at once. I am too tired. You are young and strong. You can bicycle.' He grinned at her and there was a mysterious glint in his eye.

Gracie cycled up the track. The air was chilly but the evening light was soft and pink, shining onto the castle and the houses below it. When the road got steeper she climbed off her bike and pushed it up the hill. By the time she reached the castle gates she was in a sweat. She had taken off her cardigan and wrapped it round her waist. To her horror she noticed she still had paint on her hands and in her nails. She wondered whether she should have changed out of her dungarees. But she doubted Tancredi would be there. She remembered Donato telling her that he only came to the castle in the summer months and it was now October. Surely, he'd be in Rome. For the first time she did not wish to see him. Not like this. Not looking dishevelled and wearing her least flattering painting clothes.

She rang the bell and waited at the gate, but no one came. It was after working hours so Gracie knew that Donato and his father would have gone home, as would the other gardeners. She left her bike on the grass verge and pushed the gate enough to give her a small gap to squeeze through. She walked up the drive, beneath the towering cypress trees which looked like feathers dipped in gold as the final rays of sunlight caught them before disappearing behind the hills. When she reached the castle she rang the doorbell. She waited. When no one came she rang it again. Still no one came. With a rising sense of unease she crept round to a window and put her hands to the glass and peered inside. To her surprise there were dust sheets thrown over the furniture. It looked like the contessa had left for Rome and it didn't appear as if she was planning on coming back until next summer.

Gracie was baffled. However, Rutger had assured her that he had spoken to Bagwis, so somebody must be in the castle. Perhaps the countess was round the back. She set off for the terrace where she had first met her. But when she got there she found the chairs as abandoned as the castle, the cushions having been taken away and stored for the winter. Only the birds twittered in the branches as they squabbled over the best places to roost. Confused, she didn't know what to do. Rutger would be cross if she returned having said she couldn't find her. He'd say she hadn't looked hard enough. But where could she possibly be? Gracie didn't want to be caught snooping around the property and she certainly wasn't going to shout.

Just then Tancredi appeared in the doorway of the tower. Gracie's cheeks burned with embarrassment as he stared at her in astonishment. *He* clearly hadn't been warned of her arrival. Her instinct was to turn and run, but that would have been rude, not to mention a little over-dramatic. Instead, she walked towards him, lifting her chin to hide her mortification.

As she neared him she saw that he was wearing an old, paint-spattered shirt, and dusty trousers. His hair was dishevelled and the bristle on his face looked like it was a few days old, at least. She realised he had not been expecting to see anyone. 'I'm sorry to turn up unannounced,' she said. 'Rutger sent me to speak to the countess.'

'My mother is not here,' he replied.

'Rutger spoke to Bagwis . . .'

She noticed him running his eyes over her dungarees. She

wished she had worn a pretty dress. But he smiled as he had done at the lunch table when she had needed reassurance, and rested his gaze on her face. 'Aren't we a pair,' he chuckled. 'You look like you've been at the easel all day, and so do I.'

Relieved that he wasn't furious, she smiled back. 'You're painting?' she asked.

'Come, I'll show you. I'm not very good. It's just a hobby.' He walked back into the tower. It was round, with a spacious, whitewashed room and a primitive wooden staircase leading to the levels above. The floorboards were bare and splattered in paint and against the walls were canvases, frames and other paraphernalia common to any artist's studio. On an easel was the painting that Tancredi was currently working on. It was of a man at a table, slumped over an empty glass. The colours were drab greys, browns and blues. Gracie hadn't expected to see something so depressing.

'Who is he?' she asked. There was a long pause. Tancredi studied her face. She could feel his eyes burning through her skin. She knew she looked uneasy, but she couldn't hide her reaction; there was something very raw about the painting that she found disturbing.

'It's me,' he replied at last, putting his hands on his hips. 'At least, it *was* me.'

'You?'

'Yes, I've lived many lives, Gracie.'

'He looks miserable. Inconsolable. Lost.'

Tancredi shrugged. 'Still me.' He laughed, but there was no mirth in it.

She gazed at it for a long while, wondering what misery had inspired it. At last she pulled away. 'It's dark, Tancredi. Terribly dark. But it's good.'

'Coming from you, that's a compliment.'

She smiled. 'Is all your work as dark?'

'Not all. Look, I'll show you a light one.'

They spent a long time discussing his paintings and Gracie forgot about her unattractive dungarees. They talked like old friends, laughing at the moderate paintings and admiring the good ones, although Tancredi was quick to shrug off her compliments with a self-deprecating remark. For a man so handsome and charismatic, he was very unsure of himself. This only made Gracie love him more.

'Let's have a drink,' he suggested when they had finished. 'It's been a long day.'

'I don't want to take up your time,' she said, remembering suddenly why she had come. 'Rutger sent me to tell the countess that his work has revealed a Gainsborough beneath one of the paintings.'

'Really?'

'Yes, it's very valuable. She'll be happy to hear that.'

'No, I mean, Rutger sent you up here to tell my mother?'

'Yes.'

'But my mother left for Rome in September. She hasn't been back since.'

'That's very strange. Rutger spoke to Bagwis . . . He said . . .' Then, with a jolt of clarity, Gracie realised that Rutger had sent her here on purpose because Tancredi was here. Somehow he had known. She wanted to laugh at the Dutchman's guile. 'It doesn't matter,' she said, sweeping away explanations with her hand. 'You can tell the countess for me.'

'Then we must celebrate. Come. It's not too chilly to sit outside?'

'Oh, I don't want to impose.'

'I want you to,' he said firmly. 'I haven't spoken to a soul in days.'

'Very well, then I'd love to,' she said, putting on her cardigan.

Gracie helped him bring the glasses and wine outside from the castle's kitchen and arrange cushions on a large wicker sofa placed on the semicircular terrace that looked out over the hills. The very terrace where Gracie had first met him. The sun was now little more than a dying glow on the horizon, the first star twinkling in the indigo sky. Gracie enjoyed the taste of the wine. It was cool and fresh and made her pleasantly light-headed. The joy of watching the sunset with the man she *really* loved injected her with a sense of urgency, for this might be the last time she would see him in months, possibly years. 'Why is that self-portrait so sad, Tancredi?' she asked, aware that her question was forward, but not caring.

He leaned back against the cushions, put one hand behind his head and fixed his gaze on the distant hills. 'It is a long story,' he replied with a sigh. 'But if you are not hurrying back to your studio I will share it with you.'

'I'm afraid you have aroused my curiosity so now you have to tell me.'

He chuckled. 'Very well.' He sipped his wine then leaned forward with his elbows on his knees. 'Do you remember the painting I told you about?'

'The one your uncle stole?'

'You have a good memory, Gracie.'

'For things that interest me,' she replied.

'Well, as I told you, that painting meant the world to me. Not just because it is an enchanting painting, but because it represented a time in my life when I was happy. You see, my father died when I was fifteen. Up until that point, I had no experience of loss. I was cherished, spoiled and fortunate enough to consider happiness my due. But then I lost my father and like you said, I crossed a bridge.' Gracie was touched that he remembered something she had said. She watched him drop his gaze into his wine glass and her heart went out to him. 'I could never go back to that carefree place,' he continued. 'I was young. I didn't realise that grief is something you have to learn to accommodate, not something you get through and come out the other side. You never come out the other side. You just live on, carrying it inside you like a stone in your heart. But I didn't know that. I thought I could outrun it. So, I got mixed up with a fast crowd of people. I did badly at school. I partied hard. I spent money like water. I dated unsuitable girls, took drugs and smoked, and pretty much drank myself into oblivion – and the whole of Rome knew of it. My grandfather, whom I loved, despaired of me. He tried to guide me, but I wouldn't listen. I was so full of resentment. I blamed God for taking my father away. I blamed my father for going, even though it was not his choice, and I blamed myself for my weakness, and yet I couldn't stop myself. I suppose I was crying out for help, but no one knew how to give it. I certainly didn't know how to accept it. Then, one day, my grandfather stood beside me in front of that beautiful painting and said, "Do you remember the little boy who used to linger here and gaze into this picture?"

'"Yes," I replied.

'"He is still inside you, Tancredi," he said. "His life might have changed and he might have suffered a terrible loss, but he is still inside you with all his wonder and innocence and joy. You only have to look for him." And I realised then that it was my choice how I lived my life and that I was throwing it away for nothing. Behaving like that wasn't going to bring my father back. The man I had become was not the person my father would have recognised, nor the man my grandfather could be proud of. So, I decided to turn my life around. I searched for the boy I had been.'

'Did you find him?' Gracie asked softly.

Tancredi glanced at her solemnly. 'I don't know. Let's just say that it's a work in progress, Gracie.' He shifted on the cushions and turned to face her. 'When my grandfather died I expected to receive the painting he had promised me. I don't know whether he forgot to put it in his will, or whether he thought the family would remember his wish and honour it. After all, everyone knew that he was going to leave it to me. My uncle chose to believe that he didn't *want* me to have it. I suspect the truth is that my uncle wanted to punish me for bringing the family name into disrepute. You see, his reputation is more important to him than anything else, including his family and children.' He grinned wickedly. 'How I would love to sully it, but sadly I cannot sully *his* reputation without sullying *my own*!'

'So, the painting is the despairing Tancredi who still fights for dominance. The one who lost his father, his grandfather and resents his uncle. It's a picture of despair and helplessness.'

'Very good.' He chuckled and reached for the wine bottle which sat in a bucket of melting ice on the table beside him. He topped up her glass and then his own. 'I'm sorry it's such a miserable tale.'

'Yet, it has probably inspired your best work.'

'Do you think it's that good?'

'Yes, I really do. But I wouldn't want it hanging in my hall!' They both laughed.

'Do you know, I feel better for having told you. I haven't spoken about it to anyone before.'

'As you said when you showed me round your garden, it's easier unburdening one's feelings to a stranger.'

'But you're not a stranger, Gracie,' he said and the smile he gave her had a tenderness in it that made her stomach lurch. 'Have you and Donato married yet?' he asked before putting his glass to his lips.

Gracie was surprised he remembered. 'No,' she replied.

'When is the big day?'

'Donato was a little hasty when he told you we were getting married.' Tancredi arched an eyebrow. 'When I bumped into you, he had just proposed. I had said I would think about it. That's all.'

'And have you?' he asked.

Gracie suddenly felt emotional. She turned her eyes to the hills, now silhouetted against the darkening sky. She wanted to tell him the truth, but she couldn't. 'I am still thinking about it,' she said.

'You don't love him,' he stated simply and Gracie was stunned. Her glass began to tremble in her hand for he had revealed something of himself in that intimate observation which she could not ignore.

'I'm fond of him,' she answered.

'That's not good enough.'

She drained her glass and placed it on the table. 'No,' she said, with a sigh. 'It isn't.'

He reached across and took her hand. Gracie froze. 'Don't be alarmed,' he said in a quiet voice, stroking the skin with his thumb. 'I'm glad you're not marrying Donato.' Gracie searched for something to say, but nothing came. 'You are too good for him,' he continued. His eyes shone in the twilight and Gracie hoped that she wasn't being misled by the apparent affection in them. 'I didn't think I had a chance, so I tried not to think about you. But here you are and here I am and it is as if Fate has brought us together.' He put a hand beneath her chin and placed his lips on hers. Gracie felt as if she were sinking a thousand leagues. She closed her eyes and wished she could sink for ever. Tancredi stroked her nose with his then pulled away and looked at her steadily. She opened her eyes and looked at him straight back. As she didn't protest or pull away he kissed her again, this time deeply.

Tancredi wrapped her in his arms and held her against his heart. Gracie closed her eyes again and realised that the difference between a good kiss and a bad kiss had nothing to do with technique and everything to do with love.

Chapter 11

Italy, 2010

Gracie was awoken by someone stroking her hair. She opened her eyes to find Anastasia sitting on her bed with a worried look on her face. 'Are you okay, Granny?' she asked. 'You've been asleep all afternoon. Rex said you had taken a turn.'

It took a moment for Gracie to remember where she was and what had happened. Her heart sank at the memory: Tancredi on the balcony, his raised hand, his polite, impassive smile, the fact that he had not recognised her. 'I'm all right,' she said, looking away, not wanting her granddaughter to see the hurt in her eyes.

Anastasia grinned. 'Did you drink too much wine?'

'I don't think so,' Gracie replied, putting a hand to her head, even though it was her heart that ached.

'I've spent the afternoon at the pool with Alex. He's really cool. I'm glad there's someone my own age here.'

'Yes, it's nice, isn't it.' Gracie sat up stiffly.

'He's really clever. He wants to work for the Foreign Office.'

'I think he's a charming young man.'

Anastasia laughed. 'Why don't you come down and have tea. You look really pale and I'm hungry.'

'You're always hungry,' said Gracie, climbing off the bed. 'Where does it all go?'

'I don't know, but it goes really fast, because no sooner have I eaten than I want to eat again.'

'Well, in that case, we'd better go down.' Gracie was grateful to Anastasia for forcing her back into the present. A cup of tea would be just the thing to restore her spirits. She slipped on her shoes and made for the door.

'Granny?'

'Yes, dear?'

'I'm glad I came.'

Gracie turned round. Her granddaughter was looking at her earnestly. 'I'm glad you came too, dear,' she replied. 'I'd have been lonely on my own.'

Anastasia frowned. 'Are you lonely on your own in Devon?'

Gracie was going to say that she wasn't. That she had her dogs and her friends, but for some reason she didn't want to lie to her granddaughter. 'A little,' she confessed.

Anastasia was horrified. 'That's dreadful,' she gasped.

'It's life, Anastasia,' Gracie said frankly. *So was disappointment*, she thought. That was part of life too. If Rutger had taught her anything he had taught her acceptance. Tancredi did not recognise her. It wasn't the end of the world. She had lived without him for forty-four years. She was in the most beautiful place with her daughter and granddaughter, she felt very blessed. She wasn't going to ruin it by letting her disappointment crush her.

Tea was served outside on the terrace where they had had breakfast. Gracie thought it would be more fun for Anastasia to join the larger table where Wendy, Tiff and Brigitte were now enjoying tea with Rex, Lauren and Alex, but Anastasia surprised Gracie by wanting her to herself and choosing a table at the other end of the terrace where they wouldn't be overheard, and ordering a pot of tea for two.

'Tell me,' she said, after helping herself to sandwiches and cake. 'When did you meet Grandpa and did you know, when you met him, that you would marry him?'

Gracie sipped her tea and felt a little restored. It was impossible not to be uplifted by the beautiful view and Anastasia's eager face, waiting for her to reply. *The girl had obviously taken a shine to Alex*, Gracie thought. 'Do you really want to hear or are you just being polite?' she asked.

'I really want to hear,' Anastasia replied. 'Why do you live so far away? Shouldn't you come and live in London so we can see more of you? If you lived near us you wouldn't be lonely.'

'Devon is home,' Gracie replied with a shrug. 'It's where I settled after . . .' How could she begin to explain what had happened here?

'After what?' Anastasia pressed.

'I returned to England from Italy.'

Anastasia's face showed her astonishment, which gave Gracie a frisson of pleasure. 'When did you live in Italy?' she asked.

'I came out when I was thirteen to apprentice the finest art restorer in Europe.'

'Really? I never knew that.'

Gracie's heart spluttered back to life as one of the secrets she had held on to for over four decades came slipping out. Just like that. No premeditation, no shall I, shan't I. She simply let it go. 'No one knew,' said Gracie. 'Not even Grandpa.'

Anastasia's eyes widened. 'Why didn't you tell him?'

'It's a very long story.'

'I want to hear every word of it. Please.' Gracie looked down and saw that Anastasia's hand was on hers. 'What happened in Italy?' she whispered.

'I fell in love,' Gracie said and her eyes sparkled as she thought of Tancredi, not as he was now, seeing *through* her, but as he had been *then*, seeing every inch of her. 'But not with Grandpa,' she added.

Anastasia was thrilled by this piece of information. 'Tell me from the beginning. What were you doing in Italy?'

Gracie realised now, as she began to speak, that she was ready to tell her story. That she *needed* to tell it. 'I was working as a painting restorer in a beautiful house not far from here.'

'Here?'

'Here,' said Gracie. 'It was called La Colomba and I apprenticed a man called Rutger Janssen . . .' Anastasia barely blinked as Gracie told her about Uncle Hans and the countess, although she was careful not to mention the castle or the countess's name, and to change Tancredi's to his middle name, which was the same as his grandfather's. 'I fell in love with Gaetano the first moment I laid eyes on him,' she said, reliving it.

'Truly, the first time? Love at first sight?' Anastasia was excited. She squeezed Gracie's hand. 'Did you just know, the moment you saw him?'

Gracie smiled. 'I did.'

'Was it like a bolt of lightning?'

'Well, it was, really. Yes.'

'Did he fall in love with you too?'

'He didn't notice me. Not that time.' Gracie told her about the wedding. 'I had never seen such a handsome man in all my life.'

'How old were you?'

'About your age.'

Anastasia beamed. 'Then what happened?'

'I knew he would never fall in love with a girl like me. I wasn't beautiful like you, Anastasia.'

'I bet you were!'

'No, I wasn't. But I learned that beauty really is in the eye of the beholder. What is beautiful to one person might not be beautiful to another. And beauty is as much about your heart as it is about your face. Gaetano saw my heart, Anastasia . . .'

'*When* did he see your heart?'

Gracie sighed and poured another cup of tea. 'I have to tell you about Donato first.'

Just then Carina appeared on the terrace looking very pink in the face. She had been out walking all afternoon and had forgotten to wear a hat or apply sun screen. She smiled when she saw her mother and daughter sitting together at the far end of the terrace. 'I've had the most glorious day,' she said with a contented sigh, plonking herself down and waving at Carlo for some fresh tea.

Anastasia pulled a face at her grandmother to show how irritated she was that they had been interrupted and Gracie gave her a wink, at which the girl's face relaxed into a knowing smile. Anastasia was only too happy to keep their conversation secret. 'We'll have plenty of time for the rest of the story,' whispered Gracie, patting her hand.

'This is the most gorgeous place in the world,' Carina gushed. 'The flowers are indecent! You know I walked for miles. Goodness knows where I was going, but I didn't want to stop. There are grape vines, olive groves, farmhouses . . .' She shook her head and sighed. 'I'm so happy I came.'

Gracie couldn't believe what she was hearing. 'I'm so pleased you are,' she said.

'No, really. To be honest, I didn't want to come because I was so busy, but I'm very happy I did. It's just what I need, a break like this. I've realised that holidays have always been dominated by work. Wherever I am in the world, I'm always working. For the first time ever I left my phone in my room. I don't think I've done that before. It's made all the difference. I feel like a new person and it's only the first day. Imagine how I'm going to feel by Saturday!' Carlo put a pot of tea on the table and took away the empty one. 'So, what have you two been doing?' She looked at her daughter.

'Hanging out by the pool,' said Anastasia, then she gave Gracie a sly grin. 'And hanging out with Granny,' she added.

Carina was surprised. 'Oh,' she said. 'That's nice.'

'We've had a lovely afternoon as well,' Anastasia said and Gracie heard the challenging tone in her voice as she tried to provoke her mother. 'Granny has the best stories.'

'About me as a little girl?' Carina asked, rolling her eyes.

'No, not about you, Mum,' said Anastasia irritably. 'About Gracie as—'

'Oh, they're very boring,' Gracie interrupted, giving her granddaughter a warning look.

'Not to me they're not,' Anastasia answered, then she turned to her mother. 'So, what *were* you like as a little girl?'

'Busy,' Gracie replied and Carina couldn't help but laugh.

❧

That night Anastasia waited until her mother was asleep then she crept very carefully out of bed in order not to make any noise. As she had done lots of times at school, she arranged the pillows beneath the covers so that if her mother woke up she would not notice that Anastasia wasn't there. She had left her clothes hidden in the bathroom cupboard so she could dress quietly. Moonlight shone through the window and lit up enough of the bathroom for her to check herself in the mirror. As it was a little chilly at night she put on a sweater.

Then she tiptoed out of the room and closed the door very quietly behind her.

Anastasia was in love. It had happened just as her grandmother had described it: a bolt of lightning; an instant and undeniable knowing. It had happened down at the pool. His eyes on hers; an unspoken understanding. And everything had changed. The sky looked bluer, the grass looked greener and everything about the world seemed thrilling and new. Now Anastasia couldn't think of anyone else but him. It was as if her heart had been filled with helium, almost lifting her off her feet.

They had agreed to meet in the pool house. He had promised he would be there. He had said he would wait for her all night if he had to. As Anastasia hurried down the garden towards the pool, which was hidden away out of sight of the castle, she was too excited to notice the smell of damp grass and pine or to hear the gentle chirruping of crickets. The exhilaration of doing something very naughty made her want to laugh out loud.

She scampered along the path of mown grass, between bushes of oleander and rose, and the water came into view, a silver mirror in the moonlight, reflecting the stars. The pool house was at the far end, a pretty stone pavilion which looked more like a romantic folly than a place for swimmers to change. She skipped over the paving stones, hoping he would be there. Then she smelt the smoke from his cigarette and her heart gave a little leap.

The sultry young gardener sauntered out, leaned against the door frame and grinned crookedly. 'You came,' he said in a thick Italian accent that made her stomach flip over.

'Did you doubt me, Giovanni?' she asked, walking up to him. He threw his cigarette into the bushes and wound his arm around her waist, gazing into her eyes with his dark, smouldering ones.

'I happy you came,' he said in broken English and kissed her full on the mouth. Anastasia had only kissed boys at London parties. They were wet, clumsy kisses by boys with little experience. Giovanni knew how to kiss, how to *really* kiss, and Anastasia thought she might faint with pleasure. He was masterful, sensual and she put her arms around his neck and moaned.

They didn't talk much after that. Giovanni only spoke the most basic English. But it didn't matter. They lay on the pool cover, which was folded up against the wall and served as a bed, and kissed. Indeed, they kissed all night in the semi-dark and only the silvery light that beamed in through the window knew how much. Giovanni took his time. There was no need to rush. They had until dawn. He slipped his hand beneath her sweater and felt her breasts and Anastasia's breath snagged in her throat as the unfamiliar sensations took possession of her and made her wanton. Every touch was electrifying. It was as if his hands had a special power and she wanted them to cover her, every inch of her. He toyed with her lips, brushing them gently with his, teasing them with his tongue. He kissed her neck and her collarbone, licked the well at her throat and beneath her ears, and his fingers stroked their way up her thighs and onto her underwear – and she wanted them there – and parted her thighs invitingly. He whispered in Italian, which she didn't understand, and slipped his fingers beneath her panties. '*Come sei bella . . . amore mia . . . come sei bella . . . Tesoro . . .*' He caressed her with the sensuality of a man who has caressed many women. He knew how to arouse her and for Anastasia, who had only been groped by schoolboys, the feeling was exquisite. She did not, at that point, give him her virginity, but she gave him her heart. If he took care of that, she would happily give him the rest.

❧

The following morning, Carina awoke in a panic again. Had she overslept? Was she late for the office? Then she remembered where she was. Without thinking, she reached for her phone. Just as she was about to switch it on, she recalled her resolution. She stared at it, fighting the urge to look at her messages, struggling against her need to be in constant contact with her working world and her deep desire to maintain this feeling of serenity that Italy had given her. Her thumb hovered over the on button. What if she just had a *quick* look, and turned it off? Would that count? Just a sneaky, hasty, barely-at-all glance? But what if she *couldn't* then turn it off? What if one of the messages required a response? She wouldn't be able to ignore it then. One would inevitably lead to another and down the slippery slope she would so easily fall. She hated herself for her weakness and the tranquillity she had felt the day before began to fade, replaced by something dark and heavy. She removed her thumb. No, she wasn't going to lose it. She gritted her teeth, swore under her breath, and put the phone back on the table. She had made a pact with herself and she wasn't going to break it. She would resist the lure of her phone. She rolled onto her back. Once again, the specks of dust caught in the shafts of light coming through the shutters mesmerised her. They were like tiny dancing fireflies and she couldn't take her eyes off them. That blissful sense of stillness began, once again, to grow.

Anastasia crept into the room to find her mother awake. Carina turned to see her in the doorway in a towel, her hair wet, her face aglow. 'Have you been swimming already?' she asked sleepily.

'Yes, I couldn't resist. A swim before breakfast. The water is so refreshing.'

'Maybe *I'll* swim today,' said Carina, stretching her arms and legs.

'You should, if you're not too busy making calls.'

'I'm not going to touch my phone. I've made a resolution.' Carina felt pleasantly smug. She had been faced with temptation and overcome it.

'Yeah, right.'

'I have! Anyway, you're on it just as much as I am.'

'Wrong, Mum, I haven't touched mine since yesterday and I'm not going to.'

'What's come over you?' *Giovanni,* Anastasia thought happily. 'Italy,' she said out loud.

❧

'Today, we are going to cook Mamma Bernadetta's *ragù alla bolognese*,' said Ilaria as the guests sat on their stools, pencils poised. Anastasia sat beside her grandmother and Gracie noticed that she didn't doodle or look at her phone, but listened and wrote notes. Every now and then she grinned at her grandmother and Gracie's heart inflated with pleasure at the bond that was gradually growing between them.

Mamma Bernadetta poured olive oil into the pan with a dollop of butter. 'For *ragù alla bolognese*,' Ilaria continued, 'we use two fats because this is a sauce that cooks for two hours. After thirty minutes the olive oil says he has had enough giving out flavour so the butter takes charge and keeps it alive until cooking is done. They are a very helpful pair of friends. Garlic and onions do not like each other. They divorced, you see, and are no longer speaking. So we never use them together.' Mamma Bernadetta's pudgy fingers reached for the diced carrots, celery and onion and tossed them into the pan. The delicious aroma filled the kitchen and Ilaria watched with pleasure as her students inhaled it cheerfully. *There is nothing like cooking to bring people together*, she thought, observing the group beginning to open up and talk to each other. *They are like vegetables in extra virgin olive oil*, she mused with satisfaction. *Soon they will be old friends.*

In the break, Anastasia and Alex sat on the grass in the sunshine, chatting. After a while Anastasia did a handstand and a forward roll, challenging Alex to do one too. This he declined, but he lifted her onto his shoulders and began to skip in circles while she squealed and put her hands over his eyes so he couldn't see where he was going. Eventually, they collapsed onto the ground, roaring with laughter. Gracie watched them from the shade where she was sitting with Rex, who was enjoying an espresso. 'Even the coffee tastes better here,' he said with a contented sigh. 'You know, Gracie, I was a little nervous about coming over here and joining a cookery class, but I'm very glad I did. I've met some decent folk, like you and your daughter and granddaughter, and I'm pretty sure I'll go back home and actually cook what Ilaria has taught us. My wife died, you see, and I have to look after myself now.'

'I'm sorry,' said Gracie.

'It was a while ago, but her passing taught me something important. You can't control what life throws at you and, boy, does it throw some fast balls sometimes, but you can control how you react. I've chosen to react in a positive way. I don't know how many years I have left, but I'm determined to live them to the full. See the world, learn new things, like cooking. I never was very good at the stove!' He chuckled.

'Nothing ventured, nothing gained, I say. Coming here has proven that a sense of adventure pays off.'

'I agree with you,' Gracie replied. 'My friends thought I was mad booking in to a cookery class in Tuscany, they suggested I borrow a cookery book instead and learn at home.'

'No sense of adventure!' Rex exclaimed, shaking his head disapprovingly.

'I had got into a rut and didn't even consider climbing out of it until I saw an advertisement in a magazine.'

'Is that how you found this place?'

'Yes. How did you find it?'

'I met a woman who had already been here.'

'So, you knew all about it.'

'I've always wanted to come to Italy. I think I'll head up to Rome afterwards and maybe to Venice. I might as well explore while I'm here.' He settled his blue eyes on her face and gave her a bashful smile. 'I hope you don't mind me asking, Gracie, but are you married?'

'I'm a widow,' she replied, turning her gaze to the hills. 'My husband died eight years ago.'

'I'm sorry for your loss.'

Gracie sighed. 'Thank you. I've learned to live with it. I don't think we ever get over loss, we just accommodate it. It's like crossing a bridge. You can never go back. You just have to go on only in a different way and accept that life is different. That *you're* different.' But she wasn't thinking about Ted.

'I'm sure your daughter and granddaughter give you comfort,' Rex added sincerely. Gracie looked at her granddaughter, who was still lying in the sun talking to Alex, and wondered how much more enjoyable her life would have been had she been close to Carina and Anastasia. She wondered whether the fault had been with *her*. Perhaps after Ted's death she should have moved nearer to London. But she wouldn't have had the money to do that. Perhaps she should have visited, but Carina hadn't ever insisted and she had rarely made the effort to come down to Devon. Gracie pushed those thoughts to the back of her mind. She did not want to reawaken those feelings of rejection which Italy had managed to eclipse.

'They do,' she replied. 'There is nothing like family, is there?'

❧

The cookery lesson continued until lunch. Wendy, Tiff and Brigitte drank too much wine and entertained the table with their anecdotes. Gracie marvelled at their lack of inhibition and remembered how she had sat listening to Damiana holding forth in the same way, and how she had envied her friend's ability to amuse and delight. Damiana had been a brilliant mimic, standing up and putting on performances like an actress playing many different roles. How they had laughed as they had recognised themselves in her acts. And she, Gracie, always quiet and watchful and shy.

After lunch Gracie retreated to her bedroom for a rest. Anastasia disappeared with Alex to the pool, followed by Carina, Lauren and Madeleine who put on their bikinis and lay on the sun loungers, chatting. Madeleine's skin was already a rich brown colour, which Carina envied. *She* had freckled English skin that didn't tan easily. Madeleine was also curvaceous which made her look much more appealing in her bikini. Carina had always wanted to be thin, because thin was glamorous. But now, looking at the Belgian, she wondered whether she had just been brainwashed by fashion magazines and advertising. The truth was she looked scrawny and pale. She hoped Mamma Bernadetta's pasta would pile on a few pounds – and put them in the right places.

'Do you think we will get to meet the count?' Carina asked Madeleine and Lauren as she rubbed sun lotion onto her limbs.

'I doubt it,' said Madeleine. 'Apparently he keeps himself very much to himself.'

'That's a shame. I'm rather curious.'

'So am I,' said Lauren. 'And the fact that he doesn't show makes me even more curious.'

'He is very handsome,' said Madeleine.

'Have you seen him?' Carina asked, put out that *she* hadn't. 'Have *you*?' she asked Lauren.

'No, I haven't,' Lauren replied. They both turned to Madeleine expectantly.

'I saw him the day I arrived,' she told them. 'He was in the hall.'

'Did he greet you?' Carina asked.

'Sadly not. He was talking to Ilaria at the other end with his massive dog beside him. I kid you not, that dog is as big as a pony!'

'He was lying down when I saw him,' Carina laughed.

'If he stands up he'll scare the living daylights out of you!' Madeleine took off her sunglasses to clean them on the towel. 'He didn't even acknowledge me. He just wandered out as if I wasn't there.'

Carina was astonished. 'I think it's very rude of him not to speak to you.'

Madeleine was nonplussed. 'He's opened his home to paying guests. It doesn't mean he's happy about it.'

'Wouldn't his business do better if he worked on his guests a little?' Carina was certain that, with her expertise, she could triple the count's income, at least.

'Perhaps, but the main attraction is the double act of Ilaria and Mamma Bernadetta. The count skulks about in the background, probably furious that he's been forced to open his home due to lack of funds.'

'He could always sell a painting,' Carina suggested. 'Isn't his castle full of treasures?'

'Not any more. It was once, I believe,' said Madeleine. 'But the family fell on hard times and had to sell a lot of them. The other side of the Montefosco family is very rich, so I'm told.'

'I could give him some advice, you know. My business is in public relations. I'd tell him to get out here and schmooze his clients for a start.'

'If he's angry and resentful, he'll put them off. Much better that he hides away so no one sees him.' Madeleine laughed throatily. 'Counts are two a penny in Italy anyway,' she added. 'I don't think it's such a big deal.'

'Still, it's strange that he goes out of his way to avoid us. What's he hiding, do you think?'

'A temper!' Madeleine laughed.

❧

Anastasia swam up and down the length of the pool, aware that she was being watched. Alex lay on the lounger, dozing in the sunshine, but Giovanni lurked about the roses pretending he was working. She could feel his eyes following her as she swam, then, when she climbed out and walked over the hot stones, she felt his stare burning through her bikini. Her mother was deep in conversation with Madeleine and Lauren. Alex had his eyes closed. So she looked at Giovanni directly and gave him a small, seductive smile. He shifted his eyes towards the pool house and returned her smile. Anastasia's skin prickled all over in anticipation. She tossed her head back and set off towards the folly with a purposeful step. If anyone were to see her they would assume she was making for the changing room.

A moment later she was waiting in the shadows, quivering with excitement at the prospect of a stolen kiss and the danger it posed. She could hear her heart thumping in the silence and put a hand on her chest to stifle it. 'Pssst!' She turned to see Giovanni's face at the open window behind her. '*Vieni qua, bella*,' he said and it didn't matter that she didn't understand the language for she understood what he wanted. He reached for her through the window and wound his hand around her neck. He murmured something else in Italian then kissed her. Anastasia's whole body was aroused and she longed for him to climb into the room and touch her all over. But the wall separated them, making the stolen moment even more thrilling.

'You come, tonight?' he asked and she nodded. 'I wait.'

'As soon as my mother is asleep, I'll come,' she said.

He grinned. '*Bella*!' Then disappeared into the garden.

Chapter 12

Anastasia wanted to hear more about her grandmother's past, but when she stepped onto the terrace at teatime Gracie was already sitting at a table with Lauren and her mother with pots of tea and lemon cake. The three of them looked like they were enjoying themselves and Anastasia did not wish to interrupt them. However, she was disappointed. She longed to have her grandmother to herself so that she could tell her about her budding romance with Giovanni. Even at seventeen Anastasia knew that Latin men were, by reputation, very unreliable, but she was sure that Giovanni was different. She itched to share her excitement with someone and she sensed that her grandmother would not disapprove and would give her sound advice. It didn't occur to Anastasia to tell her mother. She had never had that kind of secret-sharing relationship with Carina. The kind of relationship where the daughter confides in the mother and the mother gives the daughter guidance. Carina was always too busy for that – and too engrossed in herself. Had her father been here she might have confided in him, however. But he wasn't. So, she kept her secret to herself.

Rex was at a table with Wendy, Tiff and Brigitte. *He was like a fox in the henhouse*, Anastasia thought, ruffling their feathers with his flirting and making them laugh. She didn't feel like joining the hens or the fox. She was about to go back inside when Alex walked out. He gave her a big smile. 'There you are,' he said. 'I'm going into town. Fancy joining me?'

Anastasia was delighted. 'I'll go and get my bag,' she said and hurried to her room to retrieve it.

When she returned, the two of them set off down the avenue of cypress trees side by side. Crickets were chirruping in the undergrowth and small birds played about the branches. The sun was still hot but the light had turned a soft, grainy pink. There was a languid air to the afternoon, as if, with the sun's gentle descent, time had slowed down to a peaceful meander. Anastasia's blue toenails shone against her green flip-flops as she stepped over the stones towards the big iron gates. She felt excited to be leaving the property and venturing into Colladoro. Alex and she had settled into an easy friendship. It was as if they had known each other all their lives. *He was just the sort of boy her mother would love her to date*, she thought as she searched for Giovanni in the gardens. She peered through the trees, hoping to catch a glimpse of him, knowing he was out there somewhere. It gave her a shiver of pleasure to think of him watching her, perhaps, and being a little jealous as she wandered off with Alex.

Colladoro's paved streets were uneven, the stone worn away in places due to centuries of treading feet. The walls of the buildings glowed like rose gold in the late afternoon light and it seemed that everyone had come out of their houses to enjoy the coolest part of the day. Tourists browsed the boutiques, old men sat at café tables smoking and playing cards, young mothers gossiped while their children played and grandmothers huddled together on benches, complaining about the youth. Anastasia was drawn to the shop windows like a magpie to trinkets. Alex put his hands in his pockets and followed her patiently as she wandered from one to the other until she was finally lured inside.

It was a small boutique with linen clothes hanging on rails and jewellery in glass cases. Alex was so tall he had to lower his head as he stepped through the door. A woman with a wizened face smiled at them and said something in Italian, waving her hands encouragingly. Anastasia went straight for the necklaces and bracelets made with silver and beads. 'I want to buy something for my grandmother,' she said, suddenly inspired. The thought of buying something for Gracie gave her a warm feeling inside.

Alex joined her by the glass case. 'Are you asking me for advice?'

'Of course I am.'

'What about something green to match her eyes?'

Anastasia looked at him and laughed. 'You're very observant to notice her eyes.'

'They're the same colour as yours,' he replied and there was something in the way he was looking at her that made her turn away, embarrassed.

'So, let's find a necklace in grey-green,' she said, feeling the oncoming heat of a blush.

Alex left her side to look in the other glass displays. The shopkeeper unlocked the cabinet and began to lift pieces out to show Anastasia. When she understood what Anastasia was looking for she hurried behind the counter and pulled out a tray. She put it on the glass with a big smile. It was full of shiny bead necklaces in every possible shade of green.

'I defy you *not* to find one in there,' said Alex, putting his hands in his pockets and wandering over to take a closer look.

Anastasia's fingers hovered over them indecisively. The shopkeeper lifted one off the tray and held it up to Anastasia's face. From her gestures they both understood that she thought the green matched Anastasia's eyes exactly. 'She wants you to try it on,' said Alex.

'All right, but it's not for me, remember. It's for Granny.' She sat down in front of the mirror on the counter. The shopkeeper gave the necklace to Alex.

'Allow me to do the honours,' he said, his lips curling into a typically wry smile. She lifted her hair off her neck and Alex hung the necklace at her throat and fixed it at the back. He looked at her reflection over her shoulder. 'Well, she's right about the colour,' he said, grinning playfully. 'It's a match. It's made for you.'

Anastasia pulled a face in response to his teasing. 'Do you think Granny would like it?'

'I think your grandmother would be happy with anything you gave her. She looks like the sort of woman who appreciates a kind thought in whatever size or shape it comes.'

'Then I'll take it. Would you mind doing the honours again?' she asked Alex, lifting her hair once more. Alex unclasped it. Anastasia felt his fingers brush the skin on the back of her neck and their eyes caught in the mirror. She looked away. 'Granny is going to love this,' she said, deflecting the intimacy that had suddenly inveigled its way into the moment.

The shopkeeper dropped the necklace into a silky pouch and then the pouch into a paper bag and Anastasia left the boutique feeling very good about herself. She couldn't wait to see her grandmother's face when she gave it to her.

Alex suggested they wander into the piazza and have a drink. The sun was a blood orange sinking behind the buildings. The piazza was bustling with people. Cafés spilled onto the paving stones beneath brightly coloured awnings and waiters and waitresses weaved languidly between the tables, stopping every now and then to chat. Dominating the town was an ancient church. Doves cooed on the bell tower and locals wandered in and out of the big doors along with the odd tourist with a camera. Alex and Anastasia chose a table with a good view of the square and sat in the sunshine.

Anastasia lifted her phone out of her bag and took a photo of Alex. Satisfied with her snap she took some more. A grandfather with his grandson, feeding pigeons; a huddle of religious old women in black chatting outside the church; a beautiful young couple holding hands across the table and kissing as if they were the only two people in the world. Everything about Colladoro delighted Anastasia and she wanted to record it all so that when she was back at boarding school she would have photographs to remember it by as well as to put up on social media to impress her friends. With that in mind she suggested they take some selfies. Alex was very handsome and it would do her street-cred a lot of good to post pictures of them together. Alex rolled his eyes at her suggestion but he didn't refuse. As *she* grinned into the camera *he* smiled ironically, *cautious perhaps of making a fool of himself*, Anastasia thought as she stuck out her tongue and made the V sign for victory. She didn't want her friends to think she was taking herself too seriously, or being smug. They would want to know who Alex was and how she had met him and that gave her a kick. She would put it up on Facebook as soon as she returned to the castle.

It was evening when they wandered back up the hill. The scent of flowers hung heavy in the air, sweet and earthy. Lights twinkled in windows, candles flickered on outside tables, and the first star shone through the darkening blue. The night was approaching and with it Giovanni in the pool house. Anastasia could barely contain her excitement. She laughed and joked with Alex and he teased her affectionately, and all the while she tingled with the anticipation of Giovanni's touch.

When they arrived at the castle most of the guests were already sitting on the terrace enjoying Mamma Bernadetta's home-made wine and eating crostini. Carina and Lauren were deep in conversation while Rex was chatting up Wendy, Tiff and Brigitte, who were still tipsy and laughing raucously. To Anastasia's delight her grandmother hadn't come down yet. She hurried inside, hoping to get her on her own so she could give her the necklace. However, when she reached Gracie's bedroom she found it was empty. As she closed the door Madeleine was sauntering slowly up the corridor towards her. She beamed at Anastasia. 'Good, I thought I was going to be late,' she said, rubbing her neck beneath her hair. 'It is so hot. I've been for a lovely walk but I didn't notice the time.'

'I was looking for my grandmother. You haven't seen her, have you?' Anastasia asked.

'Yes, she is on the lower terrace, talking to Mamma Bernadetta,' Madeleine replied. 'I will now go and have a cold shower. I will be down shortly.'

Anastasia went back outside. Gracie was indeed on the lower terrace, at a small round table, with Mamma Bernadetta. The two old women were talking animatedly, and for a moment Anastasia thought her eyes were deceiving her because her grandmother didn't normally use her hands when she spoke, and she wasn't usually so vivacious. She listened more attentively, and then she realised that Gracie was speaking Italian, not in the faltering way most English people did, but fluently. Anastasia was stunned. Although she now knew that her grandmother had lived in Italy as a young woman, she hadn't expected her to speak like a local. If she hadn't known better she would have thought they were two elderly Italian ladies having a good old chin-wag.

Anastasia approached. Mamma Bernadetta saw her first because she was facing her. She gave a small smile, which was the first time Anastasia had seen her smile. Then Gracie turned round. 'Anastasia,' she said and she still retained something of the lively Italian in the way her eyes sparkled. Mamma Bernadetta pushed herself off her chair and said something to Gracie before retreating inside.

Anastasia took her chair. 'That's another secret of yours,' she said, grinning at Gracie. 'You speak fluent Italian. Why haven't you ever told anyone? Why the secret?'

Gracie sighed and shrugged. 'It's complicated,' she said, then changed the subject. 'What have *you* been up to?'

'I went into town with Alex.'

Gracie smiled. 'That's nice,' she said, wondering how the romance was going. She didn't doubt there was a romance for Anastasia was glowing in the same way that *she* had once glowed and Rutger had commented on it.

'I have a present for you,' Anastasia replied, much to Gracie's surprise. Anastasia felt a surge of pleasure at the astonished look on her grandmother's face.

'Oh, you mustn't waste your money on me, dear,' Gracie said, but she was touched that her granddaughter had.

'It's not wasting,' Anastasia retorted. She pulled the gift out of her bag and gave it to Gracie.

'What is it?'

'Open it and see. I hope you like it.' Anastasia watched with rising excitement as her grandmother lifted the silky pouch out of the paper bag and poured the beads into the palm of her hand.

'Oh, it's a necklace!' she exclaimed.

'It matches your eyes,' said Anastasia.

Gracie held it up. 'It's lovely, really lovely. How sweet of you.'

'Let me help you put it on. It will go really well with your blouse.' Anastasia stood to fix the clasp at the back of her neck, then sat down to admire it. 'It brings out the green in your eyes.'

'How thoughtful of you, dear.'

'Take it from me, it's perfect.' Anastasia was pleased.

Gracie ran her fingers over the beads, moved beyond words that her granddaughter had taken it upon herself to buy her a present. This child, who she barely knew, who had been more interested in her phone than in anyone else, had bothered to go into town and buy her old grandmother a present. Gracie felt the tears stinging behind her eyes. 'Thank you, Anastasia.'

Anastasia touched her grandmother's hand. 'It's a pleasure,' she said, feeling a little emotional herself. 'Shall I show you my photographs? You really must go into town. It's so pretty.' She rummaged for her phone, which lay at the bottom of her bag, then put it on the table in front of Gracie. Anastasia flicked the screen and the photographs slid by in quick succession. When she got to the pictures in the piazza Gracie suddenly caught her breath. 'Slow down,' she said, looking closer. 'I didn't catch them.' She dragged her finger across the screen as Anastasia had done and stopped at the photograph of the grandfather and grandson feeding the pigeons. She recognised him at once. Donato, still handsome, yet old now, as she was.

'That man reminds me of someone,' she said softly, swiping away the picture. 'He was called Donato.'

'Oh yes, you were going to tell me about him.' Anastasia rubbed her hands together theatrically. 'Goody, more secrets!' she enthused.

'Yes, *many* more secrets,' said Gracie, excited to share them at last. 'I was only nineteen, living with my uncle and learning to restore paintings. I loved Gaetano from afar, but I never imagined he would ever notice me. We were from very different worlds, he and I. He was aristocratic and wealthy. I was working class and had nothing. Donato was the town flirt. He had had his way with all the pretty girls and I was flattered when he wanted to have his way with me. I wasn't beautiful, but I learned later that attraction has little to do with that. Donato found me mysterious. He liked the challenge. My heart was elsewhere, you see, and that made me aloof with him. It drove him mad. He sensed that I was never truly his. Then he asked me to marry him.'

'He proposed?' Anastasia was astonished. 'Granny, you dark horse!'

Gracie chuckled. 'Poor Donato. I said I'd think about it. I knew I could be happy with him. I knew I should feel lucky to receive such an offer, but I didn't. I just wanted Gaetano.'

'So, what happened?' Anastasia was impatient to get to the love story part.

'Gaetano's mother had inherited half a collection of paintings from her father and Rutger and I were summoned to value them, and restore the ones that needed restoring. It was during that week that I met Gaetano and got to know him.'

'And he fell in love with you?'

Gracie smiled wistfully and his image floated into her mind amid yellow sunflowers and crimson poppies. 'He did,' she said.

'So where did it go wrong?'

'I wasn't just a restorer, Anastasia.' Gracie looked at her granddaughter steadily and felt something of the young Gracie rattle the bones inside her, as if preparing to emerge.

'What were you?'

'A forger.'

Anastasia frowned, disbelieving that her sweet and shy, law-abiding grandmother could possibly have had anything to do with such a thing. She grabbed her hand and stared at her with wide, incredulous eyes. 'Are you telling me that you forged paintings?'

'I am,' Gracie replied and there was a part of her, buried deep, that was immensely proud of the fact. 'I was not just a forger, dear. I was a brilliant forger.' She chuckled again as Anastasia looked at her with new eyes. 'There are Matisses and Renoirs and Monets out here, hanging in the houses of wealthy art collectors, which are, in fact, painted by me.'

'Granny! You could go to prison for that.'

Gracie squeezed her granddaughter's hand. 'I know,' she said. 'But at the time I didn't think of the consequences should it all go wrong. I loved my uncle. He was like a father to me, and I wanted to please him. I would have done anything for him.' At that, her eyes began to prickle with tears again. The memory of what had happened resurfaced to hurt her once more.

'Was he a forger too?'

'He was the very best,' Gracie replied. She took a deep breath and moved the story away from Uncle Hans. She wasn't ready to tell that part of the story yet. 'I told Donato that I couldn't marry him.'

'Was he broken-hearted?'

'For a while, and the whole town sympathised with him. No one could understand why I had turned him down. He was a good catch for a girl like me. But he didn't wait around. He married someone else a few months later. A pretty farmer's daughter, and I didn't care. I was in love with Gaetano and as far as I could see, there was no reason why we couldn't be together.'

'But there *was* a reason,' said Anastasia, looking at her apprehensively, and Gracie was reminded of her young self in the way her granddaughter got straight to the heart of the matter.

'Yes, there was,' she replied. 'And it wasn't class or religion or—'

'Gaetano was married,' Anastasia interrupted.

Gracie nodded. 'How did you guess?'

'I don't know. What a bastard!'

'I thought so too, at the time,' Gracie agreed. 'He was very unhappily married, but married none the less.'

'That's terrible! How did you find out?'

'It was the following spring. We had been secretly seeing each other for almost a year when his wife turned up unannounced and he was forced to introduce me.'

'What a shit! Excuse my language, Granny. But how could you go out with a man for a year and not know that he was married?'

'We were in a bubble, Anastasia. We saw each other and no one else. We didn't socialise with his friends. He lived in Rome but had a place in the countryside, near where I was living with my uncle. When we saw each other, it was either there or at my uncle's, or we wandered into the hills to picnic in the poppies.' Gracie sighed as the tender memories returned as soft as dandelion seeds on the breeze. 'It was a secret love story. I thought we had to keep it secret because his family would never approve of me, but it was because it wasn't just a love story, it was an affair.'

'When you found out, did you make a scene?' Anastasia asked.

'No, I was controlled. He introduced me as his art teacher. He was quite a good painter, you see. His wife was in a terrible mood and barely noticed me. She didn't see my stricken face, because she was only aware of her own troubles. She wanted to speak to him in private, so I made my excuses and left.'

'You must have been devastated.'

'I was. I thought my heart had snapped in two.'

'Then what happened?'

Gracie sighed. 'That wasn't an end, as I thought it would be, but a beginning . . .'

'Mum! Anastasia!' It was Carina calling them to dinner.

Anastasia sighed irritably. 'Why is it that she always interrupts at the most gripping moment? Did you carry on your affair? Did Gaetano apologise? What happened next?' In her eagerness to hear the rest of the love story Anastasia had forgotten about her own.

'Come on,' said Gracie, pushing herself up. 'We'll resume another time. It can wait.' After all, she had waited forty-four years to tell it.

❧

Gracie sat beside Rex at dinner. He settled his blue eyes onto her and there was an element of surprise in his gaze. 'You look very pretty tonight, if you don't mind me saying, Gracie.'

'It must be my new necklace,' Gracie replied. 'My granddaughter bought it for me today.'

'What a nice thought,' he said, though he knew her prettiness had nothing to do with the necklace. It was Italy, he decided, that had made her flourish.

Ilaria presented the banquet with her usual fanfare. Carina and Lauren couldn't resist the pasta. Wendy, Tiff and Brigitte were drunk on Mamma Bernadetta's wine and more boisterous than ever, telling jokes and smoking between courses. The hills were silhouetted against the indigo sky. Above them the stars twinkled and the moon shone brightly. The night was beautiful and beguiling and Anastasia couldn't wait for everyone to go to bed so that she could sneak off to see Giovanni.

It was past midnight when Anastasia's moment finally came. Her mother had drunk enough rosé to send her swiftly into a deep sleep. Anastasia dressed in the bathroom and tiptoed out without waking her. She hurried down to the pool house where Giovanni was duly waiting for her. She saw the red glow of his cigarette, like a firefly in the darkness, and her heart gave a leap of happiness. She fell into his embrace, inhaling his smell. He kissed her ardently and whispered Italian into her ear that sounded like words of love. Then he took her by the hand and led her down a path that snaked its way through long grasses and shrubs to a track below the pool, where she saw that he had left his scooter. 'You come,' he said, climbing on and grinning at her encouragingly. Anastasia didn't hesitate. She mounted the seat behind him and pressed her body against his, winding her arms around his middle. It felt good to feel him there, solid against her belly, and she rested her head on his shoulder. They set off up the track with the cool night air in their hair and the scent of the Tuscan hills in their nostrils. She didn't know where they were going and she didn't care. So long as she was with him, she was content.

It wasn't long before he drew up at the foot of an umbrella pine. The moon was sufficiently bright for Anastasia to glimpse the house through the trees. It was a farmhouse, built on one level, with a tiled roof and stone walls. There were a few other buildings in the vicinity, still like sleeping beasts, and it was towards one of these that Giovanni led her.

He pushed open the big wooden door and stepped inside. It was completely dark. Anastasia could smell the scent of hay. Giovanni pulled his phone out of his jeans pocket and switched on the torch. The barn revealed itself in the light. There were stacks of hay bales and pieces of farm machinery lying about. Rakes and brooms and other farm equipment Anastasia didn't recognise were propped up against the walls. Hoses, ropes and twine hung on hooks. There was a wooden ladder leading up to the hay loft and Giovanni took her hand and guided her towards it.

She climbed the ladder to the top. Giovanni shone his torch onto the place he had prepared for her. She gasped at the romance of it. He had laid blankets on the hay and positioned hurricane lamps on the beams which he now lit with his cigarette lighter. When he switched off his phone the candlelight illuminated the loft with its warm, flickering glow. He took her hand again and lay down on the soft bed he had made for them. If Anastasia had been nervous, his kiss reassured her. She closed her eyes and savoured the taste of him as he explored her mouth with his tongue. His hand caressed her cheek and her neck, travelling down to her breast, feeling her nipple through the thin fabric of her dress. Anastasia writhed with pleasure like a cat, growing hot beneath his touch as an aching feeling began to grow in the bottom of her belly. Giovanni was in no hurry, in fact, her impatience aroused him. He took his time, kissing her tenderly, whispering '*Ti amo*' over and over again, as he slipped his hand beneath her dress and ran it softly over her stomach.

He stopped kissing her and lifted his head to gaze into her eyes. She stared up at him and he stared down at her and she believed she saw love there, burning in the reflection of the candles that glimmered in his eyes. With deft fingers, he unbuttoned the front of her dress. She lifted her ribcage to give him access to her bra, which he unhooked with the dexterity of a man who has unhooked many, and moaned as his mouth descended onto her breast. The sensation of his tongue was almost too exquisite to bear. She thought she would go crazy with the strange intensity mounting in her core.

Then he was kissing her belly, his hands on her waist, and travelling lower. He hooked his thumbs into the sides of her panties and pulled them down her legs and over her feet. Anastasia was exposed, but it didn't frighten her. She was so overcome with desire that she was no longer thinking but following her impulses, helpless beneath Giovanni's experienced touch, thrilled by her own rampant lust.

He parted her thighs and Anastasia closed her eyes. Her breath caught in her throat as his tongue found her most intimate place and a sensation more thrilling than anything she had experienced before gradually began to build. Her body drifted on wave upon wave of pleasure. Her mind became lost in it so that she was aware only of the delicious feelings that had taken her over. She was not conscious of the noise she was making until Giovanni brought her to a climax and she slowly came back to her senses.

He grinned at her triumphantly. Her gratification was his success. He hastily wriggled out of his jeans and shirt, releasing himself for her to admire, and opened his hand to reveal a condom. His eyes shone. 'Now I make you woman,' he said, and lay down upon her.

Chapter 13

Italy, 1963

Gracie could barely see the road for the tears in her eyes. She freewheeled her bicycle down the hill, impatient to reach the privacy of La Colomba so she could sob in private. Inside her chest her heart was about to burst with unhappiness, but she held it together until she was out of Colladoro and in the open countryside. Then, when she was sure that she was alone, she surrendered to misery.

How could Tancredi have deceived her? He had led her to believe that he loved her. How could he have been so cruel? How could his mother have colluded with him, because over the past months the contessa had witnessed them together at the Castello and yet she had said nothing. The image of Tancredi's wife floated then before her eyes. Tall with an angular body, a long neck, an imperious nose and the coldest blue gaze Gracie had ever seen, Tancredi's wife was everything that Gracie was not. The woman had barely cast her a glance – she was clearly the sort of person who did not take trouble with those she deemed beneath her. 'I would like to speak with my husband,' she had said and Gracie had been left swaying, like a tree that has just survived a tornado.

Gracie had remained, rooted to the ground, as Tancredi had blanched. His wife had marched off in the direction of the castle, expecting him to follow, and he had looked at Gracie with anguished eyes. His stricken face had done nothing to compensate for the lie, however, and Gracie had turned on her heel and hurried off towards the gate where she had left her bicycle. She had wanted to be as far away from him as possible. She hadn't glanced back. She did not know whether he had hesitated, whether he had considered running after her. All she knew was that she was alone.

As she cycled up the farm track towards La Colomba she thought of Donato and was overcome with regret. She should have accepted his proposal rather than hold out for a dream, which she now knew had been nothing but a mirage. She should have taken the opportunity when it was offered and been grateful for a chance of happiness. She should have listened to Gaia and Damiana who had both told her about the count's hedonistic ways. Why had she thought she was special? How had she allowed him to persuade her that she was? Now she had nothing, just a broken heart and an empty future. She discarded her bicycle on the lawn and ran into the villa. She'd never love anyone again, she resolved. She'd grow old here at La Colomba, like Rutger, and throw all her energy into her work, which seemed to be the only thing she could control.

The house was quiet. Uncle Hans was in Paris, Rutger in Amsterdam. Only the servants were there, creeping quietly about the shadows like mice. Gracie ran to her bedroom and closed the door. She flung herself onto the bed and sobbed into her pillow. How could she not have known he was married? How could he have kept such a monumental secret from her? The questions rose and fell like waves on a tormented sea and there was nothing Gracie could do to dispel them. And all the while, Tancredi's wife dominated like a formidable ship, mighty and strong, steaming through her happiness.

At length, there came a knock on the door. A light tap-tapping that Gracie immediately recognised. She sat up and wiped her eyes. 'Come in, Gaia,' she said. The door opened and Gaia stepped into the room.

'What has happened?' she asked. The concerned look on Gaia's face made Gracie cry again. Gaia sat on the side of the bed and drew her into her arms. They remained in silence for a while as Gracie released her sorrow onto Gaia's chest. Finally, when she found her voice, she confided in her friend. Gaia did not comment until Gracie reached the end of the tale and then she brushed the stray hair off Gracie's face and smiled at her tenderly.

'I wish you had shared your secret earlier for I could have told you that he was married,' she said.

'When did he marry?'

'A couple of years ago. I don't know. In Rome, I think. I just remember hearing about it. There are people in Colladoro who look on the Montefosco family as royalty and want to know everything about them. I'm not like that, but I must have heard it mentioned somewhere. Personally, I think Count Bassanelli has always been trouble. He is one of those wealthy, entitled men who believe they can have anything they want.'

'I can't believe I didn't know.'

Gaia shrugged. 'You're detached down there in the valley. And you've been busy working. No one works harder than you.'

'I feel like a fool. I thought he loved me,' Gracie said in a small voice.

'I'm sure he does. He probably wishes he wasn't married.

But it wasn't kind to lead you on. He wasn't thinking about *you* and *your* future. He was only thinking about himself.' She smiled with compassion. 'Men like him never leave their wives. Not because they don't want to, but because they can't. Society and religion make it impossible. Don't ever be the fool who believes the empty promises of a married man! It's lucky you discovered he was married early enough to move on and find someone who is free to love you.'

'I don't have a future now.' Gracie wiped her face with her hand. 'I will be an old maid, gathering dust on the shelf, while the sensible girls like you marry and have families.'

Gaia laughed. 'Darling girl, you are so young! There is plenty of time to fall in love again.'

'I don't want anyone else.'

'Not now. Of course you don't. But you will, in time. Lots of people have their hearts broken and they survive. They grow a little wiser and a little more cautious, perhaps, but they find happiness with someone else eventually. And you will too.'

'No one will compare with Tancredi.'

'He's not so wonderful, Gracie. You'll look back in twenty years and say, "I'm so happy I never married him. Now he's fat and sweaty, with a paunch."' Gracie had to laugh at that. 'You see, I bet you didn't think you'd ever laugh again a few minutes ago, and here you are having a good laugh. He *will* be fat and sweaty, with a paunch. I know his type. Too much money, too much food, too much alcohol and too much self-indulgence. Plus, his wife will make him unhappy. I know that type, too. Spoilt and ungrateful. It's gratitude and humility that are the secrets to happiness. Rich people don't know that.'

'If he comes to the villa, will you tell him I don't want to see him? I don't want to hear his excuses. There is no justification for lies.'

'Of course.'

'I'm not going to sit in a heap and let this defeat me. I'm going to work.' Gracie knew if she remained on her bed any longer she might never get up.

'Why don't we go for a walk? The air will do you good.'

'No, I want to paint. I will be in Uncle's studio. Work is the only thing that will take my mind off him.'

'Very well. I will bring you a coffee and guard the door with my life.'

The two women went downstairs. Gaia to the kitchen to make the coffee and Gracie to her uncle's studio to continue working on the Matisse forgery.

In Hans's studio, the spring sun shone through the windows with its usual enthusiasm. Gracie wondered how it could possibly shine so jubilantly in view of her broken heart. She closed the door behind her, stepped out of her shoes and changed into overalls. The familiar smell of paint and canvas was reassuring and the routine of her work immediately soothed her aching spirit. She tried to put Tancredi out of her mind and concentrate on the painting. This she could not do, but the focus required to forge a great master was so intense that as the hours went by she did manage at least to diminish him.

She was disturbed by a sudden commotion. There came a tirade of raised voices and the sound of running feet. She sat up in alarm, paintbrush poised, and listened. One of the voices belonged to Gaia. She was shouting at someone and her staccato Italian sounded like a round of gunfire. Gracie put down her brush and went to the door to listen. When Gaia gave her adversary a moment to speak, Gracie recognised Tancredi's voice and froze.

She pressed her ear to the door and her eyes filled with tears. He had followed her after all. She imagined he had come as soon as he had been able to get away from his wife. However, the heroic image of him racing across the countryside to reach her was weakened by the reality of his lie. There was nothing he could do to make up for his deceit, nothing he could say to justify the fact that he had kept his marriage secret, and Gracie knew it. She longed for him to have an excuse worthy of her forgiveness, but there was none. He was married, and even if he was unhappily married, married in name only, or even married but separated, he was still married in the eyes of God and he should have told her.

The voices got louder as Tancredi raged around the house in search of her. Gracie could hear her heartbeat pounding against her bones. She longed to open the door and see him, but she was aware how foolish that would be. She did not want to give him the opportunity to persuade her of his innocence. For her own good, he must leave now and never return.

Suddenly the door handle rattled. It took her so much by surprise that she gasped and leapt back in panic. Just as she did so she tripped on her shoes which she had discarded so as not to cover them in paint. She stumbled, reached for a stool in an effort to save herself, but only managed to knock it over. Both she and the stool landed on the wooden floorboards with a crash. 'Gracie, are you in there?' Tancredi shouted from the other side. 'I can hear you, Gracie. I know you're in there. Don't hide. Please. Hear me out. Gracie!'

Gracie wasn't sure now whether she was crying because she had truly hurt herself, or because she loved him and wanted so badly to be given a good enough reason to forgive him. She sat on the floor, nursing her bruised hip and elbow, and said nothing. Gaia's voice set off another round of bullets.

'You can't go in there. That's Signor Hans's studio. It's private. Leave Gracie alone. She's hurt. *You* hurt her. The least you can do is leave her alone. Go on! Get out!'

Tancredi ignored her. Gracie could hear his voice so clearly it was as if he were in the room. 'Gracie, listen to me. I can explain. I never wanted to hurt you, but I wanted you so badly I couldn't risk losing you. I knew if I told you the truth you'd leave me. I need you. You've brought sunlight into my life. Before you, it was so dark.' He paused and then his voice broke and with it, Gracie's heart all over again. 'Gracie, I can't live without you. I *won't* live without you. My marriage means nothing to me. You mean everything. Please, let me come in.'

Gracie was so confused she didn't know how to respond. She wanted to tell him to go away, but she didn't *want* him to go away. 'I can't,' she said at last. Gaia fired a few more bullets but they were less certain now, as if she, too, was moved by him.

'Then I'm coming in!' he declared and before Gracie could get to her feet he had kicked the door and forced the lock. He stood in the doorway, staring down at her. She stared back at him in horror. He was standing in Uncle Hans's secret studio which only she and Rutger were permitted to enter. It was testament to Hans Hollingsworth's authority that Gracie was, at that moment, more concerned about the broken lock than Tancredi's betrayal. She scrambled to her feet, anxious to get him out of the studio as fast as possible. But Tancredi did not move. 'I'm sorry,' he said and from the distraught look on his face Gracie knew that he meant it. 'I never intended to hurt you. I was going to tell you, but I kept putting it off. The more I put it off the greater the betrayal was going to be, but I just couldn't do it. I'm a coward, Gracie. But you make me strong. Please, Gracie, forgive me.'

'Let's go outside,' she suggested firmly, her thoughts now as clear as crystal. However, there was something in the sudden officious tone of her voice that made Tancredi aware of her eagerness to get him out of the room. He shifted his eyes from her face to the canvases. Then he narrowed them suspiciously.

'My God, you are restoring a Matisse,' he said, spotting the large canvas she was working on.

'I need some air,' she said, almost pushing him through the doorway.

'But you're not restoring it,' he said, moving past her to view it more closely. 'You're *painting* it.'

'I copy, for American buyers, nothing special,' she explained weakly.

'I'm not a fool, Gracie. That's not a copy. That's a brilliant fake.' He laughed and put his hands on his hips. 'Looks like I'm not the only one keeping secrets.'

Gracie glanced at Gaia, who was still standing in the next-door studio listening to everything they said. Gracie felt as if she were drowning. Uncle Hans's business had been, up until now, watertight, but she had allowed cracks to appear and water was now seeping out at an alarming rate. 'I paint fakes, but they are always sold as fakes. I would never dupe a buyer and besides, I'm not good enough. Not to an expert eye. Gaia, would you leave me to speak to Tancredi alone?'

'If you are sure,' Gaia replied and Gracie hoped she had believed her explanation.

Gracie pushed the door shut and turned to face him. 'Okay, you are now being honest with me so I will be honest with you,' she said in a solemn voice.

'Tell me.'

'My uncle is a master forger and so am I.'

Even though he had accused her of forging the Matisse

Tancredi was stunned by her confession. 'Good God!' He shook his head and turned back to the painting. 'What a mysterious woman you are, Gracie, and how talented. This is a work of genius.'

'I hope so,' she said, standing beside him.

'How much will this make you?'

She shrugged because she didn't really care about money. 'I don't know. My uncle takes charge of the business side. I just paint the pictures.'

'I hope he gives you your fair share.'

'I don't really mind if he doesn't. I give most of it to my family back in London anyway and they are doing well enough. I need little for myself.'

Tancredi pulled her into his arms with a sudden passion. 'I wish I had married *you*. Petronella thinks only of money. I'm sorry, Gracie.' He kissed her with ardour and she was powerless to resist. She closed her eyes and felt nothing but what was familiar and right. 'I've hurt you and I will never forgive myself. I will make it up to you somehow. I will divorce my wife. Yes, that's what I will do. I will divorce her and then I will marry you.' Gracie believed him, yet, even if she hadn't, she would not have been able to leave him, such was the strength of her attachment. It would have been like ripping out her heart.

From that moment, their romance grew into an affair. Instead of being lied to, they lied to the world together. Instead of an imbalance in their relationship there was equilibrium. Gracie knew Tancredi was weak and yet it was his vulnerability that touched her where she was most tender, in the heart of her heart where she had suffered loss. Tancredi needed her and she responded to his need with the willingness of a mother with an uncertain child. As for her, Gracie needed him too. She loved the man, but she also loved the woman she was when she was with him. He made her feel beautiful. Whenever he looked at her she saw a better version of herself reflected in his eyes. She saw the woman she wanted to be.

Under the guise of his art teacher she was able to continue as before. It never occurred to his wife that her husband would look at a girl, who, in her opinion, was ordinary. The rare times Petronella came to the Castello she dismissed Gracie as 'staff' even though Gracie sat at the lunch table, invited by the countess, who enjoyed nothing more than intrigue and deception. After all, *she* was the mistress of both. Tancredi gazed at Gracie across the table, his eyes brimming with amusement and affection, and only the countess was aware of it. Sometimes, she placed them beside each other, so that they could press their legs together beneath the table and touch hands as they reached for their wine glasses.

Tancredi never discussed his wife. It was as if he didn't want his joy ruined by her negative energy. From what little Gracie saw of Petronella she was spoilt and entitled, her beauty ruined by the permanent scowl on her face. She found fault in everything – mostly her husband whom she put down at every opportunity, and was bored by the countryside, claiming it lacked excitement. She was clever, impatient and intolerant of fools. The only things that seemed to give her pleasure were jewellery and fashion. Her long, tapering fingers sparkled with gems and her lean figure was draped in expensive clothes. Gracie wondered why Tancredi had married her. What had he found in her to love, besides her beauty? Gracie wondered whether it was possible for someone with so little appreciation for the simple things in life to find any kind of real happiness.

Fortunately, Petronella did not often show up at the Castello. Tancredi divided his time between Rome and Colladoro. He was trying to start a business dealing in art, but preferred to spend his time with Gracie, pretending to learn how to paint. As for Gracie, she continued to work on the Matisse. Uncle Hans returned to La Colomba at the end of May and Rutger shortly after. Gaia had arranged for the lock on the door to be mended and Uncle Hans was none the wiser. If Gaia knew the truth about what went on in there she never said. The only other person to know about her affair was Rutger, after all, he had enabled it to begin, but besides the odd subtle remark delivered from behind his canvases, nothing was said. Life seemed to go back to normal. Then Gracie set into motion a series of events that would alter the course of her life for ever.

She devised a plan for Tancredi to get back the painting he had so loved as a child.

❧

It all started one evening in June when Tancredi and Gracie were lying in bed at the top of the tower above the studio where he liked to paint. The contessa was in Rome, the gardeners had all gone home, including Donato who still worked there with his father, and they were alone. Only Bagwis remained in the castle, but he could be relied on to be discreet. It was hot up there at the top of the tower, and airless. No breeze entered through the windows, only the golden summer sunshine and the sound of crickets. Gracie lay in Tancredi's arms, sleepy after making love, her heart full to the brim with happiness. It was then that she brought up her idea, because she so wanted to please him.

'I've been thinking,' she began. 'You know *The Temptation of Eve* that you love so much?'

She felt him grow tense at the mention of it and her excitement mounted. 'What of it?' he asked.

'I have a plan that might interest you . . .'

'Go on.'

'If you can somehow get the painting to me, I could copy it. Then you could give your uncle back the fake and keep the real one.'

There was a long pause. Gracie was beginning to doubt the brilliance of her plan when he eased her gently off him and sat up. 'Gracie, I don't know what to say. You're a genius!' He looked at her and grinned, and her excitement returned.

She drew the sheet over her naked body and knelt beside him. 'You really think so?'

'I don't doubt that you can pull off a Bartoloni. I saw the Matisse you painted. If I can just engineer a way to get the painting to you for restoration—'

'Where does your uncle live?'

'In Rome.'

'Can you invite him here? Perhaps the countess can invite him. Then you can tell him about the restoration work Rutger and I have done—'

'It's his wife we need to convince.'

'We?'

'Yes, we. If I get them down here, it's Livia we need to work on. She knows nothing about art but considers herself highly cultured. You will have to persuade her to have the Bartoloni restored.'

'How will I do that without seeing it?'

'You're the mastermind. You'll think of something.' Tancredi put his hand beneath her chin and kissed her. 'After all, I can't suggest it. My uncle is not a fool. He knows I want that painting. It has to come from his wife and you have to say something to sow the seed in her mind. She has to think it's *her* brilliant idea.'

'Not a challenge then?' she quipped.

Tancredi smiled affectionately. 'Not for you.'

❧

Getting Bruno and Livia to come to the Castello was easy. Tancredi told Gracie that he had made the suggestion to his mother, explaining that he felt it was now time to bury old resentments, and she had been delighted. After all, Bruno was her only sibling and it had grieved her to have been in the middle of the feud between her brother and son. The olive branch was duly put out and received with enthusiasm. The date was set for a weekend in August. Now all Gracie had to do was work out a way of getting Livia to give her the Bartoloni to restore. She had no idea how she was going to do it without raising suspicion, but Tancredi wanted that painting so badly she knew she couldn't fail.

Gracie had always known she was a good forger; she was about to discover that she was a good manipulator as well.

Chapter 14

The much anticipated weekend in August arrived and Gracie still wasn't sure how she was going to convince two people she had never met to send a painting she had never seen for restoration, with restorers they had never heard of. The plot was so piecemeal it was laughable. Yet, Gracie knew how important it was to Tancredi that they get their hands on his painting in order for her to copy it. Although she hadn't worked out the finer details of the plan she hoped she would somehow improvise on the day. She would be introduced to his uncle as a restorer, the countess would rave about the works she had restored for her and then Gracie would bring the subject round to the Baroque period, which she would claim was coming back into fashion. All Bruno then had to do was list the Baroque paintings he had in his possession and the rest was up to her.

Tancredi and Gracie had discussed the plot at great length and believed themselves very clever for having devised it. Were it to succeed the horrible Bruno would have a brilliant fake and Tancredi the sentimental original that meant so much to him. However, they had not taken into account Tancredi's unpredictable mother. No sooner had Tancredi suggested he invite Gracie for lunch on the Saturday of his uncle's visit than the countess declared that she would like to include Hans and

Rutger as well. Tancredi told Gracie that it was because she wanted to show off her arty friends to her brother. The siblings were notoriously competitive. As it happened both Hans and Rutger were at La Colomba, and in very good spirits having sold Gracie's Matisse to a collector in Japan. Gracie was none too happy. She couldn't lie about the Baroque period having come into fashion with her uncle and Rutger within earshot, but there was nothing she could do. Both men had accepted the invitation with enthusiasm.

On the Saturday morning Gracie awoke with her stomach in knots. The sun streamed in through the linen curtains bringing with it a chorus of birdsong and yet her nervousness prevented her from taking pleasure from the Tuscan dawn as she usually did. So much depended on today. She didn't want to disappoint Tancredi but she feared she wouldn't be able to pull it off, after all. She had been rash to have suggested such an ambitious plan in the first place. His belief in her only heightened her anxiety. What if she didn't get a chance to speak to Livia on her own? What if the subject of restoring paintings never came up? What if Uncle Hans and Rutger scuppered her plan? She felt out of control and inadequate. She wished she could back out, but she couldn't. Tancredi was depending on her.

Gracie slipped into a red-and-white sundress embellished with a bold strawberry design and tied her hair into a ponytail. Uncle Hans, holding his panama hat, admired her when she came down the stairs into the hall. 'Don't you look good enough to eat!' he exclaimed, referring to the strawberries. Gracie pulled a face which made him chuckle. 'You haven't grown tired of my jokes, have you?'

'Not at all,' she answered with an affectionate smile. 'I'd be lost without them.'

'Good. Now, I want to talk about your mission today, Gracie.' He put the hat on his head and his arm around her and led her into the garden. The smell of his spicy cologne drowned out the scents of the garden. To Gracie it was the smell of home and she loved it even more than gardenia and honeysuckle. 'Do you know who you are going to meet today at lunch?' he asked.

'The countess's brother,' she replied.

'Yes, you are going to meet Count Bruno Montefosco. Now, as you will no doubt remember, he inherited the other half of his father's art collection. There must be many paintings in his collection which need cleaning and restoring. It is your mission to convince him that we are the best people to do it.'

Gracie's heart gave a leap. Uncle Hans was playing right into her hand without even realising it. 'I will do my best,' she said, suddenly feeling a little more positive about the day ahead.

'Perhaps then he might wish to increase his collection.' He scratched his chin and gave Gracie a meaningful look. Gracie knew exactly what *that* meant.

'Yes, you never know,' she added.

'His father, Count Gaetano Montefosco, bought a few of my very best works.'

Uncle Hans began to whistle a jolly tune, *no doubt reflecting on the fakes he had painted for Tancredi's grandfather*, Gracie thought. In a sky-blue shirt with a blue-and-yellow silk cravat around his neck he looked dapper and cool in spite of the heat. Rutger stepped out of the house in a crumpled jacket and shabby-looking tie, his greying hair curling about his ears and sticking up in thinning tufts on the dome of his head. The three of them set off in Uncle Hans's recently purchased silver sports car, with the roof down and the sun on their faces, and the knots in Gracie's stomach grew tighter.

When Gracie saw the shiny cars parked on the gravel in front of the castle the knots began to give her pain. She wondered how many people the countess had invited. Having initially wished that Uncle Hans and Rutger had not been invited, she was now grateful that they had. It was reassuring to know that she wasn't going to have to walk round to the terrace and confront the strangers on her own.

No sooner had the car drawn to a halt on the gravel than Bagwis appeared with his serene, patient smile to escort them to where the party was sitting in the shade, enjoying a drink before lunch. As they approached, Gracie noticed Tancredi at once. He raised his eyes and smiled, but she detected an uneasiness in his smile that made the knots in her stomach grow even tighter. However, she felt immediately reassured by the sight of him, handsome in a linen jacket and open-neck white shirt, sunglasses glinting in the light, and thought that maybe he was just anxious, as she was. The tall, dark-haired man who stood to meet them was obviously Count Bruno Montefosco, because he resembled his sister, the countess, with his shiny black hair, aquiline nose and predatory gaze. His wife, diminutive and as scrawny as a bird who has endured a lean winter, turned her head but did not get up. She had thin, pale lips and the wan face of a woman who is never satisfied. Then Gracie's heart stalled as her gaze settled on a third woman, one she had not expected to see, and she realised why Tancredi's smile was so tense. It was his wife, Petronella, whom she knew Tancredi had *not* invited. Gracie wondered whether the countess had asked her just to cause trouble. She was perched stiffly on one of the wicker sofas with the countess, who now got to her feet and glided over the paving stones to meet them.

There was nothing rushed about the countess. She seemed to dwell in a world where time ran at a more leisurely pace. She put out a hand with a slow, languid movement, and smiled politely as Rutger shook it. 'It is so lovely to see you again, Signor Janssen.' Uncle Hans took off his hat and sunglasses and complimented her straw sombrero that was threaded with flowers from the garden. She gave him her hand and he bowed and kissed it, as gallant as a knight. Her dark eyes shone with pleasure as she responded to Uncle Hans's charm with the graciousness of a woman who is used to flattery but nonetheless thrilled by it. When she welcomed Gracie, she gave a knowing smile and said under her breath, 'No painting lessons today, then?' and Gracie felt her cheeks burn. 'Come, Signor Janssen and Signor Hollingsworth, allow me to present you to my family.' Gracie caught eyes with Tancredi and he gave a little nod, which immediately put her at ease and connected them as the pair of conspirators that they were. It didn't matter that the countess was now ignoring her as she gave Rutger and Hans her full attention, introducing them proudly as the most famous art restorers in Europe.

Petronella's face grew suddenly animated when she was introduced to Uncle Hans. Gracie noticed her smile widen as he complimented her with the same easy charm with which he had complimented the countess, bowed and kissed her hand as well, tickling her flawless skin with his moustache. The woman who had dismissed Gracie coldly now radiated beauty and charm as if she were always thus. Her mouth was no longer thin and twisted with fury but full and pouting. Uncle Hans, who was a master at making people feel special, had won her over with a few well-chosen sentences and a chivalrous kiss. When he was introduced to Livia Montefosco Gracie was reminded once again of just how handsome her uncle was. The uninspiring woman's pallor turned positively rosy as he worked his magic on her too, and the laugh that escaped her throat was entirely out of keeping with her dour, humourless demeanour.

It did not surprise Gracie that Petronella barely remembered having ever met her. She nodded politely then turned her attention back to Uncle Hans who took the place beside her on the sofa, where the countess had been sitting. Rutger had already formed a tight group with Count Bruno Montefosco, Tancredi and the countess. Gracie found herself alone with Livia Montefosco, who was now sitting frostily on her sofa, watching Petronella with envy. Gracie had no choice but to talk to her. After a few gauche attempts at conversation, to which Livia responded with a bored air and the minimum of words, Gracie dried up. There was no way she was ever going to be able to convince *this* woman to send them their paintings. She was not even attempting to hide the fact that she would rather have been talking to Uncle Hans.

Then Gracie was struck with a flash of inspiration. She looked at her uncle and said to Livia in a quiet voice, 'I'm surprised the countess invited my uncle here today.' *That* caught Livia's attention.

She looked at Gracie as if she were seeing her for the first time and said, 'Why?'

Gracie chuckled in order to appear without guile. 'Because he is her *secret* find,' she said. 'She's very possessive of him. She usually only invites him up here when she's alone. But then I suppose you and your husband have your own restorer in Rome.'

Livia looked doubtful. 'My husband has never thought of restoring his collection.'

'Really? I'm surprised. You know Hans discovered a

Gainsborough in the countess's collection. What looked like a very ordinary painting turned out to be a very valuable one. But that is Hans's genius. He and Rutger are like a pair of detectives. It would be indiscreet of me to tell you about the other amazing finds they discovered in her collection, but I can safely say that she was *very* pleased.'

Livia was now staring at her with interest. 'Really?' she said. 'You mean, paintings of little worth turned out to be valuable treasures?'

'Yes, Hans and Rutger are the best.'

'And you are Hans's niece?'

'Yes, I'm an apprentice,' she lied, hoping that Livia would put her indiscretions down to naivety and not to malice or manipulation. 'It takes years to learn the trade, but decades to gain the experience and wisdom that those two men have. I hope that one day I will be as accomplished as they are.'

'I'm sure you will be,' said Livia, looking over with a distracted air at Hans who was now talking to both the countess and Petronella. 'I understand your uncle is also an art dealer.'

Gracie was now getting into her stride. By the gleam in the woman's eyes Gracie could tell she had her attention, all she had to do to complete her mission was to slowly reel her in like a fish. 'Yes, he's like a truffle pig of the art world,' she continued. 'He's found some extraordinary works in the least likely places. It's rare that unknown works from the great masters come to light, but when they do Uncle Hans finds them. He's sold paintings to some of the greatest collectors in the world. But he'll never discuss them with anyone. He's a paragon of discretion. Sometimes he even keeps that information from me.'

'Does he really?' said Livia, narrowing her eyes, and Gracie could feel her energy, for it was prickly and competitive.

'I know that your father-in-law, Count Gaetano

Montefosco, was a client, which is why the countess was so keen to use him.' Gracie laughed, then, certain that she had done right by both Tancredi and Uncle Hans. 'Perhaps she knows that her brother is not very interested so she need not worry about sharing her secret with him.'

'Perhaps,' said Livia.

Lunch was served at the long table on one of the lower terraces, beneath trellising interwoven with vines of ripening grapes. Gracie was seated at the opposite end of the table to the countess, with Tancredi on her left and Bruno, the countess's brother, on her right. The countess presided over the meal at the head, with Hans on her right and Rutger on her left. She had generously given Hans to Livia, who was thrilled, leaving Rutger to humour Petronella, who was less thrilled. Petronella barely glanced in her husband's direction, but Gracie was nervous of talking to him in case something in her demeanour gave them away. Instead, she talked to Bruno, while Tancredi pressed his knee against hers and heightened her anxiety. To her surprise Bruno was not the mean-spirited ogre Tancredi had made him out to be. She had expected him to ignore her, as everyone else had, but he treated her like an equal, asking her questions about her life and listening intensely, as if she was the only person at the table with whom he was really interested in talking. She began to wonder, as the *spaghetti alle vongole* and wine relaxed her and the afternoon sunshine made her drowsy, whether it wasn't Bruno who refused to give up the painting, but his wife. She glanced at Livia, who was deep in conversation with Hans, her head inclined, her expression attentive and serious as if Hans were divulging the secrets of the universe, and thought it entirely possible. She had the face of a woman who was difficult to please. Bruno had the face of a man who was keen to find the best in everyone.

Tancredi was polite to his uncle but Gracie detected the coolness beneath his civility. For all his good intentions he was unable to disguise his feelings, even though he had engineered the invitation supposedly in order to make friends. If Bruno noticed he did not let on. He conversed with his nephew as if they had never quarrelled. Gracie found herself compensating for Tancredi's reticence, filling the silences when he answered in monosyllables and steering the subjects away from paintings and childhood. She wondered whether Bruno and Livia would have given Tancredi the painting if they hadn't known how much he wanted it. She sensed that Livia was holding on to it out of spite, because she was jealous of her sister-in-law, the flamboyant Countess Bassanelli. The more she observed the couple the more convinced Gracie became that the withholding of the painting had nothing to do with Tancredi and everything to do with his mother.

At the end of lunch, as coffee was served by Bagwis and a stout woman in a pink uniform with a white apron, Petronella and Livia lit cigarettes and the conversation became a general one. Bruno didn't say much. He sat back in his chair, coffee cup in hand, and listened as Hans dominated, as he always did. The countess flirted with him and he in turn flirted back. If their energy had been visible it would have been as sparks flying from one to the other in a magnificent display. Gracie watched, amused, as Petronella and Livia were forced to yield to the greater power. They puffed sulkily on their cigarettes as the countess threw back her head and laughed throatily, her Italian melodious and fluid like the sound of a stream bubbling over smooth rocks, her elegant long fingers with their manicured scarlet nails moving about her like exotic birds as she entertained with ease and elegance. She was mesmerising and Gracie felt sorry for her sister-in-law and daughter-in-law because they were thrown into shade, probably quite deliberately, by this mighty woman, greedily stealing all the attention for herself.

Tancredi's knee was still pressing against Gracie's. It felt natural there, as if his leg were an extension of her own. She glanced at him to find that he was watching her, a look of admiration on his face for all to see, were they minded to notice. Appalled that his affection should be so carelessly exposed, she pushed out her chair and put her napkin on the table and quietly excused herself. Tancredi watched her go. She could feel his eyes on her back. *Perhaps the wine had made him reckless*, she thought, as she made her way to the ladies' room.

It occurred to her as she retreated downstairs that she did not belong in Tancredi's world. As much as she wanted to be with him, she feared she did not want to be amongst his kind. These people, these wealthy, well-educated, privileged people, held no attraction for her. If anything they made her feel inadequate. She wondered whether his friends were like that. She feared they were for why else would he have married Petronella were she not the sort of woman he was used to? Gracie imagined that all the women in Rome were just like her; lofty, indulged and superior. The idea of having to be among them filled her with panic. Here in Colladoro the women were soft around the edges, not hard like Petronella and Livia. They had embraced her as one of them while Petronella and Livia had barely acknowledged her. As for the countess, she undoubtedly knew of Gracie's affair with Tancredi and had no problem with it, in fact, she readily encouraged it, but Gracie doubted she would approve of her son divorcing his wife and *marrying* her. Gracie knew she did not qualify for the position of wife. Mistress was all that was acceptable for a girl of her class.

As she wandered through the library on her way back to the terrace she was suddenly grabbed by the hand and pulled into the shadowy recess behind the door, pressed up against the wall. Tancredi's mouth was on hers, kissing her deeply and passionately. She could taste the wine on his tongue and the figs on his breath and feel the warmth of his hands through her thin dress. The weight of his body was hot, the vigour in it arousing. She forgot about Petronella and Livia and her sense of inadequacy. Nothing mattered but him and the growing desire in her loins that demanded gratification.

He lifted her knee and swiftly unbuttoned his trousers. 'You're mad!' she hissed as he pulled aside her panties and entered her.

'You love me mad,' he replied, laughing into her neck.

'But you have no protection,' she protested, suddenly anxious.

'I'll take my chances.'

'What if . . . ?'

'I don't care,' he whispered, his breath hot against her skin. Gracie laughed because she didn't care either. As he moved his hips the pleasure began to build and slowly flooded her mind and all reason in it. She wound her legs around his hips and he slowed down to a gentle rhythm.

'I love you, Gracie,' he said.

'I love you too, Tancredi,' she replied. Then she closed her eyes and let the warm feeling spread throughout her belly.

When they were spent Gracie returned to the table first, having smoothed down her dress and tidied her hair, so that they did not arouse suspicion by arriving together. However, she needn't have worried for the guests had now moved to the garden, where the countess was showing the party the newly acquired statue of a Cupid which she had placed at the end of a rose-lined walkway. Gracie joined them, hanging back a little out of shyness.

Bruno turned round and smiled encouragingly. 'Ah, there you are, Gracie. You wouldn't want to miss the garden tour,' he said.

She hoped he did not see signs of what she had just been up to. 'Every time I come here there is something new,' she replied.

'Yes, my sister loves nothing more than spending money.' His tone exposed his disapproval.

'She has beautiful taste,' Gracie said diplomatically. 'If I had her taste I would want to embellish my home too.'

He chuckled and she knew what he was thinking, that beautiful taste was one thing, but extravagance quite another. They walked on. Hans had all three women in his thrall, while Rutger shuffled along behind like a dishevelled dog, stopping every now and then to admire the view or the flowers. He was used to Hans being the showman. It was their dynamic and a very efficient dynamic at that. Gracie knew that Uncle Hans was cultivating all three ladies and, in her own way, *she* was part of their dynamic too. While they were reeling in the women, she was reeling in Bruno. The fact that she was also on a mission for Tancredi made her feel like a double agent and she felt a little guilty when Uncle Hans caught her eye and winked.

However, there was no guarantee that their charm offensive would pay off. They said their farewells at the end of the afternoon. The countess was clearly fond of Hans for she giggled like a girl when his moustache prickled her hand and lingered there a little longer than it should have. Gracie wondered whether she had ever tried to seduce him in the pavilion next to the tennis court. She wondered how far her uncle would go for business. From the way he was flirting with the countess Gracie decided he would go as far as necessary in order to complete a sale. He flirted with Livia too – Hans Hollingsworth was no fool! He made sure he charmed Petronella as well. The competitive air smouldered between the women, and Gracie could almost see it like heat quivering over hot stones. She said her goodbyes and everyone was very cordial, except Bruno whose farewell was almost affectionate. Tancredi kissed her cheek briskly and no one would have guessed they had made love behind the door in the library. They set off back down the track in Uncle Hans's dashing sports car with a triumphant air.

Yet as the weeks went by there was no word from either the countess or Livia Montefosco and Gracie began to worry that her plan had failed. That *she* had failed Tancredi. And then, at the beginning of November, Uncle Hans received a very interesting letter.

Chapter 15

Italy, 2010

'So, what did the letter say?' Anastasia asked, greedy for more of her grandmother's story.

They were sitting on a bench that was placed at the far end of the garden, overlooking the hills and the misty ocean that sparkled in the distance. It was dusk. Carina and the other guests were getting ready for supper and the grounds of the castle were quiet. The sound of crickets and roosting birds was a gentle melody they were now accustomed to.

'It was from Bruno's wife Livia,' said Gracie. 'She wanted Hans to come to their house in Rome to see their collection of paintings with a view to restoring the ones that needed restoring, and to talk about the possibility of adding to it.'

'How could you be sure that Hans would choose Gaetano's painting?' Anastasia asked.

'I couldn't be sure,' said Gracie with a smile.

'So you went with him?'

Gracie chuckled. 'You're always one step ahead of the game, just like I was,' she said, looking at her granddaughter with affection. 'I had never gone anywhere. I'd spent eight years at La Colomba, working with Rutger. I knew if I asked my uncle, he would agree to take me with him.'

'And he did?'

'Yes, he did.' Anastasia was grinning broadly, her grey-green eyes shining with excitement. It delighted Gracie that her granddaughter should be so interested. And, by telling her the story, Gracie was able to wander back down the avenues of her past and relive it. 'So, off we went to Rome in Uncle Hans's fabulous car. Rutger remained at La Colomba and neither of them had an inkling of why I wanted to go and what I intended to do when I got there. With hindsight I know that they would have discouraged me if I had told them. And of course I *should* have told them. But I was in love and I'd have done anything for Gaetano. Anything at all.'

'So, did you manage to convince Livia that Gaetano's painting needed to be restored?'

Gracie did not answer directly. She didn't want to rush through the details. She wanted to savour this part of the story, before it all went wrong. 'We arrived in Rome, which was the first time I had ever been there. What a beautiful city it is. We stayed in the famous Hassler Hotel, which was the first time I'd ever stayed in a hotel. Goodness, if you can imagine where I came from, Anastasia, a tiny house in London with an outside loo, and then imagine the glamour of this hotel, you will understand how excited I was to be there. La Colomba had impressed me, but the hotel put Uncle Hans's villa in the shade. It was like a palace. And everywhere I looked I saw ancient sculptures and buildings and magnificent works of art. It was like dying and arriving in heaven, it truly was. Well . . .' She sighed and shook her head. 'Wouldn't it be nice to take you there one day? I would love you to see it. But, I digress. Where was I?'

'You were about to tell me about Livia,' Anastasia answered, a little impatiently, because she wanted to know whether her grandmother managed to get Gaetano's painting to La Colomba.

'Ah, yes, we went to the palazzo, which was a grand palace in a square dominated by a gorgeous fountain. It was evening and the building looked pink. I remember that.'

'Did Livia know you were coming? Was she furious when she saw you?'

'No, she wasn't expecting me, but she was not furious at all. She was quite a different person on her own turf. She was gracious and warm, nothing like the frosty woman she had been at the Castello. She was excited to show Uncle Hans their collection. And my instincts had been right. *She* wore the trousers in that relationship. The reason Gaetano had not been given his grandfather's painting was entirely down to her. The seeds I had planted at that lunch had taken root. Livia was jealous of the countess, which I had sensed, and it gave her pleasure to steal what she believed to be one of her secret treasures: Uncle Hans. How she worked on him. She flirted and batted her eyelashes and treated him to a lavish meal. Me too, of course, but she wasn't interested in me. She was polite because I was his niece, but she was determined to make him like her more than her sister-in-law. That was never going to happen.' Gracie chuckled. 'She had nothing of the countess's charisma or charm. But she tried. Uncle Hans played along. He knew what she was up to. Uncle Hans was a master manipulator. No one recognised a schemer better than him.'

'Did you see Gaetano's painting?'

'I did and it was just as I had imagined it to be. It was exquisite. I could see exactly why it had appealed to the boy he had once been and why he wanted it so badly.'

'Did it need restoring?'

'Not really. A little surface cleaning perhaps,' Gracie replied. 'But Uncle Hans wasn't going to argue with me. He was so busy studying the collection – and there were many,

many paintings hanging on every wall of the palazzo – he didn't hear me making the suggestion to Livia. I got her on her own and told her confidentially that Baroque was going to be in big demand again, following a famous pop star tipping the market by buying up furniture and paintings from that period. I told her in a whisper that my uncle had been personally chosen by the pop star to source the paintings. Her greedy eyes lit up. I assured her that this little picture would soon be very valuable and it would be worth cleaning it. It was as easy as that. Of course I couldn't resist asking her whether she would ever sell it.'

'What did she say?'

'That it was sentimental so she never would.'

'Really?'

'Interesting, but not surprising. The fact that her husband's nephew wanted it so badly was reason enough to hold on to it. Had he not wanted it, I'm sure she would have sold it at the drop of a hat.'

'What a horrid woman.'

'Yes, I felt sorry for Bruno. Both he and Gaetano had married very unpleasant women.'

'Why?'

'I'm afraid the truth is rather unsavoury.'

Anastasia loved an unsavoury truth and looked eagerly at her grandmother. 'Do tell, Granny!' she said.

'Money.'

Anastasia frowned. 'I thought the family were very rich.'

'Gaetano's grandfather came from a long line of illustrious collectors. They had once been one of the wealthiest families in Europe. But buying art is an expensive business. Gaetano's grandmother had had nothing. His grandfather had married her for love, going against the wishes of his family. I discovered that later – I wish I had known that at the time. Gaetano's grandfather was extravagant. He was determined to match his famous ancestors and add to the family collection. By the time he died he had run up terrible debts. His son, Bruno, had to sell a villa he had in Tuscany and prime property he and his sister had inherited in Rome. Of course they had the paintings, but men like Bruno and Gaetano would rather cut off their limbs than sell what their families have acquired over generations. They are very proud.'

'And very foolish!' Anastasia exclaimed.

'In our eyes, yes. But one has to try to understand their culture. I believe Bruno, who had grown up with his father's extravagance, had married Livia for her money. Her family were wealthy industrialists. It was a perfect match. He gave her class and she gave him money so he could continue to live in style, surrounded by treasures.'

'Why didn't he just sell a Michelangelo?'

'I doubt he ever had a Michelangelo, dear. Bruno would rather have married money, however unpleasant it was, than sell one of his treasures. However, his sister was different. Gaetano's mother later fell on hard times and sold much of the collection she had so blithely restored, but I'm jumping ahead of myself . . .'

'Do you think Gaetano had married for money too?'

'I'm certain of it. Petronella was moneyed. I cannot think of another reason for marrying her. She didn't make him happy, otherwise he would not have come looking for me!'

'So, what did he say when you returned with the painting?'

'I had a few nerve-racking weeks while Livia had everything packed up and sent down to La Colomba. I wasn't sure she would include it in the list of paintings Uncle Hans had chosen for restoration.'

'But she did.'

'Yes, she did.'

'What did Gaetano say?'

'He held the painting in his hands and wept.'

'He cried?' Anastasia grinned, considering it embarrassing for a grown man to cry.

'Yes, he was very moved. You see, like so many material things the value is not in the paint but in what the paint represents. To Gaetano it represented his childhood. A time when he was happy. Before his father died, before he was engulfed by unhappiness, before his life went so horribly wrong. The memories attached to the painting were what held value for him.'

'He must have been so pleased with you.'

'He was pleased with me,' said Gracie and she knitted her fingers together and dropped her gaze into the black hole they made. 'And yet, that painting was what would eventually ruin everything. Everything we had. Because of that painting I lost *him*.'

Anastasia put her hand on her grandmother's and gazed at her in distress. 'How did you lose him?'

Gracie sighed and pulled her hands away. 'We should go and change for dinner.'

'But I want to hear the rest of the story. It's so sad!'

'You know it has to end sadly, otherwise I would not have married your grandfather and had your mother.'

'But I want to know how it ends.'

'And you will. But we must leave it now. Look, they're already down on the terrace, eating crostini! We don't want to miss those delicious crostini!'

Anastasia looked disappointed. 'I'd rather sit here with you,' she said.

Gracie was touched. 'And I with you,' she replied truthfully. 'We can come again tomorrow and I will tell you what happened next.' Though that part of the story would be a painful one to tell.

❧

Carina was surprised when her mother and Anastasia appeared out of the darkness, having not even changed. 'Where have you two been?' she asked, elegant in a white dress and gold belt, her hair pinned in an up-do.

'We've been watching the sunset,' said Anastasia.

'The sun went down ages ago!' said Carina, feeling a little jealous that she hadn't been included.

'We got talking,' Gracie explained. 'Anastasia is very good, humouring her old grandmother.'

'I'm not humouring you, Granny. I like listening to your stories.' Carina frowned. She wondered what stories of her mother's could be so fascinating to a seventeen-year-old. 'Come on, Granny. What are you going to wear tonight? I think I'll wear my bubble-gum-pink dress. Will you come and tell me what you think?'

Carina watched the two of them disappear inside, leaving her feeling put out. It reminded her of school when the cool girls had ganged up and excluded her from their games. In this case, she only had herself to blame; after all, she hadn't taken the trouble with either of them. She'd spent the last three days with Lauren and Madeleine and going for long walks on her own into the countryside. She tried to convince herself that she should be pleased that her daughter had taken her mother off her hands. This was Gracie's week and Anastasia was making it special for her. Yet, she didn't feel pleased. She felt ignored. There was something about Anastasia's delight at having her grandmother to herself which annoyed Carina. It was almost wilful, as if the girl was engineering a bond just to make *her* feel bad. Didn't Carina feel guilty enough about spending so much time in the office and not giving her daughter the attention she needed without Anastasia rubbing her nose in it? There was always the possibility that Anastasia genuinely enjoyed listening to her grandmother's stories, but Carina doubted that. What on earth could she have to say to entertain a teenager? Descriptions of the dances held in the church hall in the 1960s? Carina did not imagine her mother had ever done anything remotely exciting.

Yet without having to worry about her mother Carina was free to do as she pleased. She could sit in the sun and talk to Madeleine and Lauren, who were becoming firm friends. She could go out walking. She could, if she wanted to, do some work. But she didn't want to. She was becoming detached from what was going on in London. She had thought it would be a terrible wrench to be away from the office and her clients and yet it wasn't. It wasn't a wrench at all. It was as if the Universe had conspired to lure her away just to show her what life was like without her mobile phone and constant communication with her personal assistant, and been very successful.

As she joined the other guests on the terrace Madeleine appeared in a white silk blouse and trousers with shiny gold jewellery jangling on her wrists, ears and around her neck. 'How was your walk?' Carina asked.

'Early evening is the best time to go,' said Madeleine, whose cheeks were glowing from both sun and exercise. 'I relish my daily stroll. It makes me feel so alive but at the same time exhausted!' She went to the table and helped herself to a glass of wine and a crostini. 'This revives me,' she added, sipping the wine. 'The end to a perfect day.'

Wendy, Tiff and Brigitte were dressed in miniskirts, strappy sandals and sparkly tops. They had repainted their nails on both hands and feet and were fully made-up as if off to a night-club. Carina did not imagine there to be a single nightclub in Colladoro, but she was obviously wrong. 'Ilaria has told us there's a club by the sea in a place called . . .' Wendy looked to her friends for help. 'What is it called, Bee?'

'Mare something . . .' Brigitte replied.

Tiff laughed and waved her cigarette. 'Does it matter? The name won't mean anything. We have a taxi coming at ten. We thought it would be fun to have a proper night out.'

'While the cats are away,' said Wendy, a mischievous glint in her hazel eyes.

'You're all welcome to come if you like,' Brigitte suggested. 'The more the merrier.'

Carina wondered what Rufus would think of her going off to a nightclub without him. Somehow she didn't think he'd mind. But she declined anyway. 'The sun really takes it out of me,' she explained.

When Anastasia and Gracie appeared, the group were already making their way slowly to the table, escorted by Ilaria and the large shaggy dog who had decided to join them. Gracie was wearing the necklace Anastasia had given her and a green cardigan over her dress. She went straight to the dog and patted it. 'What is he called?' she asked Ilaria.

'Bernardo,' Ilaria replied. 'He belongs to Count Bassanelli.'

Carina, now beside them, took the opportunity to ask about their elusive host. 'Might we meet Count Bassanelli?' she asked. Gracie stopped breathing.

'The count is a very shy man,' said Ilaria, and Gracie sensed a change in the woman's demeanour, like air that grows cold with the prospect of rain. 'He keeps himself to himself.'

Carina sensed nothing. 'That's such a shame,' she said as Gracie took a breath. 'Though, it *is* strange not to be welcomed by our host.'

The smile did not waver on Ilaria's face, but her eyes betrayed a certain resolve. 'He just wants his guests to make his home *their* home,' she added.

'My business is in public relations and I can tell you, if he came and met his guests, and charmed them, it would do wonders for the success of this place.'

'Oh, I don't think he needs to do that, Carina. We are fully booked all summer,' Ilaria replied smoothly. Then, sensing Carina's disappointment and not wanting to indulge it, she changed the subject. 'The necklace your granddaughter gave you is lovely, Gracie.'

Carina spun round. 'Anastasia gave you a necklace?' she said.

Gracie ran her fingers over the beads. 'Yes, she did,' she replied softly. 'So sweet of her.'

Carina felt even more put out. 'Where did she buy it?'

'In the town,' Gracie replied.

'There's a lovely little boutique in Colladoro that sells necklaces and bracelets in every colour,' Ilaria rejoined. 'You should go and have a look, Carina. They are not expensive.'

'Anastasia has never bought *me* anything,' said Carina. Then she laughed cheerlessly to show that she wasn't really offended. 'But that's no surprise. She's cross with me most of the time.'

Ilaria looked at her with sympathy. 'Teenagers are always cross with their mothers. But Italy will change that. You will see.' She spoke in a tone that suggested she had seen such changes occur hundreds of times yet never tired of it. 'You are eating pasta now, no?' she said to Carina. 'You see, Italy changes people from the inside out, which is the best way to be changed. Now, how shall we sit?' And she proceeded to place everyone around the table, taking care to mix it up so they all got to know each other.

Anastasia was seated between Wendy and Alex, which pleased her because she found Wendy hilarious and was growing increasingly fond of Alex. She looked at her watch and shivered in anticipation of the pleasure to come later, when she met Giovanni in the pool house. She glanced across at her mother, who was seated between Rex and Brigitte, and wondered what she would say if she knew she had lost her virginity to an Italian she'd only known for a handful of hours. The thought made her smile. She put her water glass to her lips to hide it. Then she shifted her gaze to her grandmother, who was talking to Rex, and decided that *she*, more than anyone else Anastasia knew, would understand. She'd never have imagined that her grandmother, who had seemed so timid and ordinary, yes, *ordinary*, would have lived such an *extraordinary* life. Watching her now, talking animatedly with the silver fox, the idea was not, after all, such a strange one. Gracie's eyes were caught by the flickering glow of the candles and shone prettily, and her smile, which came readily now, had a sweetness in it that was very attractive. Since arriving in Italy she had grown in stature. She was no longer a woman who was easily ignored. There was something about her that caught the eye. *Rex had certainly noticed*, Anastasia thought. She wondered whether old people in their late sixties were too ancient for romance, or whether the silver fox might have a go. *That* thought delighted her and she smiled again, only this time her glass was not big enough to hide it.

'What are you grinning at?' Alex asked, finding her amusement infectious and grinning too.

'I wonder whether Rex and my grandmother are about to have a little romance,' she said in a low voice.

Alex looked at them across the table. 'I wouldn't rule it out. They're both single. Both around the same age, and they clearly like each other.'

'I hope so. Just think, Granny might bring more than Mamma Bernadetta's recipes back to England.'

'It would be very appropriate. After all, we *are* in the most romantic country in the world,' he said and his gaze rested heavily upon her.

Anastasia thought of Giovanni and sighed as another shiver of anticipated pleasure rippled over her skin. 'Oh, it is. *So* romantic!'

'If you're looking for a little romance, you should come clubbing with us tonight,' Wendy, who had heard the tail-end of their conversation, cut in. 'What do you say? Are you on?'

'No, thank you,' Anastasia replied, a knowing smile hovering about her lips. 'I have all the entertainment I need right here.'

Wendy caught Alex's eye and raised an eyebrow suggestively. 'Good for you,' she said and took a swig of Mamma Bernadetta's home-made wine. 'As for us married girls, we're off to do a little window shopping. No harm in looking if there's no obligation to buy.'

Carina found herself alone with her thoughts as Brigitte was talking to Wendy, and Rex was giving all his attention to her mother. She was cross with herself for minding about the necklace. After all, Gracie was Anastasia's grandmother so why shouldn't she buy her a gift? But in spite of the logic her resentment niggled. She felt cheated somehow and yet she couldn't work out why. She swept her eyes over the table. Everyone was having fun. Anastasia was giggling with Alex, their heads together like a couple of conspirators; Gracie was being charmed by Rex; Brigitte and Wendy were having so much fun they were actually talking over one another and laughing uproariously (and a little drunkenly), Madeleine and Lauren were conversing quietly and down the other end Ilaria was telling an enraptured Tiff a story about a big Hollywood star who had taken the castle over for an entire ten days for a Hen week. Carina wondered grudgingly whether the count had deigned to put in an appearance for *her.*

Later, after she had changed for bed and Anastasia had gone swimming with Alex, she called Rufus to complain. 'Darling, you've never put Anastasia first,' he said bluntly, *and a little unkindly,* Carina thought, as she was already feeling sorry for herself. 'You can't drop your phone and your focus on the office and expect her to be grateful. It'll take time. Just spend some time with her. I can assure you she's longing for you to.'

'But she's in a constant clinch with Mum.'

'Because Gracie's giving her her attention.'

'She has nothing else to do,' Carina cut in sourly.

'And what do *you* have to do out there?'

'I've been on lovely long walks.'

'Alone?'

'Yes, but it's so beautiful.'

'While everyone else has been bonding, you've been wandering off on your own.'

'You're making it sound sad, but it's not sad at all. I've been experiencing an awakening. I think we should retire here one day.' The thought of settling in some quiet Tuscan crook lifted her spirits.

'Let's live that long first,' said Rufus.

'I've just realised that I've been on a treadmill for years.'

'Hallelujah!'

She laughed. 'I'm not saying I'm going to jump off, but I might slow it down a bit.'

He sighed. 'I'll believe it when I see it.'

There was a long pause. She could hear him breathing down the line. He yawned and she imagined him in bed with his reading glasses on and his magazine in his hands and suddenly felt a pang of longing. 'I wish you were here,' she said, surprised that she meant it. 'I feel left out with Mum and Anastasia behaving like a pair of schoolgirls.'

'If you can't beat 'em, join 'em,' he said, which was so typically pragmatic of him that she laughed again. 'Look, darling. It's great that you've seen the light about work, or something of it, at least, but you now have to put as much energy into your relationships as you did into your business.' It was only after she'd hung up that she realised he wasn't just talking about Gracie and Anastasia, but about himself. She climbed into bed and hugged her pillow. What was it about this place, she asked herself, that made her feel so unbalanced? It was as if Mamma Bernadetta's home-made olive oil was pouring into her emotional joints and loosening all her hinges. She closed her eyes and let sleep take her.

In the barn a short distance from Colladoro, Anastasia lay in Giovanni's arms, revelling in her new sense of womanhood. Everything about her romance with him was beautiful; from his tanned, athletic body, his long black eyelashes and sensual mouth, to the candles that turned the hay in the barn to gold. Every sentence he spoke was like a melody, holding within each graceful syllable the power to subjugate her. His deft hands, rough from gardening, yet tender on her skin, took her to great heights of pleasure, and during these moments of ecstasy she believed she loved him as much as any heroine has ever loved her hero.

Chapter 16

Badley Compton

Flappy Scott-Booth loved nothing more than a funeral, and *this* funeral was exactly the kind she loved the most. For one, the deceased was not a close relative or friend but someone for whom she could put on a grand display of grief without actually feeling anything at all. Secondly, the deceased had no living relatives (that anybody knew of) and yet was a beloved member of the Badley Compton community, hence the responsibility for the occasion fell onto *her* broad and certain shoulders, as the most senior member of the town. Thirdly, and arguably not as important as the other two, Harry Pratt had chosen to pass away in April so the garden was bursting forth with flowers and fresh green leaves and ready to be shown off to its best advantage. There was only one snag and that was the absence of her most reliable organiser, Gracie Burton.

Seated in her immaculate drawing room, clad in a black shift dress and short black cashmere cardigan, Flappy presided over the meeting in her usual assertive manner. She fixed the other women with her sharp and unforgiving gaze and challenged them to pull the event together in no less than ten days. 'Ladies, this is going to push us *all* to the limit, not least because of the heavy hearts we carry inside us.' She put her long manicured fingers to the diamond brooch pinned strategically above her heart and gave a mournful sigh. 'Forgive me, I've been hit very hard by Harry's death. He was a dear, *dear* man.' The four women looked at each other in bewilderment, not knowing what to say. It was always surprising (and a little embarrassing) when Flappy's stiff upper lip wobbled. 'He was cherished by everyone in our community,' she went on in a trembling voice. 'Therefore, it is up to us to give him the send-off he so rightly deserves.' Again, the steely blue gaze, resting on each woman individually. 'It's a case of all hands on deck.'

Madge put up her hand. 'May I?'

Flappy could tell by the subversive expression on Madge's face that she was going to be contrary. 'You may,' Flappy replied, tensing her jaw.

'Shouldn't we wait until Gracie is back? I mean, Harry's not going to go anywhere, is he, and Gracie is so good at this sort of event.'

'I'm sure we can manage without Gracie,' Flappy said, trying not to think of Gracie in beautiful, sunny Tuscany. The fact that she had gone, in spite of Flappy's endeavours to dissuade her, had stunned her, and Flappy hadn't yet got over it. She felt personally slighted, as if Gracie's leaving had been an outrageous act of subversion. And she hadn't even had the decency to inform her. One minute she was here in Badley Compton and the next she wasn't. Without so much as a word. Flappy had had to hear it from Esther, who had agreed to look after her dogs. 'As inconsiderate as she is,' said Flappy, pursing her lips. 'We are more than capable, are we not?'

Madge looked unconvinced. 'Well, for example, when

Judith Craddock passed away Gracie organised the service sheets. I'm not even sure where she got them from.'

Flappy didn't want to be bothered with details. She just wanted to give everyone their tasks and then leave them to get on with it. Before she had time to reply Mabel put up her hand. 'You really don't need to put up your hand,' said Flappy.

Mabel swiftly dropped it and nursed it in her lap as if it had been scalded. 'I think Gracie liaised with the undertaker and *he* had them printed,' she informed them helpfully. 'But I'm not sure who she used for flowers.'

'Did Gracie organise the flowers too?' Flappy turned to Sally. 'I thought *you* were in charge of the flowers,' she said in a tone that made Sally's teacup shake on its saucer.

Sally looked uncomfortable. 'Well, I *was*, but then my son had to go abroad on business and his wife decided to accompany him and they asked me to look after their children. I couldn't very well refuse, so Gracie came to my rescue . . .' Her voice trailed off as she thought of Gracie in Italy with a pang of envy.

'Well, that is very like Gracie, isn't it,' said Flappy approvingly. 'She's always there when one needs her—'

'Except when she isn't,' Esther cut in.

Flappy sighed. 'Except when she isn't,' she repeated, a little impatiently. How *could* Gracie have gone abroad now, when she needed her the most? 'Sally, you must rise to the occasion and adorn the church with flowers. It must look like we've made a great effort for Harry. I'd hate anyone to think that we cut corners or scrimped just because he was . . .' She searched for the word without success. 'He fought in the war so we must honour him as a hero,' she added with passion. Then her busy mind stilled suddenly and a brilliant idea popped in. Harry was a war hero which gave her the perfect excuse to invite all the local grandees: the mayor, for one, and Sir Algernon Micklethwaite, the local landowner, and his wife Phyllida, Lady Micklethwaite, who chaired the Women's Institute.

'Perhaps you can find a big model plane and arrange the flowers in that,' Madge suggested to Sally, pleased with her idea.

Flappy's reverie was abruptly interrupted. 'A model plane?' she exclaimed in horror. 'Really, Madge, have a sense of decorum. This is going to be a *tasteful* funeral.' Madge glowered into her china cup. 'I will host the tea here at Darnley afterwards and everyone is welcome. With any luck the sun will shine and we can use the garden, Lady Micklethwaite has always been very kind about my garden. I will put up a marquee in case of rain. I don't want people wandering in and out of my house in wet shoes! Of course the mayor and the Micklethwaites must use the facilities inside. Kenneth plays golf with the managing director of Berry Brothers so we'll get the wine and hire glasses from there. Big Mary can make cupcakes . . .'

'We could perhaps put planes on those,' said Madge, not to be deterred. The other women thought it a splendid idea, but hid their opinions until Flappy had given hers.

'Well, if you do insist on having a theme, I can't stop you, though I honestly feel it's a little common.'

'But Harry *was* common,' said Sally – *and so are we*, she thought, glancing at Madge, Mabel and Esther for support.

'He was ordinary, for certain, but he had dignity.' Flappy sipped her tea. An awkward silence fell over the small group as they considered Harry's ordinariness. 'Very well, Sally, *you* can tell Big Mary to make cupcakes with pictures of planes on them in icing and arrange the flowers. Esther, *you* can help Big Mary organise the tea and the hiring of crockery. Mabel, *you* can organise the marquee and find some young men to serve the wine and tea. Madge, *you* can liaise with the undertaker and organise the service sheets.'

'And what will *you* do?' Madge asked.

Flappy inhaled through dilated nostrils and gave a supercilious smile. '*I* will decide what goes *on* the service sheets,' she replied. After all, *she* was the only one with any taste in music and literature. 'And of course Kenneth and I are only too happy to pay for it,' she added, which reminded everyone in the room not only of the Scott-Booths' superiority but of their right to call the shots. How apt was the proverb, 'He who pays the piper calls the tune.'

The four women left with their assignments, anxious that, without Gracie's help, they might not rise to the challenge as Flappy had instructed them to do. Flappy, happy to leave them to do all the work, though a little apprehensive of their abilities, closed the front door behind them with a sigh. As she walked back through the hall she admired the extravagant display of white lilies that swamped the antique round table and hoped that the women had been impressed. She had claimed the flowers came from her greenhouses, but in reality Karen had driven into Barnstaple to buy them. Flappy dallied a moment in front of an enormous mirror suspended on chains between a pair of portraits of herself and Kenneth by the famous artist Jonathan Yeo. She compared her reflection in the mirror to her likeness in the painting, completed five years before, and studied her skin for signs of age. Jonathan had omitted her hair, gorgeously thick and glossy though it was, and rendered her face looming out of the canvas like a medieval Madonna on an unfinished fresco. He had given her skin a golden glow – she recalled they had just been around the Aegean Islands on a yacht that summer, so her suntan was real – and her eyes a patina of indigo blue, like the sea. She examined the real thing, which she nurtured with expensive products and treatments, resisting the temptation to succumb to cosmetic surgery because she was yet to find a surgically altered face that didn't betray the surgeon's knife. *She looked natural and beautiful still*, she thought; a paragon of the gracefully ageing face. Satisfied that time had been generous – and secretly thrilled that it hadn't been so generous to Esther, Mabel, Madge and Sally, nor Gracie, for that matter – Flappy wandered into the library and pulled down a box file of old service sheets from funerals she had attended. In there she would find her poems and readings, her hymns and prayers. She would invite the vicar to lunch and tell him what she wanted then Madge could arrange with the undertaker for it to be printed. Would it be too much to put at the end of the service sheet, in small yet visible print: *With thanks to Flappy Scott-Booth for generously giving Harry this beautiful send-off*?

She took the box into the drawing room and sank into an armchair. It wouldn't take long to find a few appropriate poems for Harry's friends to read – though, if the mayor and Sir Algernon and Lady Micklethwaite were going to attend she'd have to be careful to choose the most suitable among them to have the honour of standing at the lectern. She knew Harry had liked to prop up the bar at the Bell and Dragon and shoot the breeze with the other codgers who frequented that place. He'd also whiled away the hours at Big Mary Timpson's. Flappy had asked around and no one knew of any relations. He'd never married or had children and, as far as Flappy could tell, had lived a solitary and lonely life in his tiny seafront cottage in Badley Compton, where he'd settled after the war. He'd enjoyed telling stories of his heroics over the English Channel and was once featured in an article that Gracie's late husband Ted had written for some obscure local magazine. She wondered how Harry had earned a living, but judging by his modest home and simple needs he'd clearly required very little to survive. She'd found out with a bit of subtle digging that he'd left a will and appointed a solicitor called Mr Banks to be the executor of it. She didn't think it would take very long to sort out Harry Pratt's affairs. *What a sad life he'd lived*, she thought smugly, reflecting on the full and colourful life *she* led. *Well, I'll give him a good farewell party*, she thought, opening the first service sheet. *The poor old thing deserves nothing less than that.*

Kenneth returned from the golf course in time for dinner. A pompous, portly man with a full head of grey hair swept off a low forehead and small, weaselly eyes, Kenneth Scott-Booth was a man with a very high opinion of himself. He loved golf more than anything and believed that, after having worked hard and made his fortune, he was well within his rights to play as much golf as he liked. Flappy didn't complain, as long as he wrote the cheques enabling her to live like a queen, she was happy. 'Flappy!' he shouted as he strode into the hall in a pair of primrose-yellow tattersall breeches and matching yellow cashmere V-neck sweater stretched over a ballooning stomach. 'Flappy!'

'In the drawing room,' she shouted back, reluctant to get out of the armchair.

A moment later Kenneth marched in. 'There you are!' he boomed.

'Yes, here I am,' she trilled.

He kissed her upturned cheek. 'Why are you wearing black?'

Flappy, who had changed into mourning clothes after lunch

in preparation for her meeting, replied, 'For Harry Pratt, darling. I have to set an example.'

'Ah.'

She looked him up and down. 'Nothing sombre about *your* attire.'

'*I'm* not the one setting an example.' He helped himself to a glass of whisky at the bar he had designed specifically for that purpose and perched on the edge of the club fender, knees wide, belly bulging, a man who was very much king of his kingdom.

'Did you have a good game?' she asked.

'Bloody marvellous, darling! I'm not one to boast, but I played a blinder. Two birdies, one eagle and thrashed Paul Biddling four and three. I bumped into Reg Halliday and Jimmy Brennan on the second hole, d'you remember them?'

'Of course, Reg Halliday made a fortune in packaging then lost half of it when he divorced Glenda, and Jimmy Brennan's done rather well for himself building car parks, if I remember rightly. He has a rather sweet wife called Trudy or Tilly or Tiggy or something.'

'Tamsin,' Kenneth replied, swirling the ice round his glass. 'Thought we might invite them over for dinner one evening.'

'Lovely, I'll throw something together, nothing grand, just a little soirée. I might get that quartet from Exeter again. They were terrific.'

'Reg has a new wife.'

'Really?' Flappy didn't imagine he'd gone for another old trout like Glenda.

'She's thirty-five, young enough to be his daughter, dirty devil.' Kenneth chuckled.

Flappy's lips pursed. 'How very inappropriate. I'm not going to be seen condoning *that* kind of relationship. I think we'll just have Jimmy and whatever she's called. You can keep "dirty devil" to yourself.'

Kenneth swigged his whisky. 'I see you're organising Harry's funeral.'

Flappy sighed as if she was really much too busy to take on yet another chore. 'I fear I am the only one in town who is capable of doing it, and *willing* to do it. Dear Harry had no relatives and his friends aren't up to putting together something like this. Once again, it falls upon *me* to see that things are done properly.'

'You're a saint,' said Kenneth, without any hint of irony. 'What would Badley Compton do without you?'

'I don't think they'd do very well at all.' Flappy closed the box, keeping out a few useful service sheets. 'Though I do wish Gracie were here to help. Extraordinary that she, who's never been anywhere, goes somewhere at the very moment she's most needed.'

'Do you have to give him an elaborate funeral? Can't you just leave the vicar to say a few appropriate words?'

Flappy's face crinkled into a compassionate smile. 'Darling, you know me. I'm much too generous-hearted for my own good. Harry was a war hero and beloved by the whole community. It's only right that we celebrate his life with a beautiful service. I just won't feel good about myself if I allow his life to be dismissed without any sort of ceremony.'

'My darling, you are indeed right. And you're so good at arranging these things.'

'I'm not one to boast, but I do have good taste. Goodness, if I were to leave it to those hopeless women we'd have flowers in model planes and God knows what other tackiness besides. If only Gracie hadn't gone to Italy. At least she could be relied upon to get things done.' Then her face crinkled again into a worried smile. 'I do fear for her so far from home. People like Gracie Burton ought never to stray too far from the hearth.'

The following morning dawned bright and sunny. Seagulls glided beneath puffs of vaporous cloud and Flappy watched them for a moment from her bedroom window and thought of Harry, flying his Spitfire in the heavenly sky. Dressed in black with a sorrowful expression worn heavily upon her face, she drove into town in her shiny green Range Rover. She wanted to give the locals the benefit of her grief, and buy a few essentials at the chemist at the same time. Her first port of call was Big Mary's, because that was where Harry was always to be found, either there or in the Bell and Dragon. To her delight the café was full of locals. John Hitchens was at the counter in a pair of faded Bermuda shorts and polo shirt, his grey hair wild as if he'd already been out on a boat. His granddaughter, in a floral sundress and flip-flops, was busy deciding which pastry to choose, while Big Mary was making a cup of coffee and a hot chocolate and managing to hold a few conversations at once. Every table was occupied, the air pleasantly sweet and stuffy, and a couple of scruffy dogs lay sleeping on the wooden floor, their fur wet and salty. There was an atmosphere of gaiety and laughter in the café, until Flappy walked in looking like the grim reaper and the gaiety deflated like a soufflé and the laughter fizzled out. All eyes watched her walk slowly to the counter.

'Good morning, Mrs Scott-Booth,' said Big Mary, putting the cup of coffee and hot chocolate on the counter for John Hitchens. 'What can I do you for?'

'I wish it were a good morning,' said Flappy, pressing a hand to her heart. She paused for effect, delighted to have the attention of everyone in the café. 'Wherever I turn I expect to see dear Harry.'

'Oh yes,' Big Mary exclaimed, suddenly working out why Mrs Scott-Booth was dressed in black and adopting a mournful air. 'We're all very sad at his passing,' she said, which was true, she'd known Harry all her life and in recent years, since she'd owned the café, barely a day had gone by when he hadn't popped in for a double espresso with whipped cream.

'He used to sit on that bench out there, watching the boats. I think I'm going to dedicate a bench to him,' Flappy decided, already picturing the inscription: *In loving memory of Harry Pratt, from Kenneth and Flappy Scott-Booth*. 'It would be a lovely way for the community to remember him, don't you think?'

'Oh, that would be nice,' said Big Mary.

'However, as sad as it is, there is always a silver lining to every grey cloud. At times like these the community is brought together. There is strength to be found in sharing one's grief.'

'Indeed,' Big Mary agreed. 'Why don't I make you a strong coffee? That'll lift your spirits. And a croissant? Freshly baked this morning.'

'I won't have anything, thank you, Mary. I just popped in to find out whether Sally has been in to discuss the cupcakes for his funeral.'

Big Mary smiled excitedly. 'Oh, he's to have a proper funeral, is he? With cakes and tea?'

Flappy frowned. 'Hasn't Esther spoken to you yet?'

'No, I've not seen her.'

'Really, that is very frustrating.' If it were Gracie's duty, she'd have spoken to Big Mary first thing, Flappy thought crossly.

'Would you like me to do the tea and cakes? Harry was especially fond of my cakes.'

'Well, Esther is meant to be in charge of that. I'm just the conductor, my ladies are the orchestra, but I fear they're not concentrating terribly well on the score!' Flappy didn't realise that somewhere after 'conductor' she had lost Big Mary.

'How lovely that Harry's going to get a proper funeral with tea and cakes and all,' she said, ignoring the confusing metaphor.

'I thought it only right that a war hero, such as Harry was, should be celebrated. Kenneth and I are opening the doors of Darnley for the occasion and Harry's friends are welcome.'

'There'll be plenty of people then. We were all friends of Harry Pratt.'

'That's why I felt it my duty to give him a proper send-off.'

'I'll be happy to make the tea and cakes.'

'Well, I don't want to step on Esther's toes. She's arranging all of that. So, can I leave you both to it? Esther knows the score. I'm sure she'll be in later today to talk it over with you.'

'I could make cakes in the shape of boats.'

Flappy looked doubtful. 'Planes, you mean.'

'No, boats. Harry loved boats. That's why he sat on that bench. He liked to watch the boats coming in and out of the harbour. He made model ships. His house was full of them.' *Anyone who knew Harry knew he liked boats*, Big Mary thought. 'Are you arranging the service?' she asked. 'Because I'd love to read something. A poem or a prayer, anything. I'd like to honour him in some way, if I may.'

Flappy lifted her chin. She didn't think it appropriate for Big Mary to stand at the lectern. Her platinum-blonde hair was quite a sight, and as for her size ... If the mayor and Sir Algernon and Lady Micklethwaite were going to come Flappy would need to find someone with more class. Someone who knew how to read in front of a congregation, someone who spoke the Queen's English. Then it struck her. Of course, why hadn't she thought about it before? *She,* Flappy Scott-Booth, was the perfect person to deliver the poem and do it justice.

'Thank you for offering, Mary, but cakes will be more than enough. You can honour him with those.' With that she left the café.

'Grandpa,' whispered the little girl.

'Yes, Lara?' said John Hitchens.

'Was that lady Cruella De Vil?'

Chapter 17

Italy, 1963

It snowed in December. The Tuscan hills were instantly transformed by a smooth coating of ever-changing colour. Pinky-grey in the mornings, golden in the afternoons, indigo in the hollows where the sun didn't reach and midnight blue in the light of the moon. Gracie never grew tired of the beauty and every morning, when she opened her shutters and threw wide the windows, she filled her lungs with the crisp, cold air and the sheer joy of the landscape.

The studio at La Colomba was full of Bruno and Livia Montefosco's paintings, including Tancredi's *The Temptation of Eve*. Gracie knew she would have to wait for Uncle Hans to go away again in order to copy it. She didn't think he'd approve of her plan. *That* wasn't the kind of criminal activity he was used to and she knew he'd dissuade her if she confided in him. However, Uncle Hans had no intention of travelling before Christmas. *The Temptation of Eve* and Tancredi would have to wait.

Since acquiring his beloved painting Tancredi seemed more in love with Gracie than ever. The pleasure she had derived from pleasing him was dizzying. She couldn't wait to complete the forgery so that he could take the real one home. In the meantime, they regularly made love in the tower, indulging in fantasies where there was no place for doubts and obstacles barring their future happiness. Petronella did not exist in their cosy hideaway, only the two of them and the imaginary world they had created. The Castello was deserted for the winter months with only Bagwis in residence as caretaker, but he was discreet and knew not to bother them, save to make sure there was always food in the fridge in the castle kitchen. The countess would not be back until spring.

At the end of December Uncle Hans took Gracie to London for Christmas. He had business to attend to there and he knew Gracie wanted to see her mother. Rutger travelled to Holland and La Colomba, like the Castello, was locked up and left swathed in snow.

England was enduring the worst winter in years. Gracie left a snow-covered landscape only to arrive in yet another, one decidedly less appealing. Smog choked the London air as coal fires burned constantly. The roads were icy, the trees crippled with cold, the winds bitter, blowing into the country all the way from Russia. Gracie's feelings about her home were always conflicted. She loved seeing her mother and brother yet the reality of being a guest in the house that had once been her home made her feel sad. She felt Oma's absence keenly and hated the change that had come over the place. It looked the same and smelt the same and yet it wasn't the same, because she had grown up and moved on and no longer felt the same attachment to it. As a child she hadn't noticed how shabby it was. She hadn't noticed the peeling paint and the odd corner of the room that was stained with damp. She hadn't seen the tired old furniture and the threadbare rugs because she hadn't had anything with which to compare them. Now she had experienced the grandeur of the Castello and La Colomba her mother's house had become intolerably worn-out. She didn't understand why her uncle, with all his money and fine things, didn't help his sister more. Gracie sent her mother money whenever Uncle Hans paid her for her forgeries, and yet the state her mother lived in was still dire. How was it that she didn't have the means to paint the house, fix the damp, buy the odd new piece of furniture? It wasn't until Christmas Day, when she, her mother and Uncle Hans went to Joseph's new house, situated in a more elegant part of town, that she realised where the money was going.

Joseph had married the local girl he had been seeing when Gracie had last been in London. She was a sweet, mousy young woman with a snub nose and big brown eyes and Gracie could see why he liked her. She didn't challenge him like Gracie had, but looked up to him and admired him and agreed with everything he said. She kept the house immaculate to the point of obsession. There was not an ornament out of place, or a rug laid crookedly on the floor. The cushions were plump, the surfaces shiny, the walls painted and papered, there was even a television in the front room. Joseph was keen to show off his new life to his uncle and sister. He sat smoking in a leather armchair beside the hearty fire while his wife basted the turkey, cooking to perfection in the new Belling oven he had bought for her, and boasted about his job in a local advertising firm where he was sure he was soon to be promoted to account manager. While Gracie was pleased for him, she felt guilty, for like her he was enjoying a standard of living their mother could only dream of. Yet Greet was almost bursting with pride. It was she who showed Gracie around the house, pointing out the small luxuries Gracie now took for granted.

'Why don't you keep more of the money we send you for

yourself?' she asked as her mother showed her the baby-blue bathroom suite.

'I don't need much,' Greet replied, running her fingers along the smooth rim of the sink. 'Isn't this fine, Gracie? Your father would be so proud to see what Joseph has become. I used to despair of him when he worked at the hardware shop, but then Hans managed to secure him a job at the advertising agency, and a very good job it is too. There is opportunity to climb there. Who knows where he might be in ten years. He will be able to give his children a better life than I was able to give you.'

'So, he earns well. There's no need for you to subsidise his wages.'

Greet lowered her voice. 'Oh, he is full of big talk, but the truth is he doesn't earn much at all. Of course he will, eventually. But Susan is pregnant – no, don't say I told you. It is a secret. She only found out last week and it is early days. But they are going to have a family. I am going to be a grandmother.' Her smile was so full of joy that something gave in Gracie's heart. She put her arms around her.

'Mother, I am so happy,' she said.

Her mother held her at arm's length. 'And what about you, Gracie? You are not getting any younger. It is time you found a nice man and settled down. You wrote about Donato but now you don't mention him at all.' She frowned. 'Is there no one? Are you getting out enough? Is Hans working you too hard? You have to get out and meet people. I will tell Hans. It is his responsibility. You must marry before you get too old, then no one will want you.'

Gracie longed to tell her about Tancredi, but she couldn't. It would break her to know that her daughter was having an affair with a married man. She looked at her mother's concerned face and wanted to assuage her anxiety. 'There *is* a man, Mother, but I have only just met him. Don't tell Uncle Hans.'

Greet's eyes brightened and her anxiety was swiftly alleviated. 'Is he handsome like your father was? Is he honest? Does he earn a good living? Can he look after you?'

Gracie laughed. 'He is all of those things.'

'I knew it!' Greet's delight made Gracie feel guilty. 'You are not beautiful but you are intelligent and good. If I were a man I'd be suspicious of a beautiful woman. She might run off with a younger man in years to come. But *you* can be relied on, Gracie. Any man would be lucky to be married to you.'

Gracie was happy to return to Italy and into the arms of the man who believed her beautiful.

❧

It wasn't long after Christmas that Uncle Hans went away again. Gracie set to work on the forgery at once, painting in the evenings when Rutger had retired to his cottage, and toiling away well into the early hours of the morning. She enjoyed those still, silent evenings. There was something familiar and reassuring about them. Alone in the studio she lost herself in her work and time became irrelevant, until tiredness alerted her to the lateness of the hour and the need for sleep.

Forging a seventeenth-century painting was a highly complicated process. Unlike fifteenth-century painters who used egg tempera, which was easy to emulate, Golden Age artists like Vermeer, Rembrandt and Frans Hals painted in oils, which hardened over the centuries to a consistency the forger was unable to achieve due to lack of time. It only took a dab of alcohol to expose the modern forger's brush. Hans had originally used a medium of gelatin-glue, which was unaffected by alcohol but did go soft in water, which rendered it inadequate. Then he learned from another master forger who was an expert in the chemistry of paint to use Bakelite. Bakelite was an early plastic used during the 1920s and 1930s to make brightly coloured costume jewellery, kitchenware and toys. When dry this product was impervious to anything. For Hans Hollingsworth, the discovery of this medium was a turning point in his career. He ground period-appropriate pigments into liquid Bakelite then painted it onto recycled seventeenth-century canvases. When the film hardened it mimicked to perfection an oil-paint surface hundreds of years old. In this way, he was able to forge Golden Age Dutch masters with great success. However, Bakelite was incredibly hard to use in painting and Gracie had not yet got to grips with it. She did not think it mattered. Piero Bartoloni's *The Temptation of Eve* was simply going to hang on a wall in Bruno and Livia Montefosco's house in Rome, so a good copy in oils would suffice, and it would be easy to find a matching frame, Uncle Hans's studio was full of old frames in every size. An expert would most certainly notice the difference, but Bruno and Livia were not experts.

Gracie took more pleasure from copying the voluptuous Eve and the serpent than she had taken with any previous work. The way Eve's expression conveyed a mixture of desire and fear fascinated her, the way the soft light drew her out of the murky forest and caught the head of the wicked snake, luring her into temptation. Eve's body was curvaceous, fecund, ripe, like the rosy apple on the branch above the serpent, crying out to be picked. Her lips were parted, one white hand on her breast, the other reaching out with graceful fingers, the folds of the gown that barely covered her falling away, like her innocence.

It wasn't just the painting that enthralled Gracie but the knowledge of who she was painting it for. Her love for Tancredi propelled every stroke and into her work she poured her heart. A solitary month it might have been as Tancredi was in Rome and she was busy restoring during the day and copying during the night. And yet she was content. *The Temptation of Eve* linked her to Tancredi and the tranquillity fed her soul.

The painting took Gracie five weeks to complete. Uncle Hans returned in the middle with more mysterious canvases wrapped in brown paper and her nightly activity had to be put on hold, but then he went away again, this time to Antwerp, and she was able to resume. When Tancredi returned to the Castello at the end of February he telephoned Gracie and discovered, to his excitement, that the painting was finished.

Gracie didn't have to hide her affair from Rutger, but she did have to hide the painting. As Tancredi was coming to pick her up in his car she didn't want to be seen leaving the villa with a suspicious package, so she sneaked down to the bottom of the garden and hid it beneath a bush, close to where the drive passed a little further down the slope. When Tancredi turned up she was able to greet him with nothing but a small leather handbag. She didn't imagine Rutger was watching – the studio was at the back of the villa and he wasn't the kind of man to pry into other people's affairs – but she felt so guilty for deceiving him that she wanted him to see her, just to ease her own conscience.

Once out of sight of the villa she told Tancredi to stop the car. She jumped out and scampered up the snowy bank. She reached out and withdrew the canvas from beneath the bush. 'You are devious!' Tancredi said, watching her climb back into the car with the painting, her coat dusted with white. Her face was flushed with both excitement and guilt, burning through the cold. 'You're not betraying your uncle Hans or Rutger, you know,' he said softly. 'You're cheating my uncle because I've asked you to. Let *me* be the one to carry a guilty conscience.' He leaned across the gear stick and kissed her. 'Thank you,' he said.

'You haven't seen it yet.'

'I know it will be exactly like the original.'

'I'm flattered that you have so much faith in me.'

He laughed. 'I can read you, Gracie. If it wasn't good, you wouldn't be looking so happy.'

They drove to the castle. It was a grey, cloudy afternoon. Snow still clung to the valley in pools of indigo while, on the crests of the hills, the wind had blown it away in patches. The streets of Colladoro were quiet, but had they been seen together it wouldn't have raised so much as an eyebrow for it was common knowledge that Gracie was teaching Tancredi to paint – and besides, no one would have imagined a girl like Gracie had what it took to catch the eye of the count.

Once in the tower Tancredi unwrapped the canvas. Piero Bartoloni's *The Temptation of Eve* was revealed with all the character and charm of the original. Tancredi was so surprised by the exactness of the copy that he was suddenly fearful that she hadn't copied it at all but given him the real one. She saw the look on his face and blanched. 'You don't like it?' she asked.

'Are you sure this is the copy?'

'Of course, I'm sure.'

'But I can't tell the difference.'

Gracie smiled with relief. 'You're not meant to see the difference.'

'I know, but I didn't think it would be so exact, so perfect.'

'If it is so exact and perfect, why don't you keep the copy

and leave them with the original.' Gracie didn't know why she hadn't thought of that before. If he kept the copy she'd have done nothing untoward. It wouldn't even be considered a forgery.

'Because I want my uncle to have a fake. Just knowing that he has a fake in his collection will give me pleasure.' Tancredi turned to Gracie, eyes shining. 'My grandfather promised me that painting, Gracie, and I will have it, come what may.'

'Very well,' she said, heart sinking at the thought of slipping a fake into Bruno and Livia's collection right under her uncle's nose. 'I will swap them.'

❦

The challenge of swapping the paintings was not a physical one, for that part was easy and anyone with an ounce of guile could do it, but an emotional one. Gracie did not feel happy about keeping such a secret from Uncle Hans and Rutger even though the truth would probably never come to light. The forgery would remain undiscovered in the Montefosco palace in Rome and no one would ever know of it. The only person to derive any pleasure from knowing was Tancredi, but to Gracie *he* was the only person who mattered. However, in the weeks that followed, while she worked with Rutger on the cleaning and restoring of the other paintings in the Montefosco collection, her guilt fed on itself and grew. And in the shadow of it she was able to see her uncle and Rutger not only with her eyes but with her heart, and she realised how much she loved them both.

Spring brought warm days and chilly nights and the countryside was transformed once again into the bright greens, reds and yellows that Gracie was so fond of. Tancredi hid his painting in the tower, nailed to the back of a wardrobe behind jackets and shirts and coats. When she watched him open the doors, part the clothes and gaze in wonder on his beloved painting, those were the only times her guilt lifted. In those moments, she was at peace with herself and what she had done.

She was relieved, when, at the end of June, the paintings were ready to be returned to Rome. With Gaia's help she and Rutger wrapped and crated them and sent them off in a van. Gracie was happy to see them go, knowing that her forgery was among them and no longer in the house, waiting to betray her. Livia Montefosco telephoned Uncle Hans. They spoke for a long while. When at last he hung up he reported that she was delighted with their work and had invited him to come to Rome at the earliest to discuss how to enhance her already prestigious collection. This time Gracie was not included. She was relieved. As far as *she* was concerned the Montefosco matter was closed.

It was not long after Hans returned from Rome that he suggested Gracie join him for a drink in the garden. It was a balmy, golden evening. The sweet scents of the lavender and honeysuckle lingered in the still, humid air and only the twittering of roosting birds gave a sense of movement to an otherwise tranquil scene. They sat on the terrace, she on the wicker sofa, he in the armchair, one leg crossed over the other to reveal a red spotted sock. The smoke from his cigarette filled the space around them and kept the midges away. Gracie had grown to like the smell of it for it was familiar and it was Hans. 'I need to talk to you,' he said, picking up his wine glass and taking a sip. The gold signet ring on his little finger glinted in the last rays of sun.

'What do you want to talk to me about?' she asked, her guilty conscience rising into her chest to poison the happiness there.

'My will,' he replied.

'Oh.' The relief was palpable.

'Now, it's been nine years since you came to La Colomba. During that time, you have worked hard. I could not have asked you to work harder. I could not have asked you to be more pleasant or more helpful.' He settled his intense blue eyes on her and smiled with tenderness. 'Had you been my daughter I could not have asked for a more delightful one. So, I feel it is only fair to fill you in on a few truths.' He took another sip. Gracie took one too. She liked the taste of chilled white wine and it relaxed her. She couldn't imagine the truths he was about to divulge, for surely, she knew them already. 'Now, you and I have many secrets.' At that the image of Guido Vanni on his knees in front of Uncle Hans floated distastefully into her mind. She blinked it away as Uncle Hans went on. 'But I feel you are ready to know a few more. Long before I came to La Colomba I worked as an art dealer in Amsterdam. During the war we were occupied by the Germans. I did not sympathise with them, but' – he shrugged – 'a man must do what he can to survive. I sold paintings to them in the same way that I sold paintings to my fellow countrymen. The trouble was that during that time the Germans were the only ones with the means to buy. I was already in the business of forgery. But it was not because of that that I had to leave Holland after the war, but because I had been seen to be collaborating with the enemy. I came here to Italy with Rutger and started afresh. Now, there are many forgers out there – you can wander into a grocer's or a second-hand shop and find a crude van Ostade tavern scene or a Jan Fyt game-and-fowl still life, but they are very quickly revealed as fakes – you see, few aim as high as me and have the skill to carry it off. So, I began to make money, serious money, but what is a man to do with all that money?

It cannot just be left to accumulate. I needed to put it into *things*. The most obvious thing to put it into is property. So, I began to buy properties abroad. As well as La Colomba, I have a villa in the South of France, a house in Spain, an apartment in Paris, a chalet in the Swiss mountains and a beach house in Norway. You may wonder why I am telling you this. Well, I have no children of my own. You and Joseph are the closest to children I am ever going to get. I have made a will and left all my property to you and your brother.'

Gracie was astonished. She had not expected this. 'Uncle Hans, I want to say thank you, but those properties will only come to me when you are dead and I don't want to think of you dying.'

He laughed and stubbed out his cigarette in the glass ashtray on the table, and with his long, elegant fingers, he lit another. 'My dear child, death comes to all of us, it is just a question of when. If the natural order is maintained *I* will go before *you*. Therefore, it is only wise to leave my wealth to you.'

'Have you provided for Mother?'

'Greet?' He shook his head. 'She is a complicated woman, my sister. You may wonder why I have not bought a property in London for her to live in.'

'I don't wonder about that because she wouldn't want to live anywhere but in the house my father bought her.'

'Correct, but the truth is your mother disapproves of what I do.'

Gracie was quick to disagree. 'Oh, she doesn't. She's so proud of you . . .' She remembered her mother reading out his letters to her grandmother and the excited way in which they had discussed him for hours.

Hans blew out a cloud of smoke. 'She didn't want me to bring you to Italy because she knew what I was going to teach you to do. But she couldn't refuse. She knew I would give you a better life than she could and she depended on me for survival. She only accepts the money I give her because she has to, and she accepts only the minimum. If I had my way she'd be living in Mayfair in a mansion with a maid and a butler, but she won't have it. I suppose I should admire her. On the other hand, I could condemn her as foolish.'

'She's proud,' said Gracie.

'Too proud to know what's good for her,' he added. 'Now, there is another thing I need to talk to you about, something a little more delicate.'

Gracie couldn't imagine what that was, but now her fear was gone. She drained her glass, enjoying the light-headed feeling the wine had given her, and looked at him expectantly. 'Go on,' she said.

'You work hard, probably too hard for a girl of your age. I have not indulged you with holidays in glamorous places nor introduced you to eligible men. In fact, I have been selfish and kept you to myself.' Gracie felt a blush spread over her face. 'That is my fault and I am going to put it right. It is time you started thinking about settling down.'

Gracie was embarrassed. For some reason discussing romance with Uncle Hans felt awkward. It was like speaking a language that he didn't really understand. 'Uncle Hans, I have no desire to get married.'

'Whatever happened to that nice boy Donato?'

She laughed. 'That ended a long time ago and he's married now.'

'You see, I have been neglecting you.'

'Please don't think that you have. To the contrary, I live here like a princess. You bring me beautiful dresses to wear. I want for nothing. In fact, you spoil me too much.'

'I'm not talking about spoiling you, my dear. I'm talking about finding you a husband. It is my duty as your guardian to secure your future.'

'What if I don't want to marry? *You* haven't married.'

'It is a very different matter when it comes to a man, Gracie. You are clever enough to know that. A woman needs a man and one day I will not be around to look after you.'

'I will have half of your fortune. I think I'll be more than capable of looking after myself.'

He chuckled. 'You are right and much too clever for your own good. Don't you want to have children?'

'Yes, I would like children one day,' she replied softly, but she didn't want to have children with anyone else but Tancredi.

'Then take my advice and let me assist you. We depart for the Côte d'Azur in a week.'

Chapter 18

Italy, 2010

Gracie awoke to the clamour of birds. She lay with her eyes closed and her ears alert and allowed the sound to absorb her. *It could have been forty-four years ago,* she thought, lying in bed at the top of the tower with Tancredi sleeping beside her. She remembered those dawns when the glow of the rising sun was just a blush on the horizon. The first bird would tweet, a solitary call breaking through the darkness. Then the second followed by the third until the trio of song became a cacophony as the males loudly marked their territory and attracted their mates. It was Tancredi who had told her about the dawn chorus and what it meant, before him she had always assumed it was female birds, going about building their nests. Now she listened to it and felt the melancholy that came with it wash over her.

When it was over and the racket had died down Gracie sat up. It was five in the morning, too early to rise and yet she didn't feel tired. She climbed out of bed and walked to the window. She had left the shutters open so that the scents of the garden could waft into her room. Standing at the sill she watched the Tuscan landscape slowly reveal itself as the sun peered gingerly over the skyline, lifting the curtain on the theatre of life. The indigo blue of night-time was gradually replaced by a gentle pink hue, the velvet-green fields and hills emerging out of the mist as the sun rose higher.

Gripped by an urgent longing to be outside Gracie dressed in a rush, pulling a cardigan over her blouse because the mornings at this time of year were still a little cool. She tiptoed down the corridor and crept out by the library door. The tower stood on the incline like a sleeping sentinel, shirking his duties. She could almost see Tancredi standing in the doorway, a paintbrush in his hand, a smile on his face, a twinkle in his eyes that reassured her of his love and playfully warned her of his intent. But as she passed it she saw only the inky residues of the night.

She walked down the grassy path towards the chapel, leaving a trail of footprints in the dew. The smell of roses hung sweet and thick in the air and she inhaled it appreciatively. How that smell took her back. How it lifted her spirits, as if it had the power to erase all that was negative inside her. Her step became almost a skip. It was impossible not to feel happy in the midst of such beauty. Even her memories were stripped of their potency and sparkled like the dew. Every corner of this place inspired nostalgia and yet, this morning, nothing made her sad. She felt lucky to have loved, lucky to have lived. In spite of how it had ended she felt blessed to have had another chance to see the castle and to revive something of the girl she had once been. It was like opening a book that is near the end at the beginning again and rereading the best parts. She had come to see Tancredi, of course she had, but she had also come to find the part of herself she had left here, and, in a way, she had found it. She could return to England if not wholly satisfied, pleased at least that she had come.

She found the chapel unlocked and wandered inside. It was chilly and damp and smelt the same as it had when she and Rutger had catalogued the countess's paintings. It didn't look as if anyone had been inside since those days except to clean. The count obviously used the place to store things, for there were pieces of furniture and sealed boxes. She took her time, walking slowly around, running her fingers over the walls, the back of a chair, the surface of a table, rousing the ghosts and watching them come to life with her mind's eye. She wondered what had become of Rutger. She could imagine him there, his hair curling about his ears, his face wise and intelligent and full of character, looking over the countess's paintings, eyes gleaming as each new work was revealed. She thought he had been old then but he must have only been in his fifties. Uncle Hans had seemed old to her too, but he had only been in his forties. Now as she approached seventy, forty seemed like the prime of life, and perhaps it had been for Hans. At the thought of Hans the shadows that lingered in the damp corners of the chapel seemed to spread out and envelop her, eclipsing her joy. She put a hand to her heart as a sob rose in her chest. How she had loved Uncle Hans. How she had betrayed him.

She backed away and bolted through the open door, closing it firmly behind her. Taking a deep breath she tried to expel thoughts of her uncle and recapture something of the magic she had found in the garden. Focusing once more on the smells and sounds of nature she walked on down to the vegetable garden, to the pens where the animals were kept, and there she found Ilaria.

'*Buon giorno,*' said Ilaria when she saw Gracie walking swiftly towards her.

'*Buon giorno,*' Gracie replied, grateful for the distraction.

'You're up early.'

'I couldn't resist the beauty of dawn,' Gracie said.

'I'm up every morning at five. For me it is the best part of the day. Everyone is asleep. The countryside is slowly waking up. The birds are singing and I am alone in nature. Nature doesn't even know I am here. It is a secret time, the dawn, before the sun has chased all the elves and goblins away.' Gracie laughed. She knew exactly what Ilaria meant. 'You can help me. I'm feeding the animals and saying good morning to the vine.' Ilaria's exuberance was like the sun chasing Gracie's demons away.

'Mamma tells me that you speak Italian,' she said, pouring bird food into a bucket from a large sack. 'And fluently.'

'I lived in Tuscany from the age of thirteen to twenty-three.'

Ilaria began to speak in her mother tongue. 'Then I don't need to offend you with my bad English.'

'Your English is excellent,' Gracie said truthfully. She didn't add that the charm of her English lay in her thick Italian accent. 'And bad English would never offend me,' she continued. 'I think one should be grateful when a foreigner takes the trouble to speak one's language.'

Ilaria tossed the bird seed onto the ground and watched the chickens peck it hungrily. 'You know, I love people. I love to watch them come together in this beautiful place and flower like blossoming trees. That is a great pleasure for me. I have been watching you and your daughter and granddaughter. The three of you arrived closed like winter buds but now you are opening. It is lovely to see. Anastasia in particular is like a beautiful magnolia.'

'She is a very pretty girl,' Gracie agreed.

'Not just on the outside but on the inside. She has a beautiful soul too. You have to be a little careful though that her mother does not get left in the shade. She needs to blossom too.'

Gracie frowned. 'Do you think she's being left in the shade?'

'I can only say what I observe. I think she might be a little envious of you and Anastasia. You are so alike, you see. Perhaps they need to spend some time together. I think they want to, they just don't know how to initiate it. They are like those hens over there.' She pointed to a pair of black-and-red hens who were hanging back from the feeding flock. 'They want to eat, but they don't know how to push themselves in.' She tossed a handful of food further so that some of it landed at their feet. They duly began to peck at it. 'You see, it only takes a bit of encouragement for them to get going. Now they are feeding and they are very grateful to me. They will feel warmly towards me now. Tomorrow they might even push themselves in to start with. Life is a game. You just have to know how to play it.'

'Perhaps they can go into Colladoro together this afternoon,' Gracie suggested. 'I have no wish to go into town.'

'That is a good idea. They can have a cup of coffee, look around the shops. I suggest you visit the town another day. The church of Maria Maddalena was built in the thirteenth century and is very beautiful. I think you will like it.'

They ambled up the path in the direction of the castle. The sun was now low in the sky but shining brightly, burning away the pools of mist that lingered in the valleys. As they neared the castle Gracie noticed someone sitting above them, on the bench on the terrace where she had sat with Anastasia the night before. As she looked closer she saw that it was Tancredi in a hat and sunglasses, gazing out over the hills. Her heart stalled and she touched Ilaria's arm to detain her.

'There's the count,' she said.

Ilaria followed the line of her vision. 'Yes, he likes to sit up there in the early morning with his dog. He likes to enjoy the secret dawn too, before the sun rises and nature notices him.' She began to walk on.

'Would you introduce me?' Gracie heard herself ask and it was as if someone had taken over her body and asked for her. Her voice sounded strange and otherworldly, but quite determined.

'He does not feel comfortable meeting guests,' Ilaria said and there was a determined edge to her voice as well.

'But I'd love just a moment, to tell him how beautiful his home is and how grateful I am that he has allowed us to enjoy it too.'

Gracie willed him to look round. She stared at him, silently begging him to turn. And then, as if he heard her voice in the depths of his subconscious, he turned. Gracie knew then that Ilaria was left with no choice now but to introduce them.

'Good morning, Count Bassanelli,' Ilaria said, raising her voice so he could hear her. The count looked down at them for the path along which they were walking was a little way below the terrace where he sat, separated by a stone wall exhaling puffs of purple campanula.

'Good morning, Ilaria,' he said. But he didn't acknowledge Gracie, or raise his hand as he had done that afternoon on the balcony. Gracie felt invisible and the determined person who had suddenly taken her over withdrew, leaving a hurt old woman, afraid even to speak. 'How are the hens?'

'Very hungry this morning. May I—'

'And my pigs?' he went on.

'La Fabiana is expecting her litter at any moment.'

'New life. That always pleases me.'

'Count Bassanelli, may I introduce Signora Burton.'

A look of surprise darkened his face. Gracie thought suddenly that he had recognised her for he looked so mortified, just like he had the first time they had met when he had failed to acknowledge her in the chapel. Her heart gave a hopeful leap. 'I apologise, signora, how very rude of me. I hope you are enjoying your stay and making yourself at home in my castle.'

Gracie didn't know what to say. There was no sign of recognition on his face. She couldn't see his eyes because they were hidden behind his sunglasses, but she knew, from the polite, impersonal smile, that he did not know her. 'Very much, thank you,' was all she could mutter.

'Come, we must leave you to your quiet time,' Ilaria said, setting off up the path. He raised his hat and gave her a charming smile, but it was too late. Gracie was deflated. The magic of the morning had gone, robbed by the man who had once made every morning magical.

❧

Carina awoke to find herself alone once again. She was astonished that Anastasia, who could barely drag herself out of bed before midday when at home, was getting up at the crack of dawn and going for an early morning swim. She had suggested she go with her, but it was such a pleasure luxuriating in bed and having nothing to do but wander down to a delicious breakfast and then sit listening to Ilaria's commentary while her fabulous mother cooked. She hadn't expected to enjoy herself quite so much.

Four days without her phone, well three because the first one didn't really count as it was only half a day. Carina was pleased and proud of her restraint. She wasn't so pleased, however, with the way her relationship with Anastasia was going. If she couldn't join her for the odd lap around the pool she had to find something that she *could* do with her. She could take her into Colladoro and buy her a dress, she mused. Or go for a bicycle ride. She could borrow a couple of racquets and play tennis – she had seen Rex and Alex enjoying a knock-up the day before, but she wasn't very good at tennis and neither was Anastasia. Aside from those ideas she wasn't sure what to do with her. One thing was for certain, she couldn't sit across the table and *talk* to her, because she hadn't a clue what to talk to her *about.* She couldn't imagine what Gracie was telling her and was more than a little jealous that, whatever it was, it enthralled her. Nothing *she* could say would hold Anastasia's attention. The girl wasn't interested in her business and no child wants to talk about school work (especially not Anastasia who didn't care whether she got an A or a C in her A levels).

At length she got up and went downstairs for breakfast. She didn't have long before the cookery lesson began and judging by the empty tables, she was the last down. She helped herself from the buffet and ordered a cup of strong coffee then sat gazing out over the rolling landscape. The hills filled her with serenity and peace and she sat there savouring the feeling. Savouring the sense of time passing slowly, of not having to rush, or take a call, or write something down; of just being, in this exquisite place, and not wanting to be anywhere else.

Carina drank her coffee, ate her fruit and watched and listened and relished this new way of living. Eventually, she had to leave in order not to be late for the cookery lesson. She found everyone except Wendy, Tiff and Brigitte on their stools, chatting as they waited for Ilaria to commence. She was surprised to see Anastasia, bright-eyed and smiley, chatting to Gracie, who looked oddly subdued. *Perhaps she had a bad night,* Carina thought, wandering over to find out. 'Morning,' she said, looking at her mother with concern. 'Are you all right, Mum?'

'I'm fine, why?' Gracie answered, consciously injecting some liveliness into her voice.

'You look tired.'

'No, she doesn't,' Anastasia cut in. 'She looks lovely.'

'I don't mean she doesn't look lovely, darling. She just looks like she didn't have a very good night.'

'Your mother's right. I didn't sleep very well,' said Gracie diplomatically.

'Maybe you'd like to come for a walk with me later?' Carina said, but Gracie shook her head.

'No, I'm going to lie down after lunch. You should take your mother into Colladoro, Anastasia. I hear there's a lovely old church and lots of shops and cafés.'

'That's a good idea,' said Carina, her voice a little too animated to fool her wily daughter.

Anastasia screwed up her nose. 'Maybe,' she replied and Carina sighed and left to find her stool next to Lauren.

Gracie whispered to her granddaughter, 'Darling, I think your mother would like to spend some time with you. Why don't you go for a bike ride or something? She'd love that.'

Anastasia was not enthusiastic. 'Okay,' she replied. 'But it's only because *you* don't want to come.'

Gracie smiled at her granddaughter. 'I think I'm past riding bicycles.'

'Will you finish your story later? I'm desperate to hear how it ends.'

Gracie wasn't sure she could bear to speak about Tancredi after their disappointing meeting that morning. But she didn't want to let Anastasia down. 'Of course,' she replied.

Rex had taken a shine to Gracie. He talked to her at every

opportunity, trying hard to engage her with his eyes and make her laugh with his wit. When she smiled or even chuckled he felt he had won something special. At various moments during the morning he was so keen for her attention that he whispered to her during Ilaria's commentary, which Gracie found very annoying, not least because she felt it was rude to Ilaria who took such trouble to make the lessons interesting and fun. Gracie was unaware of her own 'blossoming' and found it bewildering that Rex should be so keen to spend time with her.

But Gracie *was* slowly blossoming. The Gracie Burton of Badley Compton was but a bud of a winter passed, the flower that had opened in the Italian sun now revealed someone very different and unexpected; someone with a warm yet mysterious smile, a gentle yet wise gaze, a shy but bold personality; someone with radiance and appeal; someone with a quiet charisma. She turned to Rex, who was speaking while Ilaria was speaking, again, and rapped him on his hand with her pen. 'Shhhh,' she hissed. 'Or you will go hungry when you return to California.' Rex's smile broadened, but he did as she asked and kept his mouth shut for the rest of the lesson.

Halfway through, Wendy, Tiff and Brigitte shuffled into the class, apologising profusely. Anastasia caught Alex's eye and giggled as the three women, clearly tired and hung-over, took their stools and lifted their clipboards. Wendy's mascara was halfway down her face, Tiff's short hair was standing on end and Brigitte did not remove her sunglasses. It was only at the end of the lesson that Anastasia realised why Brigitte had not removed her sunglasses, because she was asleep.

After lunch Alex asked Anastasia whether she was going to go to the pool. She was about to say that she was (she could have done with the odd hour or two's kip), but then she remembered what her grandmother had told her. 'Mum, fancy that bike ride?' she asked and Carina's face flushed with such pleasure and surprise that Anastasia wished she had taken a photograph of it, so she could be reminded of her mother's enthusiasm when they got back to London and life returned to normal.

Gracie went to lie down. Rex was disappointed, as had she decided to go for a walk he could have accompanied her; a lie-down was as good as closing the door in his face. He resolved to find her later when she emerged. Madeleine and Lauren went to sunbathe while Wendy, Tiff and Brigitte passed out on the terrace in the sun, hoping to sleep off their hangovers.

Carina and Anastasia set off on bicycles borrowed from the castle garage. The sun was high in the sky, catching the sequins on Anastasia's silver-and-purple sandals and warming their backs as they freewheeled down the track towards the town. 'Careful!' Carina shouted as Anastasia whooped with delight and stuck out her brown legs. 'You don't know if a car is coming round the corner!'

Anastasia ignored her and felt a rush of adrenalin as the bicycle whizzed at great speed down the winding lane. She was having so much fun that when they reached the town she insisted they continue out the other end, into the countryside. Carina, who was not as fit as her daughter, envisaged the climb back up and was about to persuade her daughter to go for a cup of coffee in a café instead, but before she could suggest it Anastasia was wheeling off again without a backwards glance. Carina had no choice but to follow.

They met up again at the bottom of the hill where the road plateaued out, cutting through fields of red poppies and burgeoning crops. Anastasia glanced to the left where Giovanni's farmhouse was hidden somewhere in those hills and felt her body respond with a shiver of excitement. She couldn't wait for the day to be over and for the night to offer up its sensual pleasures. 'Let's explore,' she said to her mother, whose cheeks were pink from the sunshine and exertion.

'Ride on, darling,' she said. 'I'll follow your lead.' But Anastasia slowed down to her mother's pace and they rode side by side, chatting. If Carina had been worried about how to converse with her daughter she needn't have wasted her time. The countryside gave them plenty to discuss and Carina was surprised that Anastasia noticed so much and that she was moved by what she saw. Soon they were commenting on the changing colours of the Tuscan landscape, the pretty farmhouses with their terracotta roofs and shutters, the fields of poppies, olive groves and vineyards with the ease of two people comfortable in each other's company. Anastasia wasn't sulky and Carina wasn't bossy or dismissive. The loveliness of their surroundings brought out the best in their characters and for the first time in perhaps years they enjoyed being together.

After a while Anastasia spotted what looked like a ruined villa up a long track, almost entirely hidden by trees. 'What do you think that is?' she asked, braking.

Carina stopped bicycling and squinted in the sun. 'Looks like an abandoned house.'

'It looks gorgeous!' Anastasia enthused. 'Come on, let's go and have a snoop.'

Carina was reluctant. 'Oh, I don't think we should,' she said. 'It's private property.'

'But who's going to know?' she said. 'Come on, Mum. Don't be a scaredy-cat.'

With that she began to cycle up the drive. It was more of a slope than she had anticipated and soon she had to dismount and walk the rest of the way. Her mother was following slowly behind, at a distance now, and Anastasia didn't wait for her.

With rising excitement, because Anastasia loved ruins, she realised that this once sumptuous villa had clearly been abandoned for decades. The gardens had overgrown and like a hairy green beast had started swallowing the building whole. The roof had fallen in and grass had seeded itself on the remaining tiles, growing haphazardly in patches of defiance. The walls were stained with mildew and rot, and the windows without their glass were open to the elements. Shutters hung on rusty hinges, some had fallen to the ground, disappearing into the belly of the hairy green beast. Propelled by the romance of it Anastasia threw her bike to the ground and wandered inside.

There was no furniture. It looked as if the person who had left had taken everything with them, clearly intending never to come back. Rubble lay on the floor among other debris and animal droppings. Indeed, birds had found this quiet haven an ideal place to nest. It smelt of damp and decay. The staircase was still intact but Anastasia didn't dare climb it in case she fell through the floor above. Nothing looked very sturdy.

'Anastasia!' It was her mother shouting to her from outside. 'Are you in there?'

'I'm here!' Anastasia replied, not wanting to be deterred, or rushed.

'I think we should leave.'

'Another minute,' she called back, making her way further into the building. Carina did not want to venture inside. Ruins were of little interest to her. She waited in the sunshine, hoping Anastasia wouldn't be long. It was nearly time for tea and Carina was looking forward to a large glass of water and a cup of coffee.

Anastasia reached a spacious, airy room at the back of the villa. Big windows would once have let in a lot of light but now they were cloudy with green mould and blocked by trees. Then something on the floor caught her eye. There was paint, rubbed into the grain of the remaining wood. Once she noticed a little she began to notice a lot. She saw a wooden door that was closed and went to open it. Unlike the other doors in the house which were wide open or missing, this door was hard to dislodge. She pushed. When it didn't budge she leant on it with her full body weight and gave it a shove. It finally opened, reluctantly.

Now her curiosity was seriously aroused. This was clearly an artist's studio. There was an easel at the far end, beside the window, pots of brushes and trays of paints in tubes on a shelf. Of course everything was old and dusty. The few canvases that remained were blank, a pile of frames was stacked up against one wall, a chair stood in a shaft of light in the middle of the room. There was something strange about the chair and Anastasia couldn't stop looking at it. It was all alone; a forlorn and abandoned chair, waiting for someone who never came.

Anastasia sensed her mother's impatience although she was too far away to hear her calling. She left the room and closed the door behind her. When she emerged into the light she took a deep breath. 'Come on,' said Carina. 'I think it's time for tea.'

'Sure,' Anastasia replied, picking up her bicycle. As she did so she noticed something beneath it. She bent down to take a closer look. Carina was already bicycling down the hill. Anastasia reached out and wiped away the grass with her hand. It was a stone sign. Moving her bicycle so she could get a better grip on it, she lifted it up. It weighed more than she expected. *La* ... She gave it another wipe. The letters revealed themselves, carved into the stone. *La Colomba.* She caught her breath. It couldn't be. Surely, it was too much of a coincidence. But she distinctly remembered her grandmother saying that the villa she had lived in as a young woman was called *La Colomba.* And hadn't she worked in an artist's studio? Anastasia's heart began to beat wild and fast.

'Darling!' Carina's tone was impatient now.

'Coming!' Anastasia picked up her bike and mounted.

❧

Perhaps it wasn't such a surprise that Gracie had decided to come to Castello Montefosco after all.

Chapter 19

Hot and sweaty from her bike ride Anastasia nipped into her bedroom to change into her bikini and then headed down the path for a swim. No one was there. The pool was quiet, snuggled into the hillside, embraced by luscious shrubs and trees, and the water as still as glass, bathed in the soft light of late afternoon. She dropped her towel and dived in. The cool water instantly revived her. As she swam lengths she was grateful for the solitude as it enabled her to unravel her thoughts.

The ruined villa she had stumbled upon was obviously the same villa in which Gracie had once lived. It was too much of a coincidence to be otherwise. But why was it a ruin? What had happened to Uncle Hans and Rutger? She imagined they would be in their eighties or nineties now, if they were alive. Had Gracie returned to find them, or perhaps to revisit La Colomba? On reflection, those options seemed unlikely. Anastasia wasn't aware of her grandmother leaving the castle at all. She hadn't even gone into town. She had shown no desire to go anywhere.

It was possible, of course, that Gracie had seen the advert in the magazine and come back to relive her past, not specifically to find anybody. But that wasn't a very plausible argument.

Who lived a great love and then returned years later just to see the *place*? Maybe she had returned to find Gaetano, but again, it seemed improbable considering Gracie's lack of interest in leaving the property. Anastasia wondered whether someone in town might know of a Gaetano, older, in his mid to late seventies, and upper class. Didn't Gracie say they were from very different worlds?

As she turned to start another lap she noticed Giovanni, standing with his hands on his hips at the opposite end of the pool. Relaxed in a pair of khaki trousers and polo shirt, his black hair flopping carelessly over his forehead, a smirk curling his lips, he made no secret of what he wanted to do to her. He watched her smile back. Instantly forgetting about La Colomba and her grandmother Anastasia swam her prettiest front crawl towards him. Glancing about to make sure no one saw them, he crouched down, took her wet face in his hands and kissed her full on the mouth. 'Come,' he said, standing up and walking to the pool house. Anastasia climbed out, grabbed her towel and followed. She had barely set foot in the dark room when she was pushed against the wall and kissed, this time ardently. Giovanni pressed his body against hers and wound his hands around her naked waist. Anastasia felt her whole being respond to his touch in shivers of pleasure. His hands slipped beneath her bikini top and began to gently tease her nipples with his thumbs. It did not startle her when he pulled down her bikini bottoms and lifted her leg to more easily enter her. The naughtiness of it excited her and she lifted the other leg and wrapped them both around his hips. He laughed and said something in Italian, and she laughed with him as they moved together like a strange creature pressed up against the wall. He whispered things into her ear between gasps and moans and the sound of his deep voice and that beautiful language aroused her until her whole body shuddered and flooded with a delectable warmth.

'*Ti amo, Anastasia,*' he said, when her feet touched the ground. He lifted her chin and gazed into her eyes, a serious, melancholic look in his. '*Ti amo, veramente, Anastasia.*' And she knew exactly what *that* meant.

'And I love you too,' she responded. '*Veramente.*'

Carina found her mother at a small round table on the terrace, enjoying tea with Rex. She noticed her mother had revived a little since her siesta. The apples of her cheeks were pink again and Carina wondered whether that had anything to do with the gallant American. 'Hello, dear,' said Gracie when she saw her daughter. 'What have you done with Anastasia?'

'She's gone for a swim but I need a coffee.'

'You look like you've cycled up a mountain,' said Rex.

'I *feel* like I've cycled up a mountain.' Carina laughed.

'Where did you go?' he asked.

'Into the countryside.' She gave her mother a meaningful look. 'It was good to be just the two of us. We had a really lovely afternoon together.'

'That's nice,' said Gracie.

'It was fun to explore. Tuscany is so beautiful. I'd love to own a house here. A holiday house I could escape to for the whole summer.'

'What's stopping you?' Rex asked with a grin, for *his* adventurous spirit had come to him of late and now anything seemed possible.

'Money,' said Carina with a shrug. 'I wouldn't just want any house, you see. I'd want a pretty one, a big one, and I imagine they're dreadfully expensive.' Gracie remembered what it was like to live here. To wake up each morning to a view that took her breath away. 'I don't think it's possible to be unhappy here,' Carina continued. 'Truly, I think I'd be happy every day.'

Gracie smiled, because she knew her daughter was wrong. She was only too aware of how unhappy it was possible to be.

Rex chuckled. 'I'm sure you grow accustomed to it and experience misery just like everyone else. It's human nature to take things for granted after a while.'

'I simply can't imagine it. I think I'd wake up every morning and feel lucky.' Carina swept her gaze over the hills, shaking her head at the wonder of it to show just how lucky she would feel.

Rex looked at Gracie. 'Where do you live, Gracie?'

'In Devon by the sea and I have to agree with my daughter, I do feel lucky every morning when I look out of the window at the view. It's not Tuscany, but it's lovely too, in its own way.'

'Ah, the sea.'

'It changes every day. I love the mist in summer, the fog in winter, the way the light bounces off the water when the sun shines.' Gracie remembered her home with affection, not dwelling on the loneliness she had left there. 'I also love the drizzly days. They have their own beauty too.'

'And you live in London, Carina. Do you get to go visit your mother?' Rex asked.

Carina watched Carlo place a little cup of coffee in front of her and wished she didn't have to answer honestly. 'I don't get down to visit her nearly enough. I wish I did,' she replied awkwardly, unable to look her mother in the eye.

'She works very hard,' Gracie intervened with a smile that betrayed nothing of the hurt. 'She has her own company, you know. She set it all up and it's very successful. I couldn't be more proud of her.'

Carina put her hand on top of her mother's. If she had thought about it she might not have, but she didn't think, she just felt and responded to the feeling with a touch that surprised Gracie as much as it surprised *her*. 'No, Mum, you're very kind, but it's because I've been so self-absorbed. I should have visited you more. Much more. I regret that now. I truly do. When we return to England I'm going to make sure we come down and see you straight away.' She withdrew her hand. 'As long as you don't invite that ghastly Flappy friend of yours for dinner.'

Gracie laughed. 'She has a good heart,' she said generously.

'No, she doesn't, she just wants the world to *think* she does.'

❧

It was just before dinner when Anastasia knocked on her grandmother's door. 'Come in,' said Gracie, who had been dressed and ready for the past half-hour.

Anastasia poked her head around the door. 'Granny, can I talk to you about something?'

Gracie was lying on the bed, attempting to read a novel but not taking in a single word. 'Of course.' She put the book to one side, and Gracie shuffled along, leaving space for Anastasia to sit down. She noticed her granddaughter's glowing cheeks and shiny eyes and felt her excitement as if it were a tangible thing. 'What are you so pleased about?' she asked.

Anastasia took a deep breath. 'I have to share this with somebody and I think you are the only person who will really understand.'

'You're in love,' Gracie guessed.

'How do you know?' Anastasia exclaimed.

'Because I've been in love before and I know what it looks like.' She patted her granddaughter's hand. 'I think Alex is a lovely young man.'

Anastasia laughed. 'It's not Alex!' she exclaimed.

Now Gracie was confused. There was no one else. It certainly wasn't Rex! 'Then who is it?'

'Giovanni.' Anastasia whispered the word as if the walls might hear and tell her mother.

'Who is Giovanni?'

'The man I love!' Anastasia gushed happily.

'How did you meet him?'

'He's the gardener.'

Gracie thought of Donato and smiled. 'You and I really are much too similar.'

'It's a secret so you're not to tell Mum.'

'All right, if you really insist. I won't tell her.'

'I do. She wouldn't understand. She'd get all anxious about it.'

'What's there to be anxious about? Is he much older than you?'

'He's a gardener.'

'There's nothing wrong with that. He's probably a very good gardener.'

'That's what I think. I don't know how old he is. I haven't asked him. In fact, we don't talk much. He doesn't speak English, except the odd word, like "beautiful".' Her grin broadened. 'And "Come here".'

'I see,' said Gracie, understanding very well what sort of relationship it was. 'I think it's lovely that you've found a nice Italian man. They're very romantic.'

'Giovanni is the most romantic man, ever!'

'Tell me about him. Is he handsome?'

'Oh Granny, he is beyond handsome. I mean, he could be a film star.' Gracie recalled the boy cleaning out the rabbit hutches and realised it must be him. 'I promise you, he's better-looking than Dylan O'Brien!'

'I'm afraid I don't know who he is.'

'Better than Cary Grant!'

'I suppose *he's* more my vintage.'

'Granny, he is so hot. I don't know how I'm going to leave on Saturday.'

'Don't think about that now. Enjoy the moment.'

'But it's more than a moment. He loves me.'

Gracie smiled at the naivety of youth, but she didn't contradict her. 'I'm sure he does,' she said instead. 'I'm sure he considers himself the luckiest man in Tuscany.'

'I love him too. I'm going to have to work out a way of coming back.'

'I'm sure you'll think of something. Your mother was saying only at tea that she would like to buy a house here.'

Anastasia's eyes brightened. 'She did?'

'Well, I'm not sure it's possible. Houses in Tuscany are very expensive.'

'Oh, wouldn't it be lovely if we bought a house here. Then you could come back too. Oh, by the way,' she added, as an afterthought. 'Did you say you used to live in a house called La Colomba?'

'Yes,' said Gracie.

'Do you think there's more than one?'

'Why do you ask?' Gracie was suddenly short of breath. She put a hand on her throat.

'I found a ruin, a really cool ruin, not far from here, called La Colomba. You didn't live *here*, did you, Granny?'

They both turned as the door opened and Carina appeared in a scarlet dress and high heels, her hair swept up in a ponytail. 'Are you coming?' she said.

Anastasia jumped off the bed, oblivious of the bomb she had just dropped on her grandmother. 'Mum, Granny tells me you might buy a house here!'

Carina sighed. 'If only.'

'I'm going to talk to Dad about it.'

'You do that. You're more likely to persuade him than I am.'

'He'd love it here.'

'Of course he would.' Carina turned to her mother who was slowly climbing off the bed. There was something odd about the way she was pushing herself up, as if she had aged ten years. 'Are you all right, Mum?'

'Just a little head-spin. I often get them, standing up quickly.'

Carina reached out to steady her. 'What you need is a glass of Ilaria's home-made wine.'

'Yes,' Gracie replied flatly. But a glass of wine would not take the sting out of her memories. Anastasia had found La Colomba. Gracie wasn't surprised that it was a ruin. After everything that had happened there she was not surprised at all. She thought of Uncle Hans and felt her throat constrict with emotion. She had loved him like a father. Oh, the shame, the terrible shame ... 'I don't think I can come down tonight,' she said, sinking back onto the bed. 'I'm suddenly feeling unwell.'

Carina knelt in front of her mother and looked into her ashen face with alarm. 'What bit of you feels unwell, Mum? Is it your head?'

It's my heart, she wanted to cry out, but she put her hand on her forehead instead. 'I'm just tired, dear. Nothing to worry about. Do you mind if I don't come to dinner?'

'I'll tell Ilaria to bring something up, if you like.'

'That would be nice. Anything at all. I'm not really very hungry.'

'But you must eat. I'll tell her to bring up some soup and bread. Perhaps it's the sun. It's much stronger than it looks.' She helped her mother lie down. All the while Anastasia watched in bewilderment. Only a moment ago she had been telling her grandmother about Giovanni and she had been fine. Surely it wasn't because of what she said about La Colomba? She bit her lip, feeling guilty. Who was she kidding? She knew intuitively that it had *everything* to do with La Colomba. 'I'll come and check on you later,' said Carina.

'You don't have to,' Gracie replied.

'I know I don't *have* to, but I *want* to.'

'I want to as well, Granny,' Anastasia joined in. She moved past her mother and bent down to give her grandmother a kiss. 'We need to talk,' she whispered, then squeezed her hand. 'You need to tell me the end of the story.' As Anastasia looked into her grandmother's eyes she was shocked to find that they were filling with tears. She squeezed her hand again, a firm, meaningful squeeze, and then left the room with her mother.

All through dinner Carina and Anastasia were unable to stop thinking about Gracie. Carina worried about her health, while Anastasia wondered about Gaetano and La Colomba. If Gracie had indeed lived here then Gaetano's house couldn't be far away. She had to find out if Gaetano was still alive, but she didn't know how to. After all, perhaps it was a common name and there were loads of Gaetanos in Colladoro. It was pointless asking after a man whose last name she didn't know. On reflection her grandmother had been very happy to talk about *him*, in fact, her face had positively glowed when she'd talked about Gaetano. It was the mention of the villa that had turned her, and not just the mention of it, but the *discovery* of it. What had happened there that had so upset her? Gracie had said that the story ended sadly – had it ended tragically?

Anastasia thought of the chair in the middle of the room and shuddered.

Rex was very disappointed that Gracie had chosen not to join them for dinner. He asked after her more than once and when Carina returned from going to check on her, he asked after her again. Ilaria took soup and warm bread to her room and reported that she was feeling a little better. They all agreed it was the sun. For a woman of Gracie's age the sun could be overwhelming. 'She'll feel better in the morning,' said Ilaria confidently. 'Mamma Bernadetta's soup has magical properties. You will see.'

❦

Anxious about her mother, Carina awoke in the middle of the night. She looked across to see a lump in the next-door bed. She hadn't heard Anastasia come in after going for a midnight swim with Alex. *She must have been sleeping very deeply*, she thought. Probably aided by the few glasses of wine she had drunk. After tiptoeing to the bathroom so as not to wake her daughter she sat on her bed and tilted her watch into the moonlight. Moving it slowly back and forth she could just make out the time. Soon the birds would tweet and dawn would break. She hoped her mother was sleeping well and that she'd feel better in the morning. There was something troubling about Gracie that Carina couldn't put her finger on. She hoped she wasn't unwell, not because she didn't have the time to look after her, but because she didn't want to lose her. The sudden realisation that her mother meant so much to her was shocking. She felt winded, as if someone had driven their fist into her stomach. She stood up and went to the window and gazed out in agitation. The moon was an enormous silver globe suspended above the hills in a deep indigo sky. It was strikingly beautiful. She closed her eyes and breathed in the cool air. If she lost her mother she would never forgive herself for neglecting her all these years. She'd never forgive herself for putting her aspirations above the woman who had raised her and loved her unconditionally. She'd never forgive herself for not bothering. And she *hadn't* bothered, she admitted that now and was full of shame. Alone at the window she saw herself as she really was, as if the moon was a giant eye reflecting her faults right back at her. She could hear Rufus telling her to calm down, that one's anxieties are always amplified at night and that she would laugh about them in the morning. But she couldn't calm down. On reflection her mother had been acting strangely since the very first day. She remembered her hesitation on arrival and the way her hand had trembled as Carina had helped her out of the taxi. Hadn't she wanted to go straight to bed? Then there was the time she had felt unwell after lunch and taken to her room, leaving Rex to explore on his own. The more Carina thought about it the more her fear grew, like a shadow across her heart. What if she had been diagnosed with something terrible and hadn't told her? What if Gracie had decided to spend her savings coming here because she knew she was dying? Hadn't Flappy said she had spent *all* her savings, in which case she wasn't thinking about going back. Carina was mortified. Perhaps that silly Flappy woman had been right to worry about her friend. It *was* very out of character for Gracie to want to come to Italy. Only something like a dying wish could explain it. Carina began to cry; a dying wish that hadn't included *her.*

Her impulse was to run into her mother's room and wake her. To tell her she was sorry and to ask her whether she was really dying, but she would only wake her when she needed so badly to sleep and worry her when she needed to be tranquil. Carina realised she had been selfish all her life; she wasn't going to be selfish now. She'd wait until the morning. In the meantime she'd pray to any God who was listening for her mother's health, and she'd pray for herself too, because if her mother *was* ill, Carina was going to need all the help she could get.

Appreciative of love now more than ever before, she went to her daughter's bedside to watch her sleeping. As she bent down to look into her face she realised, to her surprise, that the lump in the bed was not Anastasia at all but a pillow stuffed beneath the blankets. She pulled them back briskly. Her suspicions were confirmed. *Typical schoolgirl*, she smiled to herself. *Sneaking off to be with Alex, no doubt.* Hadn't *she* done the same when she'd been Anastasia's age? She shook her head, half cross, half amused, because her daughter had made a fool of her. She wondered how many nights she'd been stuffing pillows down her bed and creeping out. Had it not been for the wine Carina might not have slept so deeply. *She could blame Ilaria for that*, she thought, seeing the funny side. She wondered what Lauren would make of it. Alex was just the sort of young man Carina wanted for her daughter. He was kind, intelligent, polite and clean. He wasn't going to hurt her and was mature enough to be a good influence. He was the perfect first boyfriend. The perfect gentleman to introduce her into the world of romance. Carina climbed back into bed and laid down her head. She'd pray for her mother; Anastasia, it seemed, didn't need prayers, she was doing extremely well for herself all on her own.

The dawn chorus awoke her at a quarter to five. It seemed louder than usual. Sunlight was just beginning to brighten the sky. She turned to see that Anastasia had not yet returned to her bed. Perhaps she and Alex slept beneath a tree or something, swam and then returned to their rooms, claiming they'd risen early to go to the pool. Well, Carina had been threatening to head out for an early morning swim all week but hadn't yet managed to drag herself out of bed. Now she was awake, she decided she might as well give it a go. *Maybe she'd surprise the two love-birds*, she thought with a smile. She'd make fools of *them* and get her own back.

She shrugged on a dressing gown and slipped her feet into flip-flops. As she passed her mother's room she put her ear to the door. There was no sound. Hopefully she was sleeping deeply and would wake up refreshed. Hopefully, she wasn't ill, just struck down temporarily by heatstroke. Carina thought of Rufus and how he'd roll his eyes at her overreacting. She hoped to God that *that* was all it was.

Once outside Carina was enveloped in birdsong. It seemed that birds in every bush and tree were singing their little hearts out to be heard. The discordance of it delighted her and she paused on the grass to enjoy it. In the golden light of the emerging sun the shadow in her heart dissolved and was replaced by a feeling of expansion and joy. She set off down the path, a jauntiness in her step, a childlike wonder on her face. She stopped every now and then to admire a flower, to bring it to her nose and sniff. Occasionally, she wiped a bead of dew off her nose. She took the time to watch industrious bees foraging about the lavender and their drunken flight and friendly buzzing only enhanced her pleasure. By the time she reached the swimming pool she was in an exceedingly good mood.

She swam a few lengths, relishing the feeling of being awake at this early hour of the morning, and ready for the day ahead. She looked forward to Ilaria's cookery lesson, to talking with Lauren and Madeleine who had become good friends, and to spending time with her mother and daughter.

How happy she was that she had taken the trouble to come to Italy. To think she might have missed all this because of a misguided desire to work. The idea seemed extraordinary to her now. How could anyone put work above the simple pleasures of being in a beautiful place with family and friends? She thought of Rufus and wished he were here too, then her happiness would be complete.

The rattling sound of a motor alerted her to someone on the track below. It got louder as it approached, then stopped. She heard voices, laughter and a squeal of delight that was unmistakably Anastasia's. Carina climbed out and padded to the edge of the slope from where she could see the track through the trees. Anastasia was standing in a miniskirt and cropped top, kissing a man who was definitely not Alex, sitting astride his scooter. Carina stared in disbelief. Her stomach lurched, throwing the shadow across her heart once again.

She grabbed her towel and hurried back up the slope towards the castle before Anastasia discovered her. All the joy now turned to fear. There was absolutely no way that that young man was going to have his wicked way with her daughter. But as she rushed inside she realised that in all probability he already had.

Chapter 20

Carina did not return to the bedroom she shared with Anastasia. Instead, she knocked on her mother's door. To her relief a voice that did not sound like it belonged to a dying woman responded. 'Come in.'

'I hope I'm not waking you?' Carina entered and closed the door softly behind her.

'Not at all. I've been awake for a while, listening to the birdsong.'

'Are you feeling better?' she asked hopefully.

'Much better. I just needed a good night's rest.'

'Good. Listen, Mum, I need to talk to you.'

Gracie could tell from her daughter's stricken face that something dramatic had happened. 'What is it, dear? What's happened?'

'I've just seen Anastasia with an Italian man I've never seen before. He has just dropped her back on his scooter. Down by the pool. They must have spent the whole night together. She didn't come back. She stuffed a pillow down her bed. Does she think I was born yesterday?'

'Sit down, dear,' said Gracie gently.

Carina paced the room in agitation. 'I don't think I can.' She put a hand to her forehead and let out a sob. 'I'm really, really worried, Mum.'

'About what?' Gracie asked calmly. She looked a picture of tranquillity sitting there propped up against the pillows in her floral nightdress.

'About what? I can't believe you're asking that!' Carina huffed loudly. 'How does she know him? I mean, he could be anyone: a rapist, a murderer . . . It's not safe.'

Gracie smiled sympathetically. 'He's the gardener here,' she informed her coolly.

Carina's face fell. 'You *know* about this?'

Gracie nodded. 'Anastasia told me yesterday.'

'And you didn't tell me?'

'Anastasia made me promise not to.'

'Why? Why not tell me? I'm her mother!' Carina began to pace again. 'God! Why doesn't she ever tell me anything?'

'Because she knows how you'll react.'

'And how's that?'

'Like this,' said her mother with a sympathetic smile.

Carina's jaw stiffened and she folded her arms defensively. 'Well, she's my responsibility. I can't let her run around the countryside with a man she doesn't know.'

'Now that doesn't make sense. How is she to get to know someone then?'

'Well, she could choose a boy like Alex. Someone we've all met.'

'You mean someone from *your* world. But she's fallen in love with Giovanni,' said Gracie as if it was perfectly understandable.

'Is that what he's called?' Carina walked to the window and leant back against the sill. 'She *thinks* she's fallen in love. In reality, she's fallen in *lust*.'

'Of course, and she's enjoying an exciting romance. Love or lust, at her age the two are very easily confused.'

'God, Mum, you're the one who should be disapproving, not me. I'm meant to be modern and laid-back.'

'You were never laid-back, dear,' said Gracie with a grin.

Carina did not find any of this remotely amusing. 'Old people are meant to be judgemental and "In my day . . ." blah blah blah.'

'But in my day we fell in love with Giovannis too.'

'And had your hearts broken?'

'Of course. Come and sit down.' Gracie patted the bed. Reluctantly Carina sat beside her. 'It's okay to have your heart broken,' said Gracie and Carina was surprised by her confident, authoritative tone, as if *she* had survived a broken heart herself. 'It's not the end of the world, Carina. In fact, I would say it's an essential part of growing up. A broken heart teaches you wisdom, compassion for others and understanding. It digs another layer into your being, making you more worldly and aware. It is a part of the great experience of life. It's not going to kill her.'

'But I can't bear to see her unhappy.'

'Unhappiness won't kill her either. If Anastasia experiences only joy in her life she'll never learn to empathise with others. I think the worst thing you can hope for as a parent is that your child is always happy. Unhappiness drives us deeper. It enables us to connect with people on a deeper level, to understand them and to sympathise with them. It makes us kinder. I don't want Anastasia to suffer either, but I acknowledge that suffering is an important life lesson.'

'I don't trust that Giovanni. He's much too handsome and pleased with himself. How on earth did he manage to seduce Anastasia so quickly and where did she meet him?'

'I imagine they met in the garden. I can't imagine they spoke very much because he can't speak English.'

Carina scrunched up her nose. 'He doesn't speak English!'

'I don't think they do a lot of talking, Carina.'

'Good God. It just gets worse!' She groaned and slumped her shoulders.

Gracie put a hand on her arm and left it there. 'I think it's wonderful that she's having a romance with a young man like Giovanni.'

'Why?'

'Because everyone should be madly in love at least once in their life. Some never experience it at all.'

'And I suppose it doesn't matter that she'll leave on Saturday and never hear from him again.'

'No, it doesn't matter. It's a holiday romance that she'll remember for ever.'

'Do you think she's been careful?' Carina asked suddenly. 'God forbid we have a teenage pregnancy.' She sighed heavily and shook her head. 'I wish she'd confided in me.'

'Of course she's been careful. She's a very bright girl. The young nowadays are well-educated in that department, I'm sure.'

'I hope so.'

'I know you're too old to take advice—'

'I'm not too old, Mum.' Carina smiled pathetically and put her hand on top of her mother's. 'I need your advice. I really do.'

'All right. Don't let on that you know. Anastasia asked me not to tell you and she mustn't know that you spotted her this morning. Play ignorant until *she* comes to *you*. Then act surprised. Be supportive. Enjoy it with her. If she wants to share it with you she won't want to be judged or criticised. It's a privilege if your daughter wants to include you in her life. If it all goes wrong, be there to listen and sympathise. What she needs from you is support and encouragement and not condemnation. She's young and she's having a lovely time.'

'Poor Alex.'

'No, not poor Alex at all. Giovanni is a fly-by-night romance. Anastasia will return to London having made a firm friend in Alex. Who knows what will happen down the line.'

'I suppose you're right.' Carina squeezed her mother's hand and looked at her steadily. 'Mum, you're not sick, are you?'

Gracie looked surprised, which was reassuring. 'Sick? Of course not.'

'If you were, you'd tell me, wouldn't you?'

'Yes,' she replied. 'I would.' She might not have told Carina something like that before, but Italy had brought them closer and now she realised, with certainty, that were she ever taken ill, Carina would be the first person to know.

Carina was relieved to have overreacted. 'I worried about you last night,' she confessed. 'I thought maybe you had come out here as a dying wish.'

Gracie laughed at such an absurd idea. 'That's just silly,' she chided.

'I panicked. I realised suddenly what it would be to lose you.'

Gracie's eyes shone. 'You're not going to lose me, dear,' she said. 'Not yet, anyway.'

Carina's eyes welled with tears and she reached out to hug her mother. Surprised and touched beyond words, Gracie hugged her back in silence.

❧

Anastasia returned to her room after a swim to find Carina in the bathroom drying her hair with the hairdryer. She glanced at her bed and wondered whether her mother had noticed the pillow there, moulded into the shape of a body. She poked her head round the door. 'Morning, Mum,' she said brightly, watching her mother closely in the reflection of the mirror. But Carina smiled back and went on drying her hair. Anastasia muttered 'Phew' and began to dress.

When Gracie appeared for breakfast everyone made a great fuss of her. Rex pulled out her chair and Carlo brought her a pot of tea without being asked. Lauren and Alex went to the buffet to get her a plate of pastries and fruit while Madeleine offered advice on how to deal with sunstroke were it to strike again. Wendy, Tiff and Brigitte crowded around the table asking dozens of questions all at once. Everyone agreed it had been the heat and Wendy offered to lend her a sunhat. 'It's bright pink but it will keep the sun off,' she said with a grin.

'It's so pink it might frighten the sun away all together,' Tiff added.

'Better not,' said Brigitte. 'I haven't perfected my suntan yet.'

Gracie declined for she had brought her own, but she was very touched by their concern.

Carina and Anastasia were the last to emerge; Carina in a pale blue sundress and espadrilles, Anastasia in the tiniest pair of denim shorts and sparkly silver Keds. Alex eyed her long brown legs with appreciation, the three Manchester girls with envy. Gracie watched them both with pride.

'Granny!' Anastasia exclaimed. 'Are you okay?' She bent down and planted a kiss on Gracie's cheek. 'You smell nice.'

'Thank you, dear,' Gracie replied, patting her granddaughter's hand, which was resting gently on her shoulder. 'It's rose and honey.'

'It's lovely, Granny.'

'I'm so glad you're better, Mum,' said Carina, sitting down at the next-door table. 'We'd better keep you out of the sun today.'

'I have wonderful pills for headaches, should you need them,' said Madeleine. 'I never travel without an entire medicine cabinet. I have a pill for everything.'

Anastasia went inside to help herself to the buffet. Alex followed. 'Could those shorts get any shorter?' he asked.

Anastasia grinned at him. 'Well, if they could they'd be pants.'

He laughed. 'Don't get me wrong, they look great.'

'It's much too hot to cover up.' She reached for a plate.

'And it wouldn't be fair to the only young man in the group.'

'Ah, I saw the old silver fox giving them the once-over, you know. He might be old but he's got a roving eye, that one.'

'For your grandmother.'

'Sweet, isn't it,' she said, helping herself to the pastries. 'These are so good. Have you tried them?'

'Even my mother has tried them,' he replied. 'And she usually considers wheat the enemy.'

'We're all going to return home as fat as butter.' Anastasia glanced at him, tall and slim, the sort of build that didn't easily put on weight. 'Well, *some* of us will,' she added wryly.

'I don't think *you* have anything to worry about either.'

'Isn't that lucky then,' she replied, coquettishly taking another pastry and adding it to the pile on her plate. Alex smiled admiringly and followed her back onto the terrace.

After breakfast the group assembled for their lesson. They put on their aprons, retrieved their clipboards and perched on their stools, chatting now with the effortlessness of old friends. Ilaria watched them with pleasure. 'All the buds have opened now,' she told her mother proudly.

'They always do, in the end,' Mamma Bernadetta agreed. 'Some take a little longer but others respond quickly to the magic.' She rubbed her fingers against her thumb and narrowed her eyes. 'It's all in the taste.'

❧

Ilaria clapped her hands. 'Welcome back to Mamma Bernadetta's cookery class. Today you are going to learn how to cook *crostini di fegatini*, *spaghetti alla primavera*, *pollo al Marsala e peperoni rossi*, and to finish we have chosen a big dessert, in case you haven't eaten enough, Mamma Bernadetta's very special banoffi pie. But don't be fooled, Mamma Bernadetta's banoffi pie is not like the ordinary banoffi pie you will have eaten before. No, it is certainly not. Mamma Bernadetta's banoffi pie is her own mother's secret recipe. We are going to share it with you if you promise not to tell anyone. Okay?'

The students nodded enthusiastically. Gracie remembered her grandmother's *stamppot*, for which she made the same claims as Ilaria. She wondered whether the magic Ilaria spoke of, was, in fact, all in the mind rather than in the ingredients. If they *believed* it had special qualities it most likely tasted better. If anyone had the power to seduce the mind it was Ilaria.

Anastasia was feeling sleepy. Four nights spent with Giovanni were now beginning to take their toll. Even though Ilaria was witty and entertaining Anastasia began to feel heavy between the eyes. She pinched the skin on the bridge of her nose in an attempt to wake herself up. She wished she could sneak off to bed – her own bed – and catch a few hours' sleep. And then Ilaria said something that jolted her back to her senses. 'This was Count Gaetano Montefosco's favourite dish.' Anastasia sat bolt upright and blinked at Ilaria in astonishment. Then she glanced at Gracie, expecting her to look surprised, or agonised, or both, but her grandmother did not flinch. In fact, she looked as if she hadn't even heard. Ilaria went on: 'Gaetano Montefosco was Count Tancredi Bassanelli's grandfather, a big collector of art and a lover of food, Italian food, of course.

Mamma Bernadetta's own mother, Mamma Agata, cooked for him when he was a boy and banoffi pie was his most favourite. Now you will see why.'

Anastasia was now fully awake and alert. Gaetano Montefosco's name vibrated in the air long after Ilaria had uttered it. Anastasia heard nothing of the lesson that ensued. All she could think about was Gaetano Montefosco. Yet the count's grandfather would have been far too old to have been her grandmother's lover, even Anastasia with her poor understanding of mathematics could work *that* out. But it was too much of a coincidence that he was called Gaetano *as well as* being an art lover.

Then it hit her like a ball of light in the very place where only a moment ago she had felt nothing but heaviness. The man her grandmother loved was right here in this very castle. She didn't know why it had taken her so long to work out. Obviously, Gracie had not wanted to give her lover away by using his real name, so she had used his grandfather's name instead. It all made perfect sense now. The reason for her coming here in the first place was because of *him – because of Count Tancredi Bassanelli* – the man she had loved and lost. Gracie had lived at La Colomba, which was about half an hour's bicycle ride from the castle. Hadn't she said she used to bicycle there? It wasn't surprising that she hadn't been interested in leaving the castle, because the reason for her return was *inside* the castle, not at La Colomba. That place was full of ghosts. Anastasia had felt them.

In the break Rex sat with Gracie in the shade and monopolised her with such unwavering concentration that Anastasia could no more tear her away than separate a dog from its bone. Instead, she found Alex and lay on the grass beside him and talked about nothing. After lunch Gracie went for a siesta and Anastasia and Alex headed down to the pool. Rex sat in the shade reading a book while the women lay on loungers, dozing and chatting in the sun and periodically cooling off in the pool.

Anastasia wanted to confide in her mother about La Colomba, Gaetano, Gracie's lover, and her suspicions that Gaetano was, in truth, Count Tancredi Bassanelli, but she had promised her grandmother that she wouldn't tell, so she was left with no option but to ruminate on it on her own. It would have helped to have someone to discuss it with. Two minds were always better than one. Of course, she could simply ask her grandmother. But she felt it was intrusive somehow. If Gracie had wanted her to know his identity she would surely have told her already. Of course there was every chance that Anastasia was mistaken and that it really *was* just a coincidence that Count Tancredi Bassanelli's grandfather was called Gaetano. But Anastasia sensed that she was right. It was a feeling she had, just beneath her ribcage. She would bide her time and, if the right moment arose to bring it up, she would seize it.

When the sun started to sink in the western sky, Madeleine went off for her walk. Rex wandered up to the castle in the hope of finding Gracie. Wendy, Tiff and Brigitte were still fast asleep (Wendy was snoring), and Lauren and Carina hadn't drawn breath since they had come down. Anastasia wondered what on earth they had to talk about for so long. Alex asked Anastasia if she wanted to play tennis. Tennis was not one of her strengths, but as there was nothing else to do except stroll into town, which did not appeal, or sit with Rex and Gracie sipping tea, which appealed even less, she decided that tennis was the lesser of all evils. 'All right,' she agreed, wrapping herself in a towel. 'I'll play, but only if we knock up. I don't want to have to play a game.'

'Knocking up suits me too,' Alex replied. 'Rex gave me a hard time earlier in the week. I'm all for an easy life.' They walked up to the castle together then went their separate ways to their rooms to change, agreeing to meet down at the tennis court where they hoped to find racquets and balls in the pavilion.

Anastasia slipped into her micro-shorts and a T-shirt and wandered off down the grassy path in the opposite direction of the pool. Midges hovered in the balmy air and crickets sang a noisy chorus in the long grass. She thought of Giovanni. She looked about hoping to spot him but the gardens were quiet apart from the busy endeavours of nature. She assumed he'd gone home and smiled to herself as she thought of him preparing the barn for her. Replacing the candles perhaps, smoothing down the rug, anticipating the feel of her as she anticipated the feel of *him*, and counting down the hours. *How time dragged*, she thought, as the court came into view.

She noticed at once how run-down it was. The surrounding fencing was rusted, the door completely off its hinges and leaning against one of the posts. The surface of the court was made of a strange, red-coloured earth. Strips of white tape were nailed to it to mark the lines. Some of them had peeled off. Seeds from a nearby tree had blown onto the court only to be half-heartedly brushed into mounds outside the lines. The brush was lying at one end but Anastasia was not about to use it, even though the wind had carried some of the seeds into the playing area.

Alex hadn't appeared yet. While she waited, she thought she'd look and see if there were racquets and balls in the pavilion. *That* was run-down too, she noticed. The white paint was peeling and speckled in a light green mould. She made her way towards it. As she approached she suddenly heard a woman's laugh. A deep, throaty, *dirty* laugh. She stopped and cocked her ear. Silence. She waited for it to come again, but it didn't. She looked around. However, it could only have come from the pavilion. She stepped closer, careful now not to make a sound. With mounting curiosity she reached the wall just beside the open door and held her breath. The laughter came again and this time Anastasia recognised it. It belonged to Madeleine! Madeleine then said something in Italian, followed by another throaty laugh that was indisputably hers. Anastasia's heart stalled. Who was she with? But Anastasia knew. Even before she heard Giovanni's reply, she knew; because she feared it so.

Anastasia remained a moment by the door. Her head told her they were making love, her heart told her they couldn't be. Surely there was some mistake. Perhaps they had met as Madeleine returned from her walk and Giovanni had offered to show her something in the pavilion. A nesting bird perhaps? Something so innocent that she would later laugh about it and her ludicrous imagination. But she *had* to be sure. She edged round the side of the pavilion to where a window was partly obscured by mould and ivy. Stealthily she crept like a cat across the grass until she was positioned directly below it. She took a breath, fearful of what she might see, hopeful that it was nothing more than two innocent people sharing a joke. Then, inch by agonisingly slow inch, she raised herself to her full height and peered in through the glass.

She could only just see past the moss, but the little that she saw was enough to confirm her worst fears. There was nothing innocent about the joke they were sharing. She stifled a sob and sneaked away. Just as she was setting off up the path at a run Alex was walking down it towards her.

He saw her stricken face and frowned. 'Are you all right? What's happened?'

'I don't want to play tennis any more,' she said.

'All right.' His eyes strayed behind her to the pavilion. 'I'm sorry, I got delayed talking to your mother.'

'Where is she?' she asked.

'On the terrace.'

'I need to speak to her.'

'Sure. I'll come with you.' They fell into step. 'What happened down there? You're as white as a sheet.'

'I saw a snake. A huge snake. The size of a cow. I hate snakes more than anything!'

Alex looked unconvinced. 'A snake the size of a cow is a pretty monumental snake.'

'Yes, well, it was big.' She sniffed and wiped her eyes. 'I'm never going down there again, that's for sure.'

'You didn't really want to play tennis anyway,' said Alex. He put his arm around her. 'I'm sorry you saw a snake. Had *I* been there I would have slain it for you.'

'Don't worry. It took me by surprise, that's all.' Her expression hardened and she quickened her pace. 'If I see it again, I'll slay it myself.'

Chapter 21

Carina registered her daughter's unhappy face – and the hard stare she gave her as she hurried past her table – and excused herself at once. Lauren watched her run after Anastasia then asked her son what had happened. 'She saw a snake,' Alex explained, taking Carina's empty chair for himself. This seemed perfectly acceptable to Lauren.

'Well, *I'm* not going to head down to the tennis court then,' she replied with a shudder. 'I hate snakes.'

Carina caught up with Anastasia as she headed up the stairs. 'Darling, what happened?' she asked. But Anastasia strode on purposefully without replying. Carina waited until they were alone in their room to press her further.

As soon as the door was closed Anastasia began to sob. Carina's heart flooded with compassion and, as she moved to embrace her, she was pretty sure she knew what had inspired the tears. She drew her into her arms and squeezed her tightly. Anastasia stiffened for a moment and her arms dangled by her sides as if she didn't know what to do with them. Then slowly and a little hesitantly she wound them round her mother's body. Anastasia was taller than her mother and neither of them could remember the last time they had embraced – it was usually Rufus who was ready with the hug – but it didn't feel odd. It didn't feel odd at all.

At last the sobbing quietened and Anastasia was ready to confide in her mother. They sat side by side on the bed as Anastasia shared the story of her brief romance. 'You're not going to like this but . . .' was how she had started. However, to her surprise, Carina didn't judge her or show any disapproval. She listened without interrupting as the details emerged, cautiously at first and then with greater confidence and fluidity. All the while Anastasia was speaking Carina was thinking of Gracie and remembering her advice.

'I was a fool to be taken in by him,' Anastasia said forlornly.

'No, you weren't, darling,' Carina reassured her. 'He's handsome and exotic. Lots of girls enjoy romances with foreign men. I would say it's an important part of life, falling in love and having one's heart broken.'

'Is it?' Anastasia wasn't so sure.

'You had fun, didn't you?'

'At the time, yes.'

'Then don't let what you've since discovered ruin the good times you've enjoyed.'

'I gave him my virginity, Mum!'

'Well, you had to give it to someone, sometime, didn't you? I assume he was kind?'

Anastasia managed a chuckle. 'By that you mean was he good in bed?'

'I wouldn't ask.'

'But I'll answer anyway. He was gorgeous!' Anastasia's eyes gleamed.

'Then it was worth it. Better to give yourself to someone who knows what he's doing than to someone who fumbles around awkwardly and gets everything wrong. I wish my first time had been like yours.'

'Who was your first time?'

'A boy called Tony Drake. I was sixteen. Don't tell Mum!'

'Was he a local boy?'

'Yes, I went to school with him. I didn't really fancy him. I was just grateful that he fancied me. I suppose I wanted to grow up, too. I was longing to be a woman and to make my own way in the world. But it was a real fumble and only lasted a second. I think what you've had with Giovanni is ideal.'

'But how could he . . . with Madeleine?'

'She's a beautiful woman. He's got good taste!'

Anastasia screwed up her nose. 'She's old.'

'I bet she knows a trick or two, though.' They both laughed and Anastasia began to feel a little better.

Suddenly Anastasia was seized by the desire to share Gracie's story. She didn't feel it was fair to exclude her mother. After all, the three of them had come to Italy together, it was only right that they shared the experience – the *whole* experience – and besides, Anastasia's theories about the count needed a second opinion and time was running out. Tomorrow was their last full day.

'I need to tell you something else,' Anastasia began. She faltered a moment, uncomfortable with the thought of divulging something that her grandmother had asked her to keep to herself.

'What else is there?'

'It's not about me, it's about Granny.'

Carina blanched. 'She's not ill, is she?'

'No, she's fine.'

'I just had a horrid thought—'

'She's fine, Mum. It's something else.'

'Tell me?'

'It's a whopping secret and you must promise not to let on that I've told you.'

Carina was a little put out that Gracie hadn't told her herself. 'Well, what is it?'

Anastasia took a breath. *I'm not betraying Granny. I'm helping her find the love of her life.* 'Did you know that Granny came to Italy at thirteen and lived with her uncle at that ruined house we saw the other day, until she was twenty-three?'

Carina stared at her as if she was speaking a different language. 'What are you talking about?'

Anastasia gasped. She put a hand to her mouth and stared back at her mother. 'God! You really didn't know!'

Carina stared back at her daughter in bewilderment. 'Are you telling me that my mother lived *here*? In Colladoro?'

'Yes, at La Colomba, the ruined villa we visited.'

Carina got to her feet. 'That's extraordinary!'

Anastasia was secretly excited to be revealing her grandmother's astonishing past. 'Her uncle Hans brought her out here from London to teach her how to restore paintings.'

'I didn't even know she could paint.'

'Well, she was an exceptionally *good* painter, Mum. After five years of restoring art he told her he wanted her to do something else.'

'Oh, God. I dread to think what that was!'

'Forgery.'

'Forgery? My mother was a forger? Good God, whatever next!'

'She wasn't just a forger. She was a brilliant forger, as was Hans.'

Carina sat down again. 'Why didn't she tell me?'

'She speaks fluent Italian, you know.'

Carina narrowed her eyes. 'Okay, so she didn't pick Colladoro randomly out of a magazine. Who knows, perhaps there wasn't an article in a magazine at all. But she came here on purpose. But why, after what, forty-four years?'

'She loved a man called Gaetano.'

'Hey, wait a minute! Wasn't Ilaria talking about a Gaetano Montefosco today?'

'Too old. That was this count's grandfather. I think the man might be the count himself.'

'No, it can't be. She hasn't mentioned him or shown any desire to see him. If he was the great love of her life then she would have gone and talked to him the very first day.'

'Yes, you're right,' Anastasia agreed, disappointed. 'She's shown no interest in him at all.'

'So why has she come then?'

'Not to revisit La Colomba because she hasn't left the castle grounds once.'

'No. And why has she told you and not me?'

'Because you'll get upset?'

'Do I look upset?'

'You did for a minute.'

'A minute. I'm not upset now, am I?'

'She hasn't told me the rest of the story yet.'

'*Is* there more?'

'Of course, because she left Italy and Gaetano, and went back to London. The rest you know. She must have met Grandpa, married him and hidden her past.'

'Why hide it?'

'Because she was a forger, which is a criminal, Mum.'

Carina shook her head. 'It doesn't add up, Anastasia. She could have hidden that part but been honest about living in Italy and speaking Italian. When I was a girl I remember her speaking Dutch to her mother, which I never understood, of course. But then my grandmother died when I was about twelve and apart from a brother who lived in London and who we never saw, that was the last I knew of her family. She never mentioned an uncle. It makes no sense at all.'

'You're right. It doesn't. I think I need to hear the rest of the story.'

'We have to get her away from Rex then. I'll see to that after dinner. Leave him to me. You take Granny off on your own and ask to hear more.'

'Do you think she wants to find Gaetano, but is too scared to?'

'Maybe. That's why you need to dig a little deeper and discover where he lived so we can find him for her, if, indeed, she *wants* to find him.'

'You don't mind that she loved someone else besides your father?'

Carina shrugged. 'Oh, I know she loved Dad. They were very happy together. She didn't run off to Italy the minute he died, did she? Anyway, I can hear Mum saying that there are many different ways of loving. She probably loved them both. Life is complicated. You realise that as you get older. But you're going to do a little detective work and then you're going to come and tell me and we're going to decide what to do next.'

'We leave the day after tomorrow,' said Anastasia anxiously.

'Which is why you have to extract the rest of her story *tonight*.'

Anastasia wriggled with excitement. 'Okay, I'm on a mission. I won't fail. I think I'm going to have to come clean though, at some stage, and tell her I've told you.'

'Leave that to me. I'll know when the time is right.' Carina smiled proudly at her daughter. 'You've done the right thing, darling. She'll thank you in the end.'

'She'll thank *us*,' Anastasia added, then a little nervously, 'I hope.'

❧

Mamma Bernadetta and Ilaria lingered in the doorway that led to the kitchen and watched the group assembling on the terrace for wine and crostini. Every week new guests arrived from different parts of the world, brought like seeds on a loving wind to flower in the Italian sun, and yet Mamma Bernadetta and Ilaria never grew tired of watching them bloom. Every person was different, opening in their own unique way and in varying degrees. Only the very few remained the same. *But how* these *buds had flowered*, they thought, taking pride from the magical effects of Mamma Bernadetta's recipes and this enchanting place. Ilaria folded her arms and leaned against the doorframe. 'Rex did not notice Gracie on the first night. She was like a dry flower crying out for water and yet too afraid to ask for it,' she said.

'But look how pretty she is now,' said Mamma Bernadetta, watching Gracie smile. 'Rex cannot take his eyes off her. Out of all the guests *she* has transformed the most. I did not think her particularly special, but I have learned that she is a woman with depth.' Mamma Bernadetta put her pudgy hand to her expansive bosom. 'I can feel it, Ilaria. One must never judge the quality of wine by its label.'

'But I don't think she is interested in Rex,' said Ilaria with a frown. 'I don't know why. They laugh together and walk round the gardens together and they are the only two people of their age here, and yet, I sense her interest lies elsewhere and my sensing is usually right.'

'She is a widow, Ilaria, and I know what it is to carry loss; for I carry Umberto's within me and always will, God rest his soul. It is like a stone in one's heart that is always rubbing.' She pressed her hand to her bosom again. 'Perhaps Rex will cushion the stone and stop the chafing.'

'That would be nice, wouldn't it?' Ilaria agreed. 'Ah, here come Carina and Anastasia. It fills me with joy to watch these two,' she said. 'It took them a while to look beyond their phone screens and notice the beauty around them, but they did and look how happy they are.'

'Beauty is always here,' said Mamma Bernadetta wisely. 'Ready to awaken the spirit, waiting patiently to be noticed, to be allowed to do its job.'

'Carina and Anastasia were ripe for transformation. They just needed a little help.'

'The week is not yet over,' Mamma Bernadetta said, waddling back into the kitchen. 'There is still much to be done.'

'Yes, our job is not finished. We have to mend a broken heart . . .'

'Giovanni has not broken her heart. He has introduced it to love and only bruised it,' Mamma Bernadetta said, bristling like a cat in defence of her grandson.

Ilaria was less indulgent of her nephew's antics. 'You should have a word with him, Mamma.'

'One must not interfere with nature, Ilaria. You can only observe and let it play out. Remember, everything has a purpose. Nothing happens in isolation. There is always a cause and an effect,' Mamma Bernadetta added, vigorously moving her hands for emphasis. 'We jump from experience to experience and take what we have learned with us. *That* is wisdom.'

'Yes, but really, you ought to have a word with Giovanni.'

'I'm not having a word with anyone. My grandson is part of the magic here and he is flowering too.'

'Mamma, I think Giovanni flowered a long time ago,' said Ilaria, her disapproval turning to amusement.

'Every woman needs a Giovanni at some stage in their lives. It is important to live!'

'And Giovanni?'

Mamma Bernadetta shrugged with the nonchalance of an old woman who accepts that life is an education for the advancement of the soul. 'He will have his heart broken and then he too will learn about love.'

❧

Ilaria seated the group around the table, making sure that Anastasia sat next to Alex and that Rex took the place beside Gracie. She put Madeleine as far away from Anastasia as possible, but as she observed Anastasia talking to Alex the girl did not appear to be suffering from a broken heart at all. There was an intensity about her tonight, a fiery determination in every look and gesture, as if something more important was occupying her thoughts. Ilaria noticed too how she kept glancing at her mother, who in turn acknowledged her glances with barely perceptible nods. They were like a pair of conspirators and Ilaria wondered what they were up to. Then she became aware of both women's eyes sliding towards Gracie and Rex. Did they want to encourage the old fox or discourage him, Ilaria wondered, putting the glass to her lips and savouring the fruity taste of her own wine. By the animated look on Rex's face, he was firing himself up to make his feelings known. After all, tomorrow was the last day; if he didn't do it soon he would never get the chance.

It was during dessert that the conversation evolved into a general one and the subject of snakes raised its slippery head. 'Anastasia, tell everyone what you saw this afternoon on the tennis court,' said Lauren.

'A handsome Italian, I hope,' said Wendy.

Brigitte gave a throaty laugh. 'Hmm, I might play some tennis, after all.'

'I saw a snake,' said Anastasia.

'She claimed it was as big as a cow,' Alex added, grinning at her.

'That is one hell of a big snake,' said Rex. 'Are you sure it wasn't a stick?'

'Okay, so it wasn't really the size of a cow,' Anastasia admitted. She didn't dare look at Madeleine, but she could see her looking at her in her peripheral vision.

'A snake?' Ilaria cut in. 'We only have small grass snakes here and they don't bite.' The scene that Anastasia had witnessed through the cloudy window of the tennis pavilion now materialised in a horrible vision and she felt her face grow hot.

'A snake? Did someone just say they'd seen a snake? You've got to be kidding me,' Brigitte squealed. 'Where?'

'On the tennis court,' Alex informed her.

'Then I'm going to stay up here,' Brigitte added, taking another gulp of wine.

'Did you kill it?' Wendy asked.

'*I'd* have killed it,' said Tiff. 'I'm an expert at killing cockroaches and you know how impossible *they* are to kill.'

'I ran away,' said Anastasia quietly.

Lauren turned to Madeleine. 'Have you seen any snakes on your walks?'

'The size of cows,' Alex interrupted. Anastasia elbowed him hard.

Madeleine shook her head. 'But I am not afraid of snakes,' she said coolly.

'I was rather looking forward to a game of tennis,' said Alex. 'But no one can play with a cow on the court.'

Anastasia would normally have lost her sense of humour at this point, and Carina fully expected her to do so, but to her surprise she didn't. Instead, she laughed with him. There was something irresistible about Alex's teasing. It was impossible to be cross with him. Carina was reminded of Rufus and how his refusal to take her seriously always infuriated her, and yet, seeing her daughter laugh at herself made her wonder whether the secret of happiness lay in taking oneself *lightly*.

Anastasia now looked at Madeleine. The older woman looked straight back at her. She showed no sign of guilt or shame or even apprehension at having perhaps been caught in flagrante with Giovanni. Anastasia imagined that she wouldn't even care, for Giovanni was only a diversion for her; a pleasurable way to pass the long afternoons. She gave Madeleine a small smile and Madeleine hesitated a second before smiling back. It was too dark for Anastasia to notice the shift in Madeleine's gaze as her intelligent mind now made sense of the situation.

When dinner was over Anastasia went straight to her grandmother. She put her hand on her shoulder and bent down to whisper in her ear. 'Granny, can we finish the story now?'

'You're not going to take your grandmother away, are you?' said Rex and although his tone was light his aggravation bristled beneath it.

'I'm in the middle of telling Anastasia a story and she wants to know how it ends,' Gracie told him.

'It's not a thousand and one nights, I hope,' said Rex.

Gracie laughed. 'No, it very definitely has an end.'

'I'd like to hear it, Gracie.'

Gracie was about to push herself from her chair when Madeleine appeared. 'Anastasia, can I have a word.'

Rex smiled. 'Madeleine to my rescue. Thank you, ma'am, for giving me more time.' He turned back to Gracie. 'I sure like talking to you, Gracie,' he said and his smile grew tender and his eyes softened and his attention settled on her face like the warm glow of a fire.

Gracie was not unaware of Rex's interest. At first she had thought she must be mistaken, after all, he *did* flirt with all the girls. But then it became too blatant to dismiss. She was flattered by it, of course. It had been decades since a man had shown interest in her, and he was attractive, there was no denying that. However, her heart was already taken, and had, in truth, been so since that moment in Colladoro when she had first laid eyes on Tancredi. 'Rex,' she said and something in her manner made him frown.

'Don't say another word, Gracie. Let me just talk to you and enjoy your company without the shadow of rejection. I like you and I know you like me. We're friends. You're a wise woman and I know you can see through me like I'm made of glass. We have one more day in this beautiful place and I want to spend it with you. So, tell me a story. Any story. You can even make it up. I just want to listen to you.'

'Oh, Rex, that's such a sweet thing to say.'

'I'm not being sweet. I'm being honest. I just want to bask in your light. Because you have a light, Gracie. I don't think everyone sees it because you keep it very much to yourself. But I see it and I consider it a privilege.' Gracie didn't know what to say. She smiled shyly and brought her cup of mint tea to her lips, even though there was only a drop left in it. 'I see you're lost for words,' he continued, delighted to have moved her. 'So, I'll give you time to gather yourself and tell you a story of my own. I was a musician once. I know, hard to imagine now, isn't it? But a long time ago, when I was a young man, devilishly handsome and charming too, of course, I played the drums in a band. I even played for Aerosmith once, now that was an adventure . . .'

Madeleine led Anastasia to the other end of the terrace where they could be alone. 'Anastasia, may I ask you something? Woman to woman?'

Anastasia's heart quickened. 'Of course.'

'Did you see me?' She hesitated as if unsure how to put her thoughts into words. 'You know, down by the tennis court. Am I your snake?'

Anastasia was about to lie, but Madeleine's expression was so kind, concerned even, and not at all accusatory, that she nodded. 'Yes.'

'I thought so.' She laughed. 'I didn't think you'd seen a snake the size of a cow.'

'I didn't know what to say so I said the first thing that came to mind. It was silly. Alex is teasing me mercilessly now.'

'And Giovanni has . . . with you too? Am I right? I think I am.'

Anastasia sighed and to her embarrassment her eyes began to well with tears. 'I thought he loved me.'

'Oh, darling.' Madeleine put her hands on Anastasia's upper arms and her face creased with sympathy. 'I'm sorry. If I had known I would have given him a slap.'

'It's okay. I suppose it's better to find out now rather than later.'

'What are you going to do?'

Anastasia shrugged. 'I don't know.'

'Can I tell you what *I* would do?' Anastasia nodded. Madeleine bent her head and whispered into her ear. Anastasia listened. Then her eyes lit up and she smiled. The two women laughed together. 'I'm right, no?'

'Yes, you are,' Anastasia answered.

'So, we're friends?'

'Yes,' Anastasia replied.

'Lovers come and go but friends are for ever,' said Madeleine. 'But it is important to punctuate your life with a good lover every now and then. It will keep you looking young.' It had certainly worked for Madeleine.

❦

Anastasia found her grandmother at the table, listening to Rex, their faces illuminated in the glow of the dwindling candlelight. Everyone else had moved to the higher terrace to drink coffee and gaze out over the panorama of silhouetted hills and starry skies. When Rex saw Anastasia he knew he could no longer lay claim to Gracie. He departed without a murmur, leaving the two alone in the still, quiet night.

'He likes you, Granny,' said Anastasia.

'He thinks he does,' Gracie replied. 'Italy has a way of enchanting people.'

'I think it enchanted me,' Anastasia said. Her grandmother frowned. 'It's okay. Giovanni is just a typical Italian who will seduce anything that moves.'

'What happened?' Gracie put her hand on Anastasia's. Anastasia sandwiched it with her other one.

'I'm not going to talk about me. I want to talk about you. You promised me you'd tell me the end of the story.'

'Very well. Where did we get up to?'

'You were about to go to the Côte d'Azur with Uncle Hans. He wanted to marry you off and the painting you forged had been sent back to Livia and Bruno, leaving Gaetano with the real one.'

'Ah, yes. I remember.'

'So, did you go to the Côte d'Azur?'

'I did.'

'And what happened?' Anastasia put her elbow on the table

and dropped her head onto her hand. 'Did Uncle Hans introduce you to all the eligible men there?'

'Of course he did, but I pined for Gaetano,' she said. 'However, that didn't stop Uncle Hans trying. And goodness, didn't he try!'

As Anastasia listened she was aware that her mother was watching her from the higher terrace. Nevertheless, she did not allow herself to be distracted. She did not shift her gaze. She looked at her grandmother closely. Tonight she would find out where Gaetano lived and why Gracie had not gone in search of him. She would find out why she had not visited La Colomba. She would remain here, in this chair, until she had all the answers, and then she would report to her mother and decide what to do next.

Later, she would meet Giovanni, as she had done for the previous four nights. But this time she would give him something special to remember her by.

Chapter 22

France, 1964

Gracie stood on the balcony of Uncle Hans's magnificent white villa, set high in the hills above Antibes, and gazed down onto the luxurious swimming pool below where guests, bronzed from the hot Mediterranean sun, mingled in their bikinis and swimming trunks, drinking cocktails, smoking languidly and chatting in French, Italian and Spanish, like a flock of exotic birds. The sight was overwhelming and Gracie wished she were back in the safe and familiar environment of La Colomba. But Uncle Hans was in his element. He was circulating in a panama hat, trousers rolled up at the ankles and a white shirt, cigarette in one hand, cocktail glass in the other, his smile broad and dazzling beneath a pair of fashionable sunglasses. Everyone loved Uncle Hans, Gracie noticed. Women fawned over him, men wanted to talk to him, even small children were drawn to him. He had a joke for everyone, a ready laugh and an easy charm that made all who came near him feel attractive, interesting and witty, even when they weren't. He had a gift and he clearly revelled in it.

They had been at Villa Charlene now for ten days. Gracie's skin had turned brown for Uncle Hans had insisted she buy a bikini and lie in the sun with everybody else. 'You're not going to find a husband hiding away at La Colomba or loitering in the shadows of Villa Charlene,' he said, ignoring Gracie's protestations. 'And yes, you do need a husband. You owe it to your mother, as do I. She would never forgive me if I allowed you to grow into an old maid.'

Gracie found the society in Antibes overpowering. It was moneyed, entitled and fickle. The women were beautiful and glamorous, dressed in the latest fashions, their wrists dangling with jewellery, their hair coiffed into big, elaborate styles, their confidence abundant and intimidating. The men were rich, smooth, well-mannered and handsome, and yet Gracie longed for Tancredi's arms to gather her up and take her away from a place in which she clearly did not belong.

Among Uncle Hans's friends was a young blond American called Jonas Blythe. He was not like the others. He did not look over her shoulder when he talked to her. He did not flash his wealth and he did not speak anything other than English, with a slow Boston drawl. He had eyes the colour of faded denim and long, dark lashes that framed them to dazzling effect. His lips curled up at the corners as if always on the brink of a smile or constantly ready to deliver a witticism. He was boyish and cheerful and even when critical his barbed comments were delivered in such a tone as to arouse amusement in those receiving them. Jonas and Uncle Hans had a way of playfully mocking each other that was so acerbic and snide as to be hilariously funny. They were famous for their clever repartee and people flocked around them to hear it, laughing heartily and a little nervously as the two men competed to outwit each other.

Gracie liked Jonas from their very first meeting. 'My darling, these people are trash,' he had told her, blowing smoke out of his nostrils like a benign dragon. 'They come for the cocktails and the food and because brash and wealthy people like to see other brash and wealthy people. The trick is to find enjoyment in watching them. Imagine you're at a zoo and you're observing the habits and tastes of a strange but remarkable species. That is the only way to tolerate them.'

It was Jonas who had helped Gracie choose a bikini and Jonas who educated her on social endurance, rescuing her when he noticed her looking lost and uncertain – Uncle Hans was much too busy being sociable. Jonas loved shopping whereas Uncle Hans did not. Gracie soon realised that it was Jonas who had chosen the dresses Uncle Hans had given her. 'Hansworthy loses his temper in shops,' Jonas confided as they wandered through the streets of Antibes. 'He has no patience at all. The only reason he cuts a dash is because *I* shop for him and *I* know what suits him.' Jonas had good taste and flair, and was quick to point out the flaws in Gracie's figure that needed covering up, and the positives that should be enhanced. 'You have a small waist, my darling, so flaunt it. You have pretty eyes, so choose blues, greys and greens to bring them out. They are your greatest asset so don't be shy about them, flutter those lashes and, for God's sake, don't be afraid of the mascara wand!' At that point he had inhaled sharply and scanned her body with his incisive gaze. 'You are short, so you must always wear a heel, and be careful not to eat too much starch or it will sit on your behind. Curves are one thing, dough is quite another. You will be my little project, but don't tell Hansworthy or he'll get frightfully jealous, and jealousy turns him sour.' He inhaled through his nose and pursed his lips. 'And I can't abide sourness in anybody.'

Now Gracie watched the party below with a new feeling of apprehension because the young man Uncle Hans had picked out for her was making his way round the pool with his eye on the balcony. Pierre de la Croix was wealthy but not brash; even Jonas had given his approval with the words, 'He does not stop traffic but his wallet more than compensates for his aesthetic deficiencies.' Considering the criticism he bestowed on others, this might easily have been a compliment. Indeed, Pierre was no beauty, but he wasn't unpleasant-looking either. Jonas had informed her that although he was below her on the food chain in terms of looks, he was above her in terms of wealth and status, which evened out to a perfect match. 'You see,' he had said in the tone he adopted when sharing pearls of wisdom. 'The food chain is a science that must be considered before choosing a partner. Imagine a list of animals. At the top are lions, panthers, cheetahs and tigers. At the bottom are warthogs, sloths and pigs. The levels in between are occupied by weasels, deer, monkeys and all the other animals on the planet. Now, a panther is not going to deign to date a warthog, unless the panther is a poor panther and the warthog a millionaire. On the whole warthogs find their own level and stick to sloths and pigs, perhaps going up a level if they're lucky. Panthers consider themselves above deer and horses and rabbits, so they'll look out for other panthers, lions and tigers. Do you get my drift?'

Gracie understood perfectly. Pierre, who was now making his way through the French doors, was what she deserved. She wondered what Jonas would make of Tancredi. She could just hear him saying, 'Darling, he's a panther and you are a sweet pony. You have nothing that would interest a panther. To be a success in life you have to know your place in the food chain!' But Gracie didn't want Pierre, pony or not.

'Hello, Gracie,' Pierre said, smiling. Had Gracie not been impervious to his charms on account of her infatuation with Tancredi, she might have warmed to his smile. It made his rather ordinary face surprisingly attractive. He was not tall but he was slim and athletic, and he dressed well in the way Frenchmen do. He wore an open-neck shirt, a cravat around his neck, well-cut red shorts and moccasins on his feet. He swept a hand through thick brown hair, looked at her with eyes the colour of molasses and spoke to her in an accent most Englishwomen would swoon over. But Gracie was used to accents, living with Hans and Rutger, and she did not find Pierre's particularly interesting. But she liked him. There wasn't anything about him to dislike. ('Dull, darling,' Jonas had said, but Gracie did not find him dull.)

He kissed her, wrapping her in the spicy scent of his cologne. 'You look radiant, Gracie,' he said, sweeping his eyes over the blue dress Jonas had made her buy.

'Thank you,' she replied. Jonas had also told her never to dismiss a compliment with a self-deprecating remark. That was 'so terribly English and gauche'.

Pierre leaned on the balustrade and gazed down. 'Hans always gives the best parties,' he said. 'Look at him! Working the crowd. Making new contacts for his business. He is a very shrewd man.'

'Art is a people business. It's all about contacts,' said Gracie.

'To be sure, and Hans is a people person.' He turned to her. 'And what are you, Gracie? You restore paintings but you are not about making contacts, are you?'

'I work in the background while my uncle finds the buyers and sellers.'

'A fine pair.'

'Yes, we work well together.'

He spotted Jonas who had stripped down to his swimming trunks and was posing on the diving board, waiting for everyone to notice his tanned and toned body before he performed a perfect dive, cocktail glass in hand. 'Jonas Blythe is a show-off,' he said and Gracie noticed the jealousy in his voice.

'He's an entertainer. He loves people.'

'And he loves being loved by them.'

'I think everyone loves Jonas.'

'That is because they are afraid of him.'

'Oh, I don't think so. They know his comments are designed to amuse, not hurt.'

'But often they hurt all the same. He expects people to laugh and condemns them as humourless if they don't, but really his humour is cheap and nasty.'

Gracie's cheeks burned with indignation. 'I can't agree with you,' she replied. Jonas now had the attention of all the guests and did a running jump before leaping into the air and folding into a tidy somersault. He straightened just in time, cutting through the water in a dive and causing only the slightest ripple. When he emerged, cocktail glass still in his hand, the crowd gave a roar of approval, for which he rewarded them with a beaming smile.

'What is he to you?' Pierre asked Gracie.

'He's my dear friend,' Gracie replied without hesitation.

'He is in love with you,' he said.

This was news to Gracie. 'You're quite wrong,' she said, shocked.

'Why? He dresses you and advises you on every area of your life. Do you think he would bother if he was not in love with you?'

'He bothers because he's my friend.'

Pierre shrugged. 'Have you not seen the way he looks at you? I bet that dive was especially for you.'

Gracie laughed. 'That's absurd, Pierre.'

'I wish it was.' He sighed wistfully. 'Do you love him back?'

Gracie was astonished by his directness. She would have retorted curtly, 'What business is it of yours?' but she knew why he thought it his business and she didn't want to go there. 'As a friend, I do,' she replied tersely.

'Are you sure it is nothing more?'

Pierre's probing was now irritating Gracie. If Jonas could hear him he would no longer think him dull, just graceless. 'I know my heart, Pierre. I know it better than anyone.'

This seemed to satisfy him. 'Then I believe you. Just be careful. I don't trust Jonas Blythe at all.'

'I think I would trust him with my life,' she retorted.

'Then you are a fool.'

Gracie did not want to talk to him any more. She shook her head in annoyance and made to go inside. Pierre put a hand on her arm to stop her. 'I'm sorry. I'm a little jealous, that's all, and I'm suspicious of men who pretend to be a girl's best friend.' Gracie shook off his hand. 'I like you, Gracie. I like you a lot,' he added.

Gracie remembered Donato with an inward cringe. Pierre had the same look upon his face. The pleading, sorry look of a man who cannot have what he wants and is yet to accept it. 'I like you too, Pierre. But not in the way that you want me to like you.'

'You barely know me, Gracie. Let me show you how gallant and entertaining I can be.'

'Pierre—' she began, but he cut her off.

'I won't take no for an answer. I ask for nothing from you, but your time.'

And that was the one thing Gracie was able to give him. 'All right,' she conceded. 'But I don't want to hear another word about Jonas.'

'That's a deal.' He grinned and put out his arm. 'Allow me to escort you to the party. It looks to me like the lady needs a drink.' Gracie needed more than a drink; she needed a one-way ticket to Pisa.

However, in spite of her reservations, Gracie was grateful for Pierre. Although she did not harbour any romantic feelings for him, she was happy to be escorted to parties, for it meant that she was never left on her own, feeling friendless. He was attentive, cultured and funny, and she discovered, over the following week, that he was good company. Yet, all the while she was with him she was wishing she was with Tancredi. She wondered what he was doing in Rome and wished that he could telephone her, but there was no way he could call her at the villa, and she was unable to telephone him in Rome for the same reasons. Would they ever be free to love each other in public? Would they ever be released from this life lived in secret?

When they weren't at the beach or at someone else's villa, Gracie, Uncle Hans and Jonas lounged by the pool at Villa Charlene, smoking lazily and gossiping about the people they met. Gracie loved those times the best. If she couldn't be with Tancredi, the next best thing was being with Uncle Hans and Jonas.

'Tell me, Gracie, how is your romance going with Pierre?' Uncle Hans asked one afternoon when they had returned, slightly tipsy, from a lunch party given by an American film producer.

'It is not a romance,' said Gracie, lying back on the sun lounger and closing her eyes.

'Will it become one, do you think?' Jonas asked, stretched out on the lounger in a pair of trunks, legs crossed at the ankles, a cigarette smouldering between elegant fingers.

'No,' Gracie stated firmly.

'Well, I did say he's dull.'

'He's not dull,' Gracie explained. 'He's more interesting than you'd imagine just by looking at him.'

'I don't really look at him, darling,' said Jonas with a grin. 'Really, he's not worth looking at. But if you say he's interesting, I'll take your word for it. It takes all sorts to turn the world and, as I've already told you, you are a perfect match on the food chain.'

'Oh, you and your food chain!' Hans huffed. 'You talk so much rubbish for a man who likes to think he's of superior intelligence!'

'Shhhh!' hissed Gracie. 'I'm trying to relax here. Just be nice to each other for once.'

'I will be nice to Hansworthy for *you,* Gracie, and only for you,' said Jonas.

'It is not in your nature, Jonas dear,' said Hans.

Gracie laughed. 'Pierre thinks you're in love with me, Jonas,' she said. She would not have been so bold had she not been tipsy. Sensing an energy passing between the two men she opened her eyes.

Jonas was looking at Uncle Hans, those lips curling around a secret that now struck Gracie between the eyes. She recalled that night when she had interrupted her uncle in the kitchen with Guido Vanni and her heart gave a sudden lurch. Could it be that the object of Jonas's affection was, in fact, Uncle Hans?

'Well, he's right. I do love you, Gracie,' Jonas replied.

'And I love you too, Jonas,' said Gracie, pretending she hadn't seen the look they had just given each other. 'Why do you want to marry me off, Uncle Hans? If I marry Pierre I'll live far away and you'll have to find another restorer. Besides, Rutger is very fond of me and will be sad and lonely on his own.'

'I'm not a fool, Gracie,' Uncle Hans replied. 'If you marry Pierre, you will still work for me, only you will move in a sophisticated circle in Paris. Pierre de la Croix comes from a wealthy family of collectors. Did he not tell you?'

Gracie sat up. 'No, he didn't.'

'How do you think I know him?'

'How do you know anybody?' Gracie replied.

'Touché!' said Jonas with a chuckle. 'You know *me* and I'm no collector.'

Uncle Hans dismissed Jonas with an irritable shake of his head. 'Your presence here in this villa is by no means a fait accompli, Mr Blythe,' he said, before continuing seamlessly, 'I cultivated Pierre with care and attention and determination. I have sold paintings to his family for years, and his grandmother, who sadly passed away, gave me the task of selling part of her collection when she fell into debt following a bout of uninhibited extravagance. It gave her enough to spend the next ten years being equally reckless with her money.'

'You've been set up, Gracie,' said Jonas. 'He's a cynical old bird.'

'Gracie might be a young woman of only twenty-two but she has the wisdom of a much older woman. She knows how I work, don't you, my dear?'

'I think I do,' Gracie replied. 'But I still don't want to marry Pierre.'

'You will,' her uncle assured her. 'You will realise that marriage is not always about love but about alliance.'

'But if you can acquire both why settle for half a man?' said Jonas sensibly.

Gracie laughed. 'Why, indeed?' She thought of Tancredi who would tick both boxes were she to confide in Uncle Hans.

'You can love just about anyone if you want something from them,' said Hans.

Jonas arched an eyebrow. 'The bigger the desire, the greater the love,' he said.

'Or you can simply love someone for themselves,' Gracie added, feeling increasingly drowsy in the sun. 'I don't care how much money or status a man has. I want to love a man who loves me back regardless of material things.'

'How romantic you are, darling,' Jonas gushed. 'Really, I admire your nobility of spirit. Hansworthy and I are not so pure of heart.'

'I was once pure of heart,' said Hans. 'But disappointment tainted my view of the world.'

Gracie began to doze off. The last thing she heard was Jonas, blowing out a cloud of smoke and adding, almost under his breath, 'And then you met someone who restored your faith in love, is that not so, Hansworthy?'

The day before Gracie was due to return to Italy she told Pierre that although she found him gallant and charming and all the things he had promised he would be, she did not reciprocate his feelings. He did not take it well. So convinced was he that with time he could change her mind, he refused to let the matter go. 'I will come to Tuscany and show you just how determined I am,' he said as Gracie tried her best to dissuade him. She longed to see Tancredi and she didn't want Pierre arriving on the scene and making things difficult. She knew Uncle Hans was disappointed, which made her feel guilty. After all, he had given her more than she could ever thank him for. She wished with all her heart that she could please him in another way, but he was intent on finding her a husband who suited *him,* and he too refused to let the Pierre matter go. He never once threw the accusation of ingratitude at her, but she believed he thought it all the same: the one thing he wanted from her was something she was unwilling to give.

Jonas was sorry to say goodbye. 'You must come to Paris,' he said. 'The fashion in Paris is divine.' He embraced her fiercely. 'Don't marry Pierre,' he whispered. 'You're much too far above him on the food chain.'

'But . . .'

'I know what I said and I take it back, which I rarely ever do. Darling, you're a rabbit and he's a wolf. He'll eat you. So would Hansworthy if he wasn't your uncle!'

'And he won't eat you?' she asked, cocking her head to one side and grinning at him mischievously.

'No, because I'll eat him first!'

❧

Gracie was so happy to be back at La Colomba. Driving up the dusty track towards the house was like returning into the warm embrace of an old, familiar friend. She glanced up at the hill where the Castello stood bathed in the amber glow of late afternoon and wondered whether Tancredi was there with his eye on the valley below, waiting for her homecoming.

The villa came into view and there was Rutger in his overalls, patiently anticipating their arrival. Gracie jumped out of the car and threw her arms around him. He chuckled and patted her back awkwardly, for he was not a man comfortable with physical demonstrations of affection. She inhaled the smell of turpentine and oils that clung to his hair and savoured the feeling of being home at last. Gaia hugged her so tightly her feet nearly left the ground, and the other servants discarded their reserve and hugged her too. Everyone talked at once. With all the excitement the quiet, shady villa burst into a light of its own.

Gracie didn't have to wait long before she was enfolded in Tancredi's arms again. On account of the countess filling the castle with guests they had to meet on the remote hillside beside an abandoned farmhouse where they often picnicked. It was a sheltered spot surrounded by golden fields of wheat and striped green plantations of vine. There they sat in the dappled shade of a plane tree with only the birds and crickets to witness their love.

'It has been the slowest month without you,' he said, tenderly kissing her forehead.

She leaned against him and sighed with happiness. 'And for me too,' she replied. 'I've been counting down the days.'

'Did your uncle find you a suitable man to marry?' he asked with the nonchalant chuckle of a man who knows he is loved above all others.

'He did, but I'm afraid he doesn't appeal to me.'

'What's wrong with him?' Tancredi asked, enjoying the game.

'He's not you,' she said and he squeezed her and kissed her again.

'What did you tell your uncle?'

'That he is not to my liking. Uncle Hans is not really thinking about me, he's thinking about cementing relationships that will be good for his business. Pierre de la Croix belongs to a wealthy family of collectors.'

'So do I,' said Tancredi. 'Shame we can't tell him about us, yet.'

'Yet?'

'In time, I will divorce Petronella and marry *you*. Then we can tell him. I think an alliance with the Montefosco family will please him very much.'

She smiled, encouraged by the mention of marriage. 'To Uncle Hans that would be a match made in heaven.'

'And to you?'

'And to me . . .' she replied softly, hesitating a moment for beneath the gilded fantasy of marriage lay the murky reality of entering a sophisticated, glamorous world in which she did not belong. 'It would be a match made in heaven too,' she said to please him. But the truth was she wished they could live like this for ever, meeting in secret, sharing their love with no one but each other.

'Speaking of the Montefoscos,' he continued, 'Aunt Livia now considers herself an eminent art collector. She is trying to persuade Mother to exhibit Grandfather's paintings with her in New York. She has a contact at the Metropolitan Museum of Art who thinks it's a good idea. The Great Montefosco Collection.' He laughed. 'Can you imagine?'

'Of course, I can imagine. It's a fabulous collection,' she said. 'Especially now that the paintings have been cleaned and restored.'

'They will exhibit our fake,' he said and the idea clearly tickled him because she felt him shiver with pleasure.

But Gracie did not share his delight. A feeling of unease passed across her heart. The painting she had copied was never intended to stand up to the scrutiny of experts in New York. However, Tancredi was unconcerned.

'It is a silent, passive revenge for me to know that the painting Uncle Bruno will show off at the Metropolitan is a forgery. I don't need a public humiliation. *I* know it and that is enough.'

Gracie hoped the exhibition would never happen.

Chapter 23

In the months that followed, Gracie forgot about the exhibition. Tancredi never mentioned it and Gracie assumed that the countess had decided not to lend *her* half of the Montefosco collection. For certain, Bruno's half was not likely to be sufficient on its own.

In December Gracie returned to London for Christmas with her family. It had been a year since her last visit. This time she travelled alone for Hans chose to go to the French Alps to ski. Joseph's little boy was now nearly four months old and his wife was pregnant with their next child, which everyone hoped would be a girl. Joseph himself had grown fatter. He was no longer the scrawny boy he had been when Gracie had left to live in Italy with Uncle Hans, but a broad-shouldered and sturdy young man who was account manager at a prestigious advertising company and not shy of boasting about it either. *He had certainly come up in the world*, Gracie thought. As for her mother, Greet looked a little older, a little wearier, a little thinner. Gracie hadn't seen her for twelve months and in that time, she had aged considerably. However, she insisted she was quite well and thanks to her children and brother she didn't want for anything. 'I have modest needs,' she said. 'Now I have a grandchild, my cup runneth over.

When are you going to marry and have children, Gracie? I didn't allow Hans to take you to Italy so that he could imprison you in his house and keep you away from potential husbands,' she grumbled.

'I'm still young,' Gracie insisted.

'That is debatable,' said Greet tightly. 'I was a married mother of two when I was your age. Time flies by and soon you will lose your youth and no man will want you. Mark my words, the best men are being snatched up by the clever girls right now. You will be left with only the dregs.'

Gracie brushed off her mother's comments without a care. She knew she wouldn't be left with the dregs because she already had the best.

While Gracie was in London she took the opportunity to visit the National Gallery and the Victoria and Albert Museum. She went for walks with her mother around Hyde Park and invited her to tea at Fortnum & Mason, where they ate scones with cream and jam. Joseph managed to get tickets for a West End show and they dined afterwards in a fashionable new restaurant in Soho where the maître d' knew Joseph and greeted him with much fawning, which put Joseph in an exceedingly good mood for the rest of the evening.

When Gracie left London for Italy at the beginning of January she was not sorry. She wished she could bring her mother to live at La Colomba because then she'd never have to return to London again. She and Joseph had never been close and their living so long apart had only exacerbated their estrangement. Were it not for her mother Gracie would have no reason to visit London at all.

Uncle Hans returned to La Colomba at the end of February, having spent a month in Paris following his Christmas break in Chamonix. Yet, in spite of the canvases he had brought with him and the contacts he had made, he wasn't his usual ebullient self. It was as if he had brought the Paris weather back with him and it hovered over his head in a thick grey cloud, making him morose. It was only when Gracie opened the parcels he had bought her that she realised Jonas had been there too. There were brightly coloured dresses with short skirts and pointed-toe shoes to match, lamb's wool twinsets and tights, all carefully chosen to best enhance her colouring and figure, as only Jonas could do. However, when she mentioned Jonas's name Uncle Hans gave a derisory sniff and said, 'Mr Blythe is like milk that has turned, and there is nothing worse than sour milk.' Gracie noticed the caustic edge to his humour which hadn't been there before. It sounded like their friendly teasing had gone too far.

After that Gracie knew not to bring up Jonas's name again. She hoped that, whatever had occurred between them, they would work it out and become friends again, not least because she wanted the old Hans back. But as the months passed and Uncle Hans came and went as usual, his humour did not improve.

Then, in the spring, Tancredi told her that Bruno and the countess were going to show the Montefosco collection after all, in the Metropolitan Museum of Art in New York, the following spring. 'The whole collection?' Gracie asked, hoping that the Baroque painting she had forged would not be included.

'The *whole* collection,' Tancredi replied. Then he smiled. 'Makes me happy to think of smug Bruno showing off a forgery.'

'You aren't worried that someone will notice?' Gracie asked, anxiously biting the skin around her thumbnail.

'Why would it matter? If it *is* discovered, so much the better. Uncle Bruno will be publicly humiliated. Perhaps it might create a scandal!' He laughed. 'He might even give it to me then and we can burn it. I will no longer have to hide the stolen original. I'd say that was the perfect solution to the problem.' It certainly was a solution, Gracie conceded, and she didn't know why she felt such fear. But she did. The shadow that had previously passed over her heart now lingered above it, refusing to go away.

It wasn't until October that Gracie's fears were realised. Uncle Hans received a telephone call from Livia Montefosco informing him that the museum had declared the Piero Bartoloni to be wrongly attributed, most likely a fake. Hans, who had only seen the original, not Gracie's forgery, was astonished. 'I beg to differ, Countess Montefosco, for if it were a bad fake, as you are suggesting, it would have been revealed to us in the cleaning process. As it is, neither Rutger nor Gracie noticed. It must be the work of a brilliant forger.'

Both Gracie and Rutger looked up from their easels, then they looked at each other. 'If it's a fake, it's a damn good one,' said Rutger, scratching his head. 'You cleaned it, didn't you, Gracie?'

She nodded then shrugged. 'I noticed nothing out of the ordinary,' she replied. She hid her face behind her work as the blood surged into her cheeks, threatening to expose her guilt. The fact that one of the Montefosco paintings had been found to be a forgery was not in itself worrying for Uncle Hans, she told herself, because he had played no part in its purchase. However, Gracie knew very well that he had sold Tancredi's grandfather the odd forgery, in fact he was quite proud of it, therefore it wasn't a good thing that experts in New York might be compelled to take a closer look at the whole collection. Of course, that was unlikely, but in Gracie's increasingly paranoid imagination it seemed entirely possible.

From the sound of the conversation Livia Montefosco was furious. Uncle Hans spoke to her in his smooth, impassive way, reassuring her that it wasn't, as she put it, 'a humiliation in front of the highest echelons of New York society', but a sadly all too common occurrence in a collection of that size and age. 'Just because they have discovered one wrongly attributed painting in your collection does not mean there will be others. It is highly unlikely,' he told her. '*Highly* unlikely.' Gracie remained, heart in mouth, ruing the day she ever came up with such a hare-brained idea. The only pinprick of light in the gathering darkness was the thought of Tancredi's pleasure in his uncle's humiliation. But that was not enough to allay her fears and she sat there sweating, wondering whether she should come clean and confess her crime or remain quiet and hope the whole business would simply go away.

The telephone conversation lasted half an hour, but to Gracie it appeared to last far longer. Each heavy minute was an unbearable weight to bear. Livia seemed to fluctuate from fury that Hans had not saved her from embarrassment by recognising the fake, to self-pity for what she considered to be a very public disgrace.

When at last the call ended, Hans put down the telephone and turned round to face the room. Gracie dared look at him. The cool façade he had presented to Livia Montefosco was now replaced by an expression of real anxiety and something else, something ominous. Rutger pushed his magnifying spectacles onto the top of his head and put down his brush. Gracie felt the air still around her. If she had contemplated coming clean with Uncle Hans she swiftly changed her mind. The face that glowered at her was not the usual face her uncle wore, even when he was in a bad mood. This was very different. This unfamiliar face put fear into her heart.

'We have a little problem,' he said, and the calm, quiet tone of his voice only incremented Gracie's fear.

'We have had little problems before, Hans,' said Rutger, equally calm and quietly spoken. 'And we have surmounted them.'

'Indeed we have. Forgery is not a business without risk. However, this is unexpected and inconvenient.'

'*I* cleaned it, Uncle—' Gracie began.

'No, you did not.' Uncle Hans's gaze was cold enough to freeze fire. Gracie's breath caught in her throat. 'Had you cleaned it you would have very quickly ascertained that the painting was not genuine. It is not a good forgery, but an amateur forgery any fool could have and *should* have detected.'

Again Gracie thought about telling the truth, and again she ignored the opportunity on account of her panic. If being honest was not an option the only alternative was to be entirely *dis*honest. 'I didn't clean it, Uncle,' she confessed, tears brimming. 'I didn't think it needed it. I made an error . . .'

'You made a great error, Gracie, which could get us all into trouble.'

'What can I do?'

'Pray.'

With that Uncle Hans stalked into his studio and slammed the door behind him. Gracie didn't look at Rutger. She could feel his disapproval as if it were a cloak of iron around her shoulders. Unable to withstand the atmosphere in the room, she fled. What had love driven her to do? Had she known her painting would be scrutinised by experts in a world-famous museum she would have done a proper job of it as Uncle Hans had so painstakingly taught her to do. She would rather die now than admit to having forged it herself; Uncle Hans's disappointment in her careless work would be far worse than being sent to prison for collaborating in his criminal business.

Gracie bicycled down the track into the countryside. She didn't think about where she was going, she just wanted to go far away and not come back. She had let Uncle Hans and Rutger down, two of the people she loved most in the world, and for what? To please a man whose love for her she now questioned. As she cycled, the red vines and yellow hills a wet blur through eyes blinded by tears, she began to doubt the wisdom of her choices. Had Tancredi made any move to divorce his wife? He had talked about it often, promising her a life together when the time was right, and it had always been *she* who had shrunk from the idea of it out of terror of the world he inhabited. Had he perhaps taken advantage of her uncertainty because it was convenient for him? She recalled that he hadn't tried to persuade her. He hadn't even tried to reassure her, instead he had talked about marriage as one talks about a fantasy that is unlikely ever to manifest. She knew he didn't want their affair to end, of that she was certain, but she wasn't sure he had the courage to terminate a marriage that would scandalise his family and society in Rome. The Montefosco family were very Catholic and divorce was immoral. He would not only be defying his family but also his faith. He had taken his vows before God, vows that no man could put asunder. Gracie couldn't count on his mother for her support either. As louche and bohemian as she appeared to be, Gracie sensed that when it came to the structures of her world, the countess was probably as inflexible and traditional as everyone else. A man had a mistress, some no doubt had various, but he did not marry his mistress, certainly if that mistress was from a lower class. Gracie had heard it said that no one was more snobbish than the Romans.

It was drizzling when she cycled back up the track towards the villa. She hadn't noticed the vaporous cloud moving inland from the sea. It now lingered in the valley in a cold, damp mist. Her hands were numb on the handlebars for she had forgotten, in her haste, to wear gloves. She lifted her gaze to Colladoro but the castle perched above it was hidden in the fog. Once, she had looked up at the crest of the hill with her heart full of longing, now her heart was full of doubt and it pained her to look at the castle with all the promise it had once represented. *Just as well it was concealed*, she thought miserably.

As she reached the villa Gaia was in the doorway, waiting for her. Her arms were folded and she had pulled her cardigan tightly around her fulsome body. She was shifting from one foot to the other in the cold. 'What are you doing cycling off in this weather?' she asked as Gracie left her bicycle against the wall and came running up the path, her hair wet and flat against her scalp. 'You'll catch your death of cold.'

'I had to get out of the house,' Gracie replied.

Gaia grabbed her arm. 'I have a message from Tancredi,' she whispered. Gracie looked at her wearily and Gaia noticed her eyes dim and frowned. 'He telephoned. He wants you to go to the Castello tomorrow afternoon. He's driving down from Rome tonight.'

Gracie knew why he was coming to see her. He wanted to celebrate his uncle's humiliation. She gave a wan smile; his *uncle's humiliation might just be* her *uncle's downfall*, she thought bitterly. 'Brave of him to telephone here,' Gracie said, stepping into the villa.

Gaia followed, happy to close the door on the cold. 'Must be important.'

'I don't think so,' said Gracie.

'Are you all right?' Gaia asked.

Gracie sighed and turned to her friend, her gaze heavy with resignation. 'He's not going to marry me, is he?' she said.

Gaia hesitated, which conveyed her thoughts more honestly than the words that followed. 'I'm sure he will, one day,' she said.

'No, he won't. I should have listened to you back when I discovered he was married.' She chuckled joylessly. 'The irony is that I don't want to be Countess Bassanelli living in a palazzo in Rome. I just want to be with him, here, in Colladoro.'

'You can't have both,' said Gaia. Gracie shrugged. Gaia followed her into the kitchen. 'What's brought this on? Signor Hollingsworth is in a terrible mood this afternoon and Signor Janssen is no better. Has someone died?'

That was meant to be a joke, but it was a little too close to the bone for Gracie's taste. 'I failed to clean a painting and it has been revealed as a forgery,' Gracie told her.

'I don't know why you're in trouble for that,' said Gaia, putting her hands on her hips. 'That's just unfair.'

'If I had cleaned it properly, I would have discovered it was a fake.' She was beginning now to believe her own lie.

'If anyone should recognise a fake it is Signor Hollingsworth and Signor Janssen.' Gaia noticed the surprised look on Gracie's face and grinned. 'You don't think you fooled me, do you?'

'I don't know what you're talking about.'

'That painting you tried to hide from me in Signor Hollingsworth's studio. I know what you do in there. But knowing what you do does not mean I'm going to betray you so don't look so worried. Only, those two men should be ashamed of themselves for allowing you to get mixed up in all this. You have my word that, if it ever comes to it, I will defend you with every bone in my body.'

'It won't come to that,' said Gracie, knowing Gaia meant exposure.

Gaia clicked her tongue. 'Of course not. I'm sure Signor Hollingsworth is shrewd enough to have blocked all the entrances to his lair.'

❧

Dinner was the usual formal affair in the dining room with Uncle Hans and Rutger. Hans, who had been in a bad mood since Christmas, barely made any conversation at all, which left Gracie to talk to Rutger, who was too kind-hearted to be cross with her any longer. Gracie had for years listened to her uncle's anecdotes, often at the expense of some poor soul who had somehow incited his wrath, but she had never in her wildest imaginings supposed that *she* might be on the receiving end of his fury. She wondered how long his sulk was going to last. But she needn't have wondered because when she came downstairs the following morning, he was gone.

Finding Rutger in the studio she asked him where her uncle had disappeared to. 'He had some urgent business to attend to,' said Rutger, settling onto his stool to start the day's work.

'When will he be back?'

'When the wind brings him.'

'Has he gone abroad?'

'He has gone to Paris.'

Gracie was relieved he hadn't gone to New York, *that* would have suggested the problem she had created was far worse than she had imagined. It was quite normal for Hans to go to Paris. 'Is he still furious with me?' Gracie asked.

Rutger did not look up from his easel. 'Think no more about it,' he mumbled distractedly. 'Your uncle's work would fool the greatest experts on the planet.'

'I hope you're right.'

'In that respect, I am always right. As for your uncle, well, he leads a complicated life. Of that I know nothing. What will be, will be.' Gracie didn't know what he meant, but as it had nothing to do with her, she simply nodded and set to work.

❧

Gracie cycled to the castle that afternoon. The rain had moved away in the night, leaving the countryside wet and shimmering in the sunshine. She should have been happy, after all, her plan had worked, but she felt a gnawing apprehension in the pit of her belly.

Tancredi was delighted with her, sweeping her into his arms and pulling her into the tower and kissing her. 'I have wonderful news!' he exclaimed.

'I know it,' she replied flatly. 'Livia called yesterday and told Uncle Hans about the forgery. He's not very happy.'

'It makes no difference to him,' said Tancredi sensibly. 'No one will trace it back to you.'

'I know,' she replied, not wanting to reveal that her uncle had forged paintings for his grandfather which were most certainly among those due to be exhibited and those, if discovered, could definitely be traced back to Uncle Hans. 'I should never have attempted to forge a seventeenth-century Baroque painting. It is almost impossible to do so convincingly. Only Uncle Hans can do it. I'm so ashamed.' Gracie's eyes shone.

Tancredi cupped her face in his hands. 'Gracie, you're not unhappy, are you? You've made me so happy. You've made me the happiest man in the world.'

'But I have painted the worst forgery in the world,' she explained.

'It doesn't matter. In fact, I'm delighted that you have. Uncle Bruno has been suitably humiliated. *I* have the real painting, which was meant for me, which was *always* meant for me, and *he* is left with a dud.'

'But don't you see? The humiliation is all mine because *I* painted the dud!'

'Nonsense! It's brilliant. I couldn't have planned it better had I sat down and wished for it. You're a genius! You're *my* genius!'

He went to kiss her again but she pulled away. 'Tancredi, we need to talk.' She sat on his painting stool, cold hands folded in her lap. She'd forgotten her gloves again.

Tancredi's face was expunged of all joy. 'What's wrong?'

She sighed laboriously. It hurt her to see him looking pained and yet she was compelled to confront him. 'You're not going to divorce Petronella, are you?'

The joy returned to his face. 'My darling, is that what you're worrying about? Us? I love you.' He went and knelt before her, putting his arms around her hips. 'I'm working on it. You have to trust me. It's a delicate process. Petronella's family are powerful.'

'Did you ever love her, Tancredi?' she asked.

'She was what I wanted at the time,' he replied carefully.

'Powerful?'

'Gracie, let me explain. It's complicated. Mine is a family in decline. An old family that was once rich and powerful, but which has been in deterioration for many years. *I* had the illustrious name *she* wanted and *she* had the wealth *I* wanted. But I've changed. I don't want that now. I realise that material things don't bring happiness. *You* have taught me that.' Gracie looked at him through narrowed eyes. She wanted to say that she couldn't have done a very good job, for he still prized the Piero Bartoloni painting above all else. But she remained silent as he tried to persuade her that he was no longer a material man, but a man of depth and passion and integrity. 'I was lost, Gracie. I had wasted my youth being hedonistic, thinking only of my own pleasure, squandering the money I had been given, tarnishing our family name. I realised that I had been a fool. I wanted my grandfather to be proud of me. Petronella's family were wealthy enough to restore our family to its former glory. I knew my grandfather would approve. I thought that was the way back into his favour. Marrying Petronella would go some way to compensate for the unhappiness I had put my family through.' He must have noticed the uncomprehending expression on her face and added sheepishly, 'I liked her too, of course. We were friends.'

'But she'll bear your children and then you will never leave,' she said and the words caught in her tightening throat, because that thought was intolerable.

Tancredi shook his head. 'She does not want children,' he said and Gracie realised, by his stricken look, that by marrying a woman like that he had inadvertently imprisoned himself.

'I'm sorry . . .' she began, her heart flooding with pity.

'I should have told you,' he said.

'It's all right.'

'I couldn't . . .'

'I understand,' she soothed, running a hand through his hair. 'It's unspeakable.' She wanted to reassure him that she would give him lots of children. As many as he wanted. But he pushed the subject away and Gracie knew by his change of expression that he was used to burying his disappointment.

She allowed him to draw her closer, but she felt a sense of hopelessness. In spite of his childless marriage, he was still unable to leave his wife. Gracie loved him for his faults as much as for his perfections, but it was those faults – weakness and cowardice – which would prevent him from ever standing up to his wife and asking for a divorce. She didn't believe he had the courage to defy his family or his religion. In her heart she knew he would never be hers. There would come a moment, one day, when she would have to walk away.

They made love in the room at the top of the tower – love that was made all the more intense by the inevitability of its demise – and Gracie clung to him as if these precious moments together were the last. Tancredi seemed to sense nothing of Gracie's sorrow. He was much too preoccupied celebrating his triumph. When he looked into her shining eyes he just smiled tenderly and teased her for being sentimental. 'I adore the way you feel everything so deeply,' he said. 'I can read your face like a book.' And Gracie smiled back at him sadly, because she knew he couldn't.

The following weeks went by slowly, as if time was dragging its feet. Feet that were heavy and reluctant and afraid. A gloominess hung over La Colomba too, even though Rutger and Gracie went about their work in the habitual way. When at last Uncle Hans returned he brought with him a flurry of snow. Gracie awoke to a white world outside her window, but the romance of it did little to ease her disquiet. When she saw her uncle her anxiety deepened.

Hans had lost a lot of weight. His face was gaunt so that his cheekbones protruded and his eyes appeared large and strangely startled. His clothes hung off him, like garments on a wire hanger, and he was distracted, smoking incessantly and drinking large glasses of whisky with trembling hands. In spite of returning with his usual hoard of old canvases and paintings bought at auction, he seemed not to take pleasure in them at all. Gracie wondered whether they had discovered more fakes in the Montefosco collection but she was too frightened to ask. Hans did not talk to her. Not that he ignored her, just that his mind appeared occupied with other matters. He did not bring her the usual dresses. He brought her nothing, and Gracie feared he was still cross and punishing her for her error.

He talked to Rutger, however. The two of them disappeared into Hans's studio and closed the door behind them. Gracie tried to put her ear to the wood, but she only managed to decipher the odd muffled word in Dutch. She assumed they were careful not to speak in front of her because it was *she* who had failed to recognise the forgery and therefore *her* failure that was quite possibly going to lead the detectives to their door. She bit her nails to the quick and was unable to concentrate on her work. For the first time she wished she were not at La Colomba. She wished she was at home in Camden, in the damp, dreary house where once she had belonged.

However, Gracie didn't have the heart to go home. Not even for Christmas. Rutger returned to Holland but Gracie remained at La Colomba with Uncle Hans. She would like to have invited her mother out to Italy, but she knew not to ask her uncle. She realised now that if he had wanted his sister to visit him he would have invited her long ago. As for Joseph, she barely knew him now. They were as strangers. She reflected on the family she had left behind and the family she had made in her uncle, and in her morose state of mind, she regretted leaving all those years ago. She hadn't realised then how important family was. She did now, because she felt she had lost it.

On Christmas morning Gracie awoke to a weight on the end of her bed. When she opened her eyes she noticed it was a parcel, wrapped in brown paper and tied with string. She pulled it towards her and set about opening it. Her heart gave a little flutter at the thought that Uncle Hans had forgiven her. Would he have bought her a present if he had not?

She tore off the paper to reveal an antique wooden box complete with a key in a tiny gold lock. She turned the key and lifted the lid. Inside, there was a tray of paintbrushes, all neatly lined up in their own individual slots. She lifted the tray out of its niche with loops of satin ribbon. Beneath was a compartment of tools for the trade that Uncle Hans had taught her so well. She was bewildered. Why would Uncle Hans give her a box of brushes and tools when she had all the equipment she needed here at La Colomba? She closed the lid. Only then did she notice the initials engraved in gold lettering on the top. H.E.H for Hans Edward Hollingsworth.

It was *his* box.

Gracie jumped out of bed with a sharp sense of panic. She threw on her dressing gown and hurried along the corridor to her uncle's bedroom. His door was closed. She knocked, then waited. There came no response from within. She knocked again, this time louder. She turned the knob. The room was dim, the curtains open to reveal through the window panes a white world awakening with the dawn. She swept her eyes over the bed, which was neatly made. His slippers were on the rug beside it. She noticed his dressing gown lying across the quilt. It was as if he had taken great trouble in making sure everything was tidy before leaving the room.

She padded downstairs in her bare feet. So apprehensive was she that she didn't notice the cold as she trod over the freezing flagstones towards the kitchen. 'Uncle?' she called out. The house remained silent but for the rhythmic tick-tocking of the grandfather clock in the hall. She recalled the moment she had intruded on his private moment with Guido Vanni in the kitchen, but that was unlikely to be the case now. None of the servants came in at Christmas time and besides, since then, she had not witnessed anything improper.

Gracie decided that he must have gone out. She was disappointed, albeit a little relieved, for if he had simply gone for an early morning walk, there were no grounds for concern. She felt foolish for being irrational and made herself a cup of coffee in the cafetière on the stove. While the water bubbled up through the coffee granules she thought of the box and the brushes and tools, and longed for Uncle Hans to return so she could ask him what he meant by giving her such a present.

The house was eerily quiet; the air inside it oppressive. Gracie sat at the kitchen table and tried not to feel afraid, and yet the tension grew ever tighter in her chest, as if someone were clutching her heart and squeezing it. She was restless, anxious, unable to sit still. At last she stood up, taking her coffee with her, and wandered back into the hall.

She did not expect her uncle to work on Christmas Day, but he had been acting so strangely recently that it wasn't beyond the realm of possibility that he had gone to his study to absorb himself in what he loved doing best. She took her steaming coffee cup through the house to the studio. The first rays of sunshine were breaking through the glass, falling in shafts of light onto the wooden floorboards, illuminating the room that was her and Rutger's domain. It seemed so very still and quiet. She went to the door of Hans's studio and noticed it had been left ajar. *That* in itself was unusual and the hand on her heart squeezed harder. Hans never left it unlocked. She approached with the caution of a deer advancing towards a sleeping pride of lions. Placing her hand on the door she pushed it gently and peered inside.

The first thing she saw was a chair, placed in the centre of the room. It looked forlorn there in a puddle of light. Her eyes were then drawn to the pair of feet suspended above it. Her breath caught in her throat. The feet were bare, lifeless and a queasy shade of grey. Suddenly, the room spun and a wave of nausea crashed against the walls of her stomach. The coffee cup fell out of her hand and smashed onto the floorboards. Gracie reached for the wall to stop herself from falling too; to stop the world from whirling because she needed to be sure.

When at last she was able to focus again she lifted her eyes. There, hanging from the large beam that spanned the entire room, was Uncle Hans.

Chapter 24

Anastasia stared at her grandmother in horror. It was one thing to be told that Uncle Hans had hanged himself, but quite another to watch her grandmother unravel before her eyes. She didn't know what to say. As Gracie had neared the end of the story her voice had gone as thin as ribbon. Anastasia had had to inch closer to hear – and she had not wanted to miss a single syllable. From time to time Gracie had faltered and taken a deep breath. She had massaged her throat as if trying to relieve a tightness in it, and she had stumbled on various words, the emotions they roused being at times too much. Anastasia had watched her grandmother struggle to get the story out, afraid to move in case she disturbed her stream of consciousness. In case her grandmother noticed her there, because, in truth, as the tale reached its terrible climax, it was as if she was talking to herself.

Anastasia stared at Gracie, who looked very small now, and knew that there was nothing she could say to take away the trauma of that shocking discovery, or the guilt of believing *she* was the cause. All she could do was follow her heart and put her arms around her, embracing her fiercely. Gracie allowed herself to be embraced. She also allowed herself the luxury of crying; of expressing what she had spent the last forty-four years concealing. At first her cry was a silent howl, a contraction of the diaphragm so tight as to actually cause pain as it laboured to eject her anguish in a long, drawn-out breath. And then, as she inhaled, her diaphragm relaxed so that when she exhaled again her cry found its voice. It came out in a loud, unfamiliar moan. It was as if grief, buried so deeply within her being, was at last being released, rising up through the layers and layers of resistance and secrecy accumulated over the decades. Gracie unburdened her shame, her remorse and her love.

Anastasia was alarmed. She had never heard a human, or an animal for that matter, make such a sound. The fact that it was coming out of her grandmother sent her into a sudden panic and she searched the darkness for her mother. Carina, who was on the higher terrace talking to Madeleine and Lauren, heard the strange howling and instinctively knew to whom it belonged. She excused herself and hurried down the steps to find Gracie sobbing in the arms of her daughter.

Anastasia was overwhelmed with relief to see her mother. She had managed to extract the whole story but she was too young and inexperienced to deal with the sorrow that had come with it. Carina took the chair on the other side of her mother and gently put a hand on her back. 'Mum,' she said. 'It's me, Carina.'

Slowly Gracie eased herself out of Anastasia's arms. She was unable to speak. Her body shuddered. She seemed confused by it, as if it was reacting without her consent. 'It's okay, Mum. Let it all out. Whatever it is, just let it out.' Carina remembered how her mother had once, a long time ago, said those words to her.

The three of them remained at the table in silence as Gracie's breathing gradually grew more regular and her body stilled.

'What did you do, Granny?' Anastasia asked, keen to

draw her away from the image of Uncle Hans hanging from the beam.

'I fled,' Gracie replied huskily. Carina handed her a napkin, left over from dinner, and watched her wipe her eyes.

'Where to?' Anastasia asked.

'London.'

'You didn't tell Gaetano?'

Gracie began to cry again, this time softly. 'I couldn't. I couldn't tell anybody.' Anastasia caught her mother's eye. They stared at each other in bewilderment. 'You see, *I* was the cause of Uncle Hans's suicide.' Her voice was barely a whisper now. 'They had discovered his business and were coming to get him. In which case, they'd come for me too. I knew then that Rutger hadn't gone to Holland for Christmas, but had fled too. I doubted he'd be coming back. If I stayed, I'd have to explain why I forged the Piero Bartoloni. I'd have to betray Gaetano. I couldn't do that. The only thing I could do was disappear, and hope they'd never find me.'

'What did you tell your mother?' Anastasia pressed, as Carina tried to piece the story together from what Anastasia had relayed and from what was now being said.

'I told her he had committed suicide and that I had run away out of fear.'

'Didn't she wonder why he had killed himself?'

Gracie had now stopped crying. 'I don't know,' she said, folding the napkin with shaky hands. 'She just accepted it. The body was returned to London and he was buried in Camden. She never questioned me. It was as if she knew why. As if she knew already and didn't want to discuss it.'

'Didn't you ever tell Gaetano where you had gone? Didn't he try to find you? Did he know where to look?'

Gracie shook her head sadly. 'He was never going to leave

his wife, dear. He wanted to. I don't doubt that. But he couldn't. It was a fantasy and nothing more. A fantasy we both wanted, but that sort of dream requires more than will. It requires strength and Gaetano, bless him, didn't have it. I realised while on the plane back to London that I had to let him go.'

'But you never said goodbye to Gaia, either.'

'I said goodbye to no one. I just ran, like a coward. I'm not proud of myself. But I was young. I thought by my running away the problem would just disappear.'

'Did it?' Anastasia asked.

Gracie sighed and unfolded the napkin only to fold it again. 'In one respect it did. Uncle Hans's solicitor dealt with his will and Joseph and I inherited his estate. He had given his villa in France and a great deal of money to Jonas Blythe a few months before his death. That didn't surprise me. He loved Jonas. As for my brother, Joseph accepted his inheritance with enthusiasm. He bought a big house in Belgravia. But *I* didn't want Hans's money or his homes.'

'Was La Colomba left to you?'

'Yes, it was. But I never returned. I left it to deteriorate. I shared the money with my mother, hoping she'd move out of that horrible old house, but she didn't. That was my mother. She remained there until she died.'

'What did you do with the rest? Uncle Hans was so rich.'

Gracie glanced at Carina and hesitated.

Carina stroked her mother's back and smiled sympathetically. 'Mum, Anastasia told me about your past with Uncle Hans. She didn't mean to. I coaxed it out of her. I was worried about you.'

'I would have told you, dear, but I didn't think you'd be interested.'

Carina was horrified. The fact that her mother's tone was not in the least accusatory, rather it was matter-of-fact, as if she had accepted long ago that her daughter was not interested in her, made Carina feel even worse. 'Oh, Mum!' She put a hand on her heart. 'Did you really think that? I'm so sorry. It couldn't be further from the truth. I *am* interested. I guess I've just been preoccupied with work – God, that's a feeble excuse.' Her eyes began to shine. 'I won't blame work. One can always make time if one wants to. I've been a terrible daughter and a terrible mother and I'm going to change. I don't want to be that busy, selfish person any more.' She took a breath as a tear escaped and trickled down her cheek, leaving a glistening path in her make-up. 'Will you forgive me?'

Gracie put a hand on hers and gave a small smile. 'If you forgive *me* for having kept the biggest part of my life secret.'

'It's your secret to keep, Mum.'

Gracie turned to Anastasia. 'You ask me what happened to my inheritance. I shared it with my mother, but I couldn't bring myself to use it on myself. My guilt was too great. So, it is invested. I have no idea how much is there, but it will be considerable. I have left it to your mother in my will, with a letter of explanation.'

'You weren't ever going to tell me?' Carina asked.

'No. I didn't think I could ever tell anyone. Your father never knew I had it.'

'But that's extraordinary.'

'Perhaps,' said Gracie. 'But when I said I fled, I fled in every way. I turned my back on that chapter of my life and started a new one. I met your father and married very quickly. He was everything that Gaetano was not. He was twenty years older than me. Stable, sensible and strong and he was from a world closer to the one I had grown up in. He wasn't a dashing aristocrat like Gaetano, but he was kind and I knew I'd be safe with him. I put away my brushes and I vowed never to paint again. It would have been much too painful to have opened Uncle Hans's box and used his tools, or any tools for that matter. I simply couldn't bring myself to paint again. How I regretted having painted that forgery. It wasn't even a good forgery. I hadn't taken the time or the trouble to do it properly. It was never meant to be seen by experts. It was meant to hang in Bruno's palazzo and fool only him. But Fate had other ideas and it ended in my beloved uncle's death. I will never forgive myself for that. So, my dear,' she said, looking steadily at Carina. 'The money is for you, once I am gone.'

'Don't say that, Mum.'

'We all have to go sometime.'

'But I don't want to think about it. I've only just found you.'

Gracie felt as if something soft and warm were cupping her heart. She felt strong, suddenly, as if the love she was receiving from her daughter and granddaughter was bolstering her fragile spirit with an inner coat of armour. 'Will you do something for me?' she asked them both.

'Of course,' they replied in unison.

'Will you come with me to La Colomba tomorrow? I feel ready to face it. I think I should, while I'm here. It might be my last chance. It's haunted me for so long I think I should confront it, in order to let it go.'

Anastasia took her hand. 'Of course, we'll go with you, won't we, Mum?' she said.

'Absolutely,' Carina replied. 'I'll ask for a cab to take us after lunch, unless you want to miss Mamma Bernadetta's final lesson.'

Gracie smiled. 'I don't think we could do that to her, do you? I'm sure she'll have planned something special.'

❧

That night Gracie stood at her window, staring out into the valley, which was veiled in darkness. She thought of the countless times she had stared up at this castle from her own window at La Colomba, wondering whether Tancredi was there. Whether he was thinking of her. Yet, here she was, in the castle, *his* castle, and here he was too and yet they might as well have been thousands of miles apart. She wondered whether he had ever thought of her over the years that followed her departure, as she had so often thought of him. She had written him a letter once she had arrived in London and told him not to try to find her, that her leaving was the best thing for both of them. She also told him about Uncle Hans's suicide and begged him never to divulge who had forged the Piero Bartoloni – if she was to go down for forgery she wanted to go down for a good one!

How her heart had ached for him. How it ached for them *both*. She had lost her uncle and Tancredi in the very same moment and with them she had lost her way of life and everything that was familiar to her. Now she recognised the extraordinary resilience of the human spirit, for she had withstood it all. She hadn't collapsed and refused to go on, but put one heavy foot in front of the other and taken a step into her future, without having a clue what it would hold. She remembered having told Tancredi that grief was like crossing a bridge and until you crossed that bridge you couldn't begin to understand what it meant to lose someone you loved. Well, she had crossed that bridge all over again with the loss of Uncle Hans and her lover, and another layer was duly dug into the depths of her soul. She returned to England a very different woman to the one who had come home for Christmas. She cared even less for material things. She had patience for everyone, compassion for those who needed it and a more profound understanding of the world. She had never been a religious person, but in the months that followed she thought much about God. There had to be some purpose to all of this, she argued. Oma and Uncle Hans were not dust, she was sure of that. They were out there somewhere, in another dimension, where she would one day join them. It had to be so, because when she was in nature, among the flowers and trees and birdsong, she felt it intuitively. She couldn't have explained this feeling to anyone, but it was strong, like a guiding hand on her heart.

Gracie grew to love the English countryside. After she married Ted they moved down to Badley Compton and started their life together there. She adored the sea, the pebbly beaches and rugged cliffs. She relished walking in the long grasses and watching the cows chewing the cud. She even took pleasure from the grey clouds, drizzle and fog. Loss inspired her to appreciate the natural world around her and in her appreciation that world slowly healed her. Tancredi did as she asked and did not come looking for her. She buried her past beneath the new life she had chosen and she never dug it up. When the fear of being caught and imprisoned for forging art had passed she began to enjoy her marriage. In Ted she found her level. He was the sort of man she could be content with. He didn't set her heart racing, but she had already experienced that and she knew it would never happen again. She closed the door on the sensual side of her nature and accepted a very different kind of love. Ted would not hurt her or let her down or give her empty promises. He could be relied on and she was grateful for that. They made new friends together in the town and those people did not intimidate her, or judge her, but accepted her for what she was. She had no desire to go anywhere again. Like a child whose hand has been severely burnt she had no yearning to put her fingers near the fire. She had found contentment and was satisfied with that.

Now, as she gazed down into the valley, she longed to know what happened after she left. What had become of her forgery? Had they pursued Hans only to drop the case after his death? She couldn't bear to return to England not knowing and yet, she was too afraid to confront Tancredi. He hadn't recognised her and that had cut her deeply. It had felt like a rejection although, how could it have been? He'd have had to have recognised her first in order to have rejected her. And what if he *did* recognise her and they *did* speak, and it was as if they had never known each other? That would almost be worse. A few minutes of polite conversation would hurt her even more and she wasn't sure she'd be able to take it. In that case it would be better not to speak at all.

At that moment her attention was drawn to a tear in the sky that revealed the twinkling dots of faraway stars. The sight uplifted her and she thought of Carina and Anastasia and the bond they had forged over the week they had been here. It was as if they had each been touched by something special, and transformed. When she thought of her daughter and granddaughter she experienced a wonderful expanding in her chest. Not the tight, contracting regret of before, but a warm, loving enlargement, as if her heart was rising like a cupcake in the oven. How thankful she was for that. Even if she never spoke to Tancredi and never found out what had become of her painting, she had rediscovered her family and that was more important than her past. She had a very strong feeling that the present would be the foundation upon which her future would be built. In which case, she had so much to look forward to.

❧

It was just after midnight when Anastasia hurried down the path towards the pool. She had chosen her prettiest yellow dress over which she wore a faded denim jacket. On her feet she wore sparkly sandals and she could feel the dew now, wetting her toes as she walked. Moonlight spilled through the gaps in the cloud, shining a spotlight onto the gardens, and the scent of roses was carried on the breeze. Anastasia's heart was thumping wildly with anticipation. She knew Giovanni would be waiting for her down on the track, beside his scooter, ready to whisk her off to the barn for another night of lovemaking in the den he had prepared for her. The mere thought of it sent tremors across her skin, as if her nerves were oblivious of his betrayal, or simply disinterested. If she was like Madeleine she wouldn't care and she'd enjoy him regardless. But she wasn't. She was in love and she had believed he loved her too.

The pool house came into view, bathed in the moon's milky white radiance. The pool itself was black lacquer, reflecting the night. Anastasia circled it, treading lightly over the paving stones between which little flowers had seeded themselves and flourished, thanks to Giovanni's idleness. She could make out the path that wound through the long grasses and shrubbery to the track below. She sensed Giovanni down there. She could feel him like a predator feels her prey.

She took a deep breath and set off down the bank. A glimmer of moonlight bounced off the metal of his scooter and caught her eye. She then noticed the glowing red tip of his cigarette as he put it to his lips and took a drag. He must have heard her footsteps for he turned to face her and his white teeth shone as he smiled. Anastasia fell into his arms as she always did and he pressed his mouth to hers, kissing her passionately.

She tasted the cigarette on his tongue and in his breath and her loins started to ache regardless of what was in her head, conditioned as she was, like a Pavlov dog, to anticipate pleasure. He wound his hand beneath her hair, round the back of her neck, and Anastasia had to muster all her energy to pull away, take his hand, and lead him up to the pool. At first he resisted. He wanted her to come with him, to the barn, where it was comfortable and there was no danger of being discovered. But Anastasia had other ideas. She smiled at him with promise and said the word 'Surprise', which he understood.

Once inside the pool house she pushed him playfully against the wall and kissed him. His mouth curled into a grin as he realised that *she* was going to take the lead. This clearly delighted him. His hands dropped to his sides and he lifted his chin, willingly allowing her to undress him. Slowly, she unbuttoned his shirt. Little by little his chest was exposed. She ran her fingers over it, tracing the outline of his muscles and the hair that grew there. He was indeed very fit. When his shirt was off and discarded on the floor, she started on his jeans. She unbuckled his belt, making sure she took her time, then unbuttoned his flies and pulled down the zip. He murmured in Italian and closed his eyes. She drew the trousers down his legs and he stepped out of them, kicking off his canvas shoes at the same time. She could see from the swell beneath his underwear that he was excited. This gave her a gratifying sense of empowerment. She stood up and kissed him, but when he tried to touch her she put his hands back against the wall. 'Let *me* pleasure you,' she said, and hooked her thumbs over the waistband of his underwear. Gently, she removed these too so that he was standing before her, completely naked. She looked him over, regretful that she would now have to leave him.

With a swift movement she gathered his clothes and tossed them out of the open window where Madeleine was waiting for them. Then she ran out of the pool house. Bursting into a fit of nervous giggles the two plotters ran up the path towards the castle. Anastasia dared to look back just as they turned the corner. She saw Giovanni in the doorway of the pool house, staring after them in bewilderment. He was no longer excited.

'Did you hide his scooter?' Anastasia asked Madeleine as they reached the castle out of breath.

'Of course,' Madeleine replied. 'He will have great trouble finding it, but he will of course, eventually. First, he will have to walk home naked.' She grinned, dropping the clothes onto the ground. 'That will teach him.'

'I think that's what Granny calls karma,' said Anastasia.

'And what we call revenge,' Madeleine added. 'How does it feel?'

Anastasia pulled a face. 'He is *very* handsome . . .'

Madeleine nudged her with her elbow. 'Don't start!' she said, pretending to give Anastasia a stern look. 'Come on. The job is done. We need to go to bed!' And the two walked into the castle with a bounce in their step.

Chapter 25

Anastasia and Carina awoke at the same time. They lay in bed, luxuriating in the sound of birds and in the lyrical rise and fall of Italian as a couple of retainers chatted excitedly in the garden below their window. It wasn't until Anastasia picked up the name Giovanni that she realised what they were talking about. 'They're talking about Giovanni,' she said, sitting up. 'I wonder how he got home.'

'Maybe he didn't get home. Perhaps he's still in the pool house,' said Carina with a smile. She had waited up and been told the whole story when Anastasia fell into the bedroom in a frenzy of excitement.

Anastasia grinned. 'We made sure there was nothing in there for him to clothe himself with,' she said. 'He would have had to find a leaf in the garden and wear it like Adam.' They both laughed.

'I can't help but feel a little sorry for him,' said Carina.

'He deserved it. Someone had to teach him a lesson.' Anastasia wandered into the bathroom. 'He'll regret the day he ever lured Madeleine into the tennis pavilion.'

'I hate to say it, darling, but I think it was Madeleine who lured *him* into the pavilion.'

'It doesn't matter who lured who, the fact is he has now

been punished. With any luck the whole of Colladoro knows and he is suitably humiliated.' She emerged a moment later and began to dress. 'We're taking Granny to La Colomba today,' she said.

'It's going to be very emotional for her.'

'I saw the room where her uncle hanged himself. I knew something horrid had happened in there. It felt creepy.'

'What a terrible thing to have witnessed. My poor mother,' said Carina.

'And to think she bottled it up all these years,' Anastasia added.

'You think you know someone,' Carina mused, climbing out of bed and padding into the bathroom.

'We have to find Gaetano,' Anastasia reminded her.

'I don't think she's come back for him, after all. She's come back to lay ghosts to rest.'

'You mean, facing that room?'

'Facing the past, which remains in that house. By sharing her story with us and visiting La Colomba after forty-odd years, she will finally be able to let it go.'

'You don't think she's curious to see what became of Gaetano?'

'No, you can't still love someone more than forty years later. That's the sort of thing you only read in romantic novels—'

'And in the newspapers,' said Anastasia, who was inclined to be more romantic than her mother. 'They're always printing stories like that.'

'Maybe, but it's unlikely. This is about Uncle Hans, not Gaetano.'

But Anastasia didn't agree. She sensed her grandmother's attachment to Gaetano. She didn't feel that the years had, in any way, diminished it. 'We're talking about two people who never stopped loving each other, Mum. Two people torn apart by tragedy, not because one cooled off and left the other broken-hearted. I think she longs for him. Just because she's old now doesn't mean her heart is.'

Carina laughed and zipped up her Capri trousers. 'I think you're going to be a writer of romantic novels,' she said.

Anastasia flicked her hair off her shoulders. 'If Granny lets me write her story, perhaps I will.'

'Good, then you can keep me in my old age.'

'I won't have to. You'll have Granny's money to do that!'

❧

'Today we are going to enjoy our final lesson,' Ilaria began. 'We are not going to be sad, because we are not going to say goodbye tomorrow, but farewell. Castello Montefosco will always be here, ready to welcome you back.'

Rex had noticed that Gracie had been upset the evening before, but was too polite to mention it. Instead, he took the stool next to hers and talked to her with tenderness, as if she were a wounded thing who needed looking after. Gracie noticed and was grateful, for she felt tired and raw, having not slept very well due to the emotions she had stirred up in divulging the final chapter of her story. She was anxious about going to La Colomba and what she would find there. She knew Uncle Hans would not be hanging from that beam, but in her mind he was there still, his feet grey, his face white and his lips blue.

'I hope we won't say goodbye tomorrow, but farewell,' said Rex, blue eyes twinkling with implication that was not lost on Gracie.

'Of course, we won't,' she replied. 'I hope to remain in touch with all the new friends I have made here.'

'I'd like you to see my ranch,' he said, lowering his voice as if he wasn't going to extend the invitation to anyone else. 'For a woman who appreciates nature, I think you'd find it magical.'

'I'm sure I would,' she agreed.

Seeing her agreement as an indication of her enthusiasm, he grinned, causing the crow's feet to deepen into his temples. 'Good,' he said. 'That's settled then.'

Anastasia sat beside Alex. 'What's going on between you and Madeleine?' he asked, just before the lesson started.

'What do you mean?'

'You keep looking at each other and grinning, like you've been up to a load of no good.'

Anastasia laughed. 'Let's just say we dealt with the snake,' she replied. 'It won't be bothering anyone any more, I don't imagine.'

Carina turned to Lauren. 'We'll keep in touch, won't we?' she said.

'You bet,' Lauren replied. Then she laughed and nodded towards their children. 'I don't think we'll be able to avoid each other, do you?'

Carina smiled, glad that Giovanni was now out of the picture, leaving the way clear for Alex. 'The best relationships have their beginnings in friendship,' she said. 'Whatever happens, I have a feeling that those two will always be friends.' Anastasia sensed she was being talked about. She glanced at her mother, who was watching her, and smiled quizzically.

The lesson began. The conversations stopped. The students, who had become very attentive and conscientious, took up their pencils and began to write the last notes on the final page on their clipboards.

'Today we are going to learn how to cook *gnocchi alla*

sorrentina. Gnocchi with tomatoes and mozzarella. Then we will cook something special: *coniglio con pomodori e olive*. Rabbit with tomatoes and olives.' Ilaria glanced at Anastasia and smiled. 'You don't need to look so sad, Anastasia. We are not going to cook Peter Rabbit. He is quite safe in the Beatrix Potter books.' Anastasia caught Alex's eye and they both laughed. 'Rabbit is a delicious meat and, because we look after our rabbits here at the Castello, the meat is juicy and full of flavour.' She put her fingers to her lips and kissed them. 'Delicious! And for dessert, we will make *crostata di mele*, apple tart. All the apples are from our gardens. They are sweet, but don't tell them or they'll blush! And finally, because you are my favourite pupils, I am going to teach you how to make *limoncello*, lemon liqueur. Then you can spend the afternoon sleeping it off.' She looked at her mother and grinned.

'Ready, Mamma Bernadetta?' The old lady nodded and turned her back to the group to wash her hands in the sink. Carina watched her. There was something very dear about the way she stood there, shoulders rounded, head inclined, her dress revealing thick ankles and wrinkled stockings. Carina knew she was going to miss her. She was going to miss them both. 'Let us begin,' said Ilaria, and she took a large saucepan and added to it one cup of tomato sauce.

❦

After lunch the taxi Carina had ordered arrived at the Castello just as Rex was about to invite Gracie on a walk. Gracie climbed into the front seat and folded her hands in her lap. She picked at the cuticle around her thumb and chewed her bottom lip anxiously. She wondered whether this really was a good idea. Perhaps it would be better to leave the past *in* the past and not muddy the water. She had survived forty-four years, hadn't she? Why bring it all up again? Yet, before she could convince herself to abort the plan Carina and Anastasia had got into the back seat and the driver was already setting off down the track, swerving to avoid the odd pothole and bumping over the stones.

The three sat in silence, ruminating on their thoughts, and the driver assumed that none of them spoke Italian and drove in silence too. At last the crumbling villa could be seen, peeping out forlornly between cypress trees and oleander, and Gracie caught her breath because she hadn't imagined it to have deteriorated so. Just as she was about to waver, she felt the soft pressure of a hand on her shoulder. She looked round to see her daughter smiling at her with encouragement. 'It's okay, Mum,' she said. 'We're here with you.'

The taxi rattled up the track, bouncing over the uneven ground, testing the suspension, which wasn't very well tuned even on the tarmac road. The driver was cautious, tentative even, unsure why they wanted to come here, to this desolate place. It had been a shell for as long as he had been alive.

As they got nearer, Gracie's heart began to throw itself against her ribcage in protest. 'Please stop,' she said in Italian. The driver glanced at her in surprise, but put his foot on the brake and drew the taxi to a halt. 'I'd like to walk the rest of the way. Perhaps you can wait here. We'll be an hour or so, I should think.'

'*Sì, signora*,' the young man replied, startled because the old woman looked so English yet she spoke Italian like a local.

Gracie opened the door and climbed out. Carina and Anastasia did the same. Gracie stood a moment, staring at the building, now visibly derelict, in horror. She put a hand on her heart. It was like seeing an old friend gone to ruin. The once manicured gardens were overgrown with weeds, ground elder had taken over the borders and smothered the plants, and bindweed was climbing all over the hedges, gradually strangling the life out of them. She remembered how proud Uncle Hans had been of his gardens. He'd be turning in his grave if he could see them now.

Slowly, she began to walk towards it. Memories crept out from every corner like fragile wisps of light, restoring a little life to the place, if only in her mind. She could see Gaia in the doorway and Rutger sitting at the breakfast table beneath the fig tree. She could smell the lavender and jasmine and hear the birdsong. She remembered what it felt like to be young, to be in love, to see this astonishingly beautiful world through the eyes of a child. And she felt sad because loss wasn't something that had happened to her, but something she had brought upon herself. Who knows how things might have turned out had she not forged that wretched painting?

They walked on in silence. Carina knew her mother was deep in thought and she didn't want to intrude. Anastasia swept her eyes over the place as the story her grandmother had told her brought it to life. She, too, could see Hans smoking and drinking a glass of wine on the terrace beneath the pergola. She could see her grandmother cycling up the track after having spent the day with Gaetano. She could just imagine what it had been like when it had been magnificent. Glancing at her grandmother she was sure that *she* still saw it like that. That she could see beyond the rot.

As they reached the door Gracie's face went pink. She was very hot. She wasn't sure whether it was on account of the sunshine, being the hottest part of the day, or whether she was simply overcome. This had been her home for ten years and she had been very happy here. Uncle Hans and Rutger had been her family. She felt as if she was walking among ghosts, trying to grasp hold of something lost long ago, like clutching at wood to find it turns to ash in one's hand. It was gone. All of it. There was nothing left but memory, and the one memory that frightened her the most was entombed in this building and embalmed in her imagination. Perhaps that, too, would turn to ash if she was brave enough to venture inside.

Gracie pushed the front door. It opened without a struggle. There was little of interest inside. Everything had rotted. The garden and the weather had invaded over four decades, season after season, and birds had built their nests in the corners of the rooms, animals in the upholstery, and without anyone taking care of the place it had become feral. Gracie wandered around, remembering the way it had been when it was a beloved home, and Carina and Anastasia followed behind her, trying to imagine.

They couldn't go upstairs to Gracie's old bedroom because the staircase looked too fragile. Some of the steps had completely broken and the banisters had fallen off and lay embedded in weeds on the ground. So they explored the sitting room and kitchen instead, and in some places there was no ceiling at all, just holes that exposed the skies above and the ivy falling in. As Gracie went from room to room she knew she was just marking time before she had to go to the studio, Uncle Hans's studio; the scene of his death. She knew she *must* go, she had come this far it would be cowardly not to. But she was gripped with fear. Her palms were sweating and yet she now felt strangely cold. The studio pulled at her as it always had, for the room where she and Rutger had worked had been the heart of the house. It had been forty-four years and yet she had been so deeply conditioned that her body wanted to go there by default. It was almost impossible to stop it. She could have closed her eyes and allowed her feet to find the way without her guidance. She put a hand on the wall and took a breath.

'Are you all right, Mum?' Carina asked. Her mother looked worryingly pale. She had shrunk too, like a wizened old lady, as if the weight of memory was bearing down on her shoulders and crushing her.

'It's okay, Granny,' said Anastasia, taking her hand. She knew why her grandmother was afraid. 'I've been in that room already. There's nothing in there but a chair.' She gently squeezed her hand. 'Come, I'll take you. You don't need to be afraid with me.' Gracie did not reply, but she let her granddaughter lead her slowly through the villa to the studio.

There was nothing to fear in the room where she had worked. Sunlight streamed in through the broken windows dispelling any ghosts that lingered in the shadows, and birds could be heard in the trees outside. Her easel was still there and the stool upon which she had sat was placed beside it, as if she had just got up and left. Mildewed bottles were lined up along the shelves. Some had fallen and shattered on the floor that had once been made of stone but which now looked more like the garden, for plants had grown in the cracks where the slabs had broken, and bees bumbled about the tiny blue flowers that thrived there. Gracie could see Rutger, at his easel, his grey hair curling about his ears, his glasses perched on the end of his nose, and she imagined he must be dead now, for he had been old even then.

She turned to the door of Uncle Hans's studio. Suddenly she was a young woman again. It was Christmas Day. The door was ajar. It was *never* ajar. Uncle Hans had always locked it. But here it was, open. She felt a swell of nausea rising into her solar plexus. Her hand tightened its grip. 'It's okay, Granny,' Anastasia said again. 'He's not in there any more. I promise.'

Gracie couldn't see for the tears in her eyes. Anastasia walked slowly towards the door, not wanting to force her, but keen for her grandmother to see the empty room and realise that her uncle had gone, long ago. It was only the memory that remained, and that, too, had to go.

Carina hung back, arms folded, chewing the inside of her cheek. She felt her mother's terror and it debilitated her. She watched her daughter lead her bravely in and felt a rush of pride. This young woman, only seventeen, was looking after her grandmother with surprising maturity. Carina had never imagined she could behave with such sensitivity and courage.

Gracie stepped into the room and her eyes fell upon the chair. It was in the very same place it had been when she had discovered him, hanging above it. But he was no longer there. The rope had gone and so had Uncle Hans. Nothing remained but her fear. She let go of Anastasia's hand and walked into the room which was bathed in light and warmth. She put her hand on the back of the chair.

Just then she heard a man's voice behind her. She swung round in astonishment as a ghost from the past appeared before her very eyes, demanding in Italian to know why they were trespassing in this house.

When he saw her, he blanched, as incredulous as she was. 'Gracie?' he asked.

For a moment both Carina and Anastasia thought that, by some miracle, Gaetano had found her, but that was not his name.

'Rutger?' Gracie gasped. He staggered towards her. She began to cry. 'Rutger?' she repeated, this time in a whisper. She stepped towards him, arms outstretched. They embraced with such affection that Carina and Anastasia's eyes filled with tears, too. Neither Gracie nor Rutger spoke. There was too much to say, neither knew where to begin. They remained locked in each other's arms, grateful to be reunited after so many years, grateful for the piece of their past they could at last hold on to.

Finally, they pulled away. Rutger studied her face. 'Gracie,' he said and his rheumy old eyes gleamed with their familiar twinkle. 'Gracie. It *is* you. It is really *you*.'

'I'm surprised you recognised me,' she said, thinking of Tancredi.

'Of course I recognise you. You are still Gracie, just a little older.'

'And you are still Rutger,' she laughed. 'You look the same.'

'I was born old,' he said. 'I'm ninety-six. Every dawn is a pleasant surprise.'

'Do you still live in the house beyond the garden?'

'Of course.'

'But I thought you fled to Holland.'

'I never fled anywhere. Why would I flee?'

'Because they were after you.'

'Who was after me?'

He looked confused. Gracie wondered whether he'd lost his memory. 'You know, after they discovered the Piero Bartoloni forgery, they found others and traced them back to Uncle Hans.'

Rutger frowned. 'They did no such thing.'

Gracie felt desperate. She put her hands on his shoulders. 'Yes, they did. That's why Uncle Hans … that's why he …' She began to sob. 'Why he hanged himself. Because of me. Because I forged the Piero Bartoloni and led them back to him.'

'You forged the Bartoloni?' Rutger was unconvinced. 'It wasn't even a good forgery. In fact, it was a terrible forgery.'

'But I did it for Tancredi, because he wanted the original. I did it hastily. It wasn't ever meant to be seen by experts. It was only meant to fool Bruno Montefosco.' Carina and Anastasia looked at each other at the mention of the name Tancredi. Anastasia slowly nodded.

'I am disappointed in your shoddy work,' Rutger said with a shrug. 'I have to admit, I am disappointed. I trained you better than that. But Hans did not take his own life because of a painting.'

Gracie's hands fell to her sides. 'What?'

'No one was after him.'

'But I was sure my blunder had led them to discover the forgeries Hans did for Gaetano Montefosco.'

Rutger looked appalled. 'Hans was much too good to be discovered. No one has ever discovered his forgeries and they never will. They still hang on walls all over the world. Some in the most prestigious museums. There has never been a forger of his talent before or since.'

Gracie couldn't believe what she was hearing. 'Then why did he kill himself?' she asked.

'Because of Jonas Blythe.'

'They were friends,' said Gracie.

'They were lovers,' Rutger corrected. 'But you knew that, surely.'

She shook her head. 'I wasn't sure.'

'Hans loved Jonas. He'd taken many lovers over the years, but Jonas was special. Then they had a misunderstanding. Jonas got jealous. He threatened to expose Hans's homosexuality and ruin his reputation. As you know, reputation is everything. Hans's entire business depended on that. So, Hans gave him his house in France and more money than he deserved to keep him quiet, but, Jonas wanted more. He wanted revenge.'

'Hans committed suicide because of Jonas?'

'Of course.'

'But I thought it was because of *me.* I thought he was angry with me for my blunder.'

'Yes, he was angry with you, but not for very long. He was not himself that winter because of Jonas, not because of you. If you had not run off I would have told you myself, but I assumed you knew the truth.'

'I wish I had,' she said, and the past four decades flashed before her eyes. But instead of resenting them as a waste, she felt a wonderful lightness in her spirit. A liberating sense of relief.

Rutger shook his head. 'What an unfortunate misunderstanding,' he said. 'Your friend Count Tancredi came looking for you. He took control of everything. I don't suppose you said goodbye to him, either?'

'No, I didn't. I was too ashamed.'

'Because you thought you had killed Hans.' His tone was mocking, as if he thought her foolish.

'Tancredi was never going to marry me, Rutger.'

Rutger shrugged and pulled a face. 'On reflection, you are probably right.'

'What was I to do?'

'Talk to him. He came looking for you like a lost dog, until he didn't come any more.'

'I wrote him a letter explaining.'

'That is the coward's way out, Gracie. Since when were you a coward?' As Gracie struggled to swallow his criticism, Rutger's eyes shifted to Carina and Anastasia who were listening quietly by the door. 'This is your daughter and granddaughter,' he said, scrutinising them brusquely and recognising the similarities at once.

Carina introduced herself and Anastasia, and they shook hands. 'I see you made a life for yourself, none the less,' he said, then he grinned at Carina. 'Did *you* know any of this or did Gracie keep it secret?' It was obvious that he supposed the latter.

Carina smiled, not wanting to let her mother down. 'We came here together to put the past to rest,' she said.

'Then I am glad you bumped into *me*,' he said. 'Or nothing would have been put to rest but untruths.' He turned to Gracie. 'Come and have tea with me so we can talk. We have a lot of years to catch up on and there is no tea in this ruin.'

'We'd love that,' said Carina, answering for all of them.

'Gracie?'

She looked at Rutger, ancient now and as candid as ever, and she felt the old, familiar affection for him soothe the bruise his criticism had inflicted. 'I'd like that, thank you,' she said.

As they walked out into the sunshine Anastasia whispered to her mother, 'Told you so.'

Carina grinned at her resignedly. 'Yet again, you're right,' she whispered back. 'But now we have to come up with a plan.'

'Because Granny is not going to come up with one, is she?' said Anastasia.

Carina shook her head. 'Judging by her track record, darling, no, she isn't.'

Chapter 26

Rutger's house was the simple, stark home of a man who needed few comforts. He had his own studio, in which he still restored paintings, and a terrace beneath a vine where baby grapes were just beginning to bud. The four of them sat in the shade on tatty wicker chairs and Rutger told Gracie not only about Hans's death, but about his life too, and all the secrets within it. Carina and Anastasia listened in fascination as Gracie's life was unfolded with Hans's, layer by layer like a mysterious fruit. In the light of these new revelations Carina realised that she had never really known her mother – to her shame she had never *tried* to know her. Had she asked, perhaps Gracie would have confided in her. But she never *had* asked. It astonished her to discover that Gracie wasn't the ordinary woman she had thought she was, but a criminal and a talented criminal at that.

'What I don't understand,' said Gracie, 'is why Hans never invited my mother and brother Joseph to join him out here. They would have enjoyed a far more pleasurable way of life in Italy than in England.'

'His sister disapproved of his business,' Rutger replied. 'She knew of her brother's activities in Holland during the war and that at the end he had to escape for fear of being tried for collaborating with the enemy. You see, he sold forgeries to all the top brass. That is how he first made his money. They didn't look too hard. They just wanted to amass the great works. Yes, Greet was aware of his criminal activities and she didn't like it. Therefore, he didn't want her getting too close.'

'But he supported her.'

'He would have done more had she allowed it. But she didn't want to receive money that was tarnished. She took what little she had to in order to survive.'

'She must have been very happy when Joseph started making money so that *he* could look after her.' Gracie sipped her tea thoughtfully, then added, 'Do you think she knew he was homosexual?'

'I think she knew exactly what he was. Of course, in those days, that was criminal too.'

'I liked Jonas Blythe,' she said, remembering the flamboyant young man with whom she had bonded in France. 'He was great company.'

'Hans used to get him to buy you dresses. He used to return with cases of parcels for you. It was his way of making it up to you.'

'Making up for what?'

Rutger looked at her through narrowed eyes. 'Did you never wonder how much your forgeries went for?'

'No, I was never concerned about money.'

'They went for hundreds of thousands of dollars, Gracie. The Matisse?' He sucked the air between his teeth. 'That went for three hundred and fifty.'

'Goodness, I made a fool out of somebody.'

'No, Hans made a fool out of *you*.'

'Well, he made up for it in his will.'

'He was afraid you'd leave if you had financial independence.'

'I was never going to leave,' said Gracie. 'I never wanted to leave.'

'He loved you like a daughter,' Rutger added. He smiled then, a tender smile that softened the rough contours of his face. 'And so did I.'

Gracie's eyes shone again and she dropped her gaze into her teacup shyly. 'I'm sorry I never said goodbye.'

He shrugged. 'It is all in the past. You are here now and that's what matters. It's only taken you forty-odd years!' He chuckled and Gracie couldn't help but laugh through her tears.

❧

When they walked back to the taxi they found the driver asleep with the seat back and a hat over his face. Anastasia knocked on the window and he awoke with a jolt. '*Si, signorina*,' he blurted, hastily rolling his chair back into position and turning the key in the ignition.

'Don't leave it another forty years,' said Rutger, enfolding Gracie in a firm embrace.

'I won't,' she promised.

'You know, this is a prime spot of land. You could always bulldoze the ruin and build another.'

'Please, Granny!' Anastasia enthused. 'You can't say you don't have the money.'

'I'm too old to start again,' she said.

'No, you're not!' Anastasia exclaimed, looking at her mother, who was now running her eyes over the rubble with a thoughtful expression on her face. 'Mum will do all the work for you, won't you, Mum?'

Rutger grinned at Anastasia. 'I see a chief executive in the making,' he said.

'I don't know. It's full of ghosts,' said Gracie.

'The only ghosts, Gracie, are the ones in your head,' said Rutger. 'And the old man at the bottom of the garden. I already have one foot in the grave.'

Carina opened the door and told Anastasia to get inside. 'Tell her, Mum!' Anastasia hissed as she joined her on the back seat.

Gracie sat in the front and Rutger closed the door for her. Then he put his face to the window. 'Thank you for making an old man very happy today,' he said.

'I should never have left it so long,' said Gracie.

'No, you should never have left at all. You were a good painter, Gracie. I taught you well.'

She waved as the car set off down the track. Aware of the taxi driver listening to their conversation (they couldn't depend on him not speaking English) they waited until they were back at the castle to talk about Tancredi.

'What are you going to do about him?' Carina asked as they climbed the stairs to their rooms.

'I'm not going to do anything,' said Gracie.

'But you have to let him know you're here!' Anastasia exclaimed.

Gracie stopped on the landing and looked at them sadly. 'I have seen him and he did not recognise me.'

Carina was unconvinced. 'How is that possible? Rutger recognised you immediately. You haven't changed that much!'

'I have seen him on two occasions and he has had ample opportunity to acknowledge me. He either didn't recognise me or he's avoiding me. Whichever, I am not going to embarrass myself by talking to him.'

'Didn't you say hello and introduce yourself?' said Anastasia.

Gracie folded her arms. She did not want to be thought of as cowardly. 'Of course not. It's been over forty years. I decided to tread carefully.'

'Well, you've got nothing to lose. You're leaving tomorrow,' said Anastasia.

Sensing her mother's discomfort, Carina put a hand on her daughter's arm. 'If Mum doesn't want to, she doesn't have to. You came here to make peace with the past, Mum, and that's what you've done. You don't have to do any more.'

Gracie set off down the corridor. 'I assumed Rutger had died. He was ancient when I was a child,' she said, changing the subject.

'One of those people who always looks ninety, I should imagine,' said Carina, happy to oblige and talk about Rutger. Anastasia traipsed along behind. Surely, there was something she could do.

They left Gracie in her room. She said she was tired and needed to lie down before dinner. Anastasia followed her mother into their room and closed the door behind them. 'Mum, we can't leave without having spoken to the count,' she said.

'What do you want to say?' Carina asked, throwing her straw bag onto the bed and sitting down with a sigh.

'That Gracie is here and would like to see him.'

'You can't say that. If it's said at all, Gracie has to be the one to say it.'

'How could he not recognise her? She's aged really well.'

'Yes, but if you're not expecting to see someone—'

'Rubbish!' Anastasia interrupted. 'I don't buy it.'

'Or perhaps that's the reason he's avoiding us. Come to think of it, when I asked Ilaria if we were going to be introduced she went all funny and said that he never met the guests. Do you think, and this is just a thought, that he saw her that first day and decided to hide?'

'Of course not! If he wanted to avoid her he'd go to Rome, or somewhere else. He wouldn't stay here and hide away in his apartment. That's absurd.'

'Well, I haven't been right about anything yet, have I?'

'I hope this isn't the first time you're right. It would be awful if he was avoiding us all simply to avoid Granny!'

'Don't you think it's a bit strange that the host doesn't bother to meet his guests? I've never known that happen before. It's not only rude, it's not good business.'

'I suppose he could be *pretending* not to recognise her?' Anastasia sat on the edge of her bed, facing her mother.

'Look, let's go over the facts. They have this love affair, right? Mum paints the forgery and he's thrilled. He says he's going to divorce his wife, but Mum senses that he never will, so when the painting is revealed as a forgery she fears it will lead to Hans's other forgeries and betray him. Her affair continues, however. In fact, from what we know, the count has no intention of stopping it. When Hans kills himself, Mum believes the police are after him and she flees, believing they will be coming after her, too.'

'She thinks Rutger has run off to Holland.'

'Yes, in fact, he's just gone to spend Christmas there. She leaves in a hurry and never says goodbye, only explaining her reasons for doing so in a letter later.'

'What might she have written in the letter to make him angry?' Anastasia asked, rubbing her bottom lip thoughtfully.

'Assuming she wrote something that made him furious, can he still be furious after so long?'

'He's a widower, so his wife has died. There's no reason for him to avoid her? She's not going to expose him or anything. She's an old girlfriend. What's the big deal?'

'I don't know, but we've got one night to find out.'

'I'm going to talk to Ilaria.'

Carina shook her head at her daughter's determination and grinned. 'Good luck to you then.'

❧

Gracie dressed for dinner. She put on trousers and a blouse and the necklace Anastasia had given her. She ran her fingers over the beads and felt the warm swell of tenderness permeate every corner of her chest. If she never got to talk to Tancredi she would not regret having come. Besides discovering the truth about her uncle's death and finding Rutger, she had gained something far more important: the affection of her daughter and granddaughter. She did not look too closely into the magic, but something special had occurred which had brought the three of them together. The two of them were worth a thousand Tancredis, she decided. Still, as she looked at her reflection in the mirror she knew that for her, at least, love had never died. She would leave tomorrow without having spoken to him, that was now certain. Of course she'd be disappointed, but she would tell herself how lucky she was to have loved so deeply. How many go through their lives and never experience that kind of devotion?

She went downstairs to where the others had congregated in the usual place for crostini and wine As she approached she noticed how tanned they all were, how radiant and how relaxed. Italy had been good for everyone. The sun had burned away all their cares and Mamma Bernadetta's food had bonded them, as only *her* recipes could. The castle looked radiant too. The lights glowed in the windows, throwing gold slices across the paving stones, and the walls seemed to reach out to her in a friendly embrace. She savoured the smells too, as the dew settled upon the grass and shrubs, and brought out the sweet scents of rosemary and pine. Crickets chirruped, the first stars twinkled in the cobalt sky and the faraway lights of distant dwellings twinkled with them as darkness fell.

She'd be sorry to leave tomorrow, Gracie thought to herself as she walked across the stones. The idea of returning to her old life was like a sharp stone in the midst of this perfect softness; a cold, lonely stone that almost succeeded in smothering her joy.

Rex was quick to dispel her downheartedness. He handed her a glass of wine and smiled at her with such enthusiasm it was impossible not to be rescued from her reflections. 'How was your afternoon?' he asked, but she couldn't have begun to explain what had happened at La Colomba, so she told him that it had been very agreeable and then asked him about himself. 'I finally met the elusive count,' he said. He didn't notice Gracie's smile freeze and continued, eager to share his experience. 'He was sitting on that bench up there, watching the sunset. I think he sits there often, with that big dog of his. That animal follows him everywhere. Anyway, I was walking up the path and called out in my usual jovial way, and he waved. We had a very pleasant conversation. He's a charming man. I asked him whether he was going to come and join us tonight on our last night and he laughed and said he preferred his guests to enjoy themselves without him. He said he hoped I had been treating the castle as my home. We had a little joke, you know. I told him I was growing fat on Mamma Bernadetta's food and he patted his stomach and said that it was a daily battle for him too. But as he's so slim I imagine he must take a lot of exercise. That dog needs a great deal of walking, I imagine.' Gracie listened, astonished. She wished she had been with him so that Tancredi might have had another opportunity to recognise her. She knew she should approach him herself and confront him, but she was too scared now. Too scared of being rejected. Not seeing him was better than seeing him and being snubbed. She didn't want to return to England with *that* as her final memory. She'd rather remain with the memories she already had.

Anastasia made sure she was sitting next to Ilaria by taking the chair before Ilaria could put someone else in it. Alex made sure *he* was sitting next to Anastasia, and for the first half of dinner he monopolised her while Ilaria talked to Wendy about dogs, for Wendy had an eccentric French bulldog who didn't like going out in the rain and snored louder than her husband. 'And that's saying something!' she laughed. 'Do you have a dog, Anastasia?' Wendy asked across the table.

Anastasia cut off her conversation with Alex. 'Sadly not,' she replied. 'Mum works too hard and Dad doesn't want the responsibility. I'd like a pig,' she added perkily.

'You're welcome to have one of ours,' said Ilaria.

'Or get a dog like mine and *call* him Piglet!' Wendy suggested, taking a large gulp of wine.

'The count's dog is massive,' said Anastasia, thrilled at her own mastery in swinging the discussion round to the count. 'How old is he?'

'Eight,' Ilaria replied. 'Which is very old for a big dog like him.'

'Does the count take him for walks?'

Ilaria's face assumed the quality of a mask. Her smile set and her eyes lost their animation. Anastasia sensed she did not want to talk about the count at all. 'He prefers to be with the count and goes looking for him after I take him for walks every morning,' she replied. 'I get up at dawn. The three or four hours I get before everyone else awakes are my most productive.'

'Do you look after all the animals yourself?' Wendy asked and Anastasia was frustrated that the conversation had moved on from the count. Ilaria seemed happy that it had. Her smile regained its liveliness and her eyes brightened. She was only too delighted to talk about the animals. Anastasia wondered why such reticence. Was Ilaria protecting them from the count's terrible temper? Was he unfit to be seen? Or was she aware that he was hiding from Gracie? Was that possible?

At the end of dinner Ilaria called Mamma Bernadetta onto the terrace and everyone clapped. 'My mother wants you to know that you have been her favourite guests,' she said, and they all laughed because that joke was probably made at the end of every week. 'It is very important for us to know that you will go home to your various corners of the world and continue to cook Mamma Bernadetta's recipes with love, because that is the secret ingredient she puts into all her cooking. Most important, we hope that the castle has given you a good rest from the stresses of your lives. Whenever you are tired or unhappy think of the gardens here, the lovely lavender and beautiful roses, and imagine that you are back here in the serenity of Castello Montefosco. Carry it inside you and let it warm you like a hot potato in your sweater, yes?' More clapping and then Rex stood up to reply, in his capacity as the only senior man. He raised his glass to Mamma Bernadetta, whose lips curled into a shy smile, and the guests stood up and raised theirs in a toast.

'How we would all benefit from having a Mamma Bernadetta of our very own,' he said. 'But we will have to make do with the memory. I will never forget this week. Thank you for the gift of delicious food, but more importantly the gift of friendship, because I have met some delightful folk here this week. It's been very special.' He looked at Gracie then. 'To the gift of friendship,' he said and they all repeated it and raised their glasses another time.

When they moved from the table to the terrace for coffee and tea, Anastasia managed to get her mother on her own. 'I haven't had any luck with Ilaria,' she said in a low voice. 'What are we going to do?'

'Darling, there's nothing we can do. You've done the best you can.'

'It's not good enough,' said Anastasia in frustration. 'Granny is not going back to England tomorrow without having talked to him.'

'Sweetheart, this is not your responsibility. She's probably afraid of talking to him. Have you thought of that? I mean, she could find him herself if she really wanted to.'

'I *know* she wants to,' Anastasia insisted. 'She ran away instead of saying goodbye to Rutger and Tancredi and Gaia – she's not good at confrontation. Rutger called her a coward and perhaps she is. There's nothing wrong with being frightened. She just needs us to help her, that's all.'

Carina smiled and patted her back. 'You're very sweet, darling. Granny is lucky to have a champion in you.'

'Not if I fail!' Anastasia retorted, suddenly feeling quite desperate. 'But I'm not going to. I'm going to find him tomorrow, if it's the last thing I do.'

'Just be careful,' Carina warned. 'You're delving into people's hearts. It's not a game.'

'I'll be careful, I promise.'

None of them slept well that night. Carina was worrying about Gracie. Gracie was worrying about returning to her lonely life in Badley Compton, and Anastasia was worrying about how she was going to find the count before having to take the taxi to the airport. They were due to leave at ten. That didn't give her much time.

Gracie awoke early. She saw her bag packed and waiting by the door and her stomach lurched with dread. She did not want to leave. She did not want to return to Flappy Scott-Booth and the Badley Compton Ladies' Book Club. Before, she had been content with her life, lonely as it was, for it had been familiar. But now she wanted more. The small cove represented her flight, her concealment and her cowardice. She didn't belong there any more. The only things to look forward to were her dogs, who she knew would be happy to see her. Besides them, there was no one. She climbed out of bed and spent the dawn at the window, watching the light expanding into the sky, dispelling the night, and yet today it was a melancholy sight. It filled her heart with an unbearable sorrow. Today she would leave her past behind. All of it. Uncle Hans, Rutger, Tancredi, La Colomba, Colladoro . . . Today she would leave it, most likely for ever.

Anastasia had awoken early too, not because of the birdsong but her own anxiety which had rendered her sleep shallow and fretful. Carina awoke too and stared at the little specks of light she had come to love. She felt a tightness in her belly at the thought of returning to work. She didn't want life to go back to the way it was. She wanted to bring Rufus out here so that he could enjoy the magic too. So that he could witness what the magic had done to *her.* If she returned home would she leave her contentment here at Castello Montefosco and become that brisk, stressed, selfish woman again? She turned to see Anastasia lying on her back, staring at the dust as well, and decided that she would make sure she carried the Castello inside her sweater like Ilaria's hot potato.

They went down to breakfast and sat on the terrace for the final time, gazing out onto the hills and valleys and beyond, to the sea, committing it all to memory. Anastasia sensed her grandmother's unhappiness. She sensed it so strongly that she felt as if her heart was breaking for her.

They cheered up briefly when everyone gathered round to exchange details so they could keep in touch. Rex took Gracie's hand and squeezed it. 'You promise you'll come and visit?' he said, fixing her with his china-blue eyes. 'I won't let you forget.' Gracie didn't commit, but gave him her telephone number because she didn't have an email address. 'I suggest you get one,' Rex added. 'Then we can more easily keep in touch.'

Alex and Anastasia, who both lived in London, arranged to meet up before school started in May, and Lauren and Carina set a date for lunch at an Italian restaurant on the Fulham Road so they could extend the experience for as long as possible. Madeleine, who lived in Brussels, said that she would come to London especially, just so that she could have lunch with them. Wendy, Tiff and Brigitte hugged everyone tearfully and declared that they should all return the same time the following year for a reunion. 'If I'm still alive, I'm on,' said Rex, grinning at Gracie.

'Who knows where we'll be this time next year,' said Lauren. 'But I'd happily do it all over again just to find out.'

The mood was dampened suddenly when Ilaria appeared on the terrace to announce that the taxis had arrived to take them all to the airport. Carina caught Anastasia's eye and she gave her a desperate look that propelled her to leap up from her chair and declare that she had one last thing to do. Before Carina could stop her she had run off into the garden.

Gracie said goodbye to Ilaria and Mamma Bernadetta. The

old lady felt her sadness, and instead of extending her hand, embraced her like an old friend. Carina said her goodbyes, too, and supervised the cases. She didn't want them going in the wrong taxi.

Anastasia stood on the lawn feeling fraught. She had to find the count, but she didn't know where to start looking. He could be anywhere. The grounds were large. He might even have gone out. She was close to tears. There was no way she was going to leave without finding him. She couldn't let that happen. There had to be some sort of resolution for her grandmother.

By some stroke of luck, just as she was beginning to despair, Anastasia chanced upon the count's big shaggy dog, sniffing in the bushes. She didn't know where to start looking for the count, but she thought there was a very strong chance that his dog would know where to find him. Hadn't Ilaria said he always went in search of his master? She put out her hand and gave him a pat. He wagged his tail, then continued sniffing in the bushes. Her anxiety was now so intense it was as if something were wrapping its tendrils around her chest and squeezing it. Her heart was a drumstick beating against her ribcage. She couldn't allow her grandmother to leave without at least saying hello to her old love.

The dog began to trot off up the path that led to the bench overlooking the valley. Anastasia followed it, light upon her feet, hoping that the count would be there and she'd be able to talk to him and explain. She suppressed her reservations and hurried after the dog.

The bench came into view and there, sitting on it, half facing her and half facing the valley, was Tancredi. Anastasia couldn't believe her good fortune. Drawing in a deep breath she quietly approached, letting the dog take the lead. Tancredi heard the dog's footsteps and turned his eyes away from the horizon. 'Bernardo?' he said and put out his hand. Anastasia stood there, in full view, as the dog went and positioned himself beneath his master's suspended hand, and Tancredi lowered it to pat him. She stopped. The air around her stilled. Only Tancredi's hand moved as he patted his pet. Anastasia's heart was beating so loudly now that she was sure he would hear it. But he didn't. He began to talk to the animal as if she wasn't there.

And then everything became clear, as if a veil had at once been lifted to reveal a surprising truth. In a flurry of excitement she turned and ran back down the path towards the castle. Suddenly, the world looked beautiful again. More beautiful than it had before. Her heart was so full she thought it might burst before she got there. But she reached the taxi at last to find Gracie already in the front seat, her handbag on her knee, her profile set in a sorrowful frown.

'Granny!' Anastasia cried, opening her door and crouching down to meet her grandmother at eye level.

'What is it, my dear?' Gracie replied, alarmed by the girl's urgency.

'Tancredi. You must go and see him. He's sitting on that bench.'

'But . . .'

'Oh, Granny!' Anastasia's eyes filled with tears and she took her grandmother's hand to help her out of the car. 'He didn't recognise you, not because he no longer knew you, or didn't *want* to know you, but because he's blind.'

Gracie's mouth opened in a silent gasp. 'He's blind?'

'Yes. It explains everything. Ilaria has only been protecting him. Please go, Granny. You must. He's waiting for you. I just know it.'

Carina climbed out of the car and stood beside her daughter as Gracie walked shakily across the paving stones. 'You've been right about everything so far,' she said to Anastasia. 'I just hope to God you're right about this.'

❦

Gracie made her way along the path towards the bench. She was so afraid that her body trembled all over and her legs felt like they belonged to someone else, and yet, she somehow managed the short walk without stumbling. She saw him just like Anastasia said, sitting on the bench in a blue open-neck shirt and pale trousers, his loyal dog at his side. He didn't notice her, or hear her coming, until she was almost upon him. Then he turned his face towards her and frowned. 'Hello?' he said. Gracie stopped. She was too moved to speak. Could it be possible that those beautiful eyes could no longer see? 'Who is it?' he asked, arbitrarily shifting his gaze as he tried to identify her. 'Ilaria?' Then she knew that Anastasia was right. That he hadn't failed to recognise her; he just hadn't seen her.

'Tancredi,' she said at last.

He cocked his head and frowned. 'Who are you?' he said. But there was something in his tone that suggested he might know, but was afraid to hope.

'Tancredi, it's me. Gracie.'

At the mention of her name his cheeks flushed. He blinked, as if he saw her and couldn't believe his eyes. She could have sworn they lit up with happiness like an ember that glows in an unexpected wind. 'Gracie? Is that really you?' Then he doubted. His eyes dimmed and he shook his head. 'No, it's not possible.'

Gracie's face was now wet with tears. She approached softly and sat beside him. 'It's me,' she repeated.

'Gracie.' He turned away, embarrassed. 'I'm a blind old man.'

Gracie's chest overflowed with compassion. 'I don't care,' she replied in a whisper. Then she found the courage Rutger thought she didn't have. She took his hand and held it against her cheek. 'I don't care, Tancredi, because I love you. I always have and I always will.' He closed his eyes, as if he was ashamed and didn't want her to see how useless they were. He tried to speak, but the emotion overwhelmed him. Instead, he pressed his face into her hand. Tenderly she kissed it. 'I've come home,' she said.

❦

'It feels strange driving to the airport without Granny,' said Anastasia as the taxi bumped down the track.

'We'll come back,' said Carina, folding her hands in her lap and looking out of the window at the countryside she had grown to love so much. 'I have a plan.'

'You're going to rebuild La Colomba, aren't you?' Anastasia guessed, unable to keep the excitement out of her voice.

'I'm not going to live so far away from Mum ever again,' Carina explained. 'She needs me.'

'She needs *us*,' Anastasia emphasised. Then she grinned. 'But you've been wrong about everything so far.'

Carina smiled back knowingly. 'Perhaps, Sherlock. But I'm not wrong about *this*.'

And Anastasia had a funny feeling she was right.

Chapter 27

Badley Compton

Flappy was in the garden, supervising the contract gardeners she had hired for Harry's funeral – Sir Algernon and Lady Micklethwaite had accepted the invitation (sadly, the mayor had not), therefore it was imperative that there was not a single weed in sight – when the telephone rang. She heard it inside the house and had to run across the lawn to reach it in time. When she picked up the receiver she was panting. 'Darnley Manor, Flappy Scott-Booth speaking.'

'Are you out of breath?' came the reply.

'I've been toiling away in the garden, Mabel,' said Flappy. 'Really, when it comes to horticulture I can't trust anyone to do it better than me.'

'You mustn't overexert yourself, Flappy,' said Mabel, impressed that Flappy managed to do so much.

'I'm a perfectionist, Mabel. It's a curse.' She sighed and put her hand on her thumping heart. 'What news?'

'Gracie didn't come home last night.'

'Are you sure?'

'Her daughter telephoned Esther and asked her to look after the dogs for a few more days.'

'How inconvenient. We must get a message to her to let her know that it's Harry's funeral on Thursday and we need her. I don't imagine she even knows he's died.' She gave a derisory sniff. 'Why's she staying longer? What's going on?'

'Her daughter didn't say. She said that she and her daughter came home without her.'

Flappy was confused. 'Is she in trouble? Has something happened? It would be just like Carina not to tell us. Is she unwell?'

Mabel wished she had more information. She could feel Flappy's frustration down the line. Instead of ingratiating herself, she had managed to leave Flappy feeling exceedingly dissatisfied. 'Everything is in order for Harry's funeral. It really doesn't matter whether Gracie is here or not.'

'It matters very much,' came Flappy's tart reply. 'It's her duty to be here. I need all of you to support me. I'm giving the eulogy, for goodness' sake. It's going to be very emotional. I'm not sure I'm going to get through it.'

'No one could do it better than you,' Mabel gushed.

'I know,' Flappy replied, rallying. 'I will just have to be strong. There won't be a dry eye in the house.'

Flappy put the telephone down and went back into the garden. She sat on one of the teak chairs, arranged around a low table adorned with a display of white hydrangeas, and watched the gardeners in green T-shirts labouring away in her borders. It was a warm morning and she fanned herself with *The Lady* magazine she had left on her seat. How very inconsiderate of Gracie to decide to stay on for another few days. Flappy wondered how she could afford it and presumed that her daughter was helping her with the bill. From what she had gleaned, Carina and her husband earned a considerable amount of money. *Well*, she thought sourly, *it's time her daughter stepped up to her duty and started looking after her mother.* Flappy thought of her own four children and smiled smugly. She was so very *very* lucky to have such affectionate and loving offspring. Kenneth had already bought the first-class flights and luxury hotel suites for next Christmas in St Lucia. It was a treat he liked to give his family every year. Flappy relished the fact that every single one of them came, every Christmas, not because it was a free holiday (*that* would never have occurred to her) but because they *wanted* to come. They *all* wanted to spend time with *her.* She considered herself very blessed, but then again, she had always been a very good mother.

The following day Flappy bumped into Esther in the street as she marched down the pavement on her way to Big Mary's to check on the cupcakes and tea. On the end of two leads were Gracie's dogs. 'Ah, just the person I want to see,' said Flappy. She was wearing a black trouser suit and white shirt with a stiff collar, still setting an example to the locals who had not chosen to show their grief in the same way.

'Me?' Esther replied, looking hunted.

'I wanted to check that everything is in order for the funeral on Thursday – and to find out if there's any news from Gracie.'

'The cupcakes—'

'Do we know when she's coming back?'

'Carina is driving down at the weekend to pick up the dogs.'

'Where is she taking them?' Flappy was astonished and very put out that Carina had not thought to inform *her* of her plans before telling everyone else.

'I don't know.'

'Well, for goodness' sake, someone must know something!' said Flappy in exasperation. 'Doesn't anyone know the right questions to ask!' She resolved to telephone Carina at once and find out what the devil was going on.

'We've decided—' Esther began.

'Yes, good idea,' said Flappy, hurrying away. 'I'm glad everything is in order.'

As soon as she got home she telephoned Carina. 'Flappy Scott-Booth,' she said in an officious tone of voice.

'Hello, Flappy,' Carina said breezily, because she was still carrying the warmth of Castello Montefosco in her sweater like a hot potato.

'I'm calling to find out from the horse's mouth what has happened to Gracie. I'm hoping she's all right.'

Carina smiled to herself. Really, this woman was a caricature. 'She's having a lovely time in Italy,' she replied.

'Is she not coming back?' Flappy laughed as if she thought the idea of Gracie not coming home preposterous.

'She decided to stay on a little longer.'

Frustrated with the withholding of information, Flappy asked, 'Why has she decided to stay on? Isn't she lonely on her own?'

'I assure you, she's not on her own,' Carina told her and then couldn't resist tormenting her a little more. 'She's in the very best hands.'

'Oh?' said Flappy, hoping for an explanation.

'I must go. I've got so much to do.'

'Yes, so have I. I'm arranging Harry Pratt's funeral. You will tell your mother, won't you? I know she'll want to know. The funeral is on Thursday. I'm sure she'll want to be here. Harry Pratt, local hero, you know, big occasion. Lots of important people coming. I've lent my garden. It's the least I can do for a man who fought in the Battle of Britain. We have much to thank him for. Well, I'll let you get on. Send your mother my love and do tell her about Harry. She won't want to miss his send-off. I'm giving the eulogy. A big responsibility, but really, there's no one else, it was left to me to step up to the mark. I'm so busy, you know, but I can't let Harry down.'

Flappy hung up the telephone, certain that Gracie would now race back from Italy. She was certain she knew where her loyalties lay.

❧

The morning of the funeral revealed the first concern for Flappy. It was drizzling. How dare it drizzle on her big day? She looked out of the window at the low cloud and realised, to her disappointment, that if it didn't stop and the sun didn't come out to dry the grass, no one was going to see her garden. Her beautifully trimmed and weeded garden, which she had so conscientiously prepared for her important guests, Sir Algernon and Lady Micklethwaite.

Kenneth, who was a positive man, was not at all interested in the weather. 'Everyone will be in the church and then in a tent,' he told her over breakfast.

Flappy, dressed in a black suit with a large diamond star pinned to her lapel, was not at all consoled. 'I have worked very hard in the garden and now no one will see it.'

'I'm sure the sun will come out later and everyone will get to appreciate your labour.'

Flappy put on her specs and placed her eulogy on the table. 'I'm going to read it over one more time, just to make sure I don't trip on any words. The emotion, you know. It's going to be a great challenge to get through this without shedding a tear. As for everyone else, well, I hope they bring tissues. What I've written is very moving, even if I do say so myself.'

Kenneth frowned. 'Did you know enough about him to write it?' he asked.

'He used to sit on that bench. I've put *our* bench in the

eulogy. You know, the one we're dedicating to him and gifting the town.'

'Ah, yes, that's a lovely idea, darling.'

'And he was a fighter pilot. I've put that in too. Oh, and he liked boats. Big Mary told me he used to sit watching the boats for hours. He made model boats, apparently.'

'I would have thought Big Mary might have been a better person to give the eulogy. Not because she would write it as well as you, of course, but because she knew Harry better than anyone else. They had real affection for one another.'

'Ridiculous, Kenneth. I couldn't allow her to stand up in front of Sir Algernon and Lady Micklethwaite!'

Kenneth raised his eyebrows, but he knew better than to contradict his wife. Once she got something into her mind nothing *he* could say would get it out.

The morning was busy with the coming and going of people. Sally arrived with a van full of flowers, Big Mary turned up in a minivan with her troop of helpers to set up the tea, and the local tent company departed, having finished putting the tent up, which they had started the day before. By midday the second concern was revealed. 'It's me, Mabel,' said Mabel when Flappy answered the telephone. 'I've got news.'

'Gracie's back,' said Flappy cheerfully. 'Yes, I know.'

'Oh, I didn't know,' Mabel answered in surprise.

This wrong-footed Flappy, who had to now admit that she *didn't* know. 'Is she not? I presumed—'

'No, Harry has left everything to Big Mary in his will,' Mabel declared in a trembling voice, excited to be giving Flappy a really meaty piece of information.

'Well, he didn't have any relatives, did he, and Big Mary and he were friends.'

'No, they were *more* than friends.' Mabel's voice quivered as she was about to deliver her denouement. 'He was her *father*,' she said.

Flappy sank into an armchair. 'What?' She was too shocked to pretend she already knew.

'And he's left her a considerable amount of money. Who knew he had anything like as much as that?'

'Well, how much is it?'

'Considerable,' said Mabel.

'Didn't you ask? Who did you hear this from? Is your source reliable?'

'Big Mary.'

'She told you herself?'

'She's telling everyone. The whole town knows.'

Flappy's lips twitched. She had seen Big Mary this very morning and she hadn't mentioned it. Flappy emptied her mind and waited for a brilliant idea to pop into it. A moment later she hung up and hurried through the house into the marquee.

She found Big Mary dressed as if she were going to a wedding, not a funeral, in a pink-and-white floral frock. 'Mary,' she said, smiling sweetly. 'I gather you've had some rather surprising news.'

Mary's smile was not as sweet as Flappy's. 'Harry was my father,' she said.

'And he's left everything to you in his will.'

'Well, that's a bonus, but the big news is that I now know who my father is. I'm only sorry that he never told me during his lifetime.'

'I've been thinking, actually, I should have asked you earlier, but I've been so busy arranging today that I just never got around to it. Would you mind doing me a favour and giving the eulogy? You knew Harry better than anyone, and certainly better than me. I thought of asking you even before I heard that you are, indeed, his only remaining relative ...'

Big Mary lifted her chin. 'Yes, I'd like to say a few words.'

'Good, that's settled then. This is Harry's day, I really don't want it to become all about me.'

'Regarding the other living relatives, there *is* one and she's coming,' said Big Mary.

Flappy's smile froze. 'How nice. Who is she?'

'His sister, Edda Harvey-Smith. Admittedly, they were estranged, but she would like to pay her respects all the same.'

'Very well, I will let Madge know because she must sit in the front pew. As must *you*, Mary. How nice that Harry has family, after all. Very nice.'

'Madge knows,' said Big Mary. 'It's all arranged.'

'Oh,' said Flappy, but it came out more like a squeak. 'Then I don't need to do anything, do I?' Her eyes strayed to the pyramids of cakes being laid out on the white tablecloth. They were all in the shape of boats. 'Lovely cakes,' said Flappy, because she could think of nothing else to say to Harry Pratt's daughter.

Big Mary grinned. 'He'd have loved those.'

'Yes, well, he did love boats, didn't he?'

'Oh, he did,' Mary agreed, and Flappy wandered back into the house to pour herself a large glass of wine which she would sneak up to her bedroom and drink in private.

❦

By the time of the funeral Kenneth was proved right. The wind had blown the clouds away and the sun had come out. Flappy was at the church door, greeting the vicar, when she heard a clipped, aristocratic and very assertive voice on the path behind her. She turned, cutting off the vicar, expecting to see Sir Algernon and Lady Micklethwaite. Instead, she saw an elegant woman in a black dress and jacket, with black feathers in her chestnut-brown hair and diamonds pinned to her lapel, walking up the gravel, arm in arm with Big Mary. 'What a quaint church. Adorable, like something out of a film,' she was saying. Flappy caught her breath. She had not expected Harry's sister to look – or sound – like *that*.

'You must be Flappy Scott-Booth,' said the stranger, extending her hand. Flappy noticed the diamond ring and the manicured red nails and gave it a lukewarm shake. 'I'm Harry's little sister, Edda. Mary tells me that you have gone to all the trouble of organising Harry's send-off today. I'm so grateful to you. Really, you are unbelievably generous and kind, considering you are not family. And I'm so grateful to Mary, too, for getting in touch and inviting me. I wasn't even aware my brother had died, but Harry had the foresight to put my details in the letter he wrote to Mary.' She turned to Big Mary and beamed a smile. 'Isn't it lovely that I have a niece! Harry was such a rogue. And a dark horse, too. Who'd have thought he had a love child! Now a very *wealthy* love child. He hated the way I went through money. He was the opposite, a terrible old hoarder and socialist. Money meant nothing to him. Now Mary can enjoy it and I will advise her. I'm a brilliant shopper.'

Flappy didn't know what to say. She looked at Edda steadily and instead of Edda blinking back in panic like everyone else, she returned her gaze with spirit. Bravado even, and Flappy was taken aback. 'Welcome,' she said at last. 'I have made sure you have a reserved seat in the front pew.'

'Very good,' said Edda, accepting it as her due. She headed on into the church, shaking hands and exchanging a few words with the vicar on her way.

Flappy was feeling very unbalanced when, to her relief, Sir Algernon and Lady Micklethwaite appeared on the path. Flappy swiftly composed herself, thrilled that something, at last, was going right. Lady Micklethwaite kissed her with real affection, which corrected the balance in Flappy's world and made her feel superior again, while Sir Algernon put his hand a little too low on her back, perhaps even on her bottom, but Flappy dismissed that as impossible in a man with the class to know how to behave, and kissed her too. With great self-importance, she led them into the church.

They processed slowly down the aisle, having found Kenneth dutifully waiting for them in the porch. *A stately procession of dignitaries*, Flappy thought happily, as she bestowed her smiles equally to those on her left and right. It wasn't until she reached the end that she noticed the boat. The boat filled with flowers that she had quite clearly told Madge *not* to do . . . or had it been a plane she had dismissed as 'common'? Oh horror! She groaned at the tackiness of it as her feverish mind struggled to think of a way of distancing herself from it and blaming it on someone with no taste or class. But as she showed Lady Micklethwaite to her seat, the lady turned and said, 'I do love the boat. It's darling. Whose clever idea was that?'

'Mine,' said Flappy, without so much as a blink. 'I'm so pleased you like it.'

❦

After the funeral the entire congregation arrived at Darnley Manor for the reception. Lady Micklethwaite loved the boat-themed cakes, for which, once again, Flappy took credit, and Sir Algernon and Kenneth stood on the lawn in the bright sunshine and talked about golf. Flappy, in order to restore the balance between her and Edda, took it upon herself to show off her garden. Edda followed her from border to border, making all the right noises. She admired the lime avenue where hundreds of red tulips had been planted and leaned over to sniff the *Daphne odora*. 'You have a lovely garden,' said Edda.

'Thank you,' Flappy replied graciously. 'We open it to the public, only because we feel it's unfair to keep such beauty all to ourselves.'

'How good of you.'

'People come from miles around to see it. I spend much of my time toiling away. My hands are ruined.' She held out her soft white fingers, the fingers of a woman who had never dug up so much as a weed, and pulled a despairing face. 'But it's worth it. It's a privilege to have such a splendid home.'

And then the third concern was revealed: 'I think I'm going to move here,' said Edda with the assurance of a woman whose ideas *always* manifested.

Flappy was appalled. 'Move here?' she repeated in a strangled voice.

'Yes,' said Edda, smiling as she swept her eyes over the garden. 'I think Badley Compton is divine.'

'Yes it is, but—'

'Harry loved it here and I can see why.'

'But where would you move to?'

'I'll find a lovely house. Really, after London I could do with a quaint country community of quaint country people such as you and Kenneth. The sophistication of London has become much too much. I'm longing to leave and I'm sure my husband Charles will agree with me once he's seen it.' She sighed happily. 'It's just the place. I feel at home already.'

❧

Then if that wasn't enough, a few weeks later Flappy noticed an envelope in the post, written in Gracie's neat hand. She opened it in a fury for Gracie had now been gone a month. She withdrew the letter and unfolded it. Tucked into the middle was a photograph of Gracie, radiant in a dusty pink dress, standing beside a tall, handsome man with wavy grey hair and a captivating smile. Her fury evaporated, replaced by curiosity and a strange feeling of admiration. She quickly shifted her eyes to the letter, impatient to read what Gracie had to say.

Dear Flappy

I would like to share my happy news with you and my friends of the Badley Compton Ladies' Book Club. Tancredi and I are married and starting our lives together here in Tuscany, at Castello Montefosco. I hope you will one day find the time in your busy schedule to visit us.

With affection, Gracie Bassanelli

(I know it will amuse you to learn that I am now a countess. Who'd have thought it!)

Flappy put the letter and photograph back in the envelope and took a deep and expectant breath. She wanted to be furious, she anticipated she would be, but fury never came. Instead, she smiled to herself and went to the telephone. She picked it up and dialled Mabel's number. It rang once before Mabel answered.

'Mabel, Flappy here. I have something very exciting to share with you . . .' and to her joy she was the first person with this earth-shattering piece of information. The first person to *know* it, the first person to *share* it, and the fountain from which *all* knowledge of it would be communicated. 'And would you guess, she's a countess,' she added after revealing Gracie's surprising news. 'I must say, for a small woman, that title is a little too big for her, don't you think?'

Epilogue

Castello Montefosco, a month before

'So, where have you hidden the Bartoloni?' Gracie asked.

Tancredi pushed himself off the bench and took her hand. 'Let me show you.'

They walked along the path towards the castle. The sun was now high in the sky. The dog had retreated inside, finding it too hot even in the shade. Gracie noticed how Tancredi knew every contour of his property. He didn't walk with a stick and he didn't lean on her. He had taken her hand because he wanted to hold it.

They reached the castle and he led her upstairs into his private apartment. Behind the door his rooms were cosy and humble. The few paintings that hadn't been sold hung on the walls but the furniture was shabby, the rugs threadbare. Gracie wondered how long it had been since he could see.

He showed her into his bedroom. She saw it at once, his favourite painting, in pride of place on the wall behind the brass headboard. 'What happened to my forgery?' she asked.

He shook his head and reached out to touch her. She shuffled closer so he could put his arm around her. 'That *is* your forgery,' he said.

She squinted, bewildered. 'That's the fake?'

'Yes,' he said. 'The real one is in the bottom of a cupboard somewhere. *This* is the one that means the world to me. The value of a painting is in the artist as well as in the picture, therefore, to me, this is the most priceless painting in the world – even if I can no longer see it.'

'Oh, Tancredi. I'm going to cry again.'

He pulled her close and kissed the top of her head. 'I hope they are tears of joy, Gracie.' Then he buried his face in her neck and hugged her tightly, as if determined never to let her go again. 'Because mine are.'

Acknowledgements

For this novel I travelled with four girlfriends to Italy's Amalfi coast for research. We stayed in a small *pensione* overlooking the sea and booked into a cookery course, which had been highly recommended. We were not disappointed. Mamma Agata's Cookery School is like no other cookery school on earth. It is a gem built into rock on a hillside in Ravello, with the most extraordinary view of sky, sea and the famous Amalfi coastline. The sun is hot, the smells are sensual and the food, which is all home-grown, home-made and home-reared, is out of this world. But what is even more wonderful is the family who owns it. They are warm, funny, charming, loving, big-hearted people. Old Mamma Agata cooked while her daughter, Chiara, explained, entertained and laughed; there was so much laughter! I want to thank them for a wonderful experience and for inspiring Mamma Bernadetta's cookery school in my novel. Although Bernadetta and Ilaria are my own creations, they are a tribute to Agata and Chiara and written with love and gratitude. Along life's path one occasionally has the privilege of meeting the odd jewel: these two beautiful women are two such jewels. Go to Ravello, book in to Mamma Agata's Cookery School and meet them for yourselves! You will be very pleased that you did.

I would also like to thank Aliai Forte whose stunning home in Tuscany inspired the Castello in my novel. We had the most wonderful four days there last summer, during which time I lay in the sun, soaking up the inspiration. It was hard leaving but I have relived the experience in this book, savouring every scent, sound and sight all over again.

Thank you to my mother, Patty Palmer-Tomkinson, for doing the first read and edit – she is so generous with her time and is always honest and wise. Thank you also to my dear friend, mentor and agent, Sheila Crowley, and her brilliant team at Curtis Brown: Abbie Greaves, Alice Lutyens, Luke Speed, Enrichetta Frezzato, Katie McGowan, Anne Bihan and Mairi Friesen-Escandell.

Thank you to my boss, Ian Chapman. My wise and talented editor Suzanne Baboneau, and her superb team at Simon & Schuster who give my books wings and allow them to fly! Dawn Burnett, Emma Harrow, Gemma Conley-Smith, Gill Richardson, Dominic Brendon, Laura Hough, Sara-Jade Virtue and Sian Wilson.

I would like to take the opportunity to thank booksellers everywhere from the bottom of my heart. Where would I be without *them!*

I would also like to thank my parents, Charles and Patty Palmer-Tomkinson, my mother-in-law April Sebag-Montefiore, my brother James, sister-in-law Sos and my nephews and nieces, Honor, India, Wilfred and Sam, for their incredible support during this really tough year. After Tara died I just didn't think I'd have the strength to get this book written, but thanks to my incredible family, I did.

My love and gratitude to my husband, Sebag, our daughter, Lily, and our son, Sasha.

Revisit the first story in the Deverill Chronicles

Songs of Love and War

Their lives were mapped out ahead of them. But love and war will change everything ...

Castle Deverill, nestled in the rolling Irish hills, is home to three very different women: flame-haired Kitty Deverill, her best friend and daughter of the castle's cook, Bridie Doyle, and her flamboyant English cousin, Celia Deverill.

But when war breaks out, their lives will change forever.

Wrenched apart by betrayal and swept to different parts of the globe, their friendship will be tested a thousand times over. But one bond will keep them together forever: their fierce and unwavering longing for Castle Deverill and all the memories contained within it ...

Fall in love with the penultimate story in the Deverill Chronicles

Daughters *of* Castle Deverill

It is 1925 and the war is long over. But much has been lost, and life will never truly be the same again.

Castle Deverill, cherished home to the Deverill family in the west of Ireland for hundreds of years, has burned to the ground. But young and flighty Celia Deverill is determined to restore the sad ruin to its former glory. Celia married well and has the wealth to keep it in the family . . . and she cannot bear to see her beloved home stand neglected.

But dark shadows are gathering once more, as the financial markets start to shake. And everything that felt so certain is thrown once again into doubt . . .

Don't miss the epic conclusion to
the Deverill Chronicles

The Last Secret *of the* Deverills

It is 1939 and the dark clouds of war are building over Europe. In Ireland, much has changed for the Deverill family, and a new generation is waiting in the wings . . .

Bridie Doyle is now Countess di Marcantonio and mistress of Castle Deverill, far surpassing her humble roots. But when the eyes of her dashing husband begin to stray, his identity is called into question, putting Bridie's happiness at terrible risk.

Once Bridie's best friend, but no longer, Kitty Deverill lives nearby with her devoted husband Robert. Her world is suddenly rocked by the unexpected return of Jack O'Leary, her never forgotten first love. But, this time, might Jack's heart belong to another?

Martha Wallace arrives in Dublin desperate to track down her birth mother. Her efforts are thwarted, she has no one to turn to – until JP, scion of the Deverills, catches her eye.